Stars of Ambracor

by

Sandra Valencia

Chapter One

Diana Lorenz glanced up at the clock. Fifteen minutes remained until the end of her workweek. She thoroughly enjoyed working with corporate customers in the International Division of the prestigious regional bank that had employed her since her graduation a year earlier from a local university. Pensively chewing her lip, she reviewed a few final emails before clearing her desk and leaving on time for a change. Despite a few reservations, she anticipated the upcoming weekend with growing excitement.

"Diana, it's almost five o'clock. Don't you think it's time to close down?"

Diana looked up at her department lead and smiled. She definitely wanted to avoid any detailed discussion with Jennie Clarke. Jennie was a great person with whom to work because of her work ethic, generous nature, and willingness to share her wealth of experience and knowledge. Her downside lay in ultra-conservative beliefs that often made her severely judgmental on spiritual matters failing to fit into her narrow perspective.

"Just cleaning up here. Kendra insisted that we go shopping and maybe eat out. I promised I wouldn't spend the whole weekend reading the stack of books I just bought."

Jennie Clarke grinned. "I think your roommate might have the right idea. You're too young to be so serious all the time. You need to get out and socialize more." She paused hesitantly. "My invitation is still open to join the young adults group I lead at church."

"I appreciate that, Jennie." Diana pulled her long wool coat from the hook on her cubicle partition. Slipping the cloak on, she gathered her purse, a soft-sided attaché, and a book she was reading during lunch and breaks. "Have a great weekend."

"You, too. Oh…don't let that roommate steer you in the wrong direction." Jennie hoped her warning hadn't sounded too overbearing. She had long ago recognized Diana's quiet, serious nature and her deep faith in God. On the other hand, Jennie often found it difficult to avoid openly criticizing the church Diana attended with her roommate.

A couple of items on Diana's desk suddenly tipped over for no apparent reason. Her dark amber eyes sparked with mild annoyance, but her features remained smooth and tranquil as she righted them. She felt herself growing irritated because of Jennie's obvious disapproval of her roommate. "Don't worry. Kendra is a lot more traditional and conservative than she looks. Gotta go now. See you first thing Monday morning!"

Forty minutes later, Diana tightly clutched the long straps of her purse and attaché. Sidling her way between passengers standing on a crowded bus, she stepped into the biting chill of a February evening. Especially during bad weather, she preferred riding the bus to driving the small car her parents had given her as a graduation gift. Glad that sidewalks were already cleared of nearby Lake Erie's latest lake-effect snowfall, she hurried down the street and around the corner to the building complex where she and Kendra lived.

Upon opening the door to their apartment, she welcomed a rush of warm air laden with savory aromas of the dinner Kendra was cooking. "Wow! Smells great in here!"

Kendra appeared from the eat-in kitchen. The curls of her medium-length hair had won out against the casual style she had so carefully arranged that morning. Smooth brown skin glowed with good health, and dark brown eyes sparkled with good humor. "Hey, no matter what you think, I do know how to cook."

Diana chuckled lightly. "I believe you, and I keep telling you. I don't mind at all if you commandeer the kitchen once in a while." After removing her coat and hanging it in a small closet near the front door, she sniffed appreciatively. "So, what's on tonight's menu?"

"Practicing for Lent. I'm trying my hand at pasta with homemade Alfredo sauce, garlic bread, and spinach salad."

"Pasta?" Diana asked in feigned shock. "Not exactly your specialty, is it?"

Kendra turned her nose up. "Just because I'm black doesn't mean I limit what little cooking I do to typical soul food dishes. Besides, spinach still qualifies as greens."

Diana's hands flew up in mock surrender. "I never said one derogatory word. I never even thought of one. Actually, come to think of it, I really liked all the soul food dishes you ever fixed...on those rare occasions you decided to cook."

A few minutes later, they sat at the kitchen table and enjoyed glasses of chilled white wine with perfectly prepared pasta dressed in creamy cheese sauce laced with spinach. Conversation was light in nature, touching on a few hot topics from the news and some items on sale they wanted to buy for the apartment.

Finally, Kendra laid her fork down on her plate, placed her elbows on the table, and rested her chin on her clasped hands. "Well?"

They had forged their close friendship during their freshman year of high school and often communicated with the exchange of one or two words. Even the four years spent apart pursuing bachelor degrees at different universities had not altered an almost uncanny ability to understand one another.

Diana nibbled on the last piece of crusty garlic bread. "I told you. I'm going with you tomorrow."

Obvious hints of doubt lingered in Kendra's expression. "You won't back out like you did the last time, will you?"

Diana set the bread on her plate. "Not so long as you promise to hold my hand if I get scared. You know I've never attended one of these expositions."

Kendra smiled reassuringly. "Diana, there's nothing to be afraid of. Sure, there will always be some phonies who take advantage of people's weaknesses and irrational hopes. That happens no matter where you go, but this event is one of the largest in the state. It attracts people who are some of the wisest and most knowledgeable in a variety of paranormal fields."

Diana's sigh held a nervous quiver. "I believe you, Kendra. I don't know why I get so anxious."

"Are you afraid your folks will disapprove if they find out?"

A gentle smile spread Diana's wide, sensually shaped lips. "I'm quite sure they would encourage me. When I had lunch with Mom before she and Dad left, she saw the books I was reading and actually seemed pleased. She and Dad know almost everything about my more peculiar tendencies." She stopped, mulling over a thought that had invaded her mind long ago. "Sometimes, I think they're holding back...that they know more than they're telling."

Kendra shook her head. "I can't imagine they'd do that to you. Have you ever asked them outright?"

"Not really," Diana answered. "They've always said I'm more special than I realize, and the day will come when I'll figure it all out." After an uncomfortable pause, she added, "I have the feeling I'd get that same answer if I were ever really brave enough to ask."

"Well, based on what I observed the couple of times I met her and what you've told me, you should be glad Jennie Clarke isn't your mother. She'd probably have you tied up and carried to some of those fire-and-brimstone preachers for an exorcism."

Diana couldn't hide a grin. "You're probably right about that. She's nice in so many ways..."

"But on subjects like this, her mind is like a bank safe with ten combination locks and two feet of reinforcing concrete on every wall...closed tight with no possibility of opening it."

The comment was met with a solemn nod. "I can't argue the point. All that aside, dinner was delicious. Why don't we clean up here? I'm kind of tired tonight, plus I'd like to finish reading that last book on dreams you gave me."

"Tired?" Kendra asked. "Not plotting to suddenly come down sick tomorrow, are you?"

Laughing, Diana stood and started stacking plates and silverware to carry to the sink. "Not at all. I can hardly wait to see your face when I actually walk into that convention hall."

Later, Diana sat in bed and reread the final few paragraphs of the newest book Kendra had given her. Thankfully, this author had a more dynamic style of writing than those of other books she'd read on esoteric subjects. Her current focus on books about dream interpretation resulted from an insatiable thirst as she sought to discover some significance in years of repetitive dreams that refused to fade away.

Although the material in this book held her interest, it somehow failed to *resonate.* She silently laughed at the term she'd heard Kendra use dozens of times. Now, however, she actually felt the sense that word was meant to convey as she read this writer's explanation of symbols in dreams. It seemed to Diana that her own dreams were very different from those the author described. Images meant to symbolize ideas, fears, or feelings from the subconscious did not apply to her situation. What she had experienced for years didn't fit the neatly organized categories described in any of the books she had recently read on dream interpretation.

Sleep came quickly that night. Diana had decided not to resist the dreams that had become more and more frequent over the past two years. Many nights, uncomfortable restlessness disturbed her sleep. Images were vivid, almost as if she were more alive in the dream than she was in her own bed. She saw people dressed in fashions that she thought similar to clothes she'd seen in artwork or films related to Renaissance settings. Faces and voices were achingly familiar, yet she was sure she had never met the people she saw.

Most disturbing of all had been the man who gazed at her with an intensity that stirred deep anxiety. Whenever he appeared in her dreams, she felt herself shrinking away from him. She could make out that he was quite tall. His shoulders were broad, and his body emanated strength and power. Although shadows prevented her from clearly distinguishing what she thought were swarthy features with a full beard, she felt confident that his was a presence saturated with dark, threatening mystery.

Three thirty in the morning. Diana abruptly sat up in bed. Shaking her head back and forth, she attempted to free herself from the inexplicable emotional ties binding her to this latest dream...one she had experienced dozens of times since her teens. That elusive face lingered in the shadows, haunting her. As she opened her eyes to familiar shapes inside her bedroom, nothing registered in her line of vision. Her sight was locked in place...another place she'd never been. A single tear slid down her cheek as she stared hard, seeing only brilliant blue eyes that yet again held her prisoner.

Kendra entered the kitchen. Picking up a clean mug from the counter, she poured her first cup of coffee for the morning. Casting a sideways squint at the clock on the microwave, she groaned. "I can't believe I'm actually up before five thirty on a Saturday morning. Don't tell me. You saw him again."

Diana stared into her own tall mug. Perhaps a little humor might dispel some of her tension. "He's not even my type. I've never been attracted to men with beards."

Kendra tugged her pink robe more tightly around herself. The robe's pastel color beautifully contrasted with the chocolate shade of Kendra's complexion. Sitting opposite Diana, she reached across the table and laid her hand over that of her best friend. Long, dark fingers curled around ivory ones with comforting reassurance. "Yeah, the last three guys you dated were all clean-shaven blonds...and jerks to boot."

"Joel wasn't a total jerk. He was fun when we went out...and reasonably intelligent."

"At least he waited until the third date before trying to get you into bed. Damn, I don't know what those guys didn't understand. It's not like you didn't make them well aware of your religious beliefs."

"Joel did apologize. You have to give him that." Diana's voice sounded slightly defensive.

"I suppose, and he did take you out once more before he dumped you." Kendra huffed a disgusted sigh before sipping hot coffee and dismissing the quality of Diana's dates. "All I know for sure is that you have to figure out what this all means. Sooner or later, it's going to tear you apart. I can't bear losing the best friend I've ever had...not like this."

Diana ran nervous fingers through the tousled length of her golden-brown hair. "I talked to our parish priest last week. I even went to see that therapist Damon recommended. They both looked at me as if I had two heads. At this point, I'm almost ready to surrender and go talk to the pastor at Jennie's church."

"Whoa now. That's going way too far, and I think you know it. Jennie and her church friends mean well. They're decent people who really do care. The problem is that you're different. No matter how hard you pretend, you've never fit in with most people. You need to give yourself the chance to exercise the open mind you know they're missing."

She stopped a moment for another drink of coffee. Brown eyes held compassion for her longtime friend. "Diana, life isn't only what you can see and touch in this world. You can't touch or see the air you breathe, but you know you'd die without it. You believe in God. You can't see or touch him either, but you know he's real. It's the same with spirit. It's real."

Diana's face tensed as she fought back tears. "Kendra, it's just all so confusing."

"*Confusing?* That's putting it mildly. That's also why I'm so determined to take you to that expo today. I'm convinced we'll meet someone who can give you some insight. Heaven only knows you need it, especially after that little episode last month. That even scared me, and that's not easy to do."

The very thought of that night when old, faint scars began to ooze blood stirred fresh waves of fear. Diana's melodic voice quavered. "I couldn't even tell my folks about that one, especially after you made me go to the doctor and endure that interrogation. She honestly thought I was in denial about hurting myself. Do you really think someone at the expo today might be able to help?"

Kendra smiled and nodded. "I do. A speaker named Madalyn Amador is scheduled to make a presentation on interpreting dreams. She's always in demand at these shows. Marty's working as a volunteer. I already gave him the money to pay the fee for her lecture so we'll be sure to get seats. I've heard her before, and she's awesome."

Diana slowly breathed in and out. "I'm just not sure of anything anymore."

Kendra's face assumed a stern, no-nonsense look. "Diana, we *are* going to that expo, and we *are* going to find someone to help us figure this out. The so-called normal stuff has proven useless. As the saying goes, we've got nothing to lose."

Forcing a wry grin, Diana stood and went to open a cupboard door. "How about some pancakes for breakfast before we get ready to leave?"

Arriving an hour after the expo opened, Kendra dragged Diana by the arm to volunteer tables. They picked up brochures and floor diagrams showing locations of various booths in the expansive hall. Kendra also collected listings of scheduled events and a tote full of flyers and leaflets.

While the ever-friendly Kendra chatted with some volunteers, people-watching attracted Diana's attention. Dressed casually in jackets, sweaters, and jeans, most attendees looked as ordinary as she felt. Wandering through crowded aisles, they browsed displays of artwork, polished stones, holistic health products, jewelry, and handcrafted items impossible to find in more conventional retail settings. She forced herself not to stare at some who dressed more as if they were attending a Halloween party. Others moving through the crowds were dressed somewhere in between, wearing ordinary street clothes while adorning themselves with mystical-looking accessories including amulets, feathers, and an array of unusual jewelry and embellishments.

"Hello," Kendra said. "You still with me here?"

Diana shook her head and blushed. Her girlfriend's amused grin put her immediately at ease. "Sorry. Got lost watching everyone."

"Like I said yesterday, you always get people who come more for show than content. There are even a couple exhibitors who look like they transported from silent movies while still wearing their enormous Swami turbans. Personally, those are the folks I trust least, but I guess they think that's what's expected of them."

"When is the presentation?"

"We have two whole hours to look around before we scramble to get good seats. Where do you want to start?"

Shrugging, Diana suggested they begin at the far side and work their way to the other end. Soon, initial uneasiness subsided as she stopped at various booths to admire beautifully crafted jewelry, fascinating artwork designed to soothe the spirit and inspire the soul, and extensive collections of beautifully polished stones. At one booth, glass cases held elegant hand-made jewelry set with gemstones representing every color of the rainbow.

"Hey, girl, looking at something special there?" Kendra's voice held a gentle tease as she peeked over her friend's shoulder.

Diana's fingertip touched the case. "I'm not sure why, but that one really caught my attention."

Just as Kendra laughed out loud and asked which of nearly two dozen pieces she meant, an older lady tending the booth turned her attention to Diana. Her flowing turquoise blouse highlighted sparkling blue eyes as she smiled before leaning over the case. "The ruby in that ring is a natural stone with no artificial enhancements. Would you like to see it?"

When Diana nodded, the vendor removed the ring and placed it on a black velvet pad. "This is one of the few gold pieces in the collection."

"It's beautiful," Kendra whispered. "Probably expensive, too."

Diana picked up the ring and gazed at the oval, blood-red stone. Overhead lights bounced off its many facets. Swirls of gold held the stone securely in place. Thoughtfully, Diana slid it onto the ring finger of her left hand. For one fleeting moment, she felt lightheaded. Shaking off the disconcerting sensation, she changed the ring to her right hand. Without conscious thought, she breathed out a sigh of relief. Much better there, she thought, and a perfect fit.

The vendor watched with an odd smile. Diana's jolt had been visible to her sensitive eye. "I usually don't reduce prices until the last day of the show, and I practically never discount gold jewelry. However, it seems you have an unusual connection with this stone." She paused, wondering why this young woman's aura had suddenly brightened the moment she put the ring on. "If you want to buy the ring, I can let you have it for ten percent off."

Diana glanced at the small tag. The price was more than she had ever paid for any piece of jewelry. Well, she thought, that made sense. Except for her favorite gold earrings and a small, odd collection of silver, she only purchased inexpensive costume jewelry. She turned to Kendra. "My tax refund should come any day."

Surprise clearly showed on Kendra's face. "I don't think I've ever known you to even think about buying something that expensive," she said. "You really want it, don't you?"

"I do, but don't ask me why. For the life of me, I don't have an answer." Turning back to the vendor, Diana sighed. "I really like it, but is there any possibility you could reduce the price a bit more?"

Gazing at her potential customer, the woman thought how she had instantly zeroed in on the ring that had attracted the young lady's rapt attention. Inhaling and exhaling a cleansing breath, she also felt powerful waves of energy emanating from her client. Beyond that, she questioned what it was about her customer that seemed so out of place. "The best I can do is to take off an extra ten dollars."

"Thanks," Diana said. Unzipping her purse, she pulled out a credit card. Moments later, she tucked the receipt and a velvet box into her shoulder bag. The ruby ring remained on her right hand. As Diana and Kendra changed directions to arrive on time for the dream presentation, they both cast repeated admiring glances at the shiny red gem.

An hour later, both young women paid rapt attention to the seminar. In her late fifties, Madalyn Amador's image was a perfect blend of confidence and competence. Her matronly figure, clad in a silky caftan woven in pastel colors, moved gracefully across a small stage. Expressing herself in a dynamic voice that rose and fell almost musically, she covered subject matter shifting from traditional dream-analysis techniques to mystical symbolism. After describing themes such as flying or falling in common dreams, Ms. Amador proceeded to explain differences between lucid, psychic, and epic dreams. When her talk progressed to more active dream situations, Diana leaned far forward. She concentrated on descriptions of people waking with premonitions—such as when Abraham Lincoln dreamed of his own death—or rare knowledge of events and places in the remote past.

Once the presentation ended, many from the audience tarried in hopes of having a private word with the speaker. Excusing herself for a moment, Ms. Amador moved away from the crowd toward a line of people waiting to leave the small auditorium. Reaching out an elegant hand adorned with several beautiful rings, she gently touched Kendra's arm.

Kendra turned in surprise. "Yes?"

Kindness marked the older woman's face. "Forgive me for startling you. I couldn't help but notice you and your friend in the audience. I'll be doing private readings at my booth after lunch. I wonder if the two of you might be interested in stopping by."

Diana's eyebrows lifted questioningly, but Kendra gave her no opportunity to decline a chance to talk one on one with Ms. Amador. "That would be wonderful. What time do you think you'll be back?"

With a glance at the waiting crowd, she smiled again. "I imagine I'll be here at least another fifteen minutes. Why don't you come by my booth around one thirty?"

"We'll be there," Kendra responded enthusiastically. "Thank you so much."

"Why do you think she did that?" Diana asked before picking up a flimsy plastic fork to try her first bite of lunch purchased from a vendor selling Thai food.

Kendra's arched eyebrows rose high as she shook her head. "It's hard to say. I understand she's extremely intuitive and communicates with many guides, angels, and ascended masters. What was your impression of the talk she gave?" Kendra concentrated more on her friend's face than she did on the disposable plate of food on the table in front of her.

Diana shrugged. "I'm not quite sure. At first, I thought everything was following the same repetitive, uninspired pattern as other books I read on interpreting dreams. Toward the end, I started feeling different...more like she really might understand the sort of dreams I've had."

Kendra lifted a bite to her mouth and chewed slowly. "I wonder what spices they put in this," she murmured absently before taking a second bite.

Long, silent moments passed while the two ate and pensively considered Diana's comments. Finally, after taking a drink of iced tea, Kendra sighed. "I do think we should go see her. I have a pretty strong feeling she sensed something unusual about you. It can't hurt to hear what she has to say, can it?"

Diana barely suppressed a laugh. "Only my pocketbook, especially after I bought this ring." Her eyes dropped to admire her new ruby ring.

Kendra laughed. "There is that. Tell you what. Whatever her fee is, I'll split the cost. How about that?"

A broad grin brought shining golden lights to amber eyes. "You'll do nothing of the sort. You already paid for tickets to the presentation."

"So what? Is there a law against a girl trying to help her best friend in the world keep her sanity?"

Diana finally surrendered to laughter. "Kendra, I'm not sure even the Federal Reserve has that much money!"

Huge brown eyes glittered merrily. "Why do you really think we're such good friends?"

Diana shook her head so hard that her long hair swung in front of her face. "I know, I know. We're both a couple of loony birds."

Kendra's generously full lips poked out to form an exaggerated pout. "Speak for yourself. I was thinking more like what a terrific case study you'll make when I finally get around to writing my thesis."

After discarding trash from lunch, Kendra took the lead and determinedly guided Diana through the growing throng in the aisle where Madalyn Amador's booth was located. As they got closer to their destination, Diana felt anxiety swell to the point that she finally hissed into Kendra's ear, "Hey, it's getting really crowded. If her booth is anything like her presentation, we won't even get close."

Without slowing her deliberate pace, Kendra tilted her head backward. "I told you this morning. No cold feet. We're going to see Madalyn Amador."

Hardly a minute had passed when they spotted the table at the front of Ms. Amador's booth. Diana had been right about one thing. People were rapidly closing in on the stall where books and soft lights were artfully arranged on top of a sky-blue tablecloth. Directly behind the table were two standard, stackable chairs used for large gatherings. At the back of the booth sat two additional chairs, one on each side of a small wooden table holding a crystal vase containing two roses.

Madalyn Amador glanced up from a clipboard on the front table where people were writing their names to schedule readings from the well-known intuitive. With no hint of disappointment, the crowd at the booth readily accepted Ms. Amador's gracious announcement that her first appointment had arrived. She then invited Kendra and Diana to sit at the back table.

Dropping bags on the floor and hanging purses on their chairs, Kendra and Diana sat and waited. As soon as another lady appeared to answer questions and handle book purchases at the front table, Ms. Amador quickly pulled over a third chair and joined them. "I'm very glad the two of you arrived on time."

"We were curious about why you singled us out, Ms. Amador," Kendra said after introducing herself and Diana.

A nod and a smile acknowledged Kendra's comment. "Please, call me Madalyn. It will be much more comfortable for all of us."

Receiving their nodded agreements, she placed her elbows on the tabletop and brought her hands together with only her fingertips touching. After closing her eyes and remaining silent for several moments, she began with an explanation. "I do not place my palms together because that action serves to create opposing energy. The openness of the position of my fingers actually allows me to gather energy. I suppose you might think of the connections as antennas."

While Diana struggled to suppress growing apprehension, Kendra grinned with understanding of the simple analogy. "Personally, I appreciated the depth of material in your presentation today. Your method of explaining complex dream topics in simple, straightforward terms made everything remarkably easy to follow."

"I'm glad you think so. It seems you have a unique appreciation for today's talk." A softness changed Madalyn's expression. "You were also wise to insist that your friend come here today."

Diana aimed a startled look at Kendra. "Did you arrange this in advance?"

Before Kendra could answer, Madalyn shook her head. "I assure you she did not. I saw your face near the beginning of today's lecture. I kept glancing back toward you and noticed extremely unusual fluctuations in your aura."

Clinging to skepticism, Diana met the woman's gaze as a hint of discomfort began to swell within her chest. "To be perfectly honest, I've never attended an event like this. I have no idea what to expect."

"Fair enough," Madalyn replied with a nod. "Let me see if I can help you better understand why you came. Do I have your permission to hold your hands and read your personal energy?"

Kendra's voice was quietly encouraging. "It's okay. Remember what we discussed this morning. You have nothing to lose. Just breathe deeply and relax."

Reluctantly closing her eyes, Diana obediently took a deep breath, then a second and a third. As she finally lifted her eyelids to meet Madalyn's waiting gaze, an unexpected calm flooded her body. When Madalyn took hold of her hands, she felt distinct tingling move through her fingers and into her wrists. Studying the older woman's face, she noticed raised eyebrows and an expression as if the intuitive were intently listening to voices only she could hear. Diana keenly felt every second that passed until Madalyn sighed heavily and sat back in her seat.

"You, Diana, have already discerned you're in the wrong place, haven't you?" A patient smile crossed Madalyn's face when she noted Diana's startled reaction. "I won't pretend to tell you things I don't know, my dear. On the other hand, what I sense and what I'm told by spirits who speak to me may help you achieve a measure of comfort as you await your destiny."

"I hope you'll forgive me for sounding rude, but that's a very vague statement," Diana responded.

"Indeed it is," Madalyn agreed. "Let's discuss things in a little more detail. Most important to you is your fear of the man in your dreams. Is that not correct?" Receiving a somewhat reluctant, affirming nod, she continued, "That man is part of your destiny. He represents perhaps the greatest pain you've ever known. You feel that, yet you're convinced you've never met him. Is that also correct?"

"I'm listening," Diana said, still unsure of Madalyn's direction.

"Diana, these dreams have haunted you for years now, but their intensity is increasing even more than their frequency. My guides tell me that yours watch over you more fiercely than you realize. They have even given divine assignment to your friend Kendra here to help you face this current phase of turmoil. That's because your dreams are more than surfacing subconscious desires. Your dreams hold your true reality that you will accept with reluctance. You've faced danger and death already. You will do so again. How you'll confront those events is something beyond what I can see or what my guides can reveal to me."

Diana looked bewildered. "I don't understand. What do you mean about already facing danger and death? I've led a relatively sheltered and uneventful life."

"So you think, Diana. Ask yourself questions that you know will be difficult to ask and even harder to answer. Who is the man lurking in the shadows of your dreams? Why does he watch you? What does he want? Why does he frighten you?"

Forgotten was her intention to cling to stubborn skepticism. Her breathing was quickening, and her heart was starting to throb. "I've already spent the past few years asking myself about him, but I never find any answers."

"The reason you find no answers is because of the great wall you've built around your emotions. Until you tear down those walls and allow light to penetrate your soul, you will remain in the same darkness that shields his face from you."

Kendra interrupted with a trembling voice. "Do you think he intends to hurt her?"

"That I can't answer, but it's critical for your friend to pray...to meditate and allow herself to receive the messages her own guides wait to give her. Her life has purpose she must fulfill."

"Is there nothing you can tell me about him? I mean...the man in the dreams?" Diana asked nervously.

Regret was evident in her response as Madalyn considered how pale the young woman now appeared. She always hated times when she could only share partial information. She listened to the voices speaking into her mind. "I can tell you only that he has already changed your life twice and will do so yet again."

"*What?*" Kendra asked when Madalyn suddenly stopped and became silent.

A perplexed look was quickly replaced by a more compassionate expression. "The scars on your left side...the ones that recently bled? The wound that left them was not his fault. It was yours. You failed to live by your own rules."

Tears abruptly filled Diana's eyes, and Kendra quickly grasped her friend's hands. "How did you know about her scars? How did you know about them bleeding?"

"I'm sorry. I can say nothing more than that. I share only the message I was given."

❈ ❈ ❈

Steaming chamomile tea smelled sweet and soothing as Diana tried to clear her mind after her latest unsuccessful meditation. Borrowing one of Kendra's favorite words, she repeatedly reviewed the reading she had received from Madalyn Amador and knew that it *resonated* deep within her soul. Still, two full weeks later, meditation proved fruitless while her mysterious dreams remained as troubling as ever.

Kendra appeared from the bedroom where she had been studying for her master's degree. "You're awfully quiet tonight."

Carefully setting her teacup on the glass-topped end table beside her, Diana stretched her legs out from under her before standing up. "I knew you were studying for exams."

Noticing candles still flickering in their crystal holders, Kendra asked, "No luck again with meditation?"

"Nope. None at all. Do you think something's wrong with me?"

Crossing the small living room of their apartment, Kendra reached out to hug Diana. "Hey, we're going to get you through this. There's nothing wrong with you except this strange man who seems hell-bent on torment-ing you. Remember. Your best friend isn't only one smart cookie. She also possesses several black belts in martial arts. She can defend you against that guy anytime, day or night."

Diana chuckled appreciatively. "You're the best, you know. Besides, thanks to you, I figure I can take pretty good care of myself if I need to."

"I know. You're a natural. With practice, you could earn a black belt in no time. Whatever the case, just keep in mind what old Madalyn told you. I'm your divine assignment."

Diana laughed. "I think it was more like divinely assigned."

"Whatever," Kendra said, her eyes glittering playfully. "The point is that you should be relieved to have me watching over you."

"You...my folks, too, whenever they're not traveling."

"You miss them, don't you?"

"I do. We're so close, but I'm actually glad they don't know about all this."

"Why not?" Kendra asked, sincerely puzzled by the admission. "They're well educated and very open-minded. Heaven only knows how much they love you."

"All true," Diana admitted. "There are still those times when I feel convinced they know more than they've told me."

"Do you think it's because you were adopted?"

"Possibly, but I don't believe so. They never admitted it, but I'm sure they actually knew my birth parents."

"But what about your adoption paperwork saying you were abandoned as a newborn?"

"I've overheard things more than once. I never intentionally eavesdropped, but I'm sure I heard Mom talk about how my parents still suffered over losing me."

"Maybe she was just supposing. You rarely talk about it. Does it really bother you…I mean, thinking about being adopted?"

Diana looked thoughtful as she leaned over to get her cup of tea. Sipping liquid that was now lukewarm, she asked herself that same question for the thousandth time. Deep inside, she knew the answer was still the same. "It doesn't. Maybe it should, but that's one thing that doesn't trouble me. My parents have always encouraged my interests in languages and my love of horses. They've also been so affectionate and patient, especially when things started falling over or breaking before I realized I was the cause. They seemed to know instinctively that something was upsetting me. Instead of scolding, I got hugs."

"Well, I say accept it and move on to resolve issues that do bother you."

"Yeah…like the man in the shadows who scares the hell out of me. Then, two scars I've had all my life that started bleeding two months ago for no apparent reason. Even my doctor can't explain where the blood is coming from. I feel like it's all connected, but how?"

Kendra met Diana's darkening mood head on. "Diana, we both agree that some things in this world take time to understand and others are beyond human comprehension. Right?" Receiving a nod, she continued, "I think you are your own biggest roadblock to understanding this whole dream thing. There's something you're afraid of or resisting with all your might. Whatever that something is, you've got to face it. You have to reach inside for courage to tear away veils hiding the truth that's crippling you. That's the only way you'll ever reach the heart of the matter."

A sudden shiver shook Diana from the top of her head all the way to her toes. "My God," she gasped.

Kendra grabbed her by the upper arms. "What? What happened just now?"

Diana's expression was more puzzled than frightened. "I don't know. I just suddenly felt something almost like déjà vu. Not with us exactly, but with what you said."

"Hang on to that feeling. It's likely your own intuition kicking in and giving you a starting point."

"Maybe. Maybe the meditation is starting to work. I might just get through this," she murmured hopefully.

"I have a suggestion. Let's go dig out that box of chocolates you bought and relax our overworked brains."

For the first time in days, Diana laughed aloud as she took Kendra by the arm. "That's the best idea I've heard all day. I get first dibs on the caramels."

Chapter Two

CHILLY DAMPNESS THICKENED THE CAVE'S musty air. Flickering votives sat in niches around the walls. Elongated shadows performed undulating dances as flames waved back and forth atop waxy stages. The slightest movements of brittle-shelled insects spawned faint, eerie echoes. Otherworldly stillness yielded to the occasional swift passage of dark-winged bats. Rhythmic breathing created sounds almost akin to a steady heartbeat as the cavern's visiting mistress carefully lit chunky black candles on an altar of roughly hewn stone dominating the large chamber.

The mistress's frail body, shriveled features, and graying wisps of straggly hair dramatically contrasted with the student carefully watching her. The younger woman was strikingly beautiful. Her petite frame was a sensual study of feminine curves and her face a memorable example of perfect symmetry. Black brows arched above large, dark brown eyes fringed with lush lashes. Ivory skin was taut and silken smooth from her high cheekbones to her delicately shaped chin. Curved lips were a vivid shade of dark rose. Raven tresses, drawn into a thick braid falling almost to her waist, gleamed in the candlelight.

The mistress slowly turned to look upon her rapt protégé kneeling on cold, hard stone. Craggy wrinkles stretched from hollows in the old woman's cheeks. Thin lips parted in a smile that revealed chipped, discolored teeth. The teacher highly favored this student. Nodding approval, the mistress closed drooping eyelids over colorless eyes. Her weak voice initiated a chant beginning with wavering tones that steadied quickly and strengthened with each word pronounced from an ancient, nearly forgotten language.

The apprentice's eyes had closed the moment her teacher first smiled. Bidden by carefully measured lyrics, the young woman's eyelids now fluttered open. Before her waited the mistress, the woman who stood apart from the world the novice called home. The aged crone had transformed completely and recaptured the beauty of her youth. Her student craved to obtain that same ability before the unstoppable advance of years would unravel the veil of youth and physical beauty she so valued.

"Mistress Zimda, my heart leaps with joy to see you restored to the beauty that is rightfully yours."

"This gift of transformation will one day be the legacy I leave you when my time comes to join fully in the master's ultimate power." Lips the color of fresh blood shone in candlelight. Narrow yellow flames burned in the centers of ebony eyes. Smooth skin, firm and sleek over fine bone structure, was as white as freshly fallen snow. Crimson tresses flowed freely around shapely shoulders and arms. Her tall body had become as voluptuous as it had been frail and skeletal only minutes earlier.

The novice acknowledged the promise with a reverent dip of her head. "I shall treasure such legacy, Mistress." While the student's eyes were lowered, she missed the humorless smile that reflected the true nature of the ancient conjurer who communed continuously with the darkest of demonic spirits. As she lifted her gaze again, the novice's generous lips also curved upward. Her devout expression concealed the sly, traitorous nature hidden in the coldest reaches of her heart.

Mistress Zimda looked upon her apprentice's beautiful face. Her thoughts filtered through shadowy mists of time and memory. How well she remembered the vitality and lust of youth. Gay parties filled with music and dance. Extravagant ball gowns and lavish repasts. Nights spent in the arms of lovers taken to slake the relentless demands of her body. She had gladly enslaved herself to the grim and stern master. He had promised her that the frailties and weaknesses of her mortal body would return only periodically to remind her of the magnitude of gifts that would remain hers so long as she served him well. This new devotee would deliver renewed energy to the master's ranks and refresh the beauty the mistress coveted.

"The time is come. Are you prepared to make your final pledge to the master?"

"I am."

Zimda's expression appeared much like the frozen stares etched into marble by the hammers and chisels of expert sculptors. "Rise."

The novice lifted her head high and rose to her feet. Her silk robe rustled with sounds seemingly stolen from tree boughs when summer breezes choreographed sashaying dances of abundant leaves. Shimmering black fabric clung to her curvaceous body. Her shoulders squared as her arms dropped to the sides. Erect posture accentuated her physical beauty while simultaneously enhancing an aura of haughty self-confidence.

The red-haired mistress extended her arms. Outstretched fingers waited to curl around the hands of her newest contribution to the master's fold. Master would definitely be pleased with this one. Not only would he satiate his carnal pleasures with her youthful flesh. He would also have a loyal servant readily accepted into the midst of those he prepared to conquer.

As the apprentice reached forth, Zimda's fingers instantly transmuted into long, slender serpents that tightly constricted bones in the novice's hands. The younger woman started, never expecting the appearance of such hideous creatures, let alone the pain. Instead of yielding the sweet, satisfying display of terror the sorceress had anticipated, the student's face turned livid with contemptuous resistance. She would not surrender meekly to the flaming-haired witch's betrayal.

Despite increasing pressure from the serpents as they lengthened to surround slender wrists, the apprentice uttered the most vicious of curses she had ever learned and aimed a well-placed kick into one of the mistress's legs. Mistress Zimda stumbled backward from the unexpected attack, dragging the novice with her. The younger woman swiftly braced herself, determined not to fall and become defenseless prey.

The surprise assault caused the writhing serpents to loosen their crushing compression. Making no attempt to free herself and flee, the intended victim delivered a second kick to the knee of the teacher-turned-oppressor. The mistress fell against the stone altar and wailed out in pain as the snakes released their prisoner.

The apprentice's lips curled into a furious snarl as she flexed sore, bruised hands. The voice that usually spilled forth in velvet tones assumed the cutting edge of a newly sharpened blade. "Did you honestly believe me so naïve that I would cringe in fear at such a pathetic display?"

Zimda recovered her balance. White skin swiftly flushed scarlet with fury as the flames in her eyes blazed. She seethed with burgeoning anger. For uncounted generations, she had fed on both the fearful horror and the blood of those she delivered to the master's table. All had struggled in vain to flee the serpent fingers that held them captive until Master came to claim his spoils. He had then departed with the newly captive soul, often leaving the ravaged body for his servant to feed upon.

Never had one of her initiates shown the audacity to hurl curses and actually counterattack. Incensed, the sorceress leapt forward. The novice quickly sidestepped and whirled around to face the enraged mistress, leaving both women glaring at one another. Hatred distorted otherwise beautiful faces. Rapid breaths drew damp, stale air into their lungs. Each woman studied her adversary's stance and visually measured the distance dividing them. Zimda's mouth formed a sinister smirk intended to intimidate her younger foe. The novice smiled confident arrogance, refusing to show any sign of weakness. Tension impregnated each passing second with escalating hostility.

Youth proved no hindrance as the novice concentrated on recovering the sense of inner calm she knew would be essential to surviving a violent confrontation with her tutor. She must stay composed to maintain the shield that had protected her truest thoughts from the teacher's frequent mind invasions. Many long hours of practice had perfected her ability to visualize selfish desires that projected the submissive image of want and weakness the sorceress sought. Born into a nobleman's family, the student's education had included combat training that prepared her for this moment...this one chance to work toward her goal of achieving youthful, eternal beauty.

Wrath marked the face of the demonic servant accustomed to quick, easy victories. The mind of the accomplished murderess raced. How had this petite beauty repulsed the final attack? How had she even known to expect the end delivered to countless others? Where had she learned the curses that had weakened the serpentine transmutation of the teacher's fingers? This apprentice had concealed the true nature of her thoughts, her character. Swelling antagonism collided with unwelcome angst. If this foul creature could not be defeated, then the teacher would inevitably face Master's cruel retribution. Such an end Zimda would resist with all her wiles and all her strength.

"The student dares challenge the mistress this day," Zimda hissed. "A novelty, indeed, but do not deceive yourself. You have delivered your fate into my hands. If you concede now, you will be spared agony beyond anything your paltry human brain can conceive. Death will come with greater ease as reward for your retreat from insolence."

The apprentice stood her ground in silence. She would risk no verbal sparring with the mistress. Her concentration must remain unbroken. Her only response to her opponent's comments was the slightest curve of her lips.

Zimda's lithe body swayed with the ease and flexibility of a serpent. Patience, she thought to herself. She sought to lock gazes with her victim so that her eyes' searing flames might set afire the novice's resistance. Carefully controlled features masked growing frustration. Her opponent's reaction was that of someone blind. Patience, the sorceress reminded herself. Patience.

With no change in overall stance, the wary apprentice slowly lifted a hand to the gold clasp holding her cape-like robe closed. Grasping the fastener, she tugged it open. Just as she expected, the sorceress perceived momentary vulnerability and lunged forward. The apprentice nimbly leapt aside, freeing herself from the robe and whipping it around the teacher's ankles, causing her to fall.

Shocked, the sorceress screamed obscenities as she quickly righted herself. The real battle began as unadulterated rage flooded Zimda to her very core. Years of decadent practice had honed both her skill and pleasure in bringing the stream of victims Master required. She aimed blow after blow at the student who evaded her with surprising agility. When Zimda's serpent fingers would have struck with their poisonous tips, the apprentice sprang into the air on nimble legs. She forcefully knocked the witch to the floor and pounded the vipers beneath her feet with brutal force. The two women waged personal war without the slightest hint of mercy.

Their battle raged all around the dimly illuminated chamber. Grunts and groans echoed with fearsome intensity. Creatures dwelling inside the cave scattered to avoid being crushed by the fighters or immobilized in melted wax slithering down mossy rock walls as candles toppled in the combatants' ferocious wake. Flickering lights on the altar cast rapidly moving shadows in the cave, accentuating the rising tide of violent, pervading evil.

The mistress's earlier arrogance diminished in the face of the student whose fighting abilities matched her powers of deception. Signs of strain began to line the teacher's lovely features. Ages had passed with the easy demise of all her chosen victims. Never had she faced any opponent as clever as this one.

Drawing from her deep well of evil, the sorceress renewed her attack with fresh ferocity. Uttering words of a rarely used incantation, she transformed her whole body into that of a lethal snake capable of striking with speed hardly visible to the human eye. She would make this novice suffer prolonged agony for her impudence.

Only inside herself could the apprentice's smile be perceived. Certain the mistress would rely on dark spells to achieve her goal, the novice had expected the incantation. Within the blink of an eye, the young woman withdrew a razor-sharp blade that had nestled against her midriff, hidden within a sheath sewn into her chemise. As Zimda coiled before rising into strike position, the novice lunged forward. With lightning speed, she severed the head of the scarlet-headed serpent before its pointed fangs could deliver their lethal bite.

The student's calm perusal of the battle's outcome utterly contrasted with her panting breath. The serpent had disappeared. Red hair flowed across cold rock as it mingled with crimson rivers of steaming blood running from her former teacher's decapitated body. She curiously studied the scene with absolutely no sense of revulsion or regret. The mistress had taught her well. Inflicting death sparked a uniquely euphoric climax no lover could match.

"You are wrong."

The novice turned. Dark hair had fallen loose from its restrictive braid. The still rapid pace of her breathing enhanced the sensual fullness of her rounded breasts. One strap of her camisole had slipped down onto her arm, exposing her shoulder. The slender column of her neck revealed the rhythmic pulsing of blood through her veins. Her dark eyes showed no sign of surprise, no hint of fear.

"Am I?"

The master smiled. How wrong mere humans were. Their tales told of the demon whose leathery black skin carried the putrid scent of death. Ancient stories painted pictures of a hideous being with sharply pointed teeth, mocking smile, and long claws on hands and feet.

The apprentice returned his smile as remembered legends flitted through her mind. She noted with appreciation his handsome features. Glossy black hair was straight with shining highlights. Although not exceptionally tall, his body was lean and muscular. The length and breadth of his torso and limbs were perfectly proportioned. Tawny skin was sleek and supple. Without hesitation, she openly admired the prideful display of his naked masculinity.

"You do not fear me." His voice was deep, its echoes rolling through the cavern's chambers and tunnels like the waves of a great storm raging onto deserted shores.

"Do you wish me to fear the master I have come to serve?"

The master's head tilted backward. His eyes closed. Human females always served his sexual appetite. Never had a single one completely satisfied his primal lust, but he sensed a striking difference in this fresh recruit. Her exceptional beauty belied the ferocity she had unleashed on Zimda. She demonstrated no trace of reluctance or hesitation in the face of his apparent desire. In fact, he perceived wanton yearning emanating from every inch of her body.

"We must first drink," he told her.

Crouching low, she scooped warm, glistening blood into her cupped hand. He smiled approval as she held her hand to his lips so that he might indulge in the salty fluid of life. In like form, he bent down and scooped up a portion of blood. He watched with fascinated yearning as she did not hesitate to drink the intoxicating beverage he offered. He bent forward again, this time drawing blood-covered hands slowly across his chest and abdomen.

She sensed his unspoken command and removed what little clothing she wore. Dipping her fingers back into the pool of blood, she traced crimson lines over her breasts. Filling her hands with more of the teacher's lifeblood, she drew scarlet-stained hands languorously along the curves of her body, touching herself in places sure to spark the master's interest.

When she finished, she dipped her face in respect. "May I please you, Master?"

Receiving his nod of assent, she began to tease and titillate his body with the tip of her tongue, slowly licking away blood that had power to preserve her beauty for ages to come.

Zimda had truly done well, the master thought. He then began to partake of the delights of this most desirable flesh that sought to satisfy his needs without bartering her favors for the gift of ageless beauty.

Brenna glanced upward at the sound of her name. "I apologize, Papa. My mind was wandering. What did you say?"

Her father smiled indulgently. "I only remarked how quiet you are this morning."

"I was thinking about Carola. I'll miss her when I leave school." The glib lie was nothing compared to what she had done the night before. Count Ingnan Brandere's ever-present benign smile would likely dissolve in horror if he ever learned the truth.

"When you return for this last term at school, perhaps you might reconsider withdrawing. With my position as governor, I'm sure I can convince the headmaster to allow you to continue your studies."

Brenna clearly sensed the warning from her older sister seated across the table. Forcing a smile, she replied, "No, the classes are too difficult and the rules far too rigid for me."

Casting her father a glowing smile, Breeneth Brandere defended her younger sister. "Papa, Brenna is too high-spirited to spend time in such a dull, lifeless place. That school is more suitable for girls who lack the charm and personality to flourish at our level of society."

Breeneth's comment sparked a twinge of discomfort that her father successfully concealed. He sensed undercurrents beyond simple defense of her younger sister's disdain for school. His daughters had always been close, but he sometimes worried that Breeneth might take unfair advantage of Brenna's adulation. He ignored sporadic rumors of inappropriate behavior, attributing them to jealousy of Breeneth's exceptional charm. His oldest child was beautiful and captivating. That should be a source of pride, but her haughty attitude and flashes of temper prompted occasional bouts of unease.

Dismissing the twist of unwelcome thoughts, he turned his attention to his wife. "Are the guest suites ready for the prince and his party when they arrive?"

His wife smiled and nodded. "The suites are ready and extra servants assigned. I provided the kitchen staff with formal menu plans. Stable hands are also alerted."

"My dear, your efficiency is exceeded only by your beauty." He paused. "I'm still somewhat surprised the prince plans to stay only a week."

Breeneth dropped her gaze to her plate, barely avoiding a scornful sneer as her parents abruptly moved from discussion of the prince's impending visit to their usual affectionate teases. How ridiculously boring, she thought while considering plans to further enchant her country's handsome prince. Smiling deviously, she breathed a confident sigh that he would propose marriage this time. She could finally contemplate an unending future as Ambracor's most beautiful and powerful queen ever.

Later that afternoon, Brenna smoothed yards of glistening gold silk draping from her sister's tiny waist into full skirts. "This gown is perfect for the party," she said admiringly. "The prince will never be able to resist when he sees you wearing this."

Preening as she regarded her elegant image in a gilt-framed mirror, Breeneth smiled, her confidence emboldened by the secret alliance with her demon lover. "We will make sure of it. Once I become queen, you will stay with me at the palace. You can forget about wasting away at that useless school."

Brenna's throat tightened a moment. The small puncture wound on her wrist still hurt. "You know I'll do anything for you, but I still don't understand why we had to mix our blood into that goblet."

Stretching out a delicate hand, Breeneth caressed her sister's smooth cheek. "A true blood oath carries more power than any promise. We are each bound to protect one another forever. Does that not make you happy?"

Brenna wondered how she managed to smile in agreement. How she wished she had not pretended to return home the night before. How she chastised herself for surrendering to temptation and following Breeneth to that dark cave. Never could she have imagined the scene that had unfolded before her horrified eyes. Hastening back to her father's mansion and slipping into bed, she had wondered if she would ever feel safe again.

Chapter Three

"MAY I JOIN YOU?"

Diana looked up with a blank expression on her face. For a moment, she wished she could say no. "Sure. I was just reading."

Setting her tray on the table, Jennie Clarke smiled. "I'll be so glad for warm weather so we can get outside for lunch and some fresh air. There are never enough tables in here."

"Warm weather will be welcome," Diana agreed, setting aside her book.

Showing no effort to conceal curiosity, Jennie read the title of the book now lying on the table. A shake of her head and the audible click of her tongue yielded undeniable signs of disapproval. "If you really believe in God, how can you read that kind of garbage?"

Amber eyes assumed a cool stare in response to the comment. "Jennie, we've discussed this before. I respect your right to your ideas. Please respect mine."

"It's not a lack of respect. It's a matter of concern for someone I like very much. I want the best for you. I was honest enough to express my lack of respect for your church, and I justified what I said with facts. Why won't you even give my church a chance? You could meet people your age who would share your Christian beliefs and help you build on them."

Diana started gathering her things to leave. Suddenly, she stopped. "Jennie, you know I respect your knowledge and experience here at work. On the other hand, on non-work subjects, especially when it comes to faith matters, you continuously cross the line. Your so-called facts are distorted by omissions and half-truths. Right now, I would even say you're acting like a bully. This is the last time I expect to have this conversation with you. My religion or any books I choose to study are none of your business. If I read about esoteric subjects, it's not because I'm in league with the devil. If anything, the circumstances are completely opposite."

Red-faced and obviously angry, Jennie scowled. "You're playing with fire. I only hoped to rescue you from the damnation you're letting that roommate of yours lead you into."

Quiet anger rose from some mysterious corner of Diana's soul. "You've despised Kendra since you met her. You've always been barely cordial with her. I attended one service at your church. You keep saying your church is reaching out to all of God's people, but I couldn't help noticing that its makeup is completely lopsided. Whether it's her color or her interest in the paranormal, I don't give a damn. Leave Kendra out of this." Picking up her things to go, she paused. "And, by the way, God watches out for me in ways you'll never comprehend. Remember that."

Leaving the cafeteria and going straight to her cubicle, Diana dumped her things on her desk and marched to the office of the division manager. When he invited her in, she entered, closed the door, and leaned against the wall across from his desk. He motioned for her to take a seat, but she shook her head and remained standing.

As angry as Diana felt, her voice sounded amazingly calm when she spoke. "Mr. Grant, I'm sorry. I've tried all your suggestions, but nothing works. At lunch, she just started in about the church issue and then proceeded to slam my roommate. She has no right to do that...not personally for sure, and most certainly not from a professional perspective. Considering she's my department lead, it makes circumstances extremely hard."

Mr. Grant's eyes conveyed sympathy. "From the professional side, this is the only issue we have with her performance. You once said yourself she sometimes goes overboard because of how she credits her church for saving the lives of her mother and sister after that horrible accident a few years ago."

Frustrated, Diana asked, "So what am I supposed to do? Desert my own religious faith and surrender my own interests to keep peace in a job I love?"

"Diana, take a seat and calm down. You know I'd never even suggest such a thing. I don't want to lose you. I'll have another talk with Jennie, but I honestly don't think that will resolve the tension between you two."

He pursed thin lips together beneath a graying mustache. "Look, you're a valuable employee here. Susan Grayson is leaving the FX department to have her baby. Confidentially, she isn't coming back. I was already planning to ask you. If you're interested in the job, I'll announce your transfer to take her place. It will slot you into a higher-grade position and move you out of Jennie's department. In the meantime, I'll arrange for Jennie to work with HR regarding this behavior. I don't want to ruin her career here or lose her expertise. I hope you understand."

Relief eased tension from Diana's face. "I honestly appreciate your confidence regarding the new position. I'd love learning that side of the division. As far as Jennie's concerned, this whole thing has been tough because she's really a great person except for this one issue."

"Good," Mr. Grant told her. "I'll start the paperwork. I'll have to ask your patience for a few weeks, but this should work quite well because you'll have time to train with Susan before she goes. In the meantime, leave the situation with Jennie in my hands."

By Wednesday of the following week, Diana had managed to maintain her composure while also declining extra hours she often worked to make it easier for Jennie to attend several weekly church meetings. Diana insisted she had commitments of her own, including a promise to look in on the aging mother of a college friend who was out of town. Jennie's reaction had been decidedly cool upon realizing she would have to resume more of the responsibilities expected of a department lead.

While Jennie was undeniably annoyed, Kendra heartily applauded the return of the old Diana, whose spunk and spirit had been the initial spark igniting their friendship. For months, the increasing frequency of Diana's recurring dreams had drained her. Kendra felt thrilled to see her friend standing up for herself and again performing the acts of kindness that gave her so much satisfaction. Only one nagging concern remained. If the dreams continued, Diana said nothing.

"Mrs. Merrill, is there anything else I can get you?"

"No, dear. I'm fine. I think I'll just watch a little TV and then go to bed." The elderly woman, in her mid-seventies, looked up at Diana with a broad smile that highlighted wrinkles around her mouth and eyes.

"Your nightgown and your robe are at the foot of your bed, and the covers are turned back. I set the kitchen table with dishes for breakfast in the morning. A box of your favorite cereal is on the table. I also sliced some strawberries and left them in the blue bowl in the fridge."

Mrs. Merrill laughed. "You and my Cynthia are both gems. I appreciate the help, but I'm really not so old that I can't take care of a few minor chores."

Diana looked embarrassed. "I know you're far from being an invalid. Still, you've earned a little pampering from my generation, don't you think?"

"We can agree on the pampering part. Now, give me a hug and get out of here. It's getting late, and you said you didn't drive tonight."

Pushing her arms into the sleeves of her coat, Diana frowned. "I let Kendra use my car. She needed to get some hours in at the counseling center to fulfill course requirements. With all the transfers, it would take her hours to get home. I can walk up to Broadwyn and catch a bus that will take me straight to our apartment complex."

"Be careful, sweetie. This neighborhood seems fine, but the area past Broadwyn starts to get rough. I'd hate to see something bad happen to you."

"Not to worry, Mrs. Merrill. I grew up in a neighborhood with mostly rowdy boys. I had no choice but to learn how to defend myself. Besides, I've taken a couple of martial arts classes with Kendra. She says I'm a natural. Now, keep the door locked, your phone close, and call 911 in case of any emergency. I'll check on you tomorrow, okay?"

"All right, Diana. Good night."

A few minutes later, Diana pulled the hood of her coat over her head. The weatherman hadn't said anything about rain, but the night was already dark, and a fine drizzle hung in the air. Tall lampposts dripped a kind of fuzzy, pale orange light onto deserted streets. As she walked briskly toward the bus shelter on Broadwyn, she fervently hoped the bus would be on time.

Suddenly, two men jumped onto the sidewalk from between parked cars. Both wore jeans and dark hoodies. Deliberately blocking her path, they assumed a threatening posture. She stopped and glanced around. Several more figures approached from different directions.

She stepped backward and stopped abruptly against someone behind her. A sense she had never felt before prevented her from panicking. She breathed in deeply. "May I help you, gentlemen?"

One of the men in front of her pounded something against his open palm. She couldn't tell if it was a stick or a knife. "Nice of you to offer," came the sneering reply.

"Yeah, baby, real nice. It's lonely out here tonight, and we was thinking we could use some company."

"Look, I really need to get home, and I'm positive I'm not your type. There's some cash in my purse. Take it and go find yourself some fun. Just leave me alone." She felt her heartbeat speeding up and adrenaline starting to infuse her body.

"Aw, c'mon, baby. You ain't even polite. No please or nothin' like that. We'll gladly take your money, but we already decided we wanna take you, too."

Not without a fight, she thought. In a flash, she twisted and shoved her elbow hard into the midsection of whoever had come up behind her. As the others ran toward her, she punched, kicked, and screamed for help.

Entering a house a short distance down the street, two men looked up and saw the commotion. Spotting at least seven men attacking a lone woman, one man cautioned the other. "You know we're not supposed to embroil ourselves in their affairs."

"Stay, then. I cannot let her face that alone," the second man responded tersely, dropping a bag on the old-fashioned front porch and breaking into a run. The first man groaned, dropped his bags, and chased after his companion.

Within seconds, the gang regretted their decision to prowl streets in a different neighborhood. The woman they had assaulted fought like a wild she-cat. When the two men appeared from seemingly nowhere, it didn't matter that the delinquents outnumbered them four to one. The two strangers possessed exceptional fighting skills that sent blades flying, flung assailants onto wet pavement, cracked jawbones, and dislocated at least two shoulders.

Although the apparent leader was furious, he wasn't entirely foolhardy. "Fucking bitch!" he shouted just before shoving Diana as hard as he could and then pivoting to sprint to safety.

When Diana stumbled backward, she fell against a fire hydrant. Blood spurted from a gash on her head and mingled with rain and perspiration wetting her face. No matter how hard she tried, she couldn't force her eyes to stay open. Dragging in several breaths, she struggled to cling to consciousness and softly moaned as a strong arm gently slid beneath her shoulders and slowly raised her up.

"She's bleeding badly. We need to get her back to the house."

"Leave her. Someone's coming. I think that sound is their emergency vehicles."

"I will not leave her alone out here!" Quickly gathering her into his arms, the first who came to Diana's aid stood up. "Run! Now!"

Diana was aware enough to realize she was being carried away from the wet, muddy ground where she had fallen. When her head tilted against a firm shoulder, an absurd thought crossed her groggy mind. Whoever he was, his clothes were going to be a bloody mess. Her nose crinkled at what smelled like a strangely familiar scent. How peculiar, she thought just before losing consciousness.

Chapter Four

BLUE EYES STARED OUT THROUGH a floor-to-ceiling window. Brilliant sunshine cast a ring of rays through clouds beginning to clear from afternoon skies. The heavens promised the first dry evening of the week. As heavy velvet draperies swung back into place, those striking eyes maintained their stormy expression when they shifted to face Ambracor's King Hamund.

"I cannot, Father. I *will* not."

Hamund exhaled an impatient breath. "My son, I know how much you loved her. I even led the escort to take her home in hope that Artrian and I could persuade her to change her mind. Now, six years have passed. You cannot continue this way. You must accept her death."

Thehrund's handsome face flushed with barely contained anger. "Father, we've discussed this over and over again. How many times must I tell you? I *will* find her."

Exasperation showed clearly on Hamund's face. "You were there. I know you had just arrived, but you clearly saw how she jumped off her horse and confronted the enemy warriors charging me. She fought as bravely as any man to protect her king."

"Yes," Thehrund replied, "and, as you've pointed out many times, she also took the brutal thrust of a Breyal lance." The prince grimaced as his memory replayed the sound of her scream that had accompanied both guilt and grief through years of restless nights.

"Thehrund, life has not stopped. I grow older. It will not be so many years before you assume responsibility for ruling our kingdom. You must choose a wife and produce an heir to follow you."

The king's voice softened. "Your father would enjoy the pleasures of grandchildren in these last years."

The prince's face dropped, but eyes the same blue as deep ocean waters rose beneath wide black eyebrows. "I still believe in the voices, Father. They promised I would find her. I also swore an oath that I must fulfill."

King Hamund's jaw clenched, and his back teeth ground together. His son remained as stubborn as ever. "What you experienced was nothing more than a dream...a dream born of shock and sorrow. I watched her die in the ambush near Articene. So did you and many others."

"Yes, I did. We've also discussed that point time and time again, but hers was the only body not recovered after the Breyals retreated. The only one! There was no sign of her! Nothing but her sword on the ground and her horse."

"Thehrund, the few Breyals who escaped probably took her body with them. You've studied their ways. In victory or defeat, they often take a corpse or two to display as trophies from their murderous forays. Especially when they suffer a loss, they must produce slain bodies to avoid execution by their chieftains. This time, they took hers."

The very thought of Breyal hands defiling her body triggered a rise of bitter bile that scorched the back of Thehrund's throat. Still, he obstinately clung to words from voices that had seemingly stopped time during the skirmish that afternoon. Voices...sweet and clear, yet strong and authoritative. Those angel voices had promised he could be forgiven for his transgression that had hurt her so badly. They had also warned that the path to reconciliation would severely try his patience and his resolve. He must understand that time and trials would be required to prove himself worthy. If he was absolutely sure that his love was strong enough, they had promised he would find her. After that, it would be up to him to convince her of his remorse and his love. While penitence would earn divine forgiveness, he alone must restore her trust.

"Well?" Sharpness in Hamund's voice snapped his son's retreat into private thought. "Have you heard even a single word I've said for the past five minutes?"

Long waves of black hair swung from side to side. The low pitch of his voice sounded more like a growl when he answered, "Father, it makes no difference. You drummed into my head the importance of following through on any sworn oath given of free will. I must not fail. Her life is in my hands and mine alone. I will continue the search, and I will find her."

King Hamund stared at the door through which his son departed after excusing himself to attend his afternoon training session. Compassion vied with anger. He admitted to himself how much he had adored the young woman his son once planned to marry. Years after her death, even he still missed her. She would have made an excellent wife and a wise queen who could have tempered his son's headstrong character.

When Hamund's horse had thrown him, she had swiftly dismounted and raced to the monarch's side, only to perish while defending him from advancing warriors. She had died bravely and honorably. Six years was more than long enough for Thehrund to mourn.

"Dear husband, you should be proud that he remembers and practices the values you taught him," Queen Narlina said softly, placing her hand comfortingly on the king's shoulder.

Surprised, Hamund turned. "When...how long have you been here?"

"Long enough to understand what you do not. He's convinced that she lives. Until he surrenders this quest on his own, I sincerely believe you must exercise patience. There's no need to build walls that will serve only to divide the two of you."

Hamund closed his eyes and shook his head. "I also taught him the responsibilities necessary to lead our nation when he becomes king."

"The day will come when he will be a sovereign every bit as strong and dedicated as his father. You must believe me when I tell you that. I think you must also trust your son to discover the answers he needs to live his life. Be satisfied that he works hard to earn the respect of your armies and your people. Accept his faith in God and the example he makes of himself."

"What if they find out? What if our people learn of this?"

"I know you fear ridicule if it becomes public knowledge that he remains unmarried because of these voices he claims he heard. That could happen today...or any day. It hasn't happened since her death, so it may never happen. Whatever the case, we will face events as they unfold. We mustn't seek problems where none exists."

Hamund crossed the large parlor and helped himself to a glass of brandy. He stared at the wall as if seeking some elusive solution to this divisive impasse with his son. He finally turned to face his wife. "My dear, the problem does exist. It merely remains undiscovered."

Narlina's eyes, a lighter blue than those of her son, studied her husband's features. His once-black hair had grayed. Within its length hung the two long, narrow braids on each side of his head that signified his royal station. His gray goatee was neatly trimmed and enhanced his image of intelligence and wisdom. She smiled gently into Hamund's still-handsome face and approached him with hands outstretched. "You must have faith."

Pulling her into his embrace, he wondered how he would have managed had he lost his own Narlina. There was nothing he loved more than his loyal, loving wife. As he held her, he sighed heavily. "I so worry about when he just disappears for weeks at a time. If only I had some idea of where he goes and how he gets there and back. If he should ever need my help, I would never know."

"We can only comfort ourselves with the knowledge that he is an exceptional warrior blessed with a brilliant mind. We must allow him to live his life according to his own choices, not those we would make for him."

Hamund rested his chin on the top of his wife's head. "Is there any task harder for a parent?"

Profuse sweat separated long, thick hair into soggy strands clinging to Thehrund's brow and cheeks. Drops of perspiration shone in his black beard. Rapid breaths filled heaving lungs. Lips pulled into a tight line beneath his nose. Eyes focused on his training partner's every move as the two faced off after a particularly grueling exchange of parries and counter-parries, ripostes and lunges. Again, the clang of broadswords rang through the air. Within minutes, the prince used all the might of his strong body, advancing forcefully until his opponent fell backward and lost his sword.

Leaning forward, the prince grabbed the hand of his bested partner and hauled him to his feet. "Congratulations! You must have outlasted Nagrand's best time by at least four minutes," Thehrund exclaimed to his two best friends. The low tones of his slightly gruff voice carried notes of sincere admiration.

"High praises for you," Nagrand said as he heartily patted his brother's back. To Thehrund, he added, "And it was only two minutes. I assume that's likely because you showed pity to a priest who insists on continuing the dual role as a royal bodyguard."

Karan's flushed face pulled into a grimace as he stretched muscles screaming with pain. "I still fail to understand all this practice with swords. We encountered not a single swordsman during either of our last two journeys through the portal."

Thehrund concentrated on loosening buckles of leather wrist supports before glancing up with a grim smile. "You must admit that training with the sword hones reflexes and reactions as surely as the whetstone sharpens steel blades. The resulting agility saved us from serious injury more than once."

"Ah, Your Highness, a fine point you have there. Those mobile machines we encountered last time moved faster than winter winds sweeping down the slopes of Mount Dardron."

"Nagrand, I wish to see neither you nor your brother run down by one of those infernal carriages. I also fear what other contraptions we might encounter. It seems recent excursions through that portal have been more dangerous than ever," Thehrund replied as he studied edges of his buttoned sword.

Noting the all-too-familiar shift in the prince's mood, Karan nodded. "True. The risks do seem greater, but both my brother and I understood the dangers when we swore ourselves into your service for this quest of yours."

Thehrund shoved his practice gear into a canvas duffel and hoisted the bag over his left shoulder. Expelling a heavy sigh, he shook his head. "My friends, I will always appreciate your loyalty and your company; however, I do begin to wonder if it would be better if I continue the search alone."

Nagrand broke uncomfortable silence as the three men headed toward the palace. "Thehrund, Karan and I have accompanied you not just because you are our prince. We have complete confidence in you. We also believe our journeys to these strange realms in search of Sindara must have some mystical connection meant to serve Ambracor's future."

Karan joined his brother's attempt to allay their friend's concerns. "Your apprehensions are understandable, but Nagrand is right. There can be no doubting the very real nature of these little escapades. We've been with you from the beginning, and together we shall see this through to whatever conclusion Creator God grants us."

Thehrund voiced no reply, but his expression reflected sincere appreciation. These two childhood friends, both of noble birth, had buoyed his spirits whenever sadness or self-deprecation assaulted him. Their loyalty was indeed salve for his battered soul. As they parted ways for the day, he silently prayed his quest would soon succeed. He wanted to eliminate the risks they freely accepted. Even more so, he desperately needed to end his plague of loneliness by finding the only woman he could ever really love.

Bracordia. The streets of Ambracor's capital city were festooned with banners and flags boasting every color imaginable. Excited chatter mingled with the whinnies of hundreds of horses, the jangle of harnesses, and hooves and wheels clattering over brick and stone. From high above, the nation's beloved royal family watched from a balcony as delegations from each of Ambracor's provinces processed through winding streets leading to the national palace.

King Hamund, a tall man with regal bearing, appeared exceptionally impressive wearing a sapphire-blue velvet tunic as he watched and waved at crowds below. On his left was his petite queen, a beautiful woman whose brunette hair was even longer than her husband's. His son, sole heir to Ambracor's throne, stood to the king's right. The royal family smiled greetings to those attending this year's month-long provincial conferences. Following the parade and subsequent welcoming ceremony, official meetings would begin in two days. The royal family, however, would informally receive visitors that same afternoon.

"How good it is to see you and your wife looking so well, Artrian," Hamund said later as he and another man lifted crystal glasses from a tray held by an attentive servant. "I so regret that I was unable to attend your son's wedding earlier this year. Such a joyous occasion that must have been."

Count Artrian Varacor saluted the king before tasting the drink in his hand. "It was indeed. Personally, I missed your presence, but Thehrund represented your family quite well."

"Of that I am glad. He takes little time these days to enjoy the niceties of life."

Artrian's blue-gray eyes met those of his longtime friend. "In one way or the other, I suppose we both lost children during the Breyal incursion at Articene."

Hamund nodded as his face clouded, and his voice held genuine sadness. "Too true, my friend, too true. Still, I can at least embrace my son. It pains my heart to think..."

Artrian interrupted him. "Hamund, my friend, Liana and I will never fully recover from losing our daughter. We loved her dearly, but Thehrund's continued devotion still touches our hearts."

"And mine, but I cannot deny my wish that he would finally move ahead with his life. He's still a young man…"

"As handsome as our king and with potential to become just as great a leader," Liana Varacor interjected with a gentle smile.

"Liana, I thank you for the compliment on my behalf and that of my son," Hamund said with a twinkle in his eye.

"It is only truth as I see it," Liana replied. Her light brown eyes were the same honeyed hue her daughter's had been, but her delicate features were darker and more narrow. She was slender and tall, her height enhanced by the close-fitting gown of dark green silk she wore. Although hints of sadness always lurked in her expression, kindness was forever evident in her presence.

"Why do I suspect I've become your subject of conversation?" Thehrund asked, unexpectedly joining the discussion.

"Thehrund! How glad I am to see you!" Liana greeted warmly as she accepted an affectionate kiss on each cheek.

"And I you," he replied before turning to Artrian. "How are you, sir?"

"Well, Thehrund, thank you." The count swiftly assessed the prince's appearance. "You look more like your father every time I see you."

Thehrund responded with a smile. "Thank you. Father is a great example to emulate, although I imagine he was likely boring you with the sad state of my single life."

Hamund's brow furrowed. "Thehrund, please."

"Father, I mean neither disrespect nor discourtesy."

Liana quickly noted the instant rise of tension between the two. "Your father only shares our desire for your happiness, Thehrund."

The prince nodded respectfully. "I apologize if my attempt at humor seemed out of line. Father, Minister Kardron is here. I know you wanted to speak with him as soon as he arrived."

Remaining with the Varacors after the king excused himself, Thehrund smiled wryly. "Father continues to worry that the throne of Ambracor will be left without an heir."

Count Varacor's eyebrows lifted. "He has every right to be concerned. You are his son and only heir to his throne." Pausing, he discreetly continued, "Have you made any recent journeys?"

A curt shake of the prince's head accompanied a frustrated sigh. "No. The portal has remained closed for several months."

Liana's eyelids slid closed. Fear, combined with reluctant resignation, tinged her response. "Perhaps it will now remain closed. Perhaps the portal openings were no more than opportunities for you to exorcise the demons of your grief."

"Lady Liana, I refuse to believe that. I simply cannot. As far as I can determine, this portal never existed until after my return from Articene. The voices told me exactly where to find it. They also instructed me on how to enter and leave it. Their words of warning are ones that echo through my mind each and every day."

Count Varacor placed an encouraging hand on the prince's arm. Cautious hope shone from his eyes. "With every shred of my being, I want to believe in those voices. Sindara was a light in our lives that we miss terribly. Having that light returned is a precious dream, but Liana and I would never think less of you should you decide to end your trips into the portal. There are times when one must accept the reality of death, no matter how painful that acceptance."

Thehrund swallowed hard. "The fault is mine that she broke the engagement and persuaded Father to escort her to Cahmdurn. In failing Sindara, I failed everyone, especially myself. I will not rest until either I find her or die in the attempt."

"Why do you not tell your father about the portal?"

"He already questions my sanity regarding the voices. His worries are pressing enough. I have no wish to add to them."

King Hamund interrupted the quiet exchange. Observant eyes noted his son's quick retreat into silence. "Minister Kardron and I are going to discuss a few matters in private. Since it concerns the build-up of Breyal forces just beyond Arvacon borders, I thought you might wish to join us, Artrian."

The count dipped his head in agreement. "Absolutely. Ambushes such as the one at Articene have recently resumed with increasing frequency. I must decide on a course of action for our provincial militia."

"Shall I accompany you, Father?"

Hamund sighed and shook his head. "No, my son. You and I can discuss details later. For now, I prefer that you attend guests here."

"Very well," Thehrund said. He regretted his father's occasional reluctance to include him in such meetings. At times, he wondered if his father really did think him mad. Truthfully, there were occasions when the prince questioned his own sanity regarding the continued quest. He could not deny its apparent absurdity. Still, the voices had been clear and concise. The portal had existed exactly as they had said. He had also committed himself. Accepting his chosen path, Thehrund smiled and joined his mother in welcoming new arrivals.

Midnight. Thehrund stood by the window of his bedchamber and gazed at the multitude of stars glittering against black, cloudless skies. How vast the universe appeared as he tried to imagine its length and breadth. The march of innumerable celestial bodies on their relentless, endless treks provided intriguing fodder for thought. Constellations came and left as sure markers of changing seasons. Centuries of observations by learned men offered reassurance that the celestial formations would return again and again. Recalling discussions shared with Sindara behind her telescope, he occasionally wondered where the stars went when they disappeared.

Thehrund stepped away from the window and mechanically untied the belt of his long robe. He sometimes thought too much about matters far beyond anything he could ever comprehend or control. Leave the stars in the heavens and their infinite journeys to the plans and designs of Creator God. The world of man had its own issues, many of which were too complicated ever to master. Thehrund shook off a frustrated sigh at the thought. This night, even the simplest matters escaped his control.

Moments later, he pulled a thick quilt over his shoulders and turned on his side. Would he find sleep this night? The question plagued him often. There were times when exhaustion gathered him in its embrace and carried him into deep, welcome slumber. Other nights found him tossing and turning as dreams replayed memories filled with every conceivable emotion a man might know. Dreams, he thought, as his eyelids grew heavier. When Sindara appeared in his dreams, her image provoked a potent mix of love and desire, hope and laughter, and the inevitable blend of guilt, shame, and grief.

On those few occasions when he dreamed of Breeneth, his subconscious was forced to confront his levity and indulgences upon entering manhood. He had enjoyed the wanton satisfaction of an affair with Breeneth, daughter of Count Brandere of Bramond Province. Her voluptuous, dark-haired beauty had fanned the flames of a young man's physical desires. She had proven especially adept at arranging time for them to play their roles as ardent lovers while concealing their intimate relationship behind a veil of innocent propriety. Her goal had been evident from the beginning. Ambitious for greater rank and position, she coveted the jeweled crown she hoped to claim as queen of Ambracor.

The unseen obstacle in Breeneth's way had been that Thehrund was not a man for whom mere satisfaction of his virile body's demands would suffice. With growing maturity came a surprisingly deep-rooted need. His life had been laid out for him at birth. The day would come when his father's death would place the crown of Ambracor on his head. He consciously began to note the closeness of his parents. Within their marriage, they freely shared conversation, opinions, and counsel on every conceivable subject. They were also very much in love. Thehrund was certain that, unlike many who frequented his father's court, his parents had always remained faithful to one another. In a far corner of his being, Thehrund discovered an unexpected void, a need for the same kind of love his parents knew.

When Thehrund ended their affair, Breeneth had expressed more fury than hurt and accused him of using her. The vile obscenities she had hurled were shocking, especially coming from a woman of noble birth who had been educated in religious schools. She claimed to love him, but he was far from blind to her promiscuous nature. She most certainly had not been virgin when their affair began. He had also informed her that he was well aware she still entertained other lovers. She was welcome to take her complaints to her father, but they both knew she dared not risk her father's disapproval. The parting had been bitter, made more so by the fact that they were occasionally forced to endure public occasions requiring outward civility.

Shortly after the affair ended, King Hamund dispatched his son to Cahmdurn, the flourishing economic and government center of Arvacon Province. While there, the prince would study under the tutelage of Artrian Varacor. His goal was to develop a thorough knowledge of laws of governance by actually working in a provincial administration. Hamund also expected Thehrund to improve his perception of the mentality of citizens in the most populous and prosperous region outside Ambracor's capital district. Under Count Varacor's careful guidance, the prince should gain greater insight regarding the expectations of peoples in distant reaches of the kingdom he would one day govern.

Setting aside the more carefree nature of youth, Thehrund dutifully applied himself to tasks assigned by Count Varacor. During his first week in Cahmdurn, he met key commissioners and other lesser officials. He then delved into the finer details of government operations and how various agencies cooperated to fulfill their respective responsibilities. He often went to bed late with his head aching, but he also found himself growing more appreciative of challenges facing local governments that he had once laughingly dismissed as petty circuses. Much of his change in attitude resulted directly from Count Varacor's uniquely fascinating method of explaining procedures, describing how their complexities connected, thus building new perspectives for the prince to consider.

By his fifth week in Arvacon, Thehrund had completely immersed himself in his tasks to the point he often brought questions to the dinner table. His efforts became so diligent and so consuming that Lady Liana convinced her husband to set aside a few days for a holiday at their country estate. Sensitive and compassionate, she reminded her husband of how his own father had pushed him to learn the detailed workings of state with little time for leisure. She insisted their royal charge would gain much more with a balance between work and pleasure.

At first, Thehrund protested the break. With growing maturity came a greater sense of responsibility. He found that officials reporting to the count were knowledgeable and conscientious. With their help, he began to recognize the value of analyzing and addressing the broad scope of local needs. The result established a base for implementing continuous improvements in the lives of ordinary citizens while simultaneously building success for merchants and businesses. From the prince's personal perspective, gone were thoughts of nights filled with gaming, drinking, and women. Instead, he found himself mentally challenged and with newfound respect for his father's wisdom.

Graciously, although somewhat reluctantly, Thehrund accepted the Varacors' invitation to spend a few days in the country. Upon his arrival, he was more than glad he had done so. The count's ancestral home stood on the broad crest of a low hill. The grounds sloped gently downward and were artfully divided into expansive green lawns separated by carefully tended gardens. Massive, ancient trees created a sense of connection to both land and history. Thehrund breathed in deeply of clean, fresh air and recognized even more changes in his personal perceptions. The prospect of riding and exploring the estate promised revitalizing retreat.

Making the nearly three-hour trip on horseback, Thehrund followed the Varacors' carriage until it stopped beneath the porte-cochere in front of the manor's grand entrance. Dismounting, he handed his reins to a waiting groom. Thehrund then strode toward the carriage door opened by a servant and extended his hand to assist Lady Liana as she stepped down ahead of her husband. Just as Lord Artrian joined his wife, one of the enormous double doors of the mansion's main entrance flew open.

"Mother! Father! Welcome home! How was your trip? How glad I am that I returned before you!"

"Sindara! What a delightful surprise! We didn't expect you until next month!" Liana Varacor wrapped her arms around her daughter in an effusive embrace.

"Ladies, there's also a father here who is extremely anxious to welcome his daughter home." Within seconds, Artrian held his daughter tightly and laughingly bestowed a round of affectionate kisses on her cheeks and forehead.

Sindara's voice quivered. "I've missed you all so much. Even Rezda, although you mustn't tell him I said that. He'll aggravate me to no end if he finds out."

Suddenly, Liana cast embarrassed eyes skyward before turning her attention to Thehrund. "Your Highness, please forgive our lapse in manners. Our daughter has been away for almost a year." She then formally introduced her daughter to the prince.

As Thehrund acknowledged the introduction with a formal nod, his first impression of Sindara as a bright and slightly giddy young woman changed instantly. Her features immediately drew into a smooth, demure expression. An elegant reserve swiftly replaced the unabashed joy she had shown her parents. Although she had become quiet and polite, he was positive he sensed disapproval. Such an odd response, he thought, from someone he had just met.

Later, refreshed following a brief nap and a change of clothes, Thehrund descended a marble staircase to a spacious area reserved for family gatherings. The décor was less formal than other parts of the house he had seen earlier. In front of a bank of tall windows stood a table holding an elaborately carved chess set. Comfortable chairs on either side invited the next pair of challengers. A curved sofa formed a cozy semi-circle in front of a huge fireplace framed by oak, carved in simple lines and buffed to a soft sheen. Beautifully grained oak also formed the enormous mantel supported on each side by simple wooden columns.

A painting of an esteemed Varacor ancestor hung above the fireplace, its subject an elegantly dressed man seated beside a chess table. Thehrund thought it seemed odd. Most formal portraits exhibited a striking pose that conveyed the subject's power and wealth, whereas this picture revealed a man without pretense and quite comfortable beside a game board.

"Your Highness, I didn't expect you down so early. I do hope your suite meets your expectations."

Thehrund glanced around. There she stood with that cool gaze from eyes that were an intriguing shade of gold-flecked brown. "Lady Sindara, thank you for your concern. The suite is very comfortable. I came down early thinking it would be pleasant to take a walk outside before dinner." Damn, he thought, that certainly sounded strained.

She sighed. "Although I'm sure you'd find my brother Rezda's company more entertaining, he seems to have been dallying around instead of concentrating on his studies. Father asked me to show you about should you wish."

Thehrund's eyebrows lifted in question. Somehow, he found it impossible not to ask. "And why should I find your brother's company more entertaining?"

Her manner remained indifferent. "I understand that you quite enjoy a good time with your friends. I fear you'll find a garden tour with me less than exciting. I tend to prefer more serious pursuits."

Thehrund suppressed an amused smile. "I never would have guessed considering the way you flew outside earlier to greet your parents. You appeared to possess quite a happy and excitable nature." Was that a glare she swiftly hid?

"Excitable, no. Happy, yes. I hadn't seen my family for months. Now, if you'll follow me, I'll guide you on that walk you mentioned."

Shrugging slightly and nodding his head, the prince politely followed her through the house and out a pair of rear doors. They strolled along a brick walkway crossing emerald-green lawns toward an orchard of fruit trees bearing an abundance of pink blooms. Soft breezes carried a lightly perfumed fragrance and slowly coaxed small puffs of clouds toward the horizon.

As he drew in a deep breath, he suddenly noticed that she wore what appeared to be a long skirt of dark blue but was more like trousers with very wide legs. A pale-blue pintucked blouse gathered into the waistband of her skirt. Odd, he thought yet again. Her attire was cut from beautifully draped fabrics that subtly enhanced her graceful figure but contrasted distinctively with the elaborate gowns favored by most young noblewomen her age.

"My grandfather proved himself quite the horticulturist by getting these cherry trees to grow here. This species is rare in this region." Reaching up, she grasped a low-hanging branch and gently pulled it down. "The fragrance is quite intoxicating."

The prince stepped closer and politely sniffed. The fragrance wasn't merely rich. Its complex notes prompted him to smile and take yet another whiff. "I'm not sure I've ever smelled anything like this. The scent is enchanting."

"I'm glad you can appreciate it," she said, masking minor surprise at his reaction and releasing the branch. "Just beyond the orchard is a pond we use for swimming during hot weather. Would you like to see that or some of the other gardens?"

"I have the feeling I can appreciate many things that might surprise you," he commented, suddenly wanting to ease unexplained tension between them.

"The pond is lovely this time of year," she said, seeming to ignore his comment, "but not as pretty as the spring gardens."

Breathing out a sigh, he shrugged broad shoulders. "Then we shall see the gardens."

By the time they returned to the house, Thehrund felt puzzled. The only hint to her odd behavior was a comment about his enjoyment of good times. His more rowdy years had begun when he was in his late teens and had ended when he was twenty-one. She was younger than he was and likely barely into her teens at the time. Besides, she had lived far from Bracordia. Relief presented itself when her father appeared.

"Your Highness, I hope you enjoyed a pleasant walk," Lord Artrian said. "The weather is delightful this time of year."

Thehrund graciously nodded. "Thank you, sir. We ventured through the orchard and into the spring gardens. It was quite pleasant. I look forward to seeing more of your estate."

"Excellent! Cahmdurn offers many fascinating places to visit, but I always feel most satisfied here. I find nature's surroundings to be a most effective medicine against the stress and irritations found in the city."

Lady Liana and Rezda, Sindara's younger brother, soon joined them for dinner. Over a table offering a generous array of luscious foods and local wines, Thehrund learned more about the Varacors. Erator, their oldest child, served as a lieutenant in Arvacon's militia. He was currently assigned to a post near Articene, a small, thriving city named after a nearby ancient fort. Militia presence there remained constant due to the town's proximity to the border of Breyal, a relatively primitive country of loosely allied tribes known to launch occasional raids across Ambracor's borders. Although the prince knew well the history, he had never been to Articene and inquired about the possibility of visiting the fort before his stay in Arvacon ended.

Lord Artrian was thoughtful as he tasted the wine he had just sipped from a stemmed glass. "Personally, I think it an excellent idea. In my opinion, you, as future king, should have firsthand knowledge of places like Articene. Provinces bordering Breyal must fend off unexpected attacks. I just wonder if your father would approve."

Thehrund's expression mirrored Lord Artrian's thoughtfulness. "Father instructed me to trust your judgment regarding whatever you think necessary for me to learn and observe. I understand there exists an element of danger, but I've also trained as a soldier. I pray Ambracor never again has need of a soldier king, but I would defend our country with my life."

Throughout the exchange, Sindara had remained silent. She detested the very mention of war. She had studied for years at Sacred Halls of Faith School in Berancor, a religious center located in Bramond Province. During that time, she had four times accompanied the school's finest physicians and healers to plundered border villages. Each time, she had witnessed mutilated bodies and gory injuries as she helped her teachers care for wounded citizens. She had washed blood from her hands and sometimes joined in prayers to ease passing of the dying.

When she finally addressed the prince, the sharpness in her voice surprised her more than anyone else. "Words of defending Ambracor are easily spoken. The reality behind your comment lies far beyond practice fields and raucous taverns where meaningless victories are celebrated."

"Sindara?" Lady Liana's voice held startled embarrassment. "I'm surprised at you. You must apologize immediately to Prince Thehrund."

Golden sparks flashed from Sindara's amber eyes before she drew in a huge breath. His presence aggravated her, unreasonably disturbing her usual, peaceful calm. "Your Highness, I beg your pardon. I meant no insult. Not long ago, I spent weeks in Tuutla after a Breyal attack. What I saw there remains fresh in my mind. I tended those who fought off the Breyals. Many were young men who will suffer physical reminders of the attack for the remainder of their lives."

The prince gazed at her. Tuutla, a small town in Bramond, had been a killing field. A few brave men had successfully routed the invaders, but the toll in lives had been devastating. The characteristic power of his low voice gentled. "There is no need to apologize. In a way, you're right. What you witnessed gives you far different perspective. The reality you saw is far from where and how I trained. I can only offer that my preparation makes me physically ready. My hope is that my heart and my courage will not fail should I ever be put to such a test."

As her parents diplomatically steered the conversation toward more neutral topics, Sindara closed her eyes but still felt him watching her. Memories frightened her. The thought of her beloved brother in harm's way troubled her more often than she would ever willingly admit. Prayer was her retreat...her best and only comfort in facing her fears. Thankfully, dinner was nearing an end as servants carried in trays with dessert. Smiling shyly, she declined and excused herself from the table.

"Sindara, before you leave, are you still planning to go out tonight with your telescope?"

She looked at her father and quickly tamped down invading dread. She desperately needed some time alone with her thoughts. "Yes, Father. Marnee already has everything prepared. If you wish, I can go another time."

Artrian smiled indulgently. He had sorely missed his daughter and was unspeakably glad she was home so much sooner than expected. "No, you go. I just wondered if Prince Thehrund might wish to accompany you."

Glad to do anything her father asked, she concealed reluctance. "He is welcome if he would like." She glanced at the prince, who wore a light-weight tunic, belted at the waist, snug leggings, and casual, cuffed boots.

"If you choose to go, I would suggest warmer attire. Night air will be quite chilly."

"You have a real telescope?"

His question took her by surprise. "I do. My grandfather designed it himself and taught me to use it."

"Since you appear ready, I shall regretfully leave my dessert behind and go change." He smiled at his hosts. "If you'll kindly excuse me, I do not wish to keep Lady Sindara waiting."

Half an hour later, with their horses tethered to nearby bushes, he helped her smooth a blanket over thick grass at the top of a hillock perfect for stargazing. He then watched as she laid an assortment of parts in precise order and began assembling her telescope. Without pretense while essentially ignoring his presence, she peered through the end of the complicated gadget and adjusted lenses. For a moment, he wondered if she had forgotten him.

Finally satisfied with the direction and adjustments, she looked up. He noted a slight change in her expression, although he wasn't sure what that difference was.

"We're fortunate tonight is so clear. We should be able to see a comet in the eastern sky. You'll be able to view it much easier if you sit down."

He grinned wryly as he realized he still stood at the blanket's edge. Kneeling down beside her, he pushed long hair back over his shoulder and peered through the eyepiece. Firmly holding the telescope tube of the apparatus, he felt her hand brush his as she showed him how to adjust the view and focus. When starry heavens suddenly appeared close enough to reach out and touch, he sat back and quickly glanced at her. "Amazing."

Her left eyebrow dipped as she reminded herself to be patient. "I think more than amazing. According to the Ambracada, Creator God placed more stars in the heavens than we could ever possibly count. Look again and see how many stars are visible. Then, ask yourself how many more must fill the skies."

She had mentioned the Ambracada. He remembered hearing someone say she had studied for years at the sacred religious center where the original, ancient faith writings were protected for all of Ambracor. Perhaps she intended to dedicate her life to the practice of faith. Perhaps that explained some of her odd, aloof behavior.

"You mentioned we might see a comet tonight. I've never seen one. In fact, I've never before seen a telescope such as this."

"I'm not surprised. City lights hinder stargazing. As far as the telescope, I believe this one to be far better than most schools possess."

She leaned in front of him and again adjusted the viewfinder. As she concentrated on the night skies, he discovered himself far too aware of a subtle fragrance in her hair. The scent reminded him of the cherry blossoms he had smelled earlier in the day. As well as the fragrance, her nearness prompted him to suppress an unbidden frisson that raced along the length of his spine.

"There! It just came into sight," she suddenly exclaimed, her voice carrying some of the lilting excitement he had heard when she had first greeted her parents. After what seemed an unending minute, she backed away. "Look for yourself, but be careful not to move the tube."

When Thehrund again peered through the eyepiece, what he saw transfixed him. The glowing ball eased across the sky with what looked like a tail of white fire. His lips formed an odd, crooked smile. Without taking his eye from the telescope, he asked in wonder, "How did you know you would see this tonight?"

If she thought the question stupid, her response gave no indication. "Grandfather charted much of the sky. Years ago, he noticed that the comet you see apparently has a fixed course and returns on a regular basis."

"Here," he said, reluctantly moving back so she could again use the scope. "Your grandfather must have kept detailed records to note such occurrences."

"He did," she confirmed, "and I try to update them whenever I can. I suppose the effort has few benefits except to those as curious as I am."

"One never knows when such information might prove useful. Those who sail the seas use the stars to navigate from one place to the next. It's entirely possible the data you collect might prove valuable in some other way."

She tilted her face upward. "That sounds much like something Grandfather once told me."

Images from that night remained fresh in Thehrund's mind after he returned to Cahmdurn. He paused from reading regulations recently implemented to upgrade city infrastructure. Boring material compared to his stargazing experiences with Sindara. He sighed and shook his head impatiently. If anything in this world was not boring, it most certainly was the daughter of his highly respected mentor. Such an enigma, he thought. There were moments when he had felt her gaze upon him and was quite convinced she despised his very presence. Other times, especially the evenings they sat staring through her grandfather's telescope while discussing movements of celestial bodies, her intelligence was enhanced by a vitality he knew he hadn't imagined. If only he could clear his mind of her image and focus on the task at hand.

A sound roused Thehrund from deep slumber. Something had disturbed the precious dreams that helped sustain him. He heard a knock and groaned quietly as he dragged himself from his warm bed. Stumbling across his bedchamber and through the adjoining sitting room, he opened the door. Grogginess instantly disappeared when he saw Nagrand. "The portal?"

Nagrand nodded. "Karan sent word. The air begins to move. He thinks it will be a few days before the portal is fully ready to enter, but we thought you should know."

Thehrund nodded. "Thank you, Nagrand. I shall check immediately. Come inside and wait while I dress."

Ten minutes later, both men headed along a covered path from the main palace to a small stone chapel surrounded by tall trees. They entered via a side entrance leading to the modest apartment used by the priest in residence. Karan waited, lantern in hand, by a door opening to the cellar.

Descending wooden stairs, a glance to the right provided welcome relief to the prince and his two closest friends. Near a far retention wall, just beneath the altar in the chapel above, a barely noticeable disturbance in the air evidenced the first portal opening in many months. Its slight motion was accompanied by the faintest hint of sound and sporadic, tiny sparks of light.

Thehrund filled his lungs with a deep breath of air and then exhaled a relieved sigh. "Thanks be to Creator God," he said, taking yet another deep breath. "When did you first notice it?"

"About an hour ago. It must have just begun. When I was down here after evening prayers, all was quiet."

"We must prepare. I agree with Nagrand that it will likely open soon. I think about two days."

Nagrand worriedly shook his head. "Let us hope for no delays related to the current conference. I understand there is talk of extending the meetings past tomorrow because of growing concerns regarding unusual tribal gatherings in Breyal."

"You heard correctly," Thehrund replied. "This opening could not have come at a worse time. With alarming reports now arriving daily, Father has kept me at his side. I cannot just desert him."

Karan lifted the lantern higher. The light it cast reflected off prism-like sparkles slowly moving in the soft, slowly swirling swoosh of air. "Perhaps I can request a meeting with Count Varacor. I can explain the situation and enlist his assistance."

Muscles in Thehrund's face and jaw contracted with the same tension filling his body. He imagined hearing yet again those voices that had spoken to him long ago on the battlefield near Articene. "Lord Artrian may be our only hope. How I wish there would be no need to trouble him. He and Sindara's mother have borne enough sorrow. They deserve to put their grief behind them. This is my burden to bear, not theirs."

Nagrand's hand rose to clasp the prince's shoulder. "There is reason behind all of this, my friend. You must believe that. You trusted them enough to confide in them. To my knowledge, they have never doubted you even once. I mean no disrespect toward your father, but he refuses to believe you heard the voices. The count and his wife not only believe what you heard, they accept what you explained about the portal."

"Nagrand is right, Thehrund. I think her parents are your only chance to make the journey this time. We dare not risk staying when this might be your one chance to find her."

Although Thehrund appeared to stare into the developing portal, his eyes were essentially sightless. Instead, his inner vision fixed on memories from years earlier. After prolonged silence, he nodded in agreement. "I will meet privately with Lord Artrian first thing in the morning. I leave all preparations in your hands. I'll advise as soon as possible if I expect any change in plans."

Upstairs, just as his brother and the prince prepared to leave, Karan's voice sounded firm warning. "No matter what, Thehrund, you cannot fail to enter the portal when it opens. I am convinced this is necessary for whatever future faces you personally as well as when your time comes to lead Ambracor."

Lantern light reflected from blue eyes glancing up between curtains of black waves tumbling past the prince's broad shoulders. Shadows enhanced the bleak expression on Thehrund's face. His rich voice vibrated with rising emotion. "Deep inside my soul, I understand I must obey those voices. Never should she have been exposed to that Breyal attack because of what I did, and she most certainly should not have paid for my actions with her life. Still, how do I balance my commitment to her and those voices with the needs of my father and Ambracor? How? That question plagues me every single hour of every single day."

The backward tilt of Karan's head lent an air of extreme conviction to his response. "As I've told you many times before, you must do as Sindara always encouraged you to do. Learn to trust completely in Creator God."

Chapter Five

Countess Liana Varacor had earlier resisted rapidly growing fatigue while steadfastly remaining by her husband's side. Conference meetings were fraught with heated discussions concerning risks for wide-scale Breyal invasion. Many of the day's sessions had grown contentious as delegates debated how best to defend Ambracor's more vulnerable borders. Some representatives—most surprisingly, those from Bramond—insisted threats were severely exaggerated. Meetings ended late without final accord.

Finally retiring for the night, she tossed and turned in fitful sleep. How she wanted to go home to sleep in her own bed. A fleeting moment of wakefulness dissipated into uneasy slumber, and her dreams drifted into images of a happier past.

"Where did I put my journal?" Sindara's voice was impatient. "I must be losing my mind!"

Liana exchanged an amused glance with Marnee, the beloved servant who had helped care for Sindara since she had been a precocious toddler. "I believe if you turn around, you might find it on your vanity."

"I just looked..." Sindara shook her head. Curling brown tresses, touched with golden highlights, floated back and forth as if to emphasize mounting frustration. Fair cheeks flushed with rosy color. "I apologize. With Reverend Master Zoman coming tomorrow, I feel completely flustered."

"My dear," Marnee said, her smile crinkling the corners of her brown eyes, "you've never once shown any nervousness in Master Zoman's presence. He knows better than anyone that you are one of the best-prepared candidates ever. You must have confidence."

Liana approached her daughter and stroked a silken length of shining hair. She watched while Sindara waited for Marnee to button the back of the emerald green gown she would wear to her interview with the director of the Sacred Halls of Faith. "Perhaps you should be honest with Master Zoman."

Elegant, dark brown eyebrows rose. "What does that mean?"

Affection glowed from Liana's eyes. "Sindara, I hope you'll accept a piece of well-meaning advice from the mother who adores you. You need more time. There have been recent changes that I believe you must carefully consider."

"Changes? What changes? I'm not sure what you mean."

"Daughter," Liana began, "I know you will agree that your intuition has always been exceptional. That is one of your very unique traits Master Zoman respects and highly values...and most likely needs."

"Yes, but I'm not sure I understand..."

"If you truly do not understand, then it's only because you put forth so much effort resisting intuitive voices that speak to you."

Amber eyes rolled upward. "Mother, please, what is it you think I resist?"

Liana sighed, thinking she would much prefer that her daughter reason through matters for herself. Glancing downward, she watched as Marnee slowly rose from the floor and pushed against her lower back to straighten herself.

"Listen to your mother."

Sindara's beautifully full lips pressed tightly together for just a moment. "Marnee, I'm trying, but I have yet to hear anything that makes sense."

"Oh, Sindara," her mother said, "trust me when I say you need more time before you accept any permanent position at the school or consider joining the abbey community. You can also be sure that I will speak to Master Zoman myself. You're not ready to make any such lifetime commitment."

"Are you saying my faith isn't strong enough? Is that what you mean?" The thought noticeably disturbed her.

"Not at all. I believe faith guides you more surely than anyone else I know. I also believe that you absolutely must reflect on the idea that yours might be a different path."

More confused than ever, Sindara gazed at her mother with eyes suddenly glazed by tears. "A different path? What sort of different path?"

Liana's hands lovingly ran up and down the satin sleeves covering Sindara's arms. "Daughter, only you can know for sure. What I ask is that you seriously consider the possibility of finding someone to love...a man with whom you can marry and spend your life, and perhaps have children of your own."

Suddenly still, Sindara glanced out the window. Odd lurches in her abdomen made her feel faintly nauseous. Closing her eyes, she turned back to the waiting faces of her mother and her beloved personal maid. "Except for Father, Grandfather, and my brothers, most men I've met outside our religious centers have been too threatened or too self-absorbed in their own egos to accept me for who I am."

"Men and women differ in many ways besides obvious physical differences. This is as nature and Creator God intend so we may fulfill ourselves and our purposes in life. In your case, your intelligence and your character are far too strong for many to comprehend. Whether or not you realize, you even challenge your father and me. The difference is that our love for you allows us to respect your capabilities. I also love you enough to remind you that not every man you've known is intimidated by you or lacks respect for you."

Sindara stared at her mother. Her breath caught somewhere in her throat. "You don't mean..."

"I only mean that you must carefully contemplate all possibilities before making any final decisions about your life. Now, you and Marnee finish here. I promised to help your father review some documents before dinner." With that, Liana kissed her daughter's cheek and left.

"Marnee..." Sindara said warningly as she noted the maid's stern expression.

"I *will* say it, child. He may have been here twice only, but your excessive aloofness had nothing to do with shyness or your plans for the school or the abbey. The truth will become obvious sooner or later. I consider it a blessing that it comes while you still have time to reconsider your future."

Sindara opened her mouth but found no words to counter her maid's forthright observation. Marnee knew her far too well. Evading further conversation, Sindara suggested a few minor changes to her new gown before removing the dress and turning it over to her maid for last minute alterations.

With Marnee quickly gone, Sindara picked up her diary and carried it into her drawing room. Sitting at the desk she used for reading and correspondence, she slid aside a stack of books and placed her journal down. She opened the thick, leather-bound book to a recent page of entries. As her eyes quickly skimmed the text she had written in neatly flowing script, her breath grew suddenly uneven.

> *"Ambracor's prince just left our country manor for the second time since I returned from school. His presence disturbed me from the moment I met him. I think on how upset Brenna was about him breaking her older sister's heart. From all she and her cousin discussed, the prince sounded like such a miscreant, and I understood they knew him quite well."*

She looked away from the page. Her thoughts wandered to the evenings they had spent on the hillock. How different he had been from Brenna's descriptions. Prince Thehrund's voice had held subdued excitement as he peered through her telescope at night skies. So many questions. So many astute observations. He had even asked to borrow some of the journals containing copious notes and hand-drawn charts she had made. With a heavy sigh, she glanced back at her diary.

> *"Knowing about him what I do, why did I feel such a jolt each time he came near me? Yes, he is quite handsome with those flowing waves in his black hair and those magnificent blue eyes. Still, he is just a man. Well, perhaps not just a man. He is Ambracor's future king. What is wrong with me? I have spent years preparing for my path in life. Why now are my dreams haunted by the eyes of a spoiled prince? Why now, when all is so close to fruition, do I suffer these nameless doubts? Silly. I suppose my doubts do come with a name, one I hesitate to allow across my lips for fear I may fall forever victim to his enchantment."*

She had intended to note down her mother's comments. With detached surprise, she watched the trembling of her hand. She could not possibly set pen to paper with thoughts running helter-skelter inside her head. Dropping the pen, she closed the journal without thought of the blotted stains that would underscore troubled words.

After dinner that evening, Liana suggested that Sindara join her for a leisurely walk outside. As mother and daughter admired the sounds of a summer night, Liana savored the chance to spend time with her middle child. She had watched her daughter grow from a lively toddler into a studious schoolgirl. There were times when she could hardly believe how different Sindara had always been when compared to other girls her age.

"What are you thinking, Mother?"

A gentle smile lit Liana's face. "I was just remembering when you were a little girl. I can't tell you how panicked I was the first time I went to check on you, and you were nowhere to be found."

"The first time Grandfather took me to the hillock so we could study the heavens?"

"Exactly. Grandfather Varacor once told me you fulfilled every dream he'd ever had about having a daughter of his own. The two of you were nearly inseparable. There were times when I think your father and I were almost jealous."

"Father had assumed the bulk of responsibilities for Arvacon Province by that time, hadn't he?"

Liana nodded. "He had. Your father came late in life for Grandfather Varacor, and your grandfather was thoroughly contented to spend time with his grandchildren rather than manage provincial business. Erator was always more interested in military training, and Rezda was a typical toddler demanding constant supervision. Your grandfather spent time with both boys, but you were perfect during the last years before he fell ill."

"Grandfather made learning such a joy. I also credit him with making faith such an integral part of my life."

"One thing your grandfather always possessed was deep faith. Something in you intensified that faith."

"Mother, I miss him. I've also thought about what you said today. I even looked at some of my most recent journal entries. How I wish Grandfather were still here. He understood me so well."

"A wise man he was." Liana stopped. Taking her daughter's hand, she drew her closer to gaze into the moonlit features of a lovely young woman. "Sindara, I have no doubt he would counsel you as I have. Take your time before making any final decision. I don't know what you've written in your journal, but I know you well enough to deduce the contents."

Sindara's face fell. "Mother, he frightens me. He does, and I don't know why."

Liana placed her palm against her daughter's soft cheek. "Prince Thehrund is a man who projects the power he has yet to wield. It is bred into him. Ambracor's royal family has produced a line of rulers who have defied odds. With little exception, the kings and queens before Thehrund have been well taught, well trained, and inculcated with virtues of honor and integrity rare in our world. That does not change the fact that they are essentially people just like you and me."

Sindara shook her head. "It hardly matters. There are so many beautiful, charming women who frequent court. To even think he would seriously look my way is absolute folly."

"Do you honestly think so?"

"Mother, look at me. Think about *how* I am. I would never surrender my faith or my intellectual pursuits to please a man's image of how a wife should behave. Even though Father gladly accepts your advice on practically everything, he commented on how he thinks I'm too strong for most men. If *he* thinks that way, can you imagine how the prince perceives me?"

Liana raised both hands to frame her daughter's troubled face. "My dear child, I believe growing conflicts with the Breyal tribes will become much worse during our lifetime. King Hamund shares that view. He has doubtlessly discussed all sorts of possibilities with the prince. Thehrund is an extremely intelligent and vigilant man. Once he decides to seek a bride, I'm confident that he will look for more than a pretty showpiece. He will want and need a woman who can stand by him and face all the troubles likely to confront our country."

"As true as that may be, I still can't imagine him looking twice at me."

"Oh, daughter, open your eyes. You must be the only one on this entire estate who has failed to notice how he tries not to look at you."

"Wishful thinking, Mother. That is nothing more than wishful thinking. Besides, what am I supposed to do? I would never throw myself at him the way other girls do."

"Sindara, have you ever noticed how you avoid even saying the prince's name?"

She almost denied that, but her own written words confirmed her mother's observation. "Mother, what would you have me do?"

"Oh, such a question," Liana exclaimed. "Daughter, first, trust in yourself. Allow yourself the confidence and the freedom to be the person you're meant to be. Then? Relax. Talk to him without being so aloof. Let go of your fears long enough to find out who he is and how he feels about things. If nothing more than friendship comes of it, then you have your answer and your plans for life. What matters most is that you take time to explore all possibilities."

Resuming their walk, Sindara pondered her mother's advice. As much as she loved life at the school and faith center, she had known for a long time that something was missing. Was it weakness in her resolve to commit to a cloistered life of faith? Was it some undefined emptiness rising from deep in her soul? Each time the prince had visited, she had felt inexplicable uneasiness as those questions grew more pronounced.

Her journal contained descriptions of how he had responded to things she had shown him on the estate. Recorded were his reactions to the fragrance of cherry blossoms, the sight of fat, brilliantly colored fish in the pond, the estate gardens, and their astronomical observations. Especially on those evenings spent stargazing...each time they had been close while using the telescope...she had suppressed overwhelming desire to be even closer. In truth, she had loved watching him and had secretly wished his touch might go further than accidental.

"You're very quiet," Liana commented as their path wound back toward the house.

The remark prompted a thoughtful smile. "Mother, when Master Zoman comes, I'll tell him I need more time to ponder all aspects of joining the abbey. I hope he won't be disappointed."

Pausing for a moment, Liana gazed into her daughter's pensive face. "Prepare yourself, Sindara. He will be disappointed. You would bring fresh and powerful devotion to bolster the spirits of those already committed to service there. He will also understand that such faith is often needed in other more ordinary places."

"Mother, I want you to know that I truly appreciate your wisdom. I love you very much."

Bells rang out from the palace's bell tower clock, interrupting Liana's bittersweet dream. Six o'clock in the morning. Sitting up in bed, she drew bent legs toward her chest and rested her chin on her knees. An involuntary rise of tears wet her face. Her dream had brought with it the vision of Sindara's beautiful features and the melodic sound of her voice. It had also reminded her of her daughter's loving declaration. Then, bell chimes chased away the precious memory and returned the empty hole to a mother's heart.

Artrian Varacor awakened to the one sob Liana had been unable to restrain. Lying beside her in bed, he stroked damp hair from her cheeks and gently murmured words of comfort. After that, pulling his wife close and holding her tightly until she no longer wept, he let his own thoughts drift back in time.

He had suffered profound grief when the king and prince had arrived to inform them of Sindara's death. The news had been physical in its impact, sending him staggering backward to grab on to a doorframe in order to remain on his feet. Tears fell in rivers along his cheeks. No matter how hard he tried, he could not halt the flow. That day had been the worst of his life.

King Hamund had reached Arvacon's capital city accompanied by Erator, Prince Thehrund, and a detachment of weary soldiers, many bearing minor wounds sustained in the surprise attack. Hamund's face showed strain compounded by deep sadness. Erator's stiff features showed outward control as he directed soldiers toward accommodations while holding tightly to his injured arm and stifling sorrow over the loss of his sister.

It had taken what seemed an eternity to gather enough strength to summon his wife to break such tragic news. When he began to tell Liana, her first fearful thought had been of Erator, their soldier son. Neither had known Sindara was en route to Cahmdurn. Neither could have anticipated learning that their daughter had died in battle.

Artrian would never forget the prince's appearance. Neither would he forget the profound silence during the subsequent trip to his country estate. He had watched Thehrund rebuff Hamund's initial efforts to offer comfort. Never in his life could he remember seeing any man suffer as much personal conflict as Thehrund had displayed that first night or during the days that followed.

Finally, on the fourth evening following the attack, Artrian convinced the king to accompany him to the hillock where the prince had spent the first night at the country manor and nearly every waking hour since. "Thehrund," Artrian had begun, holding at bay the tremors threatening his usual firm voice, "you cannot stay out here permanently. Grief is a burden best shared among those who care for one another."

When Thehrund slowly looked around, the desolation in his expression had been startling. "Lord Artrian, this grief is a burden I brought upon our families. My own shameful actions wrought this unspeakable tragedy."

Hamund reached out to touch his son's shoulder and was relieved when the prince didn't withdraw. "I should have brought a larger detachment. It is I who misjudged how far into Arvacon Breyals might encroach."

Thehrund swallowed hard, searching for words he knew would shock and disappoint the two men he most loved and admired in all of Ambracor. "Father, had I not hurt Sindara so badly, she never would have broken our engagement and certainly never would have demanded an escort home."

Artrian's forehead wrinkled in question. "She broke the engagement?" He turned a questioning gaze to Hamund. "Why did you not tell me? What happened?"

When Hamund would have answered, Thehrund interrupted. "Father, the blame is mine, just as it is my responsibility to explain the circumstances." Turning to face Sindara's father, he forced himself to continue. "Lord Artrian, as you know, I recently went to meet with Count Brandere regarding plans to fortify Bramond's borders to defend against Breyal incursions. I think you are both aware that I was once..."

Words stalled. He gulped in a breath that nearly choked him. His lower jaw tensed. "I once had an affair with his daughter Breeneth. That was years ago. Call it the folly of youth or the selfish stupidity of a young prince. It doesn't matter which. It was wrong, and I ended it."

Again, Thehrund paused. His very soul was awash in a flood of shame, guilt, and sorrow. "During this last visit, there was a birthday celebration for Breeneth's brother. There was plenty of food and a great deal of merrymaking. Ale and wine flowed like water. I started to leave early, but the count would not hear of it. I ended up sadly drunk and awoke the following morning in Breeneth's bed."

Artrian remained silent for several tense moments. "Sindara evidently learned of the incident. I can only imagine her reaction."

King Hamund stared at his son. "I ask not as your father but as king. Does Breeneth's father know?"

Thehrund shook his head. "I honestly have no idea how much he knows or if he even cares. When I ended our relationship years back, it was because I finally saw how selfish and shallow she is. There is something unseemly about her I cannot explain. I realized I could never take such a woman as my wife, especially one who had started a string of lovers long before we met that never ended."

Thehrund pressed on in fear of breaking down completely. "By the time I returned to Bracordia, Breeneth had already delivered a letter informing Sindara of my transgression. I will never forget the hurt in Sindara's eyes. I pleaded with her to let me explain and to grant me the chance to prove the depth of my regret and how much I truly loved her.

I even promised to ask the two of you if we could advance our wedding date so that I could make vows of fidelity that we could both hold as sacred before Creator God."

"What did she say?"

The prince's bloodshot eyes met those of his father. "She was devastated, Father, and wouldn't listen. She finally said she loved me, but she needed time to pray for God to guide her. I fell to my knees right there. I took her hands and started praying as hard as I knew how to beg Creator God to guide us both. That's when she demanded I leave."

"I remember noticing tension between the two of you. I thought you had simply quarreled. That's why I sent you to inspect border forts in Arvacon. You were gone only a few days when she told me of her decision to end the engagement. Your mother and I were both brokenhearted when she asked us to give you a letter along with her engagement ring. We had no idea what had happened. She refused to say anything more than she loved you too much to ruin your life. She pleaded with me to send her home with an escort. I tried to persuade her to wait for your return, but she said she could not and would leave on her own."

Tears scorched Thehrund's eyelids. "It was never her fault."

Knowing his daughter well, Artrian understood why she would seek refuge at home in Arvacon. "Erator said that a Breyal war party had crossed the border far north of Articene and was working its way toward the town."

"That's true. We quickly assembled a detachment of soldiers to intercept them. We never expected to encounter them already engaged in the ambush against Father and his escort." Thehrund squeezed his eyes shut to no avail. "We rode straight into the skirmish. I saw Father fall when his horse took an arrow in its flank. Before I could even move, Sindara dismounted and raced to Father's aid. I saw her fending off one Breyal when another warrior rushed to attack them. I shouted a warning, saw her swing her sword, and started running, but..." He choked on a sob. "I still... hear her...scream."

While Artrian watched Hamund embrace the inconsolable prince, part of him seethed with cold fury. Thehrund was right. His daughter never would have encountered the Breyal invaders had she not sought refuge at home. The prince's own selfish deeds had caused her to break the engagement. On the other hand, the count could not allow himself to wallow in the mire of loathing. The younger man before him had also courageously risked his life to save Erator's during that same skirmish. He wondered how he could ever reconcile himself to the fact that he had lost a daughter and kept a son because of Thehrund's actions.

As Artrian felt his wife growing calmer, a knock sounded at the door. Grimacing, he thought something must be wrong if someone was calling so early. Rising and putting on his robe, he left the bedchamber and went to open the door of their palace guest suite. Eyebrows rose sharply in surprise. "Your Highness. Good morning. Come in."

"Good morning, Lord Artrian. I apologize for such an early intrusion, but I need your help. Desperately so."

The count tilted his head toward one of the suite's sofas. "Please sit down."

"Artrian?" Hearing voices, Lady Liana had arisen and appeared beneath the arched doorway.

Thehrund instantly rose to his feet and bowed his head in greeting. "Forgive me for coming so early. I would not have done so, but the matter is urgent."

Half an hour later, Thehrund shook hands with Lord Artrian and then hugged Lady Liana. "I have no words to express my gratitude for your support."

When the prince left, Artrian returned to the sofa and sat beside his wife. He inhaled deeply. "There are times when I question his sanity as well as my own."

Liana reached for her husband's hand. "Even I face moments when I still blame him. Those times are eased only when I pray or read from the Ambracada. I remember her devotion to the teachings of faith, especially when it came to the importance of forgiveness."

"The problem is that she chose not to forgive him. If she had, she would not have been traveling to Cahmdurn that day."

Liana nodded. "True. I suppose I rely heavily on my knowledge of the child we nurtured and watched as she became such a fine young woman. She loved Thehrund; I think more than any of us knew. In time, she would have forgiven him."

"You sound so certain."

Liana closed her eyes. Her mind regressed to her night's dream. "She resisted him from the very beginning. She never wanted to love him, but she couldn't help herself."

"And that love took her life." Artrian was unable to hide the trace of bitterness that crept into his voice.

"Did it? I mean, really? Whenever Thehrund speaks of the voices he heard that day, something in him transforms completely. In every other way, he is reliable, practical, and realistic. Perhaps it is wishful thinking on my part, but intuition warns me every time I think of telling him to leave us alone. I honestly believe he heard those voices. He's also doing everything in his power to follow through on what they told him."

"Guilt can do strange things to a man."

Liana rose from the sofa. "Guilt is a relatively small part of what drives him. Artrian, he loves our daughter as no man alive could love her. He's showing that to us. He also hopes to prove it to her." Fresh tears stained her face. "Our faith allowed me to forgive him long ago. Now, my heart bids me listen to him...and help him. That is exactly what I intend to do."

Artrian watched as she disappeared into the bedchamber. Empathetic to his wife's emotions, he sighed. Memories once again intruded, bringing both comfort and torment.

"Father, when I'm with him, he makes me feel as if I'm the most special woman in the entire universe. We can discuss anything...even subjects on which we disagree. I admire the way he thinks matters through to reach opinions he can justify and defend." She paused and smiled as she reflected on the prince who was now seriously courting her. "He's so kind and thoughtful when we're together."

Wistfully, Artrian had gazed at his daughter and, for just a moment, wondered how his beautiful baby girl had grown into womanhood in what seemed no more than the blink of an eye. "What you tell me does not seem at all troublesome."

She almost laughed. "Those are only some of the good things I see in him." She trailed off, remembering his most recent visit and the way he had kissed her the night before he left for home in Bracordia. That kiss had sent shock waves roaring through every part of her body.

"Tell me, then. What is it about him that gives rise to such doubts?"

Thick, dark lashes fell upon the smooth ivory of her cheeks. She hesitated before continuing, trusting the confidence she had in her parents. "Father, when I was away at school, one of Count Brandere's daughters also attended for a while. I can't forget how angry she was after returning from a visit home."

"Angry? Why was she angry?" he prompted when Sindara fell silent. "You do know that you can discuss anything with me, do you not?" He noticed anxiety in both her posture and her expression. When she finally met his waiting gaze, she smiled shyly. Inwardly, he recognized discomfort born of innocence. "Please, Sindara, trust me. I will advise you as best I can."

With the slightest of nods, she slowly began, "Father, I quickly realized how out of place Brenna and her friends were at school. When she returned from holidays at home, there were all kinds of stories about parties that were wild and..." She stopped to search for the right words.

"Thehrund visited her father during some of those holidays…I suppose studying Bramond's defenses and the like. According to Brenna, he really enjoyed the parties they hosted. He also spent a great deal of time with Breeneth, Brenna's older sister. Breeneth expected Thehrund to propose marriage. When he left, there was no proposal, just a rather cold goodbye. Brenna was furious."

Artrian shrugged his shoulders. "Attending parties should not be construed as intentions to marry."

Sindara blushed. "It wasn't just the parties, Father. According to Brenna, the prince also…" She paused for several uneasy moments. "She said he was secretly sharing Breeneth's bed."

That revelation had cost his daughter immense effort. How to respond to her very real concerns? "I think I understand now. May I ask how long ago that happened?"

"About five years. Soon after, Brenna failed academic standards and left the school altogether."

"I see." Artrian recalled his own youthful days upon reaching manhood. "Sindara, from experience, I know young men have a knack for such antics. I don't excuse it. I only acknowledge it. I suppose it's just one of those weaknesses males seem to have. Perhaps the behavior is necessary for us to prove to ourselves that we've actually attained manhood. I won't deny that ego undoubtedly plays a role."

His daughter's eyes held questions he was loath to answer. "Yes, my darling, even I passed through that ugly phase. My only defense is that, in youth, I lacked both wisdom and experience that would have led me to more appropriate behavior. Good men quickly realize that such wayward actions lead only to unhappiness and ruin. They make note of mistakes and then set their lives on a solid track forward. I'm quite sure that is the case with your prince. He fell victim to follies typical of young men. He then rose above them."

"So, I just pretend I know nothing and ignore it?"

"I didn't say that. If it troubles you, tell him. Discuss it. Let him explain from his perspective. You can learn and better understand his character. Just be careful that you don't let his past mistakes ruin your future."

How many times had Artrian chastised himself for the advice he gave her that day? He never knew if his daughter had followed his counsel and discussed with Thehrund his relationship with Breeneth. Neither had he ever found the nerve to ask the prince. Now, he faced renewed conflict. Thehrund readily accepted blame for Sindara's loss, but he was also convinced that Creator God's angels had offered the chance to redeem himself and save her life.

The day after Thehrund had confided in Hamund and Artrian, he asked to speak privately together with them and Liana. That was when he related the mystical event he had experienced on the battlefield. Hamund immediately rejected the account and stormed from the formal parlor of the Varacor home.

Artrian had seen hope flare in his wife's eyes. For a moment, he had wanted to strike the prince for concocting such a cruel story. His hand had remained paralyzed while he studied the prince's grief-stricken features. There was no doubting the strain of shame and guilt that drew a young man's face unnaturally taut. What Artrian could not deny was the determined flame of hope burning in Thehrund's eyes.

That was all past. He and his wife had listened attentively to details of the prince's story about what the angels had said. While Hamund accused his son of wallowing in self-pity when there was a nation to govern and protect, Lady Liana had encouraged Thehrund from the start. She had reminded her husband of the times Marnee had come to them when Sindara was just a baby. The nurse had insisted that she often noticed the soft glow of angel wings above the child's crib. Liana was fully prepared to accept that her daughter might someday return from the clutches of death and that the love Thehrund proclaimed would be the inspired force to bring her back.

Artrian finally stood when his wife called his name. They had little time to prepare arguments to convince King Hamund to conclude current conferences on schedule. Perhaps they could plead for time so that provincial leaders might consult with officials back in their home capitals. A new round of meetings could then be slated to bring fresh ideas on how best to defend against the expanding Breyal menace.

❈ ❈ ❈

Karan Mezden inspected supplies assembled in the chapel cellar. Sighing continuously in frustration, he kept glancing toward the disturbance created by the portal's steadily increasing spin. How could he possibly anticipate what they might need?

Early passages had transported them to places similar to their homes in Ambracor. Blending in had been relatively easy. Whatever power controlled their trips also provided living quarters and basic means for survival. Cautiously, they had ventured out to survey their surroundings. Alert to every possible danger, they learned to communicate with local inhabitants as they purchased foods and observed challenges of life in the lands they visited. Some places had been delightful havens with serene, welcoming residents. Although they were more than willing to listen to historical accounts of how local peoples had achieved their peaceful state, all interactions had been superficial. Their goal remained to find Sindara.

Their last two crossings through the portal had carried them to places that staggered the imagination. Bewildered, they watched as people rushed about, climbing into strange-looking carriages with no horses to pull them. Rumbling sounds made by the coaches grated on strained nerves. They learned that the coaches ran with mechanical engines that spewed choking smoke into the air and rapidly propelled passengers along streets and country roads. Inside the cities, blaring horns warned pedestrians to hurry out of the way.

When they'd first left their safe house on the trip before last, clothing typical in Ambracor had drawn rude stares, jeering remarks, and outright laughter. Hurriedly returning to the house where they had arrived, they had cast furtive looks at passersby wearing unfamiliar garb. Once safely back, they discovered appropriate clothing had been provided. Whoever had sent them on these expeditions had taken great pains to ensure they would not draw unnecessary attention to themselves. If only they had realized that before going out looking so foolish.

Dressing themselves in unfamiliar clothing styles had been both hilarious and uncomfortable. Thehrund furiously complained about tight-fitting shirts and jackets that restricted freedom of movement should one need to defend himself. One other detail also created concern. All of the men they had seen wore hair cropped very short. It had taken Karan the better part of a day to figure out how to disguise the traditionally long locks that the prince stubbornly refused to cut.

Their most recent trip had been slightly easier. They had again found themselves in a world filled with horseless carriages and all sorts of devices that produced sounds or pictures. Initial encounters with the astonishing, weird contraptions had triggered shocked gasps and startled jumps. Despite the contrivances they were forced to confront and even operate on occasion, Thehrund had pushed them. He wanted them to learn as much as they could about these strange worlds while remaining focused on their primary purpose for being there.

Trusting past experience that Thehrund's spirits or angels or whoever they were would provide for them again, Karan decided to bring a minimum of items. Sufficient shirts and leggings were a must. Whenever alone in their safe houses, they preferred the comfortable familiarity of their own clothing. They would also carry a copy of the Ambracada. With Thehrund now regularly praying, their connection to sacred teachings would provide solace in strange places. They would also take the leather sheaths holding their swords and daggers. Whenever possible, they would continue practice sessions with weapons they knew well.

Soap. He mustn't forget the soap the prince insisted on using. The subtly exotic, woodsy scent was created from ingredients expensive even by royal standards. Thehrund had developed many theories about ways they might find her. The unique fragrance that Sindara had loved so well might be useful in attracting her attention.

Karan exhaled heavily. He pushed from his mind the disturbing *if* that entered his thoughts. He reminded himself that these peculiar journeys into the portal could not be mere happenstance. While preparing for this newest entry, Thehrund had insisted they cast aside all doubts. He feared the presence of any uncertainties might create self-defeating circumstances. They could not afford to think in terms of *if*. They must believe in *when*. Despite the grave and somber presence he usually projected, Thehrund was finally mastering the concept of *when* with regard to his search for the one love of his life.

❈ ❈ ❈

"Thehrund, I'm not at all happy about postponing discussions on reinforcing our borders with Breyal. Citizens in border towns and villages deserve every protection we can afford to give them."

Thehrund cocked his head to one side, causing his hair to drape down his upper arm. "Lord Artrian is committed to defending all regions in Ambracor that lie near boundaries with Breyal. He also wisely recommended that our nobles consult with leaders in those towns and villages for their suggestions. They are closest to the problems and likely have valuable ideas for curtailing the incursions."

Hamund pounded his fist on the broad arm of the chair in which he sat. "Strong military presence is the only way to stop them!"

"Your approach contains one serious flaw. Yes, strong military presence can and does stop them, but not until *after* they've crossed into Ambracor. What Lord Artrian says about preventing the incursions is right when it comes to saving lives of ordinary citizens and valuable soldiers."

"I can't begin to fathom the idea of initiating active war. We have been at peace for centuries."

"Father, I beg to disagree. Bracordia is an island of peace in the center of a country that has faced increasing attacks for nearly ten years. The topography here in the capital makes invasion foolhardy. That is not so for at least four of our provinces. Our people near the borders live daily with the specter of war. Limited it may be, but it is war nevertheless."

"Would you advocate assembling our armies to invade Breyal?" Hamund's eyes glittered angrily, and his voice rose in volume.

Remaining calm, Thehrund faced his father squarely. "Four provincial governors already deal with raids where Breyal warriors steal whatever they can carry after setting afire homes and businesses and slaughtering innocent victims. I believe the Board of Governors has every right to demand preemptive action to protect their domains. Although tardy, they now take time to canvass town mayors and sheriffs for ideas to end this plague. You granted their request for additional time to assess and develop strategic recommendations. You must be prepared to act on whatever proposals they bring when they return in six weeks."

Worried lines etched the king's forehead. "I do not want to be remembered as the king who led Ambracor into a bloody war."

Thehrund understood his father's statement referred more to his fears of destruction caused by warfare than any profaned history about his part in launching all-out war. He went to his father's side and rested his hand on Hamund's shoulder. "Father, whether we like it or not, war is already upon us. You must realize that only the scope of war will change. We will certainly seek options, but we must prepare for whatever lies ahead."

Hamund kept his eyes fixed on the polished wood table in front of him. "And you? What will you do?"

"I will continue to train and study the old books of military strategies. I will do as I have always done. And, if war escalates, I will defend Ambracor with my life."

"With us facing probable chaos, do you still intend to continue your other personal quest?"

"Father, my roles as your son and prince in this realm are ones I intend to honor so long as I live, but I must remain faithful to vows I made. I will never surrender my search until I find her." Removing his hand from his father's shoulder, Thehrund turned and left his father in brooding solitude.

Standing outside the luxurious palace apartment Sindara had used while planning their wedding, Thehrund waited patiently. He knew his beloved's faithful handmaid moved more slowly these days. When the door finally opened, the softly wrinkled face welcomed him with a smile. "Your Highness, please come in."

Closing the door, Marnee invited him to sit and offered him refreshment. He declined both offers. Instead, he closed his eyes and took a deep breath. Yes, here he could come and still detect faint traces of the velvety-soft floral fragrance Sindara had always worn. Marnee, who had remained behind to pack Sindara's belongings, had accepted his offer of employment after the Articene tragedy. She had helped keep her mistress's memory alive by ensuring that the apartment and Sindara's possessions still there were maintained exactly as they had been before the fateful trip from Bracordia.

Marnee's dark eyes questioned her prince. Her face failed to hide glimmers of hope. "Does the portal again open?"

Thehrund nodded. "It does at last, Marnee. You must pray that we will find her this time. I leave with a heavy heart because of threats facing our nation."

Marnee nodded. "Your Highness, you must allow yourself to believe you'll find her this time. Tell yourself that until you make it happen. My heart tells me she's the one to help you deliver us from the tribes of Breyal. You must bring her back...and soon."

Wise, old Marnee. Years of her unwavering encouragement had shown him why Sindara had adored her. She was one of such a tight circle who knew the full truth regarding his quest. His confidence in this aging servant was complete.

"Marnee, in case of any questions, say only that I am away because of the Breyal attacks. That is no lie. Count Varacor and his wife also know of the portal opening and will cover for my absence. Notify them immediately if you encounter any concern. I fear traitors may live among us."

"Your Highness, I will be careful as always. Do not concern yourself about me. I may be old, but I'm not as frail as I allow many to think."

Thehrund grinned. "I hope that I can soon bring great happiness for your final years."

"The angels entrusted her to my care. Ask their help, Your Highness, and then believe with all your soul they will answer."

That evening, Thehrund bade farewell to his still brooding father and walked his mother through palace corridors and up a private staircase to her rooms. Affection was evident when he stroked her cheek with long, strong fingers. "I hope you sleep well tonight."

Narlina reached for his hand, stopping him when he would have gone to his own chambers. "Your father and I worry about you more than we worry about our country. My concern for your father is even greater."

"Mother, I will do everything in my power to protect Ambracor. You know that."

Her expression stiffened with disapproval. "You're leaving again, aren't you?"

"Much must be done to strengthen our defenses."

"That's not what I mean. Tell me the truth. You're not leaving for Arvacon. You're leaving again to look for Sindara."

Blue eyes darkened, and his mouth drew into a grim line. "I will not lie to you. It is time for me to pick up the search."

"And if I tell your father?"

"I can only hope you will not."

"Thehrund, why must you go now? Ambracor needs both your strength and your courage. Your father needs you, too."

"Mother, if I could explain to you, I would. I can only swear that I honor my vows. I must find Sindara and bring her home."

Tears glazed his mother's eyes. "She's dead, Thehrund! Why can you not accept that and live your life in the here and now?"

"Mother, why is it that you and Father cannot believe in me? Why can you not trust me?"

"Because you behave like a fool when this country faces so much danger."

"Only a fool would turn his back on Creator God and promises made through his angels. I will not turn my back on God, my family, or Ambracor. Neither will I turn my back on Sindara. Someday you will understand. Good night, Mother."

Just before dawn, Thehrund awoke to light tapping at his door. He quickly climbed out of bed and let Nagrand Mezden inside. "I apologize for the hour, but Karan believes the portal is opening faster than we expected."

Thehrund said nothing. He quickly returned to his bedchamber where misty moonlight filtered through leaded windowpanes. He changed into dark clothes and dragged on a pair of boots. Snatching bundled weapons from the bottom of a massive armoire, he glanced around the room and shook his head. Not yet fully awake, he had nearly forgotten. Dropping the pack on the bed, he opened the top drawer of his nightstand. He pulled out a long chain of twisted gold that had just been repaired and pulled it over his head. Tucking the chain and the treasure it held underneath his shirt, he grabbed his things and rejoined Nagrand.

Practice had eliminated any need for spoken words. Nagrand left first, stealthily working his way through a dimly lit corridor to a doorway concealed by cleverly constructed stonework. Glancing over his shoulder to make sure the prince followed close behind, he touched the keystone that opened the door. He hurried through the opening with Thehrund only steps behind. Once the heavy door slid shut, they quietly leaned against cold stone walls for several minutes. Hearing only silence in the corridor, Nagrand picked up a small lantern he had left earlier.

Once they reached the exit from the palace, Nagrand again emerged first. The grounds were quiet. With the hour so early and damp night air carrying early spring chill, sentries preferred the warmth of wood fires in iron braziers placed at vantage points around the palace walls. From their point of exit, the path to the chapel was short and protected by rows of tall, narrow cypress trees on each side.

Despite the relative ease of reaching the chapel, both men felt distinct relief once they entered its protective shelter. For a time, extreme precautions had been necessary. Ordering guards to follow the prince, Hamund hoped to learn where his son went when he disappeared. Anticipating his father's attempts to discover his destination, Thehrund carefully planned hidden routes to avoid detection. Never sure when someone might try to trail them, stealth remained a high priority whenever they expected to enter the portal.

Reaching the cellar, Thehrund stopped at the bottom of the stairwell. The portal was indeed spinning faster and faster, emitting a humming sound that indicated it was opening much more quickly than in the past. Nagrand gathered bundles while the prince secured around his waist the broad leather belt that held his sheathed sword. The men then took up supplies and prepared to enter the swirling column.

As had become their custom, they all bowed heads while Karan prayed aloud for divine guidance and protection. Once each man followed the prayer with a personal declaration of faith and trust in Creator God, Thehrund led the way by confidently stepping forward into the churning currents that would carry them far from Ambracor.

A table lamp cast dim light inside the room. Thehrund frowned. They had once again emerged from the portal and arrived in a time full of machines and gadgets they had once thought the magic of some great wizard. He glanced around as Nagrand appeared, his boots hitting carpeted floors with a muffled thud. Karan arrived within a minute. Transit through the portal left them lightheaded. Even though repeated trips had reduced the severity, each man remained still until faint dizziness eased.

Nagrand was first to walk toward a window. Pushing aside linen-like curtains, he looked out across a long, narrow yard surrounded by a privacy fence lined with tall, slender evergreens. From what he could see, an alley divided the backyard of this house from the backs of an opposite row of homes. The sky was dark. The only noise was that of dogs barking in the distance. Leaving the window, he made his way through the first floor of the house, noting the location of the kitchen, small dining room, and front living room complete with wood-burning fireplace.

Holding his lantern in front of him, he searched for the tiny wall switches they had discovered on their last trip. He tested each one he located. As he flipped the switches up and down, he wondered if he could ever grow accustomed to the steady coldness of such lights. He much preferred the golden glow of a lantern or the lively flicker of candles.

He watched as Thehrund passed him and slowly opened the front door, stepping outside onto a spacious front porch. The prince came back inside and locked the door. "Houses along the street are dark. I expect the bedchambers are upstairs as they were last time. I think it wise that we get some rest."

The following morning, they explored the house. It was similar to the previous safe house they had occupied. Furnishings were comfortable despite their odd styles. Bedrooms upstairs were cramped but functional in Thehrund's opinion. Small closets held tailored clothing that seemed to have been made to fit each man. The kitchen was stocked with food enough for a few days. An envelope lay on the counter. On the outside, a single word was written. *Currency.* Inside was a supply of bills in varying denominations.

Thehrund picked up the envelope and carried it to the kitchen table. He glanced upward and smiled appreciatively when Karan set a mug of hot tea on the tablemat. He then stared again at the strange writing on the envelope in his hand. He was continually amazed by their ability to understand both spoken and written languages in worlds that were very different from their own. They had quickly realized their form of speech carried an accent that occasionally confused people with whom they interacted. In the evenings, the question of language inspired hours spent speculating and theorizing on how to explain yet another mystery.

"I share your questions," Karan said quietly. "How can this be? How do we understand languages not our own? Had I not lived through more than a dozen of these trips over the years, I would think myself completely mad."

Thehrund set the envelope aside and picked up his mug. The flavor of tea from home helped him maintain his focus. "I often wonder if I will awaken one day and find myself locked away somewhere for my own safety. Were it not for you and your brother, I'm not so sure I could continue."

Nagrand leaned nonchalantly against the side of an archway in the wall that divided the dining room from the kitchen's breakfast nook. "I decided long ago that the three of us share some sort of insanity. I comfort myself knowing that the adventures we've had would make anyone go at least half mad."

Thehrund gave a rare laugh. "I remember years ago when one of my tutors warned me that love was a form of incurable madness. I believe we may well have proven him right."

Nagrand joined his brother and the prince at the table. "Tell me that wasn't meant to be cynical."

Shaking his head, Thehrund answered, "Not at all. Each time we've entered the portal, I know I've brought with me a heavy heart and the mood to match. Before I fell asleep last night, I couldn't help thinking that, as reserved as she was, Sindara always found ways to make me laugh. I realized then how much I miss that feeling."

Karan smiled approvingly. "These most recent jaunts have certainly been cause for a few laughs."

"Yes," Thehrund agreed, "once we learned to avoid unexpected dangers."

"I still find myself amazed by those moving vehicles. Some are so enormous you could fit a whole house inside."

"Nagrand, I'll never forget your face the first time we saw them. You were nearly run down."

"My brother and I are both grateful for our prince's quick reflexes that day," Karan said with a shudder. "I, for one, hope we never have to face more learning experiences like those. As a priest, I much prefer the quiet serenity of our own home."

Thehrund stood up and walked over to peer out the back door. "There are many things I've seen that could prove useful. I think of that and then the stress on people's faces. I wonder if all their gadgetry is worth the sacrifice when I consider the relatively peaceful satisfaction we enjoy in Ambracor." Turning around, he sighed. "I think I shall go out and explore this place. We need to learn our surroundings before we start searching."

That night, Thehrund lay in bed and stared at the ceiling. His thoughts drifted home to happier times. He smiled into darkness, remembering her beautiful smile and musical laughter as they leaned forward to watch fish swimming in the large pond at the Varacor country estate. She was constantly amused by the reactions of the fish when she tossed breadcrumbs into the water to feed them. Although she had fed them since childhood, her pleasure always seemed fresh and new.

Memory changed scenes. Thehrund stood confidently at his father's right side. Garbed in official regalia, he exemplified the regal authority of one prepared to assume leadership from Ambracor's throne. Watching the procession of representatives who would attend the annual Provincial Governors' Conference, his interest was far from being feigned. Astute eyes observed everyone who passed the balcony where the royal family publicly greeted arriving delegates. The prince's observations of how visitors presented themselves added to the perspective rising from his developing keen sense of judging character.

Beyond politics, he anxiously awaited the appearance of representatives from Arvacon. He had personally reviewed the list of names in their entourage and had been secretly delighted to see Sindara's name among the attendees. Ever since his visits to Count Varacor's home, Thehrund had entertained more than a few daydreams centered on Lord Artrian's daughter. Daydreams yielded to nights filled with memories of her smiles, laughter, and the sharp wit and intelligence that kept him on his toes. During his most recent visit, she had relaxed in his presence, but that was hardly enough to satisfy his longing to be with her. On his journey home from that third visit, he had been somewhat dismayed to realize how much he already loved her.

His head lifted instantly when he noted the advancing rider holding the brilliant red, white, and gold banner of Arvacon Province aloft. Whereas most provincial delegates chose to travel the procession route in open coaches, those from Arvacon proudly showed both equestrian skills and breeding expertise by riding through city streets astride beautiful horses.

Thehrund could not suppress a smile the moment he glimpsed Sindara. She wore a ruby-colored riding habit and rode a magnificent golden mare that stepped elegantly high and tossed her head as if needing to ensure her mistress was the center of attention. When Sindara looked up toward the royal family, her smile brightened for brief seconds when she noted the slight forward tilt of the prince's head in recognition.

By midafternoon, Thehrund wondered if he would survive that night's welcoming banquet. He could barely concentrate on the more casual greetings when his father customarily received his closest friends and supporters prior to the first evening's celebrations. While thanking an elderly countess for a compliment that made little sense to him, he glanced upward and froze. Delegates admitted to the first afternoon's informal gathering were usually accompanied only by their wives or husbands. Count Artrian Varacor, one of his father's oldest friends, had entered the court with his wife on one arm and his daughter on the other.

The receiving line shortened so slowly that Thehrund briefly entertained the idea of bowling those in line out of the way by tripping an exceptionally rotund governor. Doing that was almost as impossible as keeping his attention on those he was expected to greet. Not very mature on the part of a prince already twenty-seven, he thought. Instead, he allowed himself the luxury of an occasional glance in Sindara's direction. He suffered disappointment each time as he watched her conversing with a couple in front of her, never once looking his way.

Just before the Varacors reached the front of the line, Thehrund surreptitiously wiped sweating palms on his tailored uniform tunic. The formal garment fell to mid-thigh, and its broad leather belt at his waist accentuated the prince's powerful physique. He warmly greeted Lord Artrian and Lady Liana before turning to Sindara. Grasping the hand she offered, he leaned forward and lightly touched his lips to smooth, fragrant skin.

Straightening, he saw her as never before. Brown hair gleamed with golden highlights and framed her oval face with graceful waves. Ivory skin was satin smooth and glowed with good health. Gold flecks shone from wide amber eyes accented by unusually long, dark lashes. Her rose-colored lips curved in a smile new to him...a smile that he realized with sudden, heart-jolting awareness was meant for him alone.

"Your Highness, how good it is to see you again," she addressed him.

Even her voice held a tone new to him. Gone was the aloof wariness of their past encounters. Even when she had excitedly discussed astronomy with him, she had always kept a noticeable distance. Something had changed...something that set his pulse racing as he acknowledged her greeting. "Thank you, Lady Sindara. I admit some surprise seeing you here. I certainly hope for an opportunity to extend to you the same hospitality you showed me during my visits to Arvacon."

She flashed him a brilliant smile. "Perhaps you might find time to give me a tour of the palace. This is my first visit."

Thehrund's sapphire blue eyes sparkled with pleasure. "I shall be delighted to make time for that tour."

When Sindara turned to answer questions from the king and queen, Thehrund forced himself to breathe evenly as he intently observed every move she made. The jacket of the red riding outfit she still wore was snugly fitted at the waist, enhancing the feminine curves of her tall figure. The pleated peplum was just full enough to show off her narrow waist as it eased outward to hug her hips. Her riding skirt had been fashioned for ease in mounting and riding a horse while retaining long, elegant lines. Both the bodice of the jacket and the side seams of the split skirt were adorned with intricate designs in white piping. Admiration swelled as her striking image etched itself into his memory.

Throughout the first week of the conference, demands on the prince's time were constant. Thehrund accompanied his father during general assemblies where he observed Hamund's mastery of diplomacy. Smaller sessions held by specialized committees provided examples of tough negotiations and tactful political finagling. The goal was to maximize benefits for the whole of Ambracor. King Hamund had crafted exceptional skills over nearly four decades as monarch. Thehrund observed and commented when he thought appropriate, all the time gaining greater appreciation for his father's knowledge and cleverness in the broad oversight of their nation's government.

He fulfilled obligations during the day that, as heir to his father's throne, he took seriously. When evenings came, dinners and entertainment often lasted until almost midnight. Fully aware of persistent attention Sindara was attracting from the many single noblemen visiting Bracordia, Thehrund made sure that she understood his intention to make time especially for her. Each morning, she received a bouquet of fresh flowers accompanied by a handwritten note.

When the initial course of conferences ended for a three-day break, Thehrund invited the Varacors to enjoy a private dinner with him and his parents. Inside an elegant dining room used exclusively by the royal family, the prince finally found time to relax. He relished the chance to engage in conversation that drew Sindara further from the cocoon of reserve that had marked their initial encounters. As she expressed opinions and ideas, he discovered growing respect for her intelligence and talents.

After dinner, he requested permission from her mother and father to escort her on a walk through some of the palace gardens. With smiling approval from both sets of parents, he tucked her arm beneath his and led her down a curved marble staircase. Walking quietly through a long corridor, they reached an arched doorway opening to stone walkways winding through the palace grounds.

The night was perfect for the stroll that was their first chance to be alone since her arrival in Bracordia. Hundreds upon hundreds of flowers filled the air with enchanting fragrance. Innumerable stars twinkled like diamonds against the velvety black dome of cloudless heavens. The full moon illuminated her distinctive features with a soft glow.

"I hope you believe me when I tell you that I've spent the entire week looking forward to spending a little time alone with you."

"Only a little time?" she asked teasingly.

A smile lit his face. "Dare I admit that I was afraid you might grow so tired of waiting for me to escape my duties that you would turn your attentions to some other exciting suitor seeking your favor?"

Her smile faded slightly as she shook her head. "Your Highness, I'm not so fickle. Besides, most of the men who have approached me are either too wrapped up in their own egos or simply too boring."

"May I consider that an indirect compliment?" he asked hopefully.

"Not at all," she replied, removing her arm from his and stepping away to admire an angel carved from marble. Her fingertips tracked along the curve of one of the statue's wings. She turned back to face him. "I hope you'll forgive my preference to be direct. When I first met you, I fully expected you to be even more arrogant and mindlessly egotistical than most of the young nobles I've met here. After all, as our future king, you are the single most privileged man in Ambracor.

"Unfortunately, my assessment resulted in several unkind remarks. During your last visit to Arvacon, I paid closer attention to your comments and opinions as well as to how you expressed yourself." She paused, wondering if perhaps she was too straightforward.

"So, my hopes are dashed that you were complimenting me." He attempted to conceal disappointment.

"Prince Thehrund, my words were not meant as an indirect compliment. To the contrary—I've discovered in you someone who surprises me with well-considered views, sincerity, and even compassion. If anything, what I said was a direct compliment."

His eyelids slowly closed as he exhaled a quiet, satisfied sigh. When he gazed at her again, he began to comprehend on a different level what it was about her that had captured his affection. She was honest and forthright. No coy games. No silly, insincere flirtations. She was a woman confident in her knowledge and abilities, and she was aware of things in life that mattered most to her.

"Sindara." Even the sound of her name felt like a caress from within his soul. "I've never known anyone like you."

"At the risk of sounding conceited, I doubt there is anyone else like me. I see myself different from most women my age...not better, just different. After six years at school studying religion and learning the art of healing, I feel gifted with an abiding faith in Creator God. And, for better or worse, I have an insatiable curiosity about most things. I tend to be far too serious. I understand those aspects of my character and long ago decided I would never mold myself into what others expected me to be. I must be who I am." She paused again. A kind of hopefulness blended with uncertainty about how to continue.

"My dear, sweet Sindara, you omit facets of who you are that have earned my admiration. You possess an extraordinary kindness and a sort of indescribable energy."

She took a single step backward. "I was also afraid of you."

Her abrupt, unexpected admission caused his forehead to furrow in question. "Afraid? I don't think I understand. What have I done to make you afraid?"

With both hands, she reached for his. "You did nothing to me. I fear I'm the one who listened to far too many rumors."

Regret briefly shadowed his face. "A young man's judgment often fails him. If those stories bore any truth, my hope is that you might find in me a man who has learned from past errors." Carefully regarding changes in her expressive features, he had not even a second to consider the irresistible desire that rose within him. Surrendering to the moment, he lowered his face and bestowed the softest of kisses on her lips.

He was almost fearful when he looked at her again. The image that filled his vision banished every shred of anxiety. Those sweet, luscious lips faintly curved into a smile that conveyed invitation. Thehrund felt himself captor and captive at once as he embraced her tightly and kissed her with a passion that astounded him. Tentative at first, she received his kiss with like ardor. By the time their kiss ended, both knew. They had lived their lives thus far so that they might always love one another.

Thehrund relished the feel of her within the circle of his arms. Her body felt warm, vibrant, and alive. For a brief moment, he thought of other women he had known. Not one had ever made him feel as she did. Her presence enveloped him, reaching deep into the core of his being and filling him with a warmth that was new and exhilarating. If ever he had doubted the existence of real love between a man and a woman, those doubts had been dashed to pieces by the intensity of the kisses they had just shared.

Eyelids slid closed. The fatigue of being in a strange world overcame him. The memory that had ushered him into sleep lingered, soothing weariness that had accompanied his soul for six years.

A long week passed. All three men spent hours walking city streets. Damp, chilly weather marked the imminent end of winter. Whenever they were out, they studied everything they saw, carefully watching people's habits and actions to learn how to perform mundane tasks. A noticeable difference in fashion provided them an odd sense of relief. Many of the men now wore their hair much longer, which made them less conspicuous on their trips out.

A new week began. Observation had taught them that this world's rhythm followed a course of five days of hectic activity, then two days at a somewhat slower pace. With few people at home during most days, Nagrand and Thehrund decided to take advantage of a warmer, brighter morning to concentrate on an intense practice session in the backyard of the house. Practices served dual purposes, keeping reflexes sharp while working off frustration related to their continuing, futile search.

As afternoon passed, dense layers of gray clouds displaced morning sunshine. Light rain came and went, leaving a damp chill that penetrated to the bone. Inside the house, Karan finished the afternoon prayer session that had become essential to all three. Prayer reminded them of home and connected them to Creator God in a place where they readily accepted their need for divine protection. Sharing prayers also reinforced bonds of both friendship and occasionally waning spirits.

Checking the kitchen pantry and that wonderful thing they had learned was called a refrigerator, they decided a trip to the market was in order. Karan remained home while Thehrund and Nagrand braved the weather to purchase groceries so unlike foods they enjoyed in Ambracor. As Karan started cooking their evening meal, what he did appreciate was the variety of food available and how easy preparation was for three bachelors whose culinary skills were severely limited.

Chapter Six

"Karan! Open the door!" Thehrund shouted from outside. Within moments, the glass-paned inside door opened. Karan shoved it all the way back and then held open the outer storm door. Thehrund turned sideways to enter without striking the woman's feet or head against the wooden doorframe.

Leaving his brother to collect bags scattered on the porch, Karan hurried inside and pushed cushions to one corner of the couch before helping Thehrund arrange the limp body on the living room sofa. "Nagrand, hurry! I need help here! Thehrund, go upstairs and change. If she awakens and sees you covered in blood, she'll likely be scared half to death."

Heading toward the kitchen, Nagrand dumped bags of groceries on the table and then snatched a handful of towels from a drawer. Returning to the living room, he passed them to his brother, who knelt on the floor beside the sofa. "What do you want me to do?"

Karan carefully placed a thick, clean dishtowel just above the woman's left temple and held it firmly. "I must stop this bleeding. In the meantime, try to remove her coat and shoes." He flinched. "See if you can also pull off those trousers. She's soaking wet and cold. We need to get her dry and warm quickly."

"Thehrund!" Nagrand shouted. "Bring a blanket when you come down!"

"Why in God's name did you bring her here?" Karan hissed in a low voice. "I thought Thehrund told us not to involve ourselves in problems here."

"You know our prince as well as I do. He saw some men attack a lone woman and immediately ran to her defense. I told him to leave her, but...."

"Never mind," Karan muttered in an irritated voice. "Bring me some clean, wet cloths so I can wash her face. Oh, turn on the overhead light, too. I need to see how bad this cut is."

Glancing upward as Nagrand disappeared with a pile of soggy clothes, Karan saw that Thehrund had brought a blanket along with several large bath towels. "Cover her with the blanket and go get the leather bag of medical supplies from the closet in my room."

"I apologize for putting you through this. I couldn't leave her."

"Just get my things."

Nagrand returned with a pan of warm water and washcloths. Watching as his brother carefully moved wet hair clinging to the woman's cheeks, he shook his head. "I find it appalling that so many men would attack a woman, but the way she fought them was almost as shocking." Kneeling by the sofa, Nagrand wrung out a fresh cloth and handed it to his brother.

With one hand, Karan continued to apply pressure to the cut still bleeding heavily. With a clean towel in his other hand, he continued to wipe the sticky mix of blood, mud, and hair away from her face. He suddenly froze and gasped out loud.

"What?" Nagrand asked in alarm.

"My God! Can it be?" Shoving a grimy dishcloth toward his brother, he said, "Quick! I need more towels! Then, tell Thehrund to hurry. I need him down here."

Gently, Karan washed as much of the remaining grime from her face as he could. Steady pressure against the gash on the side of her head had slowed the bleeding. He would need assistance keeping her still should she awaken while he examined and treated the wound.

Glancing upward, he saw Thehrund appear with the medical bag in his hand. "Give the bag to Nagrand. He can unpack bandages and the bottle of wound binder. I need you here."

Thehrund groaned. "You're the priest and physician. Can you not manage a single injured female?"

"You don't understand. I need you now. Here. On your knees...beside me!"

Biting back a sharp retort, Thehrund just stared at the priest. Karan met the prince's aggravated gaze with a stern expression. "Now, Thehrund!"

When the prince finally joined him on the floor, Karan leaned back as far as he could. "Look at her. Look and tell me if you see what I see."

Bending forward, Thehrund felt his heart lurch sharply inside his chest as bright blue eyes held first shock, then terror. Shaking hands swiftly covered still, icy fingers and lifted them to trembling lips. "Dear God! I had no idea. None...none at all. How...how...bad is the cut?"

"Bad enough. She's definitely in shock. I suspect she has a severe concussion."

"What do you want me to do?" Thehrund asked, his eyes locked on the face that had haunted him for years. Her hands were so cold and her skin so pale. "I'll do anything. Just take care of her."

Karan looked over his shoulder. His brother was already carefully setting out bandages, a medicine cup, and wound binder on a nearby table. "Nagrand, find a pillow and prop her feet up. Not too high. Get another blanket, too. In the meantime, Thehrund, you hold her still in case she starts to awaken. The last thing we need is for her to panic and injure herself even worse."

Thehrund positioned himself so that the weight of his body would prevent the young woman from making any sudden moves while Karan cleansed the area around the swelling gash in her head. Deft fingers quickly measured the thick herbal liquid that, once applied to the cut, would dry and bind the wound closed. Then, with Nagrand supporting her shoulders, Karan carefully wrapped a bandage around her head.

Giving his unexpected patient a final check, Karan stood and gathered his medical supplies while quietly suggesting that Nagrand start a fire in the grate. Without even bothering to glance at Thehrund, he knew the prince had settled himself on the floor to watch over the woman stretched out on their sofa. He then went to the kitchen to finish preparing the light supper he had started just before hearing desperate shouts from the front porch.

As Karan ladled stew into three bowls, Nagrand entered the kitchen. "I rinsed out her clothes and hung them on the screen in front of the fireplace to dry. How strange to see her wearing trousers and then to have to undress her."

"Women wearing trousers seems commonplace here. I'm not sure I could ever get used to it." He sighed. "Would you slice some bread while I make a tray for Thehrund?"

Nodding, Nagrand reached for a long serrated knife to cut a slice of hearty multi-grain bread from a loaf they'd just purchased from a nearby deli. "My head is still reeling. When we left tonight, I never expected to see a woman being assaulted by a band of men. It was sickening...like facing down Breyal raiders all over again."

"I'm glad it was too dark for him to recognize her," Karan said thoughtfully.

"A catastrophe that would have been," Nagrand readily agreed. "Had he realized we were defending Sindara, I have little doubt dead bodies would have been strewn all over the street."

"True. He came far too close to disobeying the instructions he said the voices gave him." As Karan picked up the tray, he shook his head. "We now face questions that I've feared most. How will she react when she sees him? How will we work through this?"

Minutes later, Karan set the tray on the coffee table in front of the sofa. "Supper. Eat."

Thehrund forced himself to look up. "I fear for her, Karan. She has moved not even once."

"When she does, we have no idea what to expect. You'll need all your wits about you, my friend. Eat something. Then, rest."

Dragging the table closer, Thehrund stared at his food. Taking a deep breath, he tore in half a thick slice of bread and dipped it into the stew. He half-heartedly finished the remainder without ever noticing the flavor. Instead, he attempted to marshal thoughts darting in so many directions that he felt almost dizzy.

Angel voices had promised he would find her. They had warned it would take time...that his own actions would prove if his personal devotion were deep enough to accomplish the goal of saving her life. Even his wildest imaginings had never prepared him for the journeys he had undertaken in his search. Deep within his soul, he realized this most recent trip had demanded greater dedication than all others combined. He had entered the portal this time knowing that he was leaving behind his family and his beloved Ambracor to resolve internal conflict regarding the full extent of the Breyal danger. His own voice would have carried critical influence. His decision to accept this particular portal opening reflected absolute commitment to the pledge he had made.

"Thehrund?"

Troubled blue eyes lifted questioningly.

"Midnight is nearly upon us. You've sat on the floor for hours. You should rest."

The prince's gaze dropped. With his long hair pulled back, the distress etched into his face was heartrending. "Nagrand, you know I cannot leave her."

"At least move to a chair where you'll be more comfortable. I can bring you a pillow and a blanket."

Minutes later, Nagrand dragged the coffee table out of the way and pushed an upholstered chair next to the sofa. While Thehrund settled in for the night, Nagrand added extra logs to the fireplace. In the meantime, his brother prepared a place on the floor where he could spend the night near his patient.

While Karan lay listening to her rhythmic breathing, he silently prayed. He hoped this vigil would provide answers to questions plaguing him ever since Thehrund's initial account of frozen time, angel voices, and their offer to restore the life of the prince's slain love.

Why? Why had such high value been placed on Sindara's life? Why had Thehrund been directed into the portal to search for the woman he had loved, betrayed, and lost? Why had Karan and his brother been drawn into Thehrund's quest? Why? Questions marched on and on while answers remained as elusive as clouds sailing upon winds high up in the heavens.

The grandfather clock in the upstairs hallway chimed the hour of four in the morning. Diana turned her head on the pillow. Throbbing pain filled her brain. Arms and legs were stiff and resisted every effort to move. Eyelids fluttered, opening just enough to see the orange glow of large embers in the fireplace. Her mouth felt nearly paralyzed with dryness. The tip of her tongue pushed forward to lick her lips. A breathy sigh overcame words she tried to whisper.

Karan instantly pushed himself up from the floor. As quickly as he had risen, Thehrund had been faster, shoving his blanket to the floor and landing on his knees beside the sofa.

"Who...?" Her voice shuddered.

"Do not fear. You're safe." Thehrund's voice was exceptionally gentle as he stroked strands of hair from her eyes.

"Those men..." She started coughing.

"Give her this," Karan said, handing a cup to Thehrund.

Sliding his arm beneath her shoulders, Thehrund raised her up enough so that she could take several sips of a lightly sweet tonic. "Drink slowly. This will help you feel better."

When he lowered her back to rest on the pillow, she closed her eyes. Invading memories filled her with a disturbing blend of terror and anger.

"You...were with...another man. I remember. You came to help me." She paused. "Please. Tell me neither of you got hurt."

A solid lump in his throat rendered him momentarily speechless. Her words were exactly what he would have expected from Sindara. He shook his head before finally responding, "Neither of us was hurt, but one of your attackers pushed you before we could stop him. When you fell, you hit your head. We brought you here." He nodded toward Karan. "My friend here is a physician. He treated your injury."

Reluctantly moving aside, Thehrund watched as Karan knelt and smiled reassuringly. "Nagrand, I need more light." Then, the physician gently turned Diana's face toward the back of the sofa and moved the bandage away from the cut. "The wound binder I applied is working. The gash is closing, but you need to rest. We can see the outer injury heals, but the seriousness of such a blow to the head must not be taken lightly."

"My head aches terribly." She breathed in and out. Her thought processes were slowly clearing. "Where am I? Why didn't you take me to the hospital?"

"You are in our home. We had no means to take you elsewhere."

She looked puzzled, wondering why they hadn't just called for an ambulance. Maybe they had just moved in. Sighing, she shook her head and immediately regretted it. A white-hot shaft of pain lanced through her brain, causing her to moan softly.

"Karan?" Thehrund's voice carried a sharp edge of fear.

Ignoring the prince, Karan concentrated on Diana. "I suggest you avoid sudden or unnecessary movements. Can you open your eyes again?"

Following his instructions, she squinted. "The light. It hurts my eyes."

"You may likely be sensitive to light for several days." Asking Nagrand to move the light further away, Karan continued his assessment of her condition. "Can you see my face?" Receiving the slightest of nods, he held up first two fingers, then three. He moved his index finger up and down, then side to side. Her count was correct, and her eyes followed the motions of his hand. "Splendid. Now, can you tell me your name?"

A long moment passed. She felt adrift in a fog-burdened sea. "Diana. My name is Diana Lorenz."

"Diana. Such a lovely name. I am Karan Mezden." He tilted his head. "This is Thehrund Cobrandya. He and my brother Nagrand were the ones who saw the attack. Thehrund carried you here."

"Thehrund..." She gazed for mere seconds at the somber face that stirred some profound inner sense. "I...I'm sorry...I think I...can't..." Eyelids slid closed as she surrendered to the irresistible, beckoning call of healing sleep.

Thehrund stared into a mug of hot tea. His lunch sat on the table, the food untouched. His mind reeled. He had found her. That he felt deep within his soul. Every sense and every nerve he possessed had reacted to her mere presence. She had looked at him with those hypnotic amber eyes. His heart had lurched painfully inside his chest when she had not recognized him.

"Starving yourself will change this situation not one bit," Nagrand remarked as he drank from his own mug of tea.

"You cannot know how I feel. I thought she would at least recognize me."

Karan leaned back against a kitchen counter. "You must keep in mind that she suffered a severe blow to the head...and that after fighting multiple assailants. Besides," he paused, considering his words carefully, "she awoke in an unfamiliar place surrounded by strangers."

"But we're not strangers!"

"Keep your voice down. Do you want to frighten her?"

The prince buried his face in his hands. "Does this ever end? Do I spend the rest of my life paying for a mistake I cannot even recall making?"

Karan shook his head. "Those questions I cannot answer. On the other hand, I remember exactly what you told us. The voices promised you would find her and that you would have the opportunity to earn her forgiveness. You persevered all these years and have finally found her when you least expected. Will you so easily give up now?"

"Hello?" A weak voice interrupted them.

Instantly jumping to his feet, Thehrund hurried into the living room and knelt on one knee beside the sofa. Without thinking, he took her hands in his. "I'm so sorry you awoke alone. We were in the kitchen to avoid disturbing you."

Diana managed a wobbly smile. "Then I didn't dream last night?"

"It was no dream. What can I do to help you?"

"Hmm," she sighed, feeling weak and lightheaded. "I need to..." Pausing uncomfortably, she said, "I need to get up to use the bathroom."

Thehrund's head tilted slightly backward. "Of course. I will help you..." He suddenly remembered most of her clothes were hanging on the fireplace screen. "Let me hold the blanket up to wrap around you. We had to remove most of your clothing because you were soaked when we carried you in."

Rosy blush colored her cheeks. "Was I that bad?" She then let him help her sit up. With deliberate slowness, she placed bare feet flat on the carpeted floor and stood. Dizziness caused her to sway, but Thehrund had been prepared to steady her.

As she leaned against him, he wrapped both blanket and arms around her. Waiting until she was ready to move, he savored the sweet feel of holding her in his embrace. Moments later, he guided her to the first-floor bathroom.

After assuring him she could manage without help, she used the toilet and then washed her hands. Looking into the mirror, she grimaced. Her face was ghostly pale and her hair a matted mass of tangles tumbling from the bottom edge of the bandage wrapped around her head. Leaning against the vanity cabinet, she pushed shaky fingers through long locks with little success. Unable to hide all day in the bathroom, she sighed in resignation, opened the door, and gratefully accepted Thehrund's assistance back to the sofa.

"Excellent," Karan said with a broad smile. "You look much improved. How is your headache?"

She dared not shake her head. "Not good, but better than the last time I woke up."

Karan chuckled as he sat on the sofa beside her. Her response was definitely a positive sign. "And how do you feel otherwise?"

How did she feel? "I'm not quite sure. My body feels stiff and sore. Beyond that, I just feel very strange."

"Strange? In what way?" He glanced up and exchanged a wondering look with Thehrund.

"I...I...really can't describe it." Her stomach growled. "Maybe I'm just hungry. I know I could certainly do with a cup of coffee."

"We have no coffee, but I can offer you some strong tea that should ease your headache. After that, Nagrand will fix you something light to eat."

"Thank you," she said. She lifted her gaze to Thehrund's face. "Thank you for everything. You took a serious risk confronting those hoodlums."

Hoodlums was a new word for Thehrund. "If you refer to the men who attacked you, I assure you they were the kind who only assail when they seriously outnumber their prey. They had few fighting skills, if any. Nagrand and I saw how you fought them. Had there not been so many, you likely would have prevailed."

Diana still could not believe how she had resisted them. "I took a couple of classes in self-defense, but nothing that prepared me for what happened last night. For a time, it felt almost as if someone else had stepped into my body and taken over."

Again, Thehrund exchanged looks with Karan. Perhaps he wanted to read too much into her remarks.

Later, as she started to eat, she heard the grandfather clock. One chime only. An expression of disbelief crossed her face. "Good grief! What time is it?"

Karan sat with her while Thehrund had gone up to shower and change from clothes he had slept in. "One o'clock in the afternoon. You slept quite a long time."

"What am I going to tell my boss? Worse yet, what am I going to tell Kendra?"

Karan shrugged. "Truth is always best. Now, eat. You said you were hungry, and I'm quite sure your recovery will hasten with proper nutrition."

She was hungry, and the food on her plate smelled delicious. As she chewed her first bite, she finally thought to take a closer look. Karan certainly didn't look the part of a doctor. His hair was a rich golden blond and unusually long. His clean-shaven features were quite pleasant. Gray eyes held immense kindness.

"Yes?"

She swallowed. "Yes, what?"

"You looked at me with such scrutiny. I wondered why."

She felt her face turning red. "My apologies. I just thought you don't look like any doctors I've ever met."

"And how am I supposed to look?"

"I'm really sorry. You just look...different." She needed a diversion. Taking another bite, she chewed slowly while trying to reassemble her mental faculties. "Honestly, I meant no insult. Most doctors wear their hair...well, it's usually...shorter...more conservative. May I ask where you're from? Your accent is also different."

"Observant and inquisitive. Both signs that you should have a rapid recovery." Karan looked up as Thehrund reappeared. "You will be glad to know that our patient seems to be improving rather quickly."

Diana smiled up at Thehrund. Although he smiled back, she couldn't help but think his eyes were the saddest she had ever seen. "Despite the way he took care of me overnight, I believe I just managed to insult the good doctor here."

Karan stood up and chuckled. "No insult taken," he said, meeting Thehrund's gaze. "She's curious about a physician with long hair and our accents. Perhaps you can explain while I go help Nagrand."

Thehrund finally entered the room and sat in a chair across from her. How to answer her questions was an altogether new prospect he had not anticipated. He forced another smile. "I am gladdened to see you feel better. We were quite worried."

Having eaten as much as she dared, she set her plate on the coffee table. Her head felt uncomfortably heavy with the motion, causing her to wince with pain.

He leaned forward, both his expression and posture suddenly intense. "Are you all right?"

Her answer was a slight nod of her head as she flattened her palm against the left temple near the bandaged gash. "I think so. It just hurts more when I move."

"You should lie back and try to rest. One of God's greatest restoratives is rest."

Somewhere inside her brain, she knew she should call Kendra or someone at work. She should also probably be in a hospital. Just as those fuzzy thoughts registered, she glanced at Thehrund's face. He was on the floor again, supporting her head and shoulders as he gently eased her downward.

Curious thoughts wafted haphazardly through her mind. His hair was no longer pulled back. Instead, it fell below his shoulders in a thick, waving sea of black. Unlike the others, his hair contained two tight braids on each side. Struggling to hold her eyelids open, she saw a face drawn with tension and eyes a brilliant shade of blue that nearly took her breath. She thought she managed a thankful smile as he tucked a blanket around her.

"Damn!" Kendra grabbed a potholder and quickly moved the smoking skillet from the stove. Dumping the grilled cheese sandwich that looked more like crumbling charcoal into the sink, she wondered if she could do anything right. So much for lunch. She opened a cabinet door and peered inside. Reaching for a bag of potato chips, she set it on the counter and then went to the fridge for a container of dip. Not exactly filling or nutritious, she thought, but maybe the crunching of the chips would drown out screaming inside her mind that something terrible had happened to Diana.

Just as she swallowed a bite, the phone rang. Jumping up from her chair, she grabbed her cell phone. Minutes later, she shook her head. A detective had called to advise there had been an emergency call the night before near where Diana's belongings were found, but arriving officers had seen no disturbance. Police checked the area that morning and spoke to a few residents. Except for Diana's purse and a discarded knife a block away, there was no definitive evidence they could link to Diana's disappearance. After the call ended, pacing back and forth through the apartment only made her feel more helpless.

Kendra had contacted the police department early that morning to inquire about the process for reporting a missing person. She never expected to learn that Diana's purse had been found in the middle of the street by someone on the way to catch a bus. That person had found the wallet inside and then notified the police. He later called Kendra, who was listed on an identification card as Diana's emergency contact.

Kendra considered Diana more like a sister than a friend. Years earlier, she had entered high school at a prestigious academy that cost her parents a small fortune. Although her parents earned modest incomes, they had recognized their daughter's special gifts and intellect. Wanting to give her opportunities for the best education possible, they had both taken second jobs to afford the steep tuition at the private school where they enrolled her.

Kendra's first day at that school had been utter terror. Few black students attended the school, and they had already formed a tight clique that she immediately realized would be off limits. That didn't bother her as much as she would have expected. She already understood how different she was from most people her age. Still, some longings of a fourteen-year-old girl were universal. There was a real need to fit in some place and to have friends to share the laughter and tears of growing up.

On the second day, Kendra seriously worried that she might never fit in with any of the groups she observed at school. Inside the cafeteria during her lunch period, she sat alone and looked around. Earlier, she had wondered how many of her fellow students took seriously the morning prayers everyone said as part of the school's religion-based curriculum. She watched other freshmen from feeder schools where they had spent years together. They made it obvious that outsiders weren't welcome.

That afternoon, she had stood at her open locker door, organizing things to take home. She was suddenly knocked off balance and stumbled against lockers next to hers. Her books and supplies fell into a pile on the floor. Looking around, she saw the mocking faces of two girls and a boy she knew to be upperclassmen.

"Sorry, there, missy. You weren't paying attention to where we were going." Taunting faces dared her to say something back to them.

"With three sets of eyes, I would think at least one of you might be able to find your own way through such a well-lit hall."

Kendra's brown eyes widened. Suddenly, standing in front of the three troublemakers was a tall, slender girl whose very posture made them all back away. Or was it her posture? Kendra's senses swirled on alert. She immediately felt powerful energy surging from the one person who had come to her defense.

"Look, Diana..." one of the girls started to say.

"Don't tell me to look. You three need to look at what you've done... *and* watch where you're going. Now pick her things up, give them to her nicely, and don't bother her again. Do you understand?"

To Kendra's complete surprise, the trio nearly tripped over themselves gathering things off the floor and handing them back to Kendra with a string of apologies. They may have been insincere, but the fact that they apologized at all was something of a shock.

"Are you all right?"

Kendra couldn't help but stare into eyes that reflected golden lights. "I…I'm fine. Uh, thank you."

Her rescuer suddenly smiled. "My name is Diana Lorenz. I'm sorry about those crazies over there. I may never understand why people behave that way in church-run schools. As far as I'm concerned, that's one of life's great mysteries. Now, who are you?"

Her mouth fell open, and when no sound came out, she laughed nervously. Finally, she managed an answer. "I'm Kendra Porter, and it really is nice to meet you. Forgive me, but I have to ask. Why did those kids back away from you the way they did? I don't think I've ever seen anything like that."

"I'm not always sure I understand myself. I went to the same elementary school they attended. For some weird reason, they think I have special powers."

Kendra slipped her arm through the strap of her book bag and closed her locker door. "Do you?"

Diana laughed out loud. "That would be something from a science-fiction movie, don't you think?"

Kendra laughed quietly. "Maybe. Maybe not."

Diana's face was alight with good humor. "Hey, maybe we can strike up a friendship and explore that answer of yours. What do you think?"

Tears tracked down Kendra's cheeks. That conversation had begun a friendship that stood strong through high school and continued throughout four years at different universities. Once they graduated with their bachelor degrees, they moved into an apartment together after Diana was hired by the bank where she had worked part-time during college.

During the early years of their friendship, Kendra observed many instances that explained the odd reactions she had first seen from the students who had intentionally bumped into her. Diana was slow to temper but always swift to defend against injustices. When she did become angry, things happened. The sheer power of her aura could actually force people to back away. Sometimes, objects flew off tables or desks. Her energy vibrations caused furniture, doors, and even cars to rattle or shake for no apparent reason. Electricity in her body often created shocks that startled people in her presence. Thankfully, outwardly at least, most people attributed the unusual happenings to static electricity.

Kendra watched with intense interest. Her own parents had first recognized similar tendencies in her at a very early age. They had often glimpsed a subdued glow surrounding their young daughter. By the time Kendra started kindergarten, her vocabulary often sounded like an adult's when she described her experiences at school. Unlike the majority of people who suppressed such capabilities because of social stigma, her parents had encouraged her to cultivate her abilities without making public displays that might draw unwanted attention. The Porters had been wise enough to recognize their gifted daughter needed careful coaching and time to mature until self-confidence would enable her to best use her God-given talents.

Kindred spirits in many ways, Diana and Kendra learned to trust one another with their secrets. Diana's quiet, reserved manner tended to make her protective and secretive about her puzzling abilities and experiences. Kendra's willingness to discuss their unusual tendencies gave both girls an outlet while building the firm foundation of their relationship.

Then, Kendra's parents were killed in a car accident during her sophomore year at college. Diana had refused to let Kendra give up on her hopes of working toward a doctorate. Life insurance money was set aside and carefully budgeted to help Kendra pay for education expenses not covered by scholarships and still have enough to live in reasonable comfort. All the while, Diana reminded her friend that clinging to her faith in God would ease her sorrow and help her build the future she and her parents had dreamed of achieving.

"Diana," Kendra whispered, "please be all right. I can't bear to lose you, too." She then got up, put on her coat, and left for the church a few blocks away where she could pray for her friend's safe return.

Satisfied that she had fallen asleep, Thehrund sat across from her with elbows on the chair's arms and fingertips touching. Physically, he remained inside the room to watch over her. His heart, however, drifted into the field of memories that served as his retreat whenever he had needed to bolster sagging spirits.

He had arrived for a visit on a hot summer's day. Even though his arrival was expected, she had not been inside to welcome him. Marnee appeared in the formal foyer upon hearing his voice and sent him outside to look for Sindara. Fatigue was easily ignored as he anticipated seeing her again. Walking halfway around the enormous pond, he frowned. She was nowhere to be found. Suddenly, he heard his name cried out at the same time an unexpected shove knocked him off his feet and sent him stumbling into the water. Sputtering, he pulled himself into a sitting position just as an enormous splash of cold water filled his face.

"Prince Thehrund! Welcome back to Arvacon!" She sat an arm's length away in the water and tossed her head backward. Her laughter filled the air with magic all its own.

The unexpected tumble into the pond had been surprise enough, or so he had thought. Just as he considered suitable revenge, she bounced up from the water and came to him. Throwing her arms around his neck, she kissed him soundly. When she backed away, the mischief in her grin suddenly made the abrupt drenching entirely worthwhile. The joy on her face and the fervor of her kiss filled him with optimism that he had truly won her love.

After dinner, Thehrund convinced Sindara to leave behind her telescope and notebooks so they could simply enjoy walking to the hillock where they loved stargazing. The warm evening was clear, and the heavens seemed alive with thousands of glittering stars. Staring directly at the starry firmament, the prince suddenly pointed northward where a meteor streaked across the sky. He marveled at the delight on her face. She looked so beautiful, and he couldn't wait another minute.

"Sindara, there's something I must discuss with you."

Noting changes in his expression, she frowned. "Is everything all right?"

Despite inhaling deeply, he felt almost breathless. "It's just..." He paused, having thought this would be easy. He started again. "I've been thinking of all the things we've discussed over the past few months. I realize you had a difficult time accepting me at first. Since then, I do believe I've proven that I'm not the spoiled, self-centered royal you expected me to be."

Moonlight cast a fascinating glow on her reddening cheeks. "You hadn't heard the stories about you that I did."

A frown creased his forehead. "You must tell me those stories one day."

She responded with a shy grin. "I think I would be too embarrassed."

He laughed softly. "After that wet greeting you gave me today with all the world watching?"

"That was different," she replied in a coy voice.

"I see. We can discuss that when you tell me those awful stories. Now, it's time to be serious."

She carefully molded her features into a solemn mask. "You may continue, Your Highness."

He marveled at how she demonstrated her feelings both in words and expressions. "Sindara, I don't know if I will ever match the intensity of your faith in Creator God, but I do admire and respect the way you live your faith. Your humor keeps me from taking myself too seriously. I also find your intelligence challenges me to observe and think in ways I never did before."

"Please," she interrupted when he paused, "don't tell me you've come to offer me a position as headmistress at some school in the capital."

Thehrund chuckled. "No, I wouldn't think of such a thing. What I do think is that you have changed my whole perspective on life. I told you the last time I came how much I enjoy spending time with you." He watched her features soften as she looked up at him. He took hold of both her hands. "Sindara, I hope with all my heart that you might someday come to love me as much as I now love you."

He felt her hands begin to tremble within his grasp. Her eyes suddenly shimmered with tears. "Thehrund..." For a moment, speech failed her. "I do love you. I sincerely cannot imagine loving anyone else...ever."

Stars had shone down upon them as heavenly witnesses when he surrounded her with possessive arms and kissed her with passion yet again exceeding all he had before experienced. Holding her tightly, he had felt as if their entire world suddenly belonged to him alone.

"Nothing yet, Mrs. Merrill. I'll call you as soon as I hear something." Kendra placed the handset back into its cradle. "She doesn't remember Diana mentioning going anywhere else."

The police officer, a slender black man in his mid-thirties, made a note. When he looked up at Kendra, his air of competence mixed with kindness. "We'll keep her wallet and purse for now. If you think of anything else, call us immediately. In the meantime, I promise we'll do everything we can to find your friend."

Once the officer left, Kendra double-checked locks on the door before going to pour herself a cup of coffee from a pot that had been sitting too long. She hardly noticed the burnt taste as she sat down to call Jennie Clarke to advise Diana wouldn't be at work. Ending the call, she appreciated the genuine compassion and concern she had detected in Jennie's voice. Maybe Diana was right. Perhaps the woman did have redeeming graces. The last necessity was trying again to contact Diana's parents at the secluded lodge in Africa where they were on some sort of retreat.

Kendra got up and dumped the lukewarm coffee in the sink. Her stomach was doing flip-flops. Ever since she had arrived home from her part-time job, she had known something was wrong. Diana rarely stayed out late on a weeknight and always called or texted if her schedule changed. Calls to Diana's cell phone had gone unanswered. When the call had come that morning from the kindly stranger, Kendra's level of worry had ballooned.

Looking around the neatly kept apartment, Kendra desperately needed something to do. She picked up study materials and laid them back down. There was no way she could concentrate. Going for a walk, at least for the time being, was out of the question. Whatever had happened, Diana might call or find her way home. Meditation. Maybe she could calm herself by meditating. Kendra went to her bedroom, sat on the floor, lit a candle and incense, and then initiated her prayer for protection before slipping into a comforting meditative state.

Holding her head between her hands, Diana gave out a little groan. "What a headache."

Tucking away precious memories of happier times, Thehrund rose from his chair and went to her side. Perching on the edge of the solid wood coffee table, he did his best to smile. "Hello again."

She opened one eye and peeked up. "I have new sympathy for people who suffer migraine headaches. I need to get up. Would you mind helping me?"

Saying nothing, he dropped onto one knee and supported her as she slowly sat up. "If you'd like, I can help you into the bathroom. Nagrand washed your clothes out last night. They're dry now if you feel up to putting them on."

Shyly, she nodded. "That would be nice. Thank you."

Emerging from the bath a little later, she felt better after having washed her face and rinsed her mouth with some mouthwash she had found. She made a mental note to replace the bottle and then hoped her rattled brain would remember. Feeling less vulnerable now that she was fully dressed, she looked forward to going home to shower and change into clean clothes. She was relieved that her rescuers had not found it necessary to remove her panties. A quick glance had revealed fresh blood from scars that were bleeding again for no apparent reason.

Finding her way back to the living room, she met Thehrund's gaze with an appreciative smile. "How can I ever thank you for all you and your friends have done for me?"

"Trust me when I say we are all more than glad that we were able to help you."

Something in his response struck an odd chord in her. She shook off the strange feeling. "Is my coat here?"

"Of course." Within seconds, Nagrand appeared with her coat in hand. "Nagrand cleaned off mud from where you fell and hung it downstairs to dry."

How peculiar, she thought. She had barely asked the question before Nagrand entered the living room. Thanking him, she reached into her pocket. "Thank heavens I didn't lose this," she said, raising her cell phone. "I only hope it still works. By the way, you didn't by chance save my purse, did you?"

Nagrand frowned. "I'm afraid not. When you fell, heavier rain was beginning to fall. We didn't think to look for anything else. It seemed more important to get you out of the cold where we could take care of your injuries."

"It's all right. I hope you'll excuse me. I need to call my roommate. She'll come and take me home." She started to enter the number but stopped. "What's the address here?"

Nagrand gave her the information while Thehrund remained mute. The idea of her leaving was one that prompted rising fear of losing her again.

A few minutes later, Diana sat in the kitchen. With a mug of fragrant herbal tea in her hand, she fought back tears. "My roommate was scared to death. I felt awful when she started to cry."

"The two of you must be very close," Karan said kindly.

"Kendra is the best friend I've ever had. She knows me better than anyone and keeps my secrets like no one else would."

"You do not strike me as the kind of person who would have secrets to hide," Nagrand remarked.

Diana forced a grin. "Not bad secrets. Just unusual ones...the kind most people can't understand."

Half an hour later, Nagrand met Kendra at the door and invited her inside. She immediately ran to Diana and threw her arms around her. Tears coursed down the cheeks of both women. When Kendra finally loosened her embrace, fearful eyes quickly examined her friend's appearance and noted the bandage still wrapped around Diana's head. "You look awful. What in the world happened?"

"Long version later. Short version is that a gang attacked me on the way to the bus stop. I was blessed to have two heroes come to my rescue because I was slammed to the ground, hit my head, and got knocked out for the count." She then turned and formally introduced Thehrund, Karan, and Nagrand.

"Why didn't anyone call me or the police or an ambulance? Someone found your purse this morning and called both the police and me. I've been worried sick."

"I'm sorry, Kendra. There's no phone here. On the brighter side, Karan is a doctor. Believe me. I've received excellent care."

A short time later, Diana hugged Karan and Nagrand, thanking them profusely for their kindness and promising a visit when she was better.

Turning to Thehrund, she felt a sharp tug at her heart. His eyes once again filled with the sadness she had noted earlier. Stretching her arms up around his neck, she whispered, "I know you're the one who actually made sure I was safe. I will never forget."

On their way to the car, Diana stumbled. By the time she fastened her seatbelt, she felt a fresh onslaught of lightheadedness and worsening pain in her side. Despite a flood of protests, Kendra drove straight to the hospital emergency room instead of going to their apartment.

Fortunately, the emergency room wasn't especially busy that evening. In less than an hour, Diana was being examined by a physician. Once blood had been drawn, the doctor ordered both X-rays and scans. Between rounds of tests and questions, she rested against the raised head of her hospital bed and quietly described details of the ordeal and then awakening inside the home of her rescuers. As she talked, fatigue such as she had never known began to overtake her. She felt so exhausted that she didn't even argue when the ER doctor decided to admit her.

When Thursday arrived, Diana was more than ready to leave the hospital. Resting had been hard enough Tuesday night as nurses and technicians kept waking her either to draw blood or check her temperature and blood pressure. A neurologist had stopped in late Wednesday morning to check her reflexes and responses to visual stimuli. Thankfully, her X-rays were clean, but he had expressed grave concern about her brain scans revealing anomalies he had never seen before. He instructed her to contact his office after leaving the hospital to make a follow-up appointment.

While she answered questions from a police detective on Wednesday afternoon, her personal physician stopped in with another colleague. The detective departed quickly, leaving the medical staff to examine her side where old scars still showed signs of bleeding. The soreness had improved, but there was no explanation for blood seeping from wounds that appeared old and completely healed. Her own doctor also insisted that she come in the next week for a follow-up examination.

Kendra and Diana finally made it through the door of their apartment, carrying a small overnight bag and several floral arrangements sent from Diana's job and people from church. Kendra first ordered Diana to sit down and follow doctor's orders to rest. She then headed to the kitchen to fix a light lunch.

Tired of spending nearly her entire week either lying on a sofa or stuck in a hospital bed, Diana decided to take her overnight bag to her bedroom and unpack. Looking at the clothes she had worn the night of the attack, she wondered if she would ever wear them again. Sighing, she dumped them into the hamper in her room. Maybe she would just wash them and donate them to charity.

The final item she pulled out was a linen shirt that was much too large for her. Thehrund had given it to her so she would have something clean to wear when she left their house. She planned to return the shirt after washing and ironing it.

Pausing to examine the garment more closely, she noted the fine, tight weave of white linen fabric. The styling was quite unusual, more like something a hero from a bygone era might have worn in some romance novel. Curiosity prompted her to look inside. Her eyebrows lifted high with astonishment. The seams had all been sewn by hand. Holding one section of the shirt close to her face to admire tight, even stitches, she drew in a sudden breath. Bringing the shirt closer to her nose, she realized the fabric was permeated with a distinct, subtle scent. She sniffed again. Yes, she thought, she remembered that same fragrance whenever Thehrund came near. Adding the shirt to the pile of laundry, she puzzled over its unique smell. What was that scent, and why did it disturb her so?

By Friday, feeling as if she had lost a week of her life, Diana decided she couldn't tolerate another day of forced inactivity. Once Kendra left for class, Diana drove to the police station to finalize her statement about the attack and sign release papers to get her purse back. She declined to reveal specific details about the men who had saved her. One thing she had definitely noticed was that they lived quietly and kept to themselves.

She had told Kendra she would not repay their kindness by disrupting their solitude. Besides, no one had seen the gang members well enough to identify them. Diana insisted that her rescuers had simply been anonymous good Samaritans.

After returning home, she cast a disgusted look at the hamper nearly full of laundry. She went to the kitchen, where she decided she really wasn't hungry. Looking at the table, she saw that Kendra had left a list of doctors' names and numbers along with a reminder to call for follow-up appointments. Sighing in exasperation, she admitted to herself that the trip to the police station had drained her. A nap was definitely in order.

The privacy fence around the backyard, lined on the inside with tall arborvitae trees, provided perfect space for Thehrund and Nagrand to bring out their swords for practice. They had sparred nearly twice as long as usual. Spring temperatures were comfortably cool, and bright sunshine was welcome after days of rain or constant drizzle. With a sudden lunge, Thehrund caught Nagrand's sword and sent it flying into the air.

"Again!" Thehrund growled.

Shaking his head, Nagrand bent to retrieve his sword. "That's enough for me. I'm too tired for more."

"We need to practice. When we return to Ambracor..."

Karan stepped off the back porch and walked over to the prince. "You both need to stop for a while and rest."

Sweat beads dripped from Thehrund's face. "I need more practice," he said gruffly.

"We both know what you need, and driving yourself and Nagrand into a state of exhaustion will not resolve your problem."

Thehrund glared angrily at Karan. His nerves were nearing a breaking point, but he knew his friend was right. Thrusting the point of his sword into soft, damp earth, he said nothing as he turned and stalked into the house.

The two brothers looked at one another. Nagrand removed a towel dangling from his pocket and wiped his face. "As long as I've known him, I have never seen him as he is now. Not even after Articene."

Karan shared his brother's opinion. "I can almost understand how he must feel. To find Sindara after all this time and for her not to recognize him at all..."

Nagrand approached his brother and placed a hand on his shoulder. "Karan, in my opinion, we must convince Thehrund to remember and believe all that the angel voices said. How many times have they led us safely into and out of the portal? This time, we finally found her. He said the angels told him it would be up to him to regain her love and her trust. We need to remind him of that. There must be no hint of doubt if we're to succeed here."

Karan smiled sheepishly. "Such wisdom should have come from your brother the priest."

Nagrand grinned. "Perhaps the priest has influenced his wayward brother more than anyone realized."

When evening arrived, the still-brooding Thehrund returned to the backyard. Leaning against a tree near the center of the yard, he stared heavenward. Budding tree branches framed random patches of sky. City lights undoubtedly reduced the visibility of the heavens, but those stars that could be seen filled him with a sense of ironic sadness. The brightest star for his soul was as patched and dimmed as the view above his head. While caring for Diana, he had thrilled at momentary glimpses of the woman he loved. In the end, this world's Diana had seemingly eclipsed the existence of his beloved Sindara. Peering between branches at dark skies, he found his thoughts yet again slipping back in time.

Thehrund had arrived a day earlier to deliver documents to Lord Artrian containing approvals for expanding military fortifications near Arvacon's border with Breyal. King Hamund normally would have sent a trusted aide, but he was well aware of his son's profound affection for Artrian's daughter. Dispatching his son achieved two purposes. The first was honing skills that would one day serve Thehrund upon his ascension to the throne. The second was fulfilling a father's hope that his son would be one of the lucky royal heirs who might wed for love as well as political stability. The prince had already received his father's wholehearted blessing to seek Sindara's hand in marriage. He had also spoken with Count Varacor about his intentions to propose marriage.

Dinner that evening with the Varacor family was a lighthearted affair. Lord Artrian and his wife avoided questions concerning political issues in Bracordia. Instead, they discussed cultural topics related to new plays coming to the theater. Over a light and creamy dessert, their conversation also turned to a local composer and a much-anticipated symphony premiere scheduled later that autumn.

Autumn. The night was velvety warm with little hint of winter to come. The few clouds in the sky looked like long, wispy fingers attempting to pluck diamond-bright stars from the heavens. He immensely enjoyed the hours they spent stargazing whenever he visited Arvacon. This night, however, was one of those times he had convinced Sindara to leave behind her telescope and collection of pens, ink, and paper.

He glanced at her profile as they strolled through gardens clinging to the last vestiges of summer flowers. How hard it was to believe the woman at his side was the same aloof and severe person who had admonished him concerning what she perceived as frivolities while those in religious service tended victims of Breyal raiders. The Sindara whose hand now fit so perfectly within his had revealed a zest for life, thirst for knowledge, compassion, and fun-loving nature that had captured both his imagination and his heart.

As they ambled along, both thoroughly enjoyed the cheerful sounds of night birds and insects. Long hair bounced around her shoulders with each step she took. Knowing how deeply he was immersing himself in affairs of state, she questioned him regarding his opinions on critical issues. Listening carefully to his responses, she offered well-considered ideas of her own.

Upon reaching the hillock where they always studied the skies, Thehrund tightened his grasp on her hand and stopped her. Gazing down at her, he couldn't help himself. He leaned forward and lightly kissed her. His reward was one of her expressions that always teased his memory when he was far from Arvacon. Her mouth spread slightly, not quite forming a smile. Instead, her lips conveyed a rare combination of tranquility mixed with invitation. And those eyes...pure gold glistening within light brown irises...how those eyes sparkled with vitality and love.

"For a man who just stole a kiss, Prince Thehrund, you look positively solemn." The slight tease in her voice accentuated the amused rise of delicately arched eyebrows.

Thehrund pulled his face into a mask of disappointment. "My dear Lady Sindara, your words are as a knife into my heart. I had hoped the kiss was freely given by my lovely companion."

Humor added warmth to her light, musical laugh. Then, catching him completely off guard, she threw her arms around his neck and initiated a kiss of her own. Mere seconds passed before Thehrund crushed her body against his, marveling at the power of a kiss that set his heart racing and his nerves ablaze. Every aspect of the kiss was perfect, most especially the sweet taste of her as his tongue slipped past moist lips clinging to his. When they finally parted, he noticed her flushed cheeks as her full breasts rose and fell in rapid rhythm.

Catching her breath, she smiled tremulously. "*That*, Your Highness, was a kiss freely given."

Enclosing both her hands within his, he leaned forward and kissed her fingers. "You must try to be serious for a moment."

She tilted her head slightly to the right and pursed her lips together in amusement. "I'm disappointed. I thought that kiss was quite serious."

He couldn't help himself. He laughed out loud before throwing his arms around her in an enthusiastic, happy embrace. "Indeed it was, My Lady! Indeed it was!" He then pushed her slightly away, enjoying the lighthearted expression on her face. "But...I have another matter we must discuss. A serious one."

Watching him carefully, she wondered at what appeared to be a swift change in his mood. All kinds of ideas raced through her mind. One of those ideas prompted an involuntary note of fear. She had remained faithful to virtues instilled throughout years of studies at school. What if he had grown bored with her? What if he had just toyed with her feelings to see if she would fall victim to his charms as others had? Her breath caught, and she hardly dared to breathe. Swallowing hard, she nodded. "All right. Tell me."

"Sindara," he began, "I want you to know that I've never known anyone quite like you." He stopped, unsure how to continue.

"But?"

Noting the hint of anxiety creeping into her eyes, he took a deep breath and continued in a gentle voice. "There is no but. What you see before you is a man who realizes that the woman in front of him fulfills more than he ever dreamed of finding. Sindara, I love you. With all my heart, I love you. I know that life with me will not be an easy one. The future I face as Father's successor already involves heavy demands and carries responsibilities for the whole of Ambracor. I must be honest. My future holds stresses and sacrifices far different from what most marriages would ever encounter. My most fervent hope is that you can accept the challenges life with me would bring. Sindara, I am asking you to marry me."

"Thehrund," she whispered. She then raised her hand and placed it against his cheek. Her gaze held his. A single tear slipped from the corner of her eye. "Do you have any idea how hard I've tried not to love you?"

A puzzled look crossed his face. "Why would you not want to love me?"

Her gaze dropped, and she stared at the ground. Her lips quivered. Her voice faltered before words rose in a whisper. "So many reasons, most that I'm certain words could never express. Mostly, I think I could not bear the thought that you might someday have a change of mind. To lose your love? That I could not bear."

Reaching out, he tucked long fingers beneath her chin and lifted her face. "My beloved Sindara, that is one thing you need never consider. That I swear. I will love you until the day I die."

"I sometimes fear how much I love you."

"Please don't. All I want is for you to say you love me enough to be my wife."

She swallowed and blinked back tears. "I..." It was her turn to search for words that emerged in yet another whisper. "Are you so sure I can be the wife you really need?"

"Sindara, as I already said, I cannot promise our lives will be easy. With all that is even now expected of me, circumstances will sometimes serve to part us. One thing is sure. I will always carry you in my heart."

Her eyes had captured his in a gaze so intense that tremors ran the length of his spine. How lovely she looked in the moonlight. How much did he love and desire her!

When she finally rediscovered her voice, it came as sweet as any ballad he had ever heard. "When I left the abbey, it was because I felt something was missing from my soul. You, Thehrund, fill that emptiness."

She moved forward into his embrace. With his arms around her and the heat of his body against hers, she knew already how much she loved him and how very much she wanted him. He had inspired her heart and awakened her body to wants and desires she had never imagined. Gently pushing braids and thick locks back from one side of his face, she placed her lips against his ear. "Thehrund, I do love you. I would be honored to marry you."

Muscles in his arms contracted, tightening his embrace. He exhaled a sigh replete with the satisfaction seeping into his soul. Holding her beneath Creator God's starry skies and brilliant moon, he kissed her again, slowly, deeply...wanting to convey how much he truly loved her. Reluctantly, he released her.

Dipping his hand into a pocket of his tunic, he withdrew a velvet pouch closed with a ribbon drawstring. Opening the bag, he removed a ring. The band of gold flared into swirled prongs that held a large, multi-faceted ruby. The swirls at the top and bottom of the stone were studded with glittering diamonds. "This ring has been in my family for generations. I hope you will wear it as a symbol of my love for you and our engagement."

"Thehrund," she gasped softly as she watched him slide the ring into place on her finger. "It's so beautiful!"

Embracing her yet again, he was contented for the moment just holding her. One thing he was learning from her was to appreciate each moment that life brought along. As often as he dreamed of making love to her, he knew that waiting until they wed would only make sweeter the time he could claim her fully as part of his life.

"Thehrund? *Thehrund!*"

The prince blinked several times before Nagrand's insistent voice drew him from his lapse into memories and back to the present.

"It's late. You should sleep."

"Sleep brings dreams too painful to bear."

Nagrand cocked his head to the side. "Yes, and memories torment your waking hours. Memories also create conflict with what you know to be critical duties awaiting us in Ambracor." He paused, noting the faint scowl on Thehrund's face. "You know the portal must reopen soon, and we shall have to return home."

"You need not remind me of what I know only too well."

"There's no need to be angry. You alone hold the key to resolving the problem at hand."

"If I held any such key, do you think for even a moment I would not have used it already?" Thehrund's voice was low and gruff.

Nagrand crouched down and stared at the ground. "So, you fail to realize what we've accomplished this time and the reason behind that progress?"

Thehrund's mood was growing more agitated by the minute. "Am I to suppose you know that reason when I do not?"

Shaking his head in exasperation, Nagrand stood again. "Thehrund, remember what you told us before we entered the portal this time. You cautioned us to allow no hint of doubt into our thoughts. You told us to think not in terms of *if* because we would invite failure. Karan and I are more convinced than ever that the Divine wishes you to learn lessons through this quest that will strengthen you for the sake of all we hold dear at home. We consciously decided to cling to that belief, and we now see the result. You must recover the determination you had when we entered the portal to come here. With all that I am, I believe that is your key to returning home with Sindara by your side."

Thehrund's head fell backward. His eyes clamped tightly closed. "I grow so weary, Nagrand. You know we face war at home. I worry that the strain will claim Father's life far too soon. I fear what anxiety and grief might do to Mother. I dread making decisions I know will cost lives." He faced his longtime friend. "How? How can I do all that is expected of me?"

Hair the same golden color of his brother's swung to and fro. "You start by remembering how often Sindara urged you to have faith and pray. Deliver all your doubts and fears into Creator God's hands that He might guide you. Then, believe with all your might that the power of the love you and she shared will mend the rift that divided you. After that, we return home to defend our people and our country."

Thehrund watched as Nagrand turned and walked back to the house. Doubts had indeed crept into his mind when she had awakened and shown not even the slightest hint of recognition. Perhaps doubt was the wrong term. Fear. That was it. Fear had crept in...fear that the journeys had led to finding her and the ultimate punishment of knowing he had lost her forever. His heart and mind had sunk into the mire of bitter self-deprecation.

As he stood alone in the middle of the night in a dimensional world so strikingly different from his own, chilly breezes stirred. He closed his eyes, feeling cold air sting his cheeks. A gentle voice wafted on soft winds, that voice speaking to him from another time, another place, another world.

"Thehrund, I know it's hard to believe, but Creator God is everywhere...even in places we cannot see. Believe in him. Have faith in him. Pray to him. Always, Thehrund, protect your faith because it is the source of all joy, all love...all miracles."

Falling to his knees, Thehrund obeyed that ethereal voice and prayed as tears coursed down his cheeks.

Chapter Seven

"I'm bored stiff already. How am I ever going to last two more weeks here on my own?"

Kendra chuckled at Diana's impatience. "It's not my fault Mr. Grant won't let you come back to work sooner than the doctor's release. Maybe you can catch up on your reading and practice your meditations. Unless, of course, you want to rewash all the laundry you did yesterday when you were supposed to be resting."

Peeved, Diana stuck her tongue out at Kendra. "Some sympathetic counselor you'll make, Ms. Porter."

"Being sympathetic does not include condoning outright stupidity. You suffered a severe head injury. You need time to heal."

Diana plopped down on the sofa with an unopened chocolate bar in her hand. "Yes, plus time to gain ten pounds eating these."

Kendra laughed out loud. "At the rate you're going, I think I'll put some of my investments in that candy company. I predict a sharp rise in the value of their stocks."

Scowling, Diana tossed the bar onto the coffee table. "Speaking of laundry, I think maybe I'll drive over to return Thehrund's shirt."

"You've got to be kidding! You just got out of the hospital Thursday, went to the police station Friday morning, and washed everything in the apartment after you came home! Today's only Saturday! What is it you don't understand about getting some rest?"

"He might need the shirt. Besides, I'd like to thank them again."

"Diana, the shirt can wait a few days."

"I want to take it to him today. Don't fuss at me, okay?"

Kendra's irritated expression softened. "Diana, what is it you're not telling me?"

"I don't know what you mean," Diana answered truthfully.

Studying her friend's features, Kendra thought sure there was something different, something escaping her own keen intuition. "I know they probably saved your life. That kind of thing creates special emotional bonds, but I keep feeling like there's a missing piece here. Are you absolutely sure they didn't do something to you?"

"They were all as gentle and kind as they could be. I remember waking up in the middle of the night, and they were right there, watching over me."

"This whole thing strikes me as so weird. You've got three men living together in a house. One claims to be a doctor. Who knows about the other two? Their mannerisms are very different, plus I've never heard an accent quite like theirs." She stopped, took a breath, and added, "Their hair is longer than yours."

"Is that all?" Diana asked, her expression comical.

Kendra shook her head. "I don't know. It's like they really don't belong here."

"Hmm, I wonder where I've heard that before."

"That's different," Kendra retorted.

"Is it?" Diana asked thoughtfully. "Is it really? I mean, think about it. You and I have talked for years about how I've never really felt like I fit in, no matter where I go. Oh, and don't forget your Madalyn Amador. Remember what she said about having already discerned that I was in the wrong place? Seriously, what did that mean? And what do you mean by it right now?"

Brown eyes grew distant. Her instincts had definitely started humming upon meeting Diana's rescuers. Something about them perplexed her. She honestly hadn't sensed danger, but she couldn't deny feeling a powerful energy permeating the very air around them.

"Kendra?"

"Sorry. I didn't mean to drift off. There was just something about their energy that caught me unawares. I don't know how to explain it."

"Something bad?"

"No. That I can say for sure."

"I'm glad for that. Look, I have an idea. I need to get out of here for a while. I'm going to return Thehrund's shirt. As a thank you, I'm going to invite them to dinner. That will be a personal way of thanking them, plus we'll have a chance to learn more about them without the stress we had Tuesday."

"Not a bad idea. In fact, I think that's a terrific idea. When do you plan to have this little shindig?"

Diana shrugged. "A nice Sunday dinner sounds good to me."

Kendra frowned. "Next Sunday? Can't. I'll be finishing a major project."

"I was actually thinking about tomorrow." Ignoring Kendra's fresh onslaught of protests, Diana went to her room for the shirt and her purse and was quickly out the door with a cheerful goodbye.

Fifteen minutes later, she parked her car, got out, and looked up at the two-story home that had sheltered her after the gang attack. The large brick house had probably been built in the late forties. A concrete walk led to four steps rising to the wide front porch. The front yard was small, its thick grass still clinging to winter browns. The home appeared entirely ordinary.

With Thehrund's freshly laundered shirt protected by a bag pulled from her own dry cleaning, she walked up to the door and rang the doorbell. While waiting for someone to answer, she looked around. Plain. Everything looked really plain. No hooks for hanging plants. No kind of adornment at all. There was nothing to make the house stand out. Why that bothered her, she really couldn't say. She thought of it as an oddity. Kendra would have called it intuition.

Hearing footsteps from inside, she turned and waited. When Nagrand opened the inside door, his look of surprise quickly transformed into one of the widest smiles she had ever seen.

"Diana! We were just talking about you and wondering how you were. Please! Come in!"

"I hope my timing isn't too inconvenient. I came to return Thehrund's shirt."

"Your timing is perfect. I'll call him."

Within a few short moments, she heard Nagrand's call for Thehrund followed by the sound of boots hitting hardwood steps as he hurried from upstairs. As soon as he entered the living room, she stood and held up his shirt. She smiled comically. "Your shirt! Safely returned. I even washed and ironed it myself."

"Diana! How wonderful to see you again! The shirt worried me not at all, but my concern for you is definitely relieved." Thehrund nodded ever so slightly just before Nagrand took the shirt and excused himself to put it away. His breath caught for a brief moment as he noted the way her lacy white sweater clung to beautiful curves. "Please, sit down and tell me. How are you?"

Dismissing her observation of how Nagrand swiftly disappeared with the shirt for later consideration, Diana sat on the sofa, carefully tucking folds of her long, tiered skirt around her legs. "I'm much better. When we left here, Kendra insisted on taking me to the hospital. They kept me there for a couple of days, more for observation than anything else. My doctors want to see me next week, but I think everything will be fine."

"For that, I am exceedingly glad," Thehrund said with heartfelt relief. "My confidence in Karan's skills as a physician is yet again justified."

"I do appreciate everything you all did for me." She looked down at her hands and noticed she was fidgeting with the ring on her right hand. Looking up, she was surprised to see Thehrund also staring at the ring.

"I'm sorry if I still seem nervous."

"You need not apologize. Your ring...may I see it?"

"Uh, sure." She started to take it off, but he was at her side in an instant and had taken hold of her hand.

"Your ring is beautiful. Rubies are my favorite gemstones."

Her smile hid the question that flashed through her mind. Why did she feel she already knew that? Ignoring the impossible notion, she shrugged and said, "I just bought it recently. I saw it at a show and...I sort of fell in love with it. Kendra thought I was crazy because I never buy expensive jewelry."

Astonished by how much the ring resembled the one he wore beneath his shirt, Thehrund slowly released her hand. "Why we feel compelled to do certain things can be perplexing. When one discovers the reasons, there is often fascinating satisfaction."

Although his comment added to an expanding list of puzzling observations, she decided to ignore it, at least for the moment. "Thehrund, there's another reason I wanted to stop by today."

"Yes?"

His bright blue eyes gleamed with anticipation she couldn't help but notice. "I really want to thank you all for the way you took care of me. If you're not busy tomorrow, I'd like to invite all of you for a home-cooked dinner." Okay, another strange thought. Where had the others gone?

"We have no plans for tomorrow. Your invitation to dinner is very kind, but..."

"I know you don't have a car. I could pick you up tomorrow afternoon and bring you back after dinner. Kendra will be there, and she's looking forward to seeing you all again under more pleasant circumstances."

Stopping at the market on her way home, Diana found it difficult to concentrate on a dinner menu suitable for three men, each with a vigorous, athletic build. Her imagination wandered in all sorts of directions as she considered various details of her earlier visit. As she contemplated preparing a pasta dish or meat for the main course and cake or ice cream for dessert, she finally decided she and Kendra would have a serious talk that evening. Maybe Kendra had been right all along. Diana thought maybe…just maybe…her intuition was as sensitive as her friend had always insisted.

Later, Diana and Kendra ordered in pizza so they could concentrate on a thorough cleaning of their kitchen without having to deal with cooking supper and cleanup afterward. As they meticulously brushed corners, polished cabinets, and wiped counters, Diana finally found the courage to broach the topic of her observations of Karan, Nagrand, and Thehrund. Taking a break after their food arrived, they sat on the floor in the living room to eat.

"One thing I noticed when I picked you up was that Thehrund definitely seems to control everything that goes on there," Kendra said as she took her first bite of pizza.

Diana nodded and swallowed a mouthful. "I agree. Even today, when I was holding Thehrund's shirt, he nodded toward Nagrand…and when I say nodded, I mean it was almost impossible to notice. Without a single word, Nagrand took the shirt and disappeared. I didn't see him or his brother until just before I left. Oh! Speaking of the shirt, I noticed something really odd about it when I got ready to wash it. That shirt was entirely handmade. Every single seam was stitched by hand."

"Handmade?" Kendra's curiosity was quickly rising. "What else did you notice?"

Diana thought back. "As much as I hate to admit it, you were right about something else. They do seem totally out of place. Everything about them…" She paused for a drink of soda. "Karan is supposedly a priest as well as a doctor. I've never seen either a doctor or a priest with hair that long. I have no idea what Nagrand does. For that matter, I don't know what Thehrund does for a living." Grinning mischievously, she added, "One thing's sure. They all are built."

Kendra almost strangled on the cola she was swallowing. "*Built* is one way of putting it. They're definitely extra-fine specimens of the male gender of our species."

Diana giggled. "I noticed that even with my cracked head." Her expression turned serious. "I've tried to place their accents, but I keep coming up with zilch."

"That's interesting, considering your skill with linguistics," Kendra commented. She noticed a sudden change in Diana's expression. "What? Tell me what you're thinking."

Standing up, Diana walked over to the window and stared down at the street below. "Kendra, this probably makes no sense at all, but I feel as if I should know them. Whenever the feeling hits, I get this strange sensation in the pit of my stomach that I can't begin to understand or explain."

"Such as?" Ignoring her food, Kendra leaned forward intently.

"The best way I can put it is that it seems like I anticipate what they're going to do or say, especially with Thehrund."

"Ah, yes, the blue-eyed hunk with the waves and braids," Kendra teased, feeling Diana was starting to show signs of emotional distress. When Diana glanced around, the look in her eyes was more than enough to confirm Kendra's perception. "Can you give me an example?"

Diana's gaze dropped to the ring on her finger. The weird feeling she'd had earlier returned with a jolt. "This afternoon, I felt a little nervous and started twisting the ring on my finger. Thehrund took my hand to look at it. The strangest look crossed his face. I swear, Kendra, when he said his favorite stone was a ruby, I felt like I already knew that. No, that's not right. I *did* already know it."

Diana finally turned away from the window and came back to sit down. "Something else. The scars. They stopped bleeding for almost a month. By the time I saw my doctor at the hospital, they had started again. It makes no sense at all, but I keep feeling it has something to do with them."

Kendra scooted over and put an arm around Diana. "Maybe you strained something during the fight. You haven't had any of the dreams for a while, have you?"

Diana shook her head. "I have to pull myself together. I sure wish Mom or Dad would call."

"They will as soon as they get back to civilization. In the meantime, I'll take care of you the best I can."

Diana smiled. "I appreciate that. On the other hand, I feel like I can take care of myself. I just need answers to all these questions colliding inside my mind."

❈ ❈ ❈

"Artrian, whatever is the matter?" Liana gently grasped her husband's arm and gazed up at him.

"Trouble," he replied with a curt shake of his head. "Hamund sent word that he wants Thehrund to return to Bracordia immediately. He apparently has new information regarding Breyal tribes gathering near the border of Bramond Province. He plans to discuss possible strategies to defend against invasion."

"I was afraid of this when I saw the courier arrive. What will you do?"

"That, my dear, is a troubling question. I will not lie to him. When I told him we needed time to further assess current defenses and plan for augmenting our fortifications, it was no lie. When I agreed that Thehrund would also study and compare our present situation to prior history, my only deception was in omitting the fact that Thehrund would make his assessments away from Ambracor."

"Hamund will be furious when he finds out."

Artrian glanced down at the letter in his hand. "He will have every right to be furious. Liana, leave me for a while. I must consider carefully how to handle this."

"All right. If you need me, I'll be at the chapel."

Just as she opened the door of her husband's office, Artrian's voice stopped her. "Pray hard, Liana, but before you go, have someone start packing. I must leave immediately for Bracordia."

Liana smiled. "*We* must leave..." She then closed the door quietly behind her.

The next morning, Artrian dispatched the king's courier back to the capital. After sealing the brief document, he prayed it would suffice to buy an extra day or two in hope that Thehrund would return soon. His letter informed King Hamund that word was being sent via Cahmdurn for a party to depart Articene as soon as possible. Again, deception by omission. Articene lay almost three days from the Varacor country estate.

Once the messenger departed, Artrian joined his wife for prayers at the small chapel near their manor house. He prayed for forgiveness for his role in deceiving his king and, more importantly, his friend. He also prayed for Thehrund's quick and safe return. For the first time since his daughter's death, he allowed himself what he considered the greatest indulgence of all. He prayed that Thehrund's voices had been truly divine and that the prince would return with Sindara safe at his side.

Late that night, he lay awake, unable to sleep. How many times since Sindara's death had he spent hours trying to fall asleep? He most certainly had not bothered to keep count. Tonight...tired, worried, and riddled with guilt...he decided that perhaps Liana's approach was best. It was hard for him to accept that parts of his life were always just beyond his control. His daughter had often told him that the most difficult part of life was trusting Creator God enough to allow him to assume full control. When one learned to do that, one could rely on resolution of life's worst trouble or, at the very least, strength to find peace amid the turmoil.

Long after midnight, slumber finally overcame him. Within the invasion of dreams, he saw himself as a young man, delighted with his vibrant, beautiful wife and their small children. He had been conscientious about the example he showed his sons. He had wanted them to enjoy their childhood while still learning the responsibilities they would shoulder upon reaching manhood.

His daughter had been a puzzle. She could go from her usual sunny disposition to stormy aggravation in a flash, especially if she thought someone close to her was being mistreated. She was fiercely protective of people she loved. Her mind was intelligent, her curiosity always a burning fire. His own father had been the one person upon whom they could rely to stimulate her interests and keep her entertained, especially when he took her out for stargazing.

"Sindara," Artrian whispered, turning in his sleep. As was expected of all women of noble birth, she had undergone extensive training in basic combat skills and the use of weapons. Her distaste for violence had been the one point over which they had argued most. Liana had finally convinced her husband that their daughter was more suited to an extended religious education that would also provide her training in caring for the sick and injured. While most young noblewomen studied at schools until they were sixteen, Sindara had elected to continue her religious schooling until her twenty-second birthday.

How he had looked forward to the completion of her studies and her return home. From regular correspondence, he had fully expected her to commit to life in religious service. What he had not foreseen was her surprise arrival home that had coincided with Prince Thehrund's initial visit to the Varacor country manor.

Artrian and Liana had watched with serious trepidation those first encounters with the prince. Religiously educated as she had been, Sindara could also be stubborn and opinionated. Prince or no prince, she had no qualms whatsoever about expressing her viewpoint on any subject that arose. What had shocked everyone was that, despite initial verbal sparring, there seemed to be an immediate, undeniable connection between Sindara and Prince Thehrund.

Dreams unfolded memory after memory. The odd expressions when she had tried so hard to avoid Thehrund's gaze. Her uncommon nervousness during the prince's first two visits. Her surprising decline of Master Zoman's offer to join the religious community in Bramond. The joy of watching his daughter fall in love with a man who appeared completely enchanted by her.

Artrian's dreams shifted. He had been in Cahmdurn when Breyal raiders had attacked the king's escort near Articene. A local deputy had burst into his office to alert the count that the king and a band of soldiers had just passed the outskirts of the city. Hearing there had apparently been a skirmish, Artrian immediately instructed his aide to prepare for the arrival of the king's party. Waiting outside, he could still remember the shaft of fear upon seeing bloody bandages around Erator's arm. King Hamund appeared shaken but otherwise unharmed. The despair on Prince Thehrund's face was beyond description.

Lord Artrian had rushed to his son's side and helped him dismount. His son dismissed the wound on his arm as superficial. His presence exuded a combination of dread, anger, and sorrow. The muscles in Erator's face twitched with stress. "Father, some of the others have injuries that need treatment. First, there's something I must tell you. Sindara..." He choked, unable to continue.

King Hamund limped toward his old friend, firmly grasped Artrian's arm, and led him inside. "I was escorting your daughter home when we happened upon a band of Breyal warriors. A stray arrow grazed my horse's flank. He reared and threw me. Sindara was by my side within the span of a heartbeat. She...she gave her life defending mine."

Artrian would never forget the horrid, nauseating pitch in his stomach upon hearing those words. Sindara...his beautiful, golden-eyed daughter... gone. His chest ached as he struggled for breath. Barely audible words emerged from a throat choked with anguish. "Why? Why were you bringing her home when the wedding in Bracordia is only weeks away? How could this have happened?"

Thehrund, his expression beyond bleak, stepped forward. "Erator's injury needs attention. I will explain everything later. We must first go with your sheriff and deputies to arrange treatment for others who need it and accommodations for everyone else."

After the Breyal raiders had been defeated, troops from Fort Articene had gathered injured comrades, secured Breyal prisoners, and returned to their post. Although wounded, Erator stayed with Thehrund to gather together bodies of Ambracor dead until fresh troops arrived to dispose of Breyal corpses and transport their own dead home for burial.

Erator had witnessed his sister's courageous actions that undoubtedly saved the king's life. He had spared a swift look upward when Thehrund's resounding voice had desperately shouted Sindara's name in warning. That glance had filled his vision with horror as a Breyal warrior pierced his sister's side with a spear. Thehrund had started toward his father but stopped abruptly. For a moment, it seemed all had frozen in time. The next thing to pierce Erator's awareness was Thehrund veering sharply toward him just as another Breyal warrior lunged in renewed attack. The prince's quick action had deflected the attacker's weapon so that it hit Erator in the arm instead of the back.

Lord Artrian listened to every detail. He would forever recall the anguish he saw on Thehrund's face and heard in the young man's voice. The prince was inconsolable as he readily assumed all blame for Sindara's fate. He alone accepted without question that her body had disappeared with no trace whatsoever. When he finally shared his account of voices that had spoken to him on the battlefield, there had been no sign of mental instability, only determination such as Artrian had never seen before or since.

"Artrian?" Liana asked, abruptly roused from sleep when her husband had bolted upright and called out his daughter's name. "Artrian! Are you all right?"

Sitting up in bed, Artrian breathed heavily. His heart pounded. Sweat beaded on his forehead. "Sindara... Liana, I feel her. I'm sure of it."

"Lie down, dear. You must have been dreaming."

He let his wife pull him backward onto the bed. He breathed raggedly. "We leave tomorrow for Bracordia. I must face Hamund."

A silent maid carefully folded delicate petticoats, lace-trimmed corsets, and fine gowns of silk and satin. After placing the garments in a large travel trunk, she was glad for Breeneth's curt dismissal. She never felt comfortable in Breeneth's presence and hurriedly left for Brenna's rooms to finish packing for the upcoming trip to Bracordia.

Alone in her chambers, Breeneth sat on the velvet-upholstered bench in front of her vanity. Ebony eyes gleamed with dark thoughts. Beginning with the ambush at Articene that resulted in Sindara Varacor's death, Master's plan to use Breyals to escalate tensions was successfully pushing Ambracor toward unavoidable war. The subsequent death and destruction would empower her master sufficiently to enable his escape from the bowels of their world.

She smiled at her image in the mirror. The timing of this trip to Ambracor's capital was perfect. It was common knowledge that Hamund was insisting that Thehrund marry. She had already manipulated her father into departing early for Bracordia. With her continued influence over him and his access to the king, her long-awaited success was imminent.

"Queen Breeneth Cobrandya," she murmured in a light, satisfied voice. Proudly admiring her own lovely reflection, she happily anticipated being wedded to Thehrund and receiving Master's lavish rewards.

Chapter Eight

Soft, classic melodies provided a relaxing background. Clusters of candles on living room tables created a tranquil, appealing ambience. Carefully suppressing his innermost thoughts and feelings, Thehrund remained quietly observant as Nagrand jovially entertained their hostesses with animated tales of riding mishaps after learning of Diana's interest in horses.

When the oven timer chimed and Diana excused herself, Thehrund rose from the sofa and followed her into the kitchen. "Can I assist in any way?" he asked.

"You can, thank you." She handed him a pair of insulated oven mitts. "Bending over still makes me lightheaded. If you wouldn't mind, you could lift the pan from the oven and put it here on the counter."

Savoring precious moments alone with her, he gladly moved the heavy roasting pan to the insulated mat she had indicated. "That was simple enough. May I help with anything else?"

Diana's eyebrows lifted. His eagerness to help somehow seemed so out of place in the kitchen. Glancing around, she pointed to a small serving cart holding several bottles of red wine and a corkscrew. "While I get everything ready to serve, perhaps you could open a bottle of wine and fill the glasses on the table.

Following her instructions to open and pour wine, Thehrund constantly shifted his glance to watch as she deftly filled serving dishes and expertly cut juicy slices from an aromatic, perfectly prepared roast. Memory teased him with visions of her quiet efficiency with her telescope. She worked as competently here as she had in Ambracor.

Gathered around a somewhat crowded table, Kendra prayed brief, heartfelt grace, including thanks for both Diana's recovery and her brave rescuers. After serving dishes were passed and then set aside on the serving cart, she said little. Occasionally adding a remark or replying to a question, she preferred watching and listening to exchanges over a delicious dinner.

By the time Diana served cherry-topped dessert and coffee, Kendra felt perplexed. Their guests displayed excellent manners. They also maintained captivating conversation that revealed surprisingly little about their private lives. Their more formal speech fascinated her as she tried to pinpoint their exotic accents. Thehrund's covert attentiveness to Diana was almost as puzzling as Diana's discussions with their three handsome guests. She sensed some missing link but had no clue what it might be.

❋ ❋ ❋

"Delivered them all home safe and sound?" Kendra greeted her roommate's return Sunday evening.

"Safe and sound. If ever I've had an interesting evening, this was it."

"No kidding. By the way, congratulations on supper. That prime rib must have been a major splurge, but it was melt-in-your-mouth tender and absolutely delicious. The mashed potatoes were perfect and the veggies... okay, we both know I really don't like veggies, but that cheesecake was supreme."

"I'm glad dinner earned your approval," Diana said with a laugh.

"Those guys must not have had a decent meal in ages. Did you see how much they ate?"

"I do think they enjoyed the meal," Diana agreed with a grin. "Anything left to clean up in the kitchen?"

Kendra shook her head. "All bright and shiny again."

"Great. Thanks."

"The least I could do." Kendra saw the subdued expression that suddenly draped over Diana's face. "Ready to talk?"

Diana went to the sofa, slipped off her shoes, and sat with her feet tucked under her. "Part of me is."

"And the other part?" Kendra asked as she sat at the opposite end of the sofa and turned to watch Diana's changing expressions.

"The other part of me feels more confused than ever."

Kendra's smile was reassuring. "We've muddled through worse."

"Maybe, but never have I personally encountered anything so perplexing in my whole life." She looked down and plucked nervously at the edge of the cushion she had pulled onto her lap. "Kendra, you have to admit they were completely charming and had excellent manners. Nagrand was as entertaining a guest as we've ever had."

"Okay, so far."

When Diana remained quiet, Kendra picked up the conversation. "I watched them all evening without being too obvious. I stick by my original conclusion that they're out of place here. I do need to include an addendum that I thought about the whole time you were gone."

"What's that?" Diana asked without looking up.

"I saw...no, I *heard* something that brought me face to face with what you've always said about your own feeling of not belonging." Diana glanced upward with a puzzled expression as Kendra continued, "I know this is going to sound strange, but the longer conversation continued, the more I noticed you picking up the cadence...the rhythm...of their speech. It was downright weird."

Diana shrugged. "I still get the strangest feeling whenever I'm around them. Especially Thehrund."

"Thehrund is a case all unto himself. It's more than an observation about him being in charge. The others defer to him automatically. They totally respect him, and he totally calls the shots."

"So I told you already," Diana reminded her.

"You did, but another thing I noticed is that there's a closeness, some special bond they share. I only wish they weren't so secretive about their background. Maybe if we understood more about their culture, we'd feel more comfortable around them."

"I have to confess. I almost dread looking directly at Thehrund." Diana's admission came with an unexpectedly powerful emotional toll. "I can't recall ever seeing anyone with eyes so expressive or so sorrowful."

Kendra's voice dropped, the rich notes softening as she studied Diana's faraway look. "I agree. I also noticed how closely he watched you...as if he was waiting for something. Are you sure you've never met before?"

Diana shook her head. "Thehrund is one man I would surely remember meeting."

Kendra nodded. "He would be hard to forget." Diana's apparent fatigue concerned her. "Look, you're tired after cooking dinner and then entertaining. Why don't you turn in and get some sleep? We can let all this settle and discuss it again tomorrow when I get home from class."

Diana gratefully accepted the suggestion. Inside her bedroom, she realized how close she had come to tears while talking with Kendra. In fact, she had felt herself on the verge of tears for days. Why? It made no sense at all. Maybe she had tried to do too much after the head injury. Maybe she was starting to worry because her parents hadn't called yet. Climbing into bed and beneath the covers, she fell into a fitful sleep.

The following morning, she woke up without knowing why. Peeking at her alarm clock with one eye, she stifled a groan. Not even five in the morning. Knowing that going back asleep would be impossible, she reluctantly got up and dressed. Not even bothering with her usual morning cup of coffee, she drove to a nearby park for a long walk.

Leaving her car in the park's main lot, she decided the morning's crisp, fresh air certainly helped clear her mind. The earliest signs of sunrise were just becoming visible. Tree limbs were full of buds promising an explosion of green within the next few days. Birds soared across the sky or perched on branches. Tweets and chirps created a cheerful morning symphony.

She wandered aimlessly for nearly half an hour before coming to an abrupt halt. So absorbed in thoughts flitting in and out of her mind, she had no idea why she had stopped so quickly. Suddenly fearful someone might be following her, she glanced around. The path was empty.

Water gurgling in the nearby fountain caught her attention. Perhaps the rippling waters had drawn her away from purposeless meandering. Turning toward a circle of benches surrounding the fountain, she took several steps before stopping again. She spotted a tall man leaning against a tree, his back turned toward her.

Approaching slowly, she finally found the nerve to speak. "Thehrund?" She saw his head tilt slightly...as if he only thought he'd heard something. "Thehrund, is that you?"

When he turned, his features reflected surprise. "Diana, good morning. I never expected to see you here, especially so early."

What was it in his manner that stirred anew the questions filling her mind? "I couldn't sleep. I thought maybe a walk in the park would help calm me."

His forehead creased in question. "Is something wrong?"

She started to lie and say no. "To be honest, I'm not sure. The past few months have been really unsettled. After the attack last week, I..."

He rescued her from sudden muteness. "Would you like to sit a while? We can watch the sunrise from this side of the fountain."

"That would be nice. I've been walking for some time now."

After several silent minutes sitting together on a wooden bench, he cast a sideways glance at her. His heart skipped a beat as he recognized a pensive mood typical of Sindara. How much he wanted to say something. Warnings from angel voices remained clear in his mind. No matter how strong the temptation, he dared not reveal details of their shared past beyond answering any direct questions she might ask. He clasped his hands together to keep from balling them into tight fists.

Diana's was the first voice to break the silence. "I must say how surprised I was to see you. It's very early, and this park is miles from your house."

"I'm quite accustomed to walking and hiking. Since I woke early and couldn't go back to sleep, it seemed a good idea to start the morning surrounded by nature." Wondering if it might be a mistake, he continued, "You mentioned that you've felt unsettled. Do you know why?"

She sighed. "I suppose that's the biggest problem. I can't find a reason to explain it. I've had all kinds of dreams that make no sense. Faces I think I should know. Familiar voices. And pain."

"Pain? What kind of pain?" His alarm was immediate and obvious.

"You wouldn't believe me if I told you. I don't even believe it. For that matter, neither does my doctor."

"You've actually consulted a physician about the pain?" Blue eyes suddenly reflected worry. "Perhaps you could speak with Karan."

"I wouldn't want to trouble him. Besides, it's pointless." Her shoulders lifted with the deep breath she took. "I'm sure I'll work through it sooner or later. What about you? What kept you awake? My cooking perhaps?"

Needing to suppress rising nervousness, he stood and walked over to the fountain's edge. "Dinner last night was exceptional. Quite honestly, I cannot remember the last time I enjoyed a meal so much."

She stood and walked over to him. She couldn't resist a grin. "I'm glad for that. It would be awful to think my cooking had made you ill."

A glint of light reflected off one of the gold bands that bound the ends of his braids. "Your hair... You're wearing it loose this morning."

The sudden change of topic startled him. "I often pull it back to avoid too many strange looks."

"I see," she murmured. Without conscious realization, she lifted her hand and caught the end of one braid between her fingertips. "I think I like it better this way. It suits you."

Thehrund wondered if he might strangle on the sudden knot in his throat. Her gesture was exactly the same as one of Sindara's that he always cherished.

Diana felt her gaze drawn upward. His blue eyes held such mystery... such profound emotion. The briefest of thoughts rushed through her mind. Before she could begin to define the thought, she felt her head tilting backward and her lips trembling as his mouth lightly touched hers.

She backed away slowly before responding to some mystifying inner force that swept away every shred of sanity. It didn't matter who had kissed whom. All that mattered was the kiss itself, a thrilling invasion of elation and sorrow, fear and excitement. As his mouth covered hers, she responded with a vibrancy that sent curling tendrils of fire coursing through her veins. The tip of his tongue touched her lips before gently probing more deeply, allowing her to share more fully the feel and taste of the bond they had formed. Their tongues met, spawning torrents of tantalizing sensations.

When the kiss ended, her head rested against his shoulder. She could hardly breathe. Tears stung her eyelids. She desperately wanted to resist when strong hands grasped her arms and held her away. A shimmer of tears also shone in his eyes. What had just happened? Her mind suddenly reeled, and she stepped backward.

"I...I..." For the life of her, she had no idea what she wanted to say. Inhaling sharply as tears finally began to fall, she shook her head. "I'm sorry. I have to go now."

Stunned and speechless, Thehrund watched as she turned and ran away.

❈ ❈ ❈

Relief flooded Diana when she arrived home to find Kendra already gone. Inside the bathroom, she stared into the mirror at her ghostly pale reflection. Slight redness colored sensitive skin likely affected by the texture of Thehrund's beard. Her lips quivered. Wisps of hair feathered around her face. Long, silken tresses were tousled. Yes, she remembered the feel of his hand in her hair. That's why it was such a mess.

What had happened at the park? How was it possible they had each admitted an inability to sleep and had both gone to the same park at the same strange hour? There was no way he could have known she would be there. In fact, she was the one who had spotted him leaning against that tree. How forlorn and alone he had looked just before she called his name. What she could only describe as a moment of quiet harmony had existed between them until...

Her eyelids fluttered as she touched two fingertips to lips still sensitized by the intensity of the kiss they had shared beneath the newly risen sun. She felt a sudden, hollow shudder inside. Thoughts stalled yet again. Her entire soul filled with the lingering power of their unexpected kiss.

"Why has he not come in?" Karan asked.

Nagrand huffed in exasperation. "I have no answer. After dinner last night with Sindara and Kendra, I was so heartened by the return of his optimism. For now, I prefer to stay out of the way of a foul mood such as I have not seen in many months."

Karan handed his brother a cup of steaming tea. "I believe we both would gladly trade this for a barrel of ale, but tea will have to do for now."

More than an hour later, Thehrund finally left the backyard and entered the kitchen. Tired and drenched with sweat after a prolonged solo workout, he filled a glass with water and drank it straight down. Without uttering a word as he passed through the living room, he disappeared upstairs. Stripping and climbing into the shower, he stood as warm water mingled with tears running down his cheeks.

Fear had tensed his muscles to the breaking point once he finally regained his senses in the park. He had never intended to kiss her, but when she had looked up at him, his soul had reacted to the essence of Sindara that he felt each time he found himself in Diana's presence. Pure emotion had conquered deliberate thought processes. Her response to that kiss had been identical to Sindara's. Driven by the image of her running away, he had also broken into a run, not stopping until he returned to the house.

He didn't bother going downstairs after he dried off. For that matter, he didn't bother getting dressed. Naked, he went to his bedroom and collapsed on the bed. Adjusting the chain he almost always wore around his neck, he slid her engagement ring around until he could hold it up and gaze at the stone. Why? Would there ever be an answer to why?

When Kendra arrived home, she was surprised to find the only light in the apartment coming from above the kitchen sink. She knew Diana was home; her car was in the lot outside. Flipping the switch for the living room lights, she dropped her purse and computer case on a chair and shrugged out of her coat, dumping it on top of her other things instead of hanging it up. Heading into the kitchen, she saw that everything was neat and tidy. The kitchen whiteboard had a note written in bright red marker. A plate of leftovers from Sunday dinner was in the fridge and just needed to be heated in the microwave.

Kendra had begun the day with concern when she got up and found Diana gone already. Now worry was starting to mushroom. Going to Diana's bedroom door, she tapped lightly before slowly pushing the door open. "Diana?" she said in a hushed voice.

"Hmm?"

"What's wrong?" Kendra hurried to the side of the bed where Diana lay with her arm across her forehead.

"Just a bad headache. I took the pain medicine the hospital prescribed. The pain is almost gone, but I feel groggy."

"Must be a bad headache if you actually took medicine. Can I get you something?"

"No, thanks. I'm afraid I won't be much company this evening."

"Just feel better. I'll check in on you before I go to bed."

"Thanks. You're the best." She paused. "Kendra?"

"Yes?"

For just a moment, she had intended to ask Kendra to stay. A sudden, inexplicably cold emptiness filled her. "Nothing. Well, something. Would you mind getting me an extra blanket?"

Just before dawn, the extra blanket flew off the bed along with her other bedclothes. Diana's nightgown was soaked with perspiration. Hair clung to her cheeks in sodden streaks. She rolled from one side of the bed to the other and back again. She felt the bounce of her body on the hard leather of a saddle. Her breathing was labored. Her nostrils filled with flying dirt and the mingled scents of animals, sweat, and blood. Her ears rang with the clash and clang of steel, shrieking horses, groans of injured men, and moans from the dying. Suddenly, she leapt from bed with a loud thud when her feet hit the floor.

"Your Majesty!" she screamed in fearful warning. She twisted and fought against arms trying to pin her down. Struggling to free herself, she turned and again saw the face that had haunted years of dreams. Once more, she heard panic and fear as he desperately shouted out her name. Again, she felt the searing thrust of the lance piercing her side just before she collapsed to the floor.

The typically jovial innkeeper respected the solemn mood of the guests who regularly lodged at his establishment. Count Varacor, his wife, and their staff were among the kindest and most generous of any of the visitors who frequented his inn on the well-traveled road to and from Bracordia. The innkeeper poured a round of after-dinner liqueur and inquired if they needed anything else. He then left when they thanked him for his attentions and wished him goodnight.

Liana held a crystal cordial glass in her hand. "Have you thought further about what you will tell him?"

Her husband shook his head and tipped his glass, draining it in a single gulp. "I can only think that three days of tiresome travel stand between me and the very real possibility of losing my best friend."

"So you will tell him the truth?"

"To do otherwise would be dishonorable as well as disrespectful, especially now that the situation is further complicated by Hamund's order to advance the next round of meetings. I wish I had your brother's great gift for words. I could likely tell the truth in such a way that would leave our king confounded long enough for Thehrund to return."

"Why not spend our first day in the capital with Cleotis? He would gladly help you craft suitable wording for your conversation with Hamund. After all, with only one or two exceptions, we've only concealed knowledge of Thehrund's trips."

Artrian stared at the tiny drop of liqueur remaining in the bottom of his glass. "I find it difficult to decide which I dread most, waiting to inform the king or actually divulging circumstances sure to fuel displeasure with Thehrund."

"And, of course, bearing that displeasure yourself for supporting Thehrund."

Artrian blew out a sigh heavy with resignation. "Truthfully, Liana, do you not think we look foolish for going along with this crazy notion of Thehrund's?"

"Did I even hint that I thought you were foolish a few nights ago when you awoke at midnight saying you were sure you felt Sindara?"

"That's not quite the same. The Ambracada explicitly speaks about the eternal nature of the spirits of Creator God's people. It is one of the greatest of his divine gifts."

"Yes, but the Ambracada says very little of how Creator God might choose to use those spirits. How many times have we discussed this? Thehrund is the last person I would expect to hear spirit voices. He loves and respects his father, but even if Hamund were to issue a royal mandate that Thehrund marry, I have no doubt whatsoever that our prince would refuse to obey."

"That thought has crossed my mind more than once. It is one I find difficult even to consider."

Liana reached across the table and took her husband's hand. "Artrian, you must stop tormenting yourself over our support for Thehrund. Easy it has not been. Place your full faith in Creator God. Then, trust Thehrund. He has flaws just as everyone does, but at the core, he is a very fine man. Sindara would not have loved him otherwise."

Artrian's eyes closed for a moment as he swallowed hard. "Had it not been for his flaws and the love she bore him, we would have no need for this conversation."

"Bitterness accomplishes nothing. I admit I had to work on that concept. I still falter because I miss her so much that it often hurts. I also know there's something not right about that whole set of circumstances."

"What about his ready admission of guilt?"

"He never once denied the content of that letter Sindara received...that is, as far as waking in bed with Breeneth. He was also very clear that he couldn't remember how he got there. Does that sound like the Thehrund we both know?"

Artrian shook his head. "We will likely never know the full truth. For now, I'm tired. We have much travel still ahead. I think we should go up and get some sleep."

Hours later, Liana awoke. High winds whistled and howled in the night. Brilliant flashes of lightning burst into the room's inky darkness. Booming roars rattled walls and panes of glass in the windows. A mighty thunderstorm had rolled in with rain that pelted the outside of the inn. Glancing at her husband, she wondered how he could possibly sleep through such a storm.

Crossing the room in bare feet, she pushed aside curtains and stared at skies seemingly consumed by the storm's fury. In some ways, her very soul felt in complete harmony with the wild tempest raging in the night. A sudden thought penetrated her sleepy mind. This storm would last for hours, and the torrential downpour would leave many roads muddy and impassable for days. She smiled and said a prayer of gratitude. Her heart told her that any extra time Thehrund might need was coming as a gift directly from Heaven.

❈ ❈ ❈

"She's in here," Kendra said as she guided paramedics through the apartment and into Diana's room. "I covered her up, but I didn't move her."

One paramedic knelt down on the floor and spoke to Diana in a soothing voice while the other started checking her vital signs. "We hear you're not feeling so well."

Diana resisted rolling her eyes. "My friend worries far too much. I had only a terrible nightmare. Nothing more."

The paramedic examined Diana before addressing his partner. "Her blood pressure is elevated, and her pulse is rapid." He then followed with a stream of numbers and observations, none of which sounded especially good to Kendra.

The senior paramedic glanced at Kendra. "Has she been sick recently?" Learning of her stay in the hospital following a severe head injury, both medics showed greater concern. "Miss, did the doctors give you any medicine that you took?"

She nodded. "Pain medicine. The bottle is on the nightstand. I took one capsule early this afternoon and another just before bedtime."

Taking the bottle she pointed out, he read the label and then opened it to count the pills inside. "Only three missing. The script was filled last Thursday. I think we can safely rule out an overdose here," he said.

His partner picked up the questions. "Do you remember if you fell out of bed?"

"I was dreaming. I leapt from bed. The simple conclusion is that I tripped over the blankets and fell."

"Your roommate says she heard you scream and that you fought with her when she came to check on you. Do you think you hit your head when you fell?"

"My head is fine, thank you. For now, I wish only to return to bed so I might go back to sleep."

Kendra frowned and touched the elder paramedic's arm. As one medic continued talking with Diana, the other took Kendra aside. "What do you think?"

"Although it was several months ago, she had a series of nightmares. None quite as serious as this, but..."

"She's not in top-notch condition now, but she isn't in crisis. What's bothering you?"

Kendra inhaled slowly. "The way she's talking. I mean, it is Diana's voice for sure, but the way she's putting her sentences together... Something doesn't sound right."

The medic returned to his patient. "Miss, I'm going to ask you a few questions, just to make sure everything's all right here. Can you tell me your name?"

"My name is Sin..." Stopping abruptly, she shook her head and took a deep breath. "My name is...Diana Lorenz. My roommate here is Kendra Porter. Also, if it isn't especially inconvenient, I must use the bathroom. Now. Please."

"Ms. Lorenz, you shouldn't get up yet."

"I am quite sure I cannot wait." Pushing them away, she twisted and, grabbing on to the mattress, hoisted herself up. "Gentlemen, I shall return in just a moment so you might finish your questions."

The younger medic insisted on escorting her to the bathroom. The other turned a puzzled gaze toward Kendra. "Is she always like that?"

Kendra closed her mouth and shook her head hard. "I've known her since ninth grade. I've never seen her like this."

"And?"

"Nothing," Kendra answered, suddenly recalling another night when Diana's speech pattern and cadence had matched those of her rescuers.

Within minutes, Diana returned with the insistent aid of the paramedic. Looking over at his partner, he said, "There's blood on her gown, but she says she's not having her period."

Kendra spoke up. "She has a scar on her left side. Actually, two scars... one on the front and one on the back. They started bleeding several months ago. She went to her doctor for an exam, and they checked her at the hospital. There's nothing wrong with the scars to explain the blood."

Half an hour later, the paramedics decided there was no critical need to transport Diana to the hospital. They recommended that she keep follow-up appointments with her doctors and stay in bed to rest as much as possible. Once the medics left, Kendra went to Diana's room to help her change into clean nightclothes. While Diana made a second trip to the bathroom, Kendra straightened sheets and blankets.

"I sincerely apologize for all the aggravation."

Kendra's face still showed clear signs of worry. "You're not mad?"

Amber eyes held nothing but affection as Diana reached out to caress her friend's cheek. "You are more than a blessing, especially now. How could I possibly be angry when you look out only for my well-being?"

The next morning, Diana lay in bed listening to a string of stern instructions from Kendra. Meekly, she nodded. "Yes, I understand. You see I am still in bed. Yes, I shall most certainly call you if anything feels wrong."

Half an hour after Kendra left for class, Diana got out of bed, showered, dried, and dressed. Staring into the mirror as she brushed her hair, she knew she dared wait no longer. She had to know, and there was only one way to find out. Consumed by questions riddled with anxiety, she quickly donned a three-quarter-length jacket over a wine-red sweater and matching pleated skirt. Grabbing her purse, she hurriedly left her apartment and went to her car.

Sitting inside the vehicle, she felt sheer energy rush at her from all directions. More by habit than conscious thought, she fastened her seatbelt. Pushing the ignition button and starting the engine, she drew in several deep breaths. Carefully, she told herself. Very carefully. She then backed her car from her assigned spot and pulled out into traffic.

By the time she stopped and parked the car, she felt exhausted. Still, she pushed herself without mercy. She had to ask. She simply had to know. Exiting the car after checking for traffic, she straightened her back, walked up to the house, rang the doorbell. It was barely past nine in the morning. Someone should be up.

She heard the sound of the door unlocking inside. She watched as the brass doorknob turned. When the door opened, a surprisingly familiar face greeted her.

"Nagrand, good morning," she greeted, her voice subdued. "Thehrund. Is he here? I need to speak with him."

Sensing urgency in her manner, Nagrand opened the door all the way and allowed her to enter. "Are you all right?"

Before she could respond, Thehrund appeared in the living room. Stunned by her unexpected arrival, he had no time to greet her before she crossed the room to stand directly in front of him. The moment her eyes met his, he watched as tears welled up and spilled down her face.

"Thehrund! The truth! You must tell me the truth! Your father. Erator. Did they survive the attack? I must know! Tell me!"

Shock prevented him from answering her immediately.

"Thehrund! Answer me! Did they survive?"

Tears suddenly glistened in sapphire eyes. "Sindara..." He gulped in a deep breath. "Erator suffered a minor injury to his arm. Thanks to you, Father still sits upon the throne of Ambracor."

An involuntary sob escaped her. "All thanks be to Creator God!"

Regaining his senses, Thehrund gently reached out to her. "Sindara, come. Sit."

"I can't...I..." she stammered, backing away to escape his touch.

"Please. Sindara, we must talk. I beg you. Please."

Her chin quivered as she used the sleeve of her coat to wipe tears from her face. "I feel so confused! Nothing makes sense right now! Nothing!"

"Sindara..."

"You're certain my brother and your father are all right? What about my parents?"

"Sindara, I cannot begin to imagine how you must feel. Karan just made fresh tea. Let's have a cup while you calm yourself. We can talk then."

"I don't want to talk! Just tell me about my family!"

"Your family was fine when last I saw them. That was only a few weeks ago. You must let me explain..."

"Nothing makes any sense! I...I can't do this, Thehrund! I just can't!" Emotionally overwhelmed, she spun around and nearly knocked Nagrand over as she raced out the door to her car.

"Sindara! Sindara!" Following her, Thehrund called out, his voice thick and hoarse. Leaping out over the steps from the porch and landing solidly on the ground, he could only stand helplessly in the front yard and watch as her car sped away.

Chapter Nine

When Kendra returned home that evening, total darkness greeted her. Her heart sank as she dumped her things in a heap on the floor. "Diana? Diana!"

She turned on lights and went straight to Diana's room. Not bothering to knock, she walked in. The dresser mirror reflected the darkened room's only light from the flame atop a small candle. Suddenly, she realized Diana was sitting on the floor, her back to the bed and a pillow clutched to her chest. A tissue box sat beside her along with a pile of crumpled tissues.

"Diana! Dear God, what's wrong?" Kendra dropped to the floor. She reached out and pushed wet strands of hair back from her friend's face. "Oh, Diana, please! This has to stop! Tell me. What's wrong?"

Huge, body-jarring sobs blocked any words of explanation Diana might have tried to say. That she had wept for hours was evident. A second attempt to speak only served to heighten the impression of absolute despair.

Kendra stood up long enough to drag off her coat and then sat down again, wrapping her arms around her friend. For the longest time, they sat until the sobbing subsided. Finally, Diana grew quiet, and Kendra dared to speak again. "Diana, I can't possibly help if you won't tell me what's wrong. C'mon, girlfriend. Let's get off the floor and go get something to drink."

All resistance subsided. Diana placed her hands in Kendra's and accepted help up from the floor. Without protest, she followed Kendra into the kitchen. Quietly, she sat down in a chair and waited for her friend to bring two glasses of water to the table. When Kendra told her to drink, she drank.

Minutes passed. Diana's hands rose in a gesture that her friend understood. They waited until she felt able to speak. "First of all, I must apologize. By the time I arrived home, I had lost all sense of time..." She emitted a tiny, cynical laugh. "That cliché seems especially ironic considering present circumstances."

"I'm not sure humor is such a good idea right now." Worry etched deepening lines into Kendra's face. "Besides, you promised to stay home today and rest."

Swollen, bloodshot eyes lifted to meet her friend's patient gaze. She took a napkin and blew her nose. Once was certainly not enough. She blew again and sniffled. "I know, but my reason for going felt urgent at the time, and so it was. Details remain for which I have absolutely no comprehension."

"Diana, you're doing it again...that speech thing."

"Dear Kendra, I know this is difficult to understand. It may be even harder to explain, but I shall try...at least the parts I remember."

"Remember? What do you mean *remember*?"

"I finally understand many things...especially the dreams."

"How? What happened? Where did you go today? You have to help me, Diana."

Leaning back in her chair and rolling tense, aching shoulders, Diana nervously smiled. "I shall begin by telling you something that will sound completely preposterous. I ask only that you hear me out before you think me mad."

"Go ahead," Kendra prompted, unsure what to expect.

Inhaling deeply, she said, "I shall begin by telling you that Diana is not my real name. In reality, I am Sindara Varacor."

Sitting back, Kendra shook her head. "Wait. I've known you how long? Your parents, too. Now you tell me..."

Sindara interrupted her. "I warned you it would sound outlandish. Just let me finish. Please?"

"Maybe I'm the one who's going crazy," Kendra muttered. "Okay, go ahead. I'm listening."

"As I said, my name is Sindara. My real father is Count Artrian Varacor. He is governor of a place I know as Arvacon Province. The people you know as my parents are, for the time being, as great a mystery to me as they are to you. As of yet, I only now begin to assemble pieces of this puzzle.

"In answer to your earlier question, I went to see Thehrund. I had questions I could ask him only. You were right when you told me they were out of place. I was correct all those times I said I didn't belong here. We all come from somewhere else...a country called Ambracor."

An hour later, Kendra sat with her head between her hands. "So, let me be sure I understand. Thehrund is actually a prince and heir to the throne of this place called Ambracor. Just to spice up the story, you and he were going to get married, but you broke the engagement when you found out he had slept with another woman. His father, the king, escorts you back home because you basically threw a tantrum. Then, while on the way home, you were killed. Oh, and the scars that bleed here are from where you were skewered there by some warrior's spear."

"Your summary is rather blunt and cold, but it is essentially accurate." Sindara continued, "Kendra, as of yet, I have no idea how all this happened...or why."

Kendra's face became a study in changing expressions as she tried to absorb all she had just heard. "Di...I'm sorry. Di—" Kendra huffed an exasperated sigh before continuing. "Sindara, I guess my first question is how this affects us."

"From my perspective, you remain the finest friend I've ever known, here or in Ambracor. I think nothing could ever change that. As for the rest..." Her voice trailed off. As confusion began to fade from her mind, thoughts and memories slowly began to crystallize. "I don't know. Once I knew my family was safe and the king unharmed, I saw only Thehrund. It was as if all the hurt that drove me from Bracordia flooded me entirely. He wanted me to stay today...to talk. I had no heart to face him."

Rising from her chair, Kendra went to the refrigerator and pulled out plastic containers of cut veggies and a package of thick, deli-cut American cheese. She then busied herself by making a quick relish tray and fixing grilled cheese sandwiches for the two of them while she considered events of the past week and a half. In the meantime, Sindara sat in silent contemplation.

"Not fancy like prime rib, but we both need to eat," Kendra said as she set plates and napkins on the table. "Would you like something more to drink?"

Sindara nodded. "Thank you so much. I must admit my stomach begins to roar."

Kendra dared a feeble smile. "That sounded a little more like Diana. If it weren't for Thehrund and the others, I would definitely use you as a subject for my thesis."

"I'm confident Thehrund can explain better. The problem is that, every time I think of him, I remember the shock when I read that letter and then the attack. I can close my eyes and almost feel that lance thrusting into my side."

Nibbling a corner of her sandwich, Kendra studied her friend's features. Her eyes were still red and puffy. Her skin was pallid, her lips swollen. Never had she seen such grief on anyone's face.

"Sindara," Kendra began, wondering how long it would take to get used to the new name, "I'm going to say something that may sound odd to you."

Sindara's eyebrows rose high. "After all I just told you, I can hardly imagine anything sounding more bizarre."

Kendra had to smile, this time with honest humor. "True, but a thought keeps coming to the forefront of my mind. I remember something Madalyn Amador told you that day at the expo. Then I think of the two times I've been around Thehrund. Madalyn said something about your getting hurt wasn't his fault. It was yours...that you hadn't followed your own rules. When Thehrund was here, he watched your every move. It suddenly dawns on me that it's because he's in love with you. Deeply in love. Is there some way you can match what Madalyn said with what happened between you and him?"

Sindara thought long and hard as she finished her sandwich. Searching through still-jumbled memories, she relived the day he had returned from Bramond. Instead of going to meet with his father, Thehrund had come straight to her apartment in the palace and found her weeping. His whole demeanor had revealed immediate recognition of the cause of her distress.

"I was so hurt. I knew he once had an affair with Breeneth, the woman the letter said he had been with. Humiliation was the least of my feelings. He betrayed my love and my trust. He tried to explain, but I refused to listen. I was sure that anything he might say would be nothing more than a lie." Sindara swallowed several times, resisting fresh tears as she recalled the defeated look on his face as she ordered him to leave.

"How long had you known before he came to you?"

Sindara struggled to recall details to answer Kendra's question. "The letter arrived one afternoon. Thehrund returned early the next morning. He didn't deny he had been with her. He said he had departed immediately and then begged for a chance to explain."

"You mentioned that Ambracor still relies on transportation by horse and carriage. Do you think it's sort of strange that a letter could beat him if he came directly home? I can't help but wonder what would have happened if you had listened instead of sending him away."

Sindara rose and went to put dishes in the sink. Reaching into a cupboard, she pulled out a small box of cookies. Back at the table, she offered Kendra some and then took one for herself. Biting into delicately sweet wafers, she tried to make sense of wildly churning memories. Her thoughts shifted. "I studied for years at a private religious center. My plans were to commit to a life of religious service. That all changed when I met Thehrund."

"Going back to what Madalyn said, how do you think that might relate to what happened between you and Thehrund?"

Sindara picked up a second cookie. "We have a book of faith called Ambracada. It's very much like the Bible here. The book contains the original guidelines given to us by our Creator God so that we might live life in harmony with the Divine One and each other. Those rules require our people to honor life, to practice kindness and service to others, and to forgive when asked." Facing a painful past was no easy task. "In my state of shock and hurt, I gave Thehrund no real chance to explain... no chance to redeem himself. I could not see myself forgiving him for such a betrayal. All I wanted was to escape...to return home where I could remain secluded with my sorrow."

"So, Madalyn was right when she said you didn't follow your own rules."

Kendra's gentle, logical insight prompted a tearful smile. "I suppose so, but that fails to explain why I have lived a life here or why Thehrund is here...or even how we came here in the first place."

"It won't be easy, but if you honestly want to understand all of this, you have to talk to him. I don't see any other way." Kendra knew her friend needed to reach that strong core of character that she believed to be as much a part of Sindara as it had been part of Diana. In fact, she thought, they were indeed the same person, only coping with a single problem from two entirely different perspectives.

"The more I think about this, the more convinced I am that Thehrund was the man in your dreams, the one always watching you. He wasn't just watching you. He was actually searching for you. I know that doesn't make much sense, but an inner voice tells me it's true. Some force put you two on a collision course because you both need to resolve this conflict. Do you mind if I ask another question?"

Perceiving more than a kernel of truth in Kendra's words and fully appreciating her impressive intuition, Sindara nodded and waited.

"Was it the nightmare last night that triggered all this, or was it something else?"

Nervously rubbing the palms of her hands together, Sindara dared to relive her encounter with Thehrund at the park. At the time, she had been unable to understand why she had responded so passionately to his kiss or why she had then run from him. Comprehension dawned on her.

"I went walking in the park early yesterday morning. To my surprise, I encountered him there. We walked and then sat to talk. Something happened that I could not understand at the time. He kissed me, Kendra, and I kissed him back. I was helpless to stop myself. Then, I ran from him, just as I did this morning. I think the kiss triggered the nightmare, and the nightmare finally freed all of these hidden memories."

Ever one for diffusing tension, Kendra held up a hand. "Stop." She sucked in her breath. "Damn! I wish a man that sexy would kiss me!"

For the first time that evening, Sindara laughed. "Oh, Kendra, you are absolutely incredible."

Early the following morning, Sindara gazed at her reflection in the mirror. The wonders of makeup had helped minimize the dark circles under her eyes. Kendra stood behind her and brushed her hair.

"You can do this. I know you can. And remember, I'm just a phone call away."

Sindara faintly smiled. "I haven't made the last two weeks easy for you."

Kendra chuckled. "No lie that. One thing I can say is that this has been over-the-top fascinating. I can hardly wait to see what happens next."

By the time Sindara reached her destination, she wondered if it might be too early. The clock in her car showed the time as seven o'clock. Bolstering her resolve, she parked halfway down the block in the only space available. As she walked back toward the house, part of her wanted to retreat. She could not surrender to the urge. Her soul would never find any peace until she finally faced him.

Standing on the porch and pushing the doorbell proved harder than she had imagined. Finally watching the doorknob turn prompted an abrupt lurch in her stomach. This time, Karan answered the door. Judging by his appearance, he had either been asleep or had just gotten up when she rang the bell.

"Karan, I apologize for coming so early. It's just..." Words caught in her throat. "I don't know if he'll see me, but I wish to speak with Thehrund."

Karan pushed mussed hair away from his face. "He's upstairs. Asleep. This past week has been trying for...for all of us...but especially exhausting for Thehrund. I finally convinced him to take a sleeping draught. I expect he should sleep another few hours."

Her face dropped, and she nodded understanding. She had come this far. There could be no turning back. "Do you think I might go up to sit with him?"

Her request startled Karan. "Why are you here?"

"Karan, I know how angry you and Nagrand must be with me. Please try to understand. When I came yesterday, I had only begun to remember my life in Ambracor. I was terrified that I had lost my brother and failed to save King Hamund. Beyond that, I had also just learned that I was not the person I always thought I was. You cannot imagine such a shock as that was."

Karan sighed heavily. "Sit down for a minute. Please," he said, pointing toward the sofa. Following, he sat in a chair across from her. Leaning forward and staring at nothing in particular, he searched for words. "Have you any idea how long we've searched for you?"

"No, truly I do not." Her eyes met his. "What I thought I knew was that I was a twenty-three-year-old woman starting a career in banking and sharing an apartment with her best friend. Yesterday morning, I awoke from a nightmare and realized I was an entirely different person from an entirely different world. My current concept of time is practically non-existent."

He blew out a long, slow breath. "That explains much," he finally said with a note of sympathy in his voice. "For almost six years, Nagrand and I have accompanied Thehrund while he searched for you."

"Six years? Karan, how can that be? You must believe me when I say I don't understand. I remember a Breyal warrior rushing at me. I died. I must have."

"So everyone there that day thought. Thehrund was the only one who knew differently."

"How? How could he have known? The last thing I remember was his voice calling my name. I looked toward him, and there was nothing more until yesterday...except for a full life here."

"You have no idea what Thehrund has endured in order to search for you."

"But why? Why would he look for me if he saw what happened?" she interrupted.

"The questions you ask are best answered by Thehrund. I will take you upstairs to him, but you must understand something. I've never known a man so willing to risk everything because of his love for a woman. Thehrund does love you, and that love has brought him years of great suffering."

She was almost surprised that her eyes remained dry. "Karan, just take me to him. Please."

Opening the bedroom door where Thehrund slept, Karan entered and quietly placed a chair near the bed. As he turned to go, she stopped him. In a whisper, she asked him to leave the door open and then waited for him to return downstairs before going inside.

Sitting on the upholstered, straight-backed chair, Sindara thoughtfully gazed at the man she had once promised to marry. He had changed little since she had last seen him. What had Karan said? Six years. Looking closer, she noticed the faintest hint of lines etched across his forehead. His beard was still coal black. So were the thick strands of hair that strayed in every direction around his pillow and along his shoulder.

Her mind calmly accepted an invasion of memory as she noted the two long braids on his side nearest her. On Monday morning, she had automatically reached out to touch one. A subconscious reaction, no doubt. How often had she toyed with his braids while he held her and talked about his feelings and dreams for their future? The gesture had become an affectionate habit that had apparently remained imprinted on her psyche.

For the life of her, she couldn't resist reaching out to touch the braid closest to her. Just as she did, he rolled over in his sleep, his face turning away from her. As he settled, the blanket covering him slid down, revealing the breadth of his shoulder, the sculpted muscles of his arm, and the supple skin covering them. More memories. The warmth and security whenever he held her in the circle of those arms had been both comforting and electrifying.

Her throat tightened. She blinked back tears. She refused to cry again... not yet anyway. On the other hand, she desperately needed to touch him, to convince herself this was not some new dream meant to challenge her sanity. With deliberate slowness, she eased her weight onto the edge of the mattress. Gentle fingers smoothed long locks into some order. Without thinking, she slowly stroked her fingertips along the length of one slightly frayed braid. As she did, the tip of a fingernail barely grazed the skin on his arm.

Stirring, he turned again. Sleep-heavy eyelids struggled to open. Black pupils were wide, the azure irises surrounding them barely visible in the darkened room. The grief that crossed his face knifed into her heart as surely as the Breyal spear had once pierced her side. With a muffled groan, he tugged the blanket over his face as he sought escape from the torment of yet another unfulfilled dream.

Again, she refused to weep. Instead, she leaned forward and kissed hands tightly clutching the blanket's satin edge. She then watched as he slowly slid the cover from his face.

He blinked several times before pushing himself up on one elbow, his hair tumbling into a mass on the pillow as his eyes widened in disbelief. "Sindara?" He sounded as if he could barely force her name across his lips.

Straightening, she met his disbelieving expression with a steady gaze. "I apologize for disturbing you. I just couldn't resist the temptation to touch you. I needed to be sure you were real."

Defying lingering effects of the sleeping draught Karan had given him, he woke abruptly and sat up. Pushing his fingers backward through his hair, he stared. "How long have you been here?"

"I'm not quite sure. A short while."

Twisting, he shoved pillows against the headboard and leaned back. "I... After yesterday, I thought never to see you again." The low tones of his voice were thick with sleep and sadness.

"Thehrund..." Her thoughts stalled. What could she say? She swallowed and tried again. "Night before last, I awoke from another nightmare. This time was different. I finally began to recall life in Ambracor. When I came yesterday, all I clearly remembered was the Breyal attack. I was terrified for Erator and that I had failed to protect your father."

Her face dropped, and she stared at hands now trembling in her lap. "I heard you call out my name that day just as I felt the stabbing pain of the spear. That was the only other thing I remembered yesterday morning. I cannot begin to describe the terror and confusion that consumed me. I wasn't even sure what was real or what wasn't, whether I was Diana Lorenz or Sindara Varacor."

Thehrund's broad chest expanded with a deep breath. "When you refused even to talk yesterday, I thought I had failed and that you were forever lost to me."

"You were right when you said we need to talk. I admit I was afraid of you. The explosion of memories and hurt was more than I was prepared to face. Thehrund, I know I hurt you, too. That was never my intent."

Despite fear that she might flee yet again, he dared to reach for her. This time, she willingly moved into his arms and rested her cheek against the firmness of his bare chest. Rhythmic beating of his heart filled her ears. His warm breath teased the sensitive skin of her neck. Never had she felt him so close.

Sounds drifted from downstairs and through the open bedroom door. Reluctantly, she withdrew from his embrace. "What now, Thehrund? What do we do now?"

"Tell me you will go downstairs and wait until I can dress and join you. Then, we can sit and talk. I will try to help you understand. You must realize there remains much I really don't yet comprehend." When she started to stand, he grasped her hand tightly. "Sindara, promise you'll wait for me."

His apprehension was justified. How many times had she run from him already? Leaning forward, she touched her lips to his. "I promise, Thehrund. I promise to wait for you downstairs."

Two pairs of gray eyes looked at her with apprehension when she entered the kitchen. She could hardly blame either man for being so concerned. The smile she gave them was weary, but it came more easily than she expected. "He's awake. He will come down after he dresses. I was wondering if I might beg a cup of tea."

Karan's relief was instantly apparent. "A pot is brewing now. Would you like toast or biscuits with the tea?"

"Either sounds perfect."

"Karan, please make that two cups and two plates." Thehrund had just appeared in the doorway.

When Sindara turned, she indulged herself with a long, admiring gaze at the man whose tall, muscular frame dominated the arched entry to the kitchen. He had obviously dressed in a hurry. Thick socks were pulled up over leggings. A generously cut white linen shirt was untucked and fell loose around his lean hips. Long hair was far from being tamed into order, giving him an almost leonine appearance that exuded impressive, sensual masculinity. His face, framed by his black beard, bore no hint of the fearsome warrior he could be. Instead, his mouth formed an adoring smile, and azure eyes shone with tender regard.

With quiet speed, breakfast plates, mugs, a pot of tea, and a platter piled with toast and pastries appeared on the kitchen table. Karan and Nagrand quickly disappeared. The smile she gave Thehrund was tentative as her mouth opened soundlessly, revealing her loss for words.

Thehrund rescued her by reaching for her hands and guiding her to the table. He pulled a chair out for her before sitting across from her. Bending his head, he grasped trembling hands yet again and pressed a lingering kiss on them. Glancing upward and tenderly smiling, he did not hesitate to offer quiet, heartfelt grace for the food before them and the immense blessing of both their lives and this reunion.

Conversation began hesitantly. Sindara had so many questions, but she hardly knew where to begin. Thehrund expected some of her questions would be difficult. Others would be impossible for him to answer. Indeed, he already realized that the entire set of circumstances surrounding them at that very moment was mysterious beyond imagination. He wondered how he could ever convey that to her.

He watched as she lifted a mug to her lips. "I'm trying to recall when I ever saw you so quiet."

His words prompted a shy smile. "It's so hard to know where to begin. I find myself in the rather peculiar circumstance of being two people at once."

"Are you really two people?"

The straightforward question activated analytical thought processes that set her mind racing. Thankfully, he remained silent as he ate a slice of toast spread with butter and jam. That silence gave her time to consider events over the past week and a half. His simple, perfectly worded inquiry finally set her mind on a clear course toward recovery.

"For the past few days, I felt trapped on a ferry being reeled first one way and then the other at breakneck speed. On one side, I had knowledge of the life I've lived here. On the far side, Sindara's life and all her memories were rushing to invade." She paused, wondering how to continue. "I suddenly realize Diana was always Sindara. The only real difference is that, as Diana, I struggled with imbalances and uncertainties that existed because the foundation that makes Sindara who she is was lost in a state of confusion. Now, the more the haze clears, the more confident I am in knowing that I am but one person. I am Sindara."

Thehrund's solemn features settled with relief. "It seems this journey has not been easy for either of us."

Compassion softened her features. "From what little I know, it seems what you have faced has been clearly worse."

He looked away for a moment. Bitterness would always tinge his memory of that day. "The afternoon before the attack, a messenger rode into Articene with news that a band of Breyal raiders had crossed Arvacon borders. Erator and I decided to lead a detachment from the fort to intercept the raiders before they reached any towns or villages. We weren't sure what was happening when we heard sounds of battle. When we realized a royal escort had been ambushed, we raced headlong into the fray. I saw Father's horse throw him. Within seconds, I watched you dismount and join the fight. Because of you, Father had time to free himself."

Drinking tea to soothe his constricted throat, Thehrund forced himself to continue. "While you fended off one Breyal, I saw a second run directly at you. I shouted a warning, but I was too far away to help. I saw when the lance struck you...and I heard you scream."

Sindara noted the way his hands helplessly balled into tight fists. Sliding her chair closer, she extended her own hand to stroke his face. "That part is over now. You must let it go."

His face dropped, but his right hand lifted, covering hers and pressing it flat against his cheek. "Sindara, that memory I can never let go. That one moment in time was frozen for me to watch while I listened to the voices of angels. They are the ones who told me you could be saved...but only if I was willing to commit to a quest that could lead to redemption for the actions that caused you to break our engagement. They offered me a choice. I could swear an oath to undertake a search for you, but I would have to earn forgiveness for what happened in Bramond. If I accepted and fulfilled the offer, your life would be spared. It would be up to me to win back your love and your trust." His voice broke as words faltered. A track of tears formed on his cheek.

"Thehrund, I have no idea what to say. I..."

His gaze intensified. Tremors marked words he struggled to say. "Sindara, you must understand. Guilt was not the driving force behind my decision to give my oath to Creator God and his angels. This I swear to you. I knew that I had failed you, but I also loved you beyond anything else in my life. I could not conceive of living out my years without you. If there was any chance to save you, I was willing to assume whatever risks necessary to do so."

Smiling was impossible. Truth infused every word he spoke, and every word filled wounds her soul had suffered. "And now? How do you feel now?"

His lips pressed tightly together. Drawing in a deep breath, he decided that, whatever the consequences, he needed to explain details of the story she had been too hurt to hear those many years ago. "I want you to know what happened in Bramond."

Her involuntary wince revealed pain the memory still prompted. The difference now was that she could better manage sorrowful emotions. "Tell me."

Thoughts carried him back in time to Bramond's provincial capital and Count Brandere's mansion. There had been a lavish celebration of a family birthday. Food and drink were served in abundance. The count had insisted that the departing prince stay to enjoy the festivities. He recalled someone pushing another tankard into his hand. After that...

"Thehrund?"

When he met her gaze, he realized he had lost himself in a past that had cost him dearly. He wasn't sure when he had stopped talking or how much he had told her.

"Thehrund, do I understand correctly that you don't even remember going to her room, let alone..."

He gripped Sindara's hands tightly, fearful she might bolt again. "Sindara, years before I met you, I had no qualms about joining friends for a good time and getting drunk. Very drunk. I tell you with no pride, but never was I so drunk that I couldn't get myself home while also avoiding Father's wrath for foolishness unbecoming to his heir. You are free to confirm that with Nagrand. This was the only time I could remember nothing...not going to Breeneth's rooms...or bedding her. The time between the party and my waking beside her remains a total blank."

Sindara's mind drifted back to her years at school. Brenna had occasionally bragged about plots and tricks she and her sister played on people. She wondered about the possibility of Thehrund being one of their victims. "Do you think they might have put something in your drinks that caused you to black out?"

Thehrund squarely faced her question. "Sindara, I must be honest. I don't know. I suppose it is possible. What I can say is that I was so furious when I woke up that I left immediately. That is something else you can verify with Nagrand. I wanted nothing more than to escape that place and return home as fast as we could ride."

Sindara pondered details that did not fit. "I need not ask Nagrand. I trust you to tell me the truth. The question that comes to my mind is this. If you left immediately and rushed home to Bracordia, how did Breeneth's letter arrive the day before you did?"

Thehrund sat back, his expression pensive. "I pushed my escort hard on that ride back. Our horses were bred in Arvacon specifically for speed and endurance. I have no explanation for how any messenger from Bramond could have reached you first."

She got up and carried her mug and plate to the sink. Leaning over the counter, she wrestled with a barrage of thoughts and ideas. Had he held to his original intention to leave the party early, he never would have been at risk for a drunken stupor, a drunken blackout, or whatever else had happened in Breeneth's bedroom. Still, she also had to accept that, as heir to Ambracor's throne, he was often expected to attend events for the sake of appearances and nothing more.

His arms encircled her waist and pulled her backward against the hard planes of his virile male body. Resisting his embrace was impossible. Resting her hands on top of his, she sighed. "I wish I could express how deeply I regret giving you no real opportunity to explain."

"There is so much more to this tale than either of us yet comprehends. Your memories of a full life here are in absolute conflict with the six years I have searched for you. I must believe there is some reason this has all occurred." His face nuzzled against the smooth skin of her neck. Moist lips tracked kisses up to her earlobe. His breath was warm as he whispered in her ear, "What I do know is that I love you, Sindara. There is nothing I want more than to take you home and to marry you as soon as a wedding can be arranged."

Turning in his embrace, she looked up into those haunting blue eyes that had followed her through countless dreams. Lifting her face closer to his, she briefly captured his lips with hers. When he responded to her unspoken invitation, the rekindled fusion of their mouths reflected the bonding of their souls. By the time he breathlessly ended the kiss, her body quaked with desire to fulfill love long denied.

"Thehrund?" Karan's hushed voice called their attention. "Forgive my interruption. The portal begins to open. I thought you should know."

Her expression held fresh questions as she stared into eyes that had momentarily shifted to acknowledge Karan's report. "Portal? What does he mean?"

"Come. I will show you." Leading her by the hand, Thehrund followed Karan to the room where a faint disturbance of air revealed early stages of the portal's formation. Seeing the puzzled look on her face, he explained, "This is the means we have used to travel many places throughout our search. It always begins this way. Once it takes on the appearance of a full-fledged whirlwind, we step into it and are transported. This is how we came here and how we will finally take you home."

Uplifted eyebrows revealed her misgivings. "How long does it take?"

Thehrund gave a single shake of his head. "It varies, but it usually takes two to three days for it to completely form. Once it's ready, we have a matter of hours to enter. Travel time is perhaps a minute or two."

"So, you're telling me we can return home through...this?"

His smile reassured her. "A strange mode of travel to be sure, but it is safe nonetheless. The only aftereffect is a mild dizzy sensation."

"That's all?" she asked skeptically.

Chuckling, he wrapped his arms around her, his embrace transferring the rush of relief inundating him as he anticipated taking her back to Ambracor. "I promise," he murmured in husky tones. "We will enter together and together arrive safely home."

Once he released her, she slowly backed away from him. She paused for several moments and then shakily walked to the living room. Her feelings threatened fresh collapse into chaos, trapping her on an emotional seesaw. Retrieving her things from the sofa, she put on her coat and reached into a pocket for her keys.

"What are you doing? Are you leaving?" Distress instantly lined his features.

She managed a faint smile. "Two days. That is so little time. I have a life here...people I care about...responsibilities. This all comes as so much, so fast."

Unnerved, he grasped her arms. "I thought... You said..." Stammering to a halt, he drew in a shuddering breath. "Just moments ago, we spoke of going home. Together."

Delicate fingers stroked the bearded line of his jaw. "Thehrund, I need time...time to think, time to organize my thoughts..."

He suppressed rising panic. "The portal is opening. I dare not miss it when it does. Sindara, when we left, Ambracor was on the verge of war. I am needed at home, and I need you with me. If you don't go now, we will likely be parted forever. You must believe when I say I would prefer death over losing you again. Please, Sindara, forgive me for hurting you. Please come home."

His words swept like a mighty gust through her mind and into her heart. At that moment, everything about him...the tilt of his head, the look in his eyes, the intensity in his voice...exposed the powerful blend of turmoil, fear, and dread filling him. She realized she could never simply dismiss the massive mantle of obligations awaiting him in Ambracor. Neither could she ever escape her love for him. Still, she could not deny the validity of her own responsibilities in this world, and she needed to place her thoughts in order.

Opening her purse, she withdrew her cell phone and walked over to Karan. Placing it in his hand, she showed him how to use it to contact Kendra's cell or the apartment's landline in case the portal began to open faster than expected.

Turning to face Thehrund, even her posture showed how weary she really felt. "I need to go home. I cannot simply walk away and leave things in total disarray, and I cannot sort things out from here. Karan can advise me about the portal. It takes only twenty minutes to drive here."

"No. I come with you. I cannot risk letting you go alone." His response was decisive. "Perhaps I can even help."

Her response was steady, almost curt. "Then I suggest you bring a change of clothes and expect to sleep on the sofa tonight. I shall wait for you outside."

Once inside her car, she rested her forehead on the steering wheel. Even a few moments of solitude seemed exceedingly precious. Her life was transforming too quickly...too drastically. She was losing count of how many times she had been on the verge of tears this one single morning. Still, she resisted. Enough tears had been shed yesterday. And the day before. Earlier, she had felt trapped on a seesaw; now it seemed more like a roller coaster out of control. Anger, hurt, and dread one minute. Love and elation the next.

Sound snapped her from sinking deeper into contemplation. Thehrund had lifted the handle and opened the passenger side door of her small sedan. She watched as he tossed a small duffel into the back seat and then climbed in beside her. She noted the downward tilt of his head and the somber lines of his distinctive, angular profile. The regular rhythm of her pulse changed as his sadness weighed down her heart.

Realization was not quick, but with it came liberation. The heaviness that affected her breathing had nothing to do with her own feelings of anger and betrayal. Instead, on an empathic plane rising from her love for him, his distress, full of regret plus worries for their homeland, had found its way into the core of her being. With empathy came fresh clarity. Words would not suffice. Turning slightly in the driver's seat, she reached out and touched his arm.

Thehrund could not bear to look at her. A knot in his throat blocked speech. His stomach ached. His heart pounded an uneven rhythm. Unsettled conditions at home heavily burdened his sense of duty. Fear for the lives of his parents and his people swelled within his heart. Profound anxiety had displaced relief when she mentioned needing time to think. He had lived too many years on fragile threads of hope. His mind questioned whether he possessed sufficient strength to continue clinging to that hope.

"Thehrund," she said softly, "look at me."

As if in slow motion, he lifted his head and finally turned to meet her waiting gaze. Troubled eyes were filled with questions, yet he remained mute. His image, dejected and unspeakably weary, reminded her of her state of mind the day she had delivered a letter and her engagement ring to King Hamund.

Leaning across the car's center console, she kissed him. "Forgive me, Thehrund. My mind is clear, and my heart is full. I love you. Worry no more. I will somehow get things here sorted out, and then I will go home with you to Ambracor." She gave him a teasing smile. "One thing must be absolutely clear. I expect you to follow through immediately on what you said about marrying me as soon as you can possibly arrange it."

His voice again sounded deep and husky. "Are you certain, Sindara? Really certain?"

Her gaze dropped for just a moment to the console effectively separating them. Frowning, she caught his lips in yet another brief kiss. "I promise a more convincing kiss when we reach my apartment."

Following a quiet ride, she parked her car and led him upstairs to her apartment. Once inside with the door closed, she stretched her arms up around his neck and initiated a kiss unlike any they had ever shared. Soft lips parted, demanding from him the startling pleasures created by his tongue touching hers. Tiny whimpers formed in her throat as she deepened her kiss until he reached a point where he knew he had to stop...had to recover self-control.

Tears finally spilled down her cheeks. Different tears this time. Tears from a heart overfilled with love discovered anew. "Do you now believe I'm sure?" she murmured.

Clutching her tightly, he answered, "I believe, my love. I finally, truly believe."

He then led her to the sofa. "I have something for you." Reaching behind his neck, he unfastened the clasp of the gold chain he had worn for years and pulled it from beneath his shirt. Taking her left hand, he slid her engagement ring into place.

She gasped softly. "My ring," she whispered. "I had forgotten how beautiful it is."

"Did you really?" he asked as he held up her right hand. Although the ring she had bought for herself was smaller and less intricate, design similarities were undeniable.

Later, setting her laptop aside as something she would soon find useless, she located pen and paper to start a list of things to do. They laughed. The following day would be hectic beyond belief. Go to the bank to turn in her immediate resignation. She would explain that the hospital neurologist had found problems with her brain scans, which was true, and that her fiancé had insisted she consult with his personal physician. Heaven help her explain how she had gotten engaged so suddenly. Go to the title agency to transfer her car to Kendra. Try again to contact her adopted parents. Close bank accounts and go shopping for a ton of lingerie that she would make Thehrund carry back to Ambracor. Kendra could use any leftover funds as she saw fit.

So absorbed in plans slowed by kisses and caresses, they were surprised when the door opened. Kendra had come home early. The second she saw them, a beaming smile crossed her face. "I see things worked out just as I expected," she said with a laugh as she quickly went to Sindara and squeezed her in a tight hug. Thehrund, who had immediately stood upon her arrival, also received a warm embrace.

Later, Kendra and Sindara decided to cook a light supper while Thehrund pulled boxes down from closet shelves in Sindara's bedroom. Frowning upon hearing a knock at the door and then struggling to maintain a welcoming expression, Kendra invited in unexpected guests. Offering them a seat, she excused herself to return to the kitchen.

"Sorry, but you have visitors," she said while making a genuinely apologetic face.

When Sindara reached the living room, she forced a friendly smile. "Jennie! Such a surprise. I did not expect you to stop by."

Jennie stood up. "I was in the neighborhood and thought I'd stop to see how you're really doing. You remember Marlene here from my church, don't you?"

"Of course. I am pleased to see you again, Marlene."

Jennie carefully appraised Sindara's appearance. "Those bruises on your face! What a terrible thing to happen! We've been praying for a fast recovery."

"I appreciate that," Sindara said. "It has been difficult, but I am better."

"Sindara, the boxes are all down..." Appearing from her bedroom, Thehrund suddenly stopped. "My apologies. I did not intend to interrupt."

Sindara crossed her eyes at Kendra, who was making a sad attempt to stifle laughter. Meanwhile, Jennie and her friend openly gawked in stunned curiosity. Not even in movies had they ever seen a man quite like Thehrund.

"Jennie, please, allow me to introduce you to Thehrund Cobrandya. Thehrund, this is Jennie Clarke and Marlene Thomas. Jennie works at the same bank as I do. Marlene is her friend."

"I am honored to meet you both," Thehrund said as he bowed his head respectfully.

"Likewise," Jennie replied in a strained voice, her expression still registering shocked inquisitiveness. "Thehrund, is it? You must be new here."

"I am visiting only."

"I see. And how do you know Diana?"

Nosy of her, Sindara thought as she barely avoided rolling her eyes. Thehrund only smiled graciously. "We met years ago at the home of her parents."

"Oh, that's nice. It's a shame her parents are out of the country. I'm sure you regret missing them."

Sindara's smile stiffened. She could see how intensely Jennie studied him, and that spark of disapproval was impossible to miss. "Actually, he saw them just a few weeks ago. By the way, aside from Kendra, you are the first to hear our news. Thehrund and I are to be married."

Jennie positively gaped as her mouth dropped open in astonishment. "Married?" Her voice actually squeaked.

Sindara silently chided herself. She shouldn't enjoy the other woman's apparent discomfort so much.

At the same time, Jennie was convinced Diana must be suffering more from the brain injury than anyone knew. This man with his long hair and strange attire...this Thehrund looked more like a throwback to some bygone age...or worse. "Oh...well...congratulations. I had no idea you were seeing anyone. This is...a real surprise."

"I'm quite sure it is. Thehrund is helping me collect some of my things. You may as well know that I'm leaving the bank. When the hospital ran brain scans after the attack, they had serious concerns about the results. Thehrund is taking me home to his country where his personal physician will coordinate my care and any necessary treatment."

"You're kidding." Tact was definitely not Jennie's strong suit. "You can't be serious."

"I am completely serious. We have already consulted with his physician. My care will be in excellent hands."

"I can assure you," Thehrund added, noting visible strain between the two women, "she will receive finer care nowhere else."

Jennie shook her head. "There's no better care available anywhere else. Our medical advances and facilities here are the best."

"I do not doubt the quality of medical services here, but exceptional care also exists in other places. What concerns me is my understanding of the length of time patients here often wait for care. My personal physician will see to it that her treatment receives the highest priority."

"I'm sure you have good intentions, but if you'll excuse my candor, are you sure you have the means to ensure such care?" Jennie started when Kendra snorted and promptly excused herself to return to the kitchen.

"Jennie," Sindara said firmly, "that question was rude. You make your usual judgments based on a narrow view of how people should look, behave, and believe. I realize Thehrund doesn't fit any images you consider acceptable, but he is an exceptional man who carries with him deep faith in God. He relies on that faith because he holds responsibility for the lives of thousands. In his country, he is a prince...a true, blue-blooded, crown-on-the-head prince and successor to the throne of his father. Yes, his father is king."

Thehrund's black eyebrows lifted as he recognized the rising levels of both Jennie's disapproval and Sindara's irritation. He turned a steady, daunting look toward Jennie and reached for Sindara's hand. His patience was limited where his fiancée's well-being might be at stake. "I ask you to please excuse us. My Sindara tires easily after her ordeal. I am sure you understand. She needs to eat supper and take her medicines before I make sure she goes early to bed."

Grasping a red-faced Jennie by the arm, Marlene finally spoke up. "Diana, we need to be going anyway. I apologize for barging in unannounced. I do hope all goes well with your recovery. Oh, and good luck with your upcoming wedding."

Sindara watched with mixed emotions as Jennie barely nodded goodbye before Marlene practically dragged her from the apartment.

"Damn! The nerve of that woman!"

Thehrund looked shocked. "Such language from my betrothed!"

Sindara heaved a frustrated sigh. "My apologies, Your Highness. That woman has annoyed me for too long."

"Her manners were somewhat...churlish."

"I probably shouldn't have answered her as I did. I've endured so many incidents like this. I finally lost all patience."

"Look on the bright side, girlfriend," Kendra interjected with a thoroughly amused grin on her face as she reappeared from the kitchen. "Supper's ready, and you can enjoy it knowing that's probably the last time you'll ever have to deal with Ms. Jennie Clarke."

Chapter Ten

"You're up early," Kendra greeted Thehrund as she entered the kitchen to start the morning pot of coffee. "I hope the sofa wasn't too uncomfortable."

Thehrund greeted her with a smile. "The sofa was fine, thank you. I actually slept quite well."

"Good. I'm surprised Sindara isn't up. She's always what we call the early bird."

Thehrund's expression was extraordinarily gentle. "I checked on her when I first awoke. She was peacefully asleep."

Kendra's voice was soft. "She hasn't slept well for months. I'm glad she's finally getting the rest she needs. I guess we owe that to you."

Thehrund's head shook back and forth. "Real gratitude goes to Creator God and his angels who watched over her."

"From what I understand, you had six years when you could have given up. You didn't, so you also deserve thanks. I've never seen her so happy." Kendra sat down across from him. "The story you told about frozen time, angel voices, and the portal is astounding. I wonder what's behind it all."

Thehrund shrugged. "At home, Sindara's intense faith was widely recognized. All who knew her expected her to commit to a cloistered life. That changed when we met. Despite her devotion to her faith, I believe she was never meant to live in such seclusion. I think of that, but I, too, ask the same question. Why?"

Kendra got up, poured two cups of coffee, and returned to the table. "I, for one, can't complain that she was saved, but you're right. The questions behind all that's happened are perplexing."

Thoughtful blue eyes looked up at Kendra over the cup he had just lifted to his mouth. "I believe she is destined to perform some great task."

Kendra gazed at his face. She noted the sweep of his eyebrows, the light bronze shade of his skin, the line of his beard, the drape and waves of his hair. Intuition rose on a gentle tide. "I believe the task belongs to both of you. This event...Sindara's near death and the quest you were offered...now this reunion...everything was meant to prepare both of you for something significant in your future. Whatever lies behind this also involves Nagrand and Karan."

"You sound very sure," he remarked as he studied the distant expression in her eyes.

"I am." She shrugged. "Just don't ask why."

Thehrund sighed. "If you divine an explanation you can share, I hope it comes before we leave." Finishing his coffee in silence, he excused himself to check on Sindara.

The tips of his fingers lightly traced the contour of her cheek. Dark bruises were slowly fading. Rose color defined the shapely curves of her lips. Long eyelashes fluttered as eyelids slowly opened to reveal sleepy eyes the shade of dark honey. That first waking smile held sweetness he had never before seen.

"Four mornings in a row I am blessed to see your beautiful face."

"Thehrund," she whispered as she reached for him.

Minutes later, after placing her pillows against the headboard with one hand, he reluctantly loosened his embrace. As she settled back, he breathed a satisfied sigh. "We have much to do today."

Her smile widened with the joy of hearing again those wonderfully resonant tones of his voice. "I didn't mean to sleep so late."

Although he did not smile, his expression reflected his soul's returning tranquility. "You needed rest. Were it not for the tasks you planned and the opening of the portal, I would have let you sleep longer."

"You were right to wake me. Let me get up and get ready." Leaning forward, her lips grazed his with the lightest of touches. "I love you, Prince Thehrund."

❈ ❈ ❈

Walking upstairs to the second-floor apartment proved something of an adventure. Sindara's purse dangled from her shoulder as she manipulated three bulky shopping bags while fumbling with her keychain and then inserting correct keys into the door locks. Balancing several boxes tucked beneath his chin while also laden with shopping bags, Thehrund followed close behind. Sindara laughed when he dryly remarked that he had never before heard of using a prince as a pack animal.

Pushing open the door and entering the apartment, Sindara stopped so abruptly that Thehrund staggered into her, causing bags and boxes to tumble to the floor. Across the living room, Kendra had just risen to her feet, a shocked expression on her face as she looked from Sindara to the two visitors seated on the sofa.

"Mom! Dad! I had no idea..." Sindara's words trailed off as she turned suddenly speechless. Shoving packages out of the way with her foot to create a path, she hurried forward to the couple who had adopted her as an abandoned newborn. Both reached out to receive her tearful, welcoming hugs.

An hour later, she sat in stunned silence as she turned a small, shining disk over and over in her hand. A frame of gold filigree securely cradled the highly polished, silver-white crystal that looked almost like a mirror. She exchanged glances with Kendra, who looked just as amazed at an identical disk resting on her lap.

"We apologize for deceiving you, Sindara. Never would we have done so had your life not hung in the balance. We did everything possible to be the parents you needed. Our love for you was no deception. We hoped it might suffice to gain your understanding and earn your forgiveness should the right time come."

Grateful beyond words for Thehrund by her side, Sindara swallowed hard. "I never once suspected you were..."

Thehrund rescued her. "Angelic guardians taking the form of humans is written in the Ambracada. To know that you did so for Sindara's sake both humbles and inspires me. Master Garen, I know I also speak for Sindara when I say that we shall be forever grateful for what you and Lady Aminta have done for her."

Aminta's smile brightened the soft glow surrounding her. "We gladly serve Creator God as directed. This experience in human form has given our spirits new dimensions of understanding human nature. It is especially satisfying seeing that you both cherish the blessings you rediscover in your love."

"You must never forget. The faith you each possess granted this chance for reunion and reconciliation. There is another reason, too," Garen said, his voice deeper than even Thehrund's and ringing with the faintest of echoes. "Deliberate, evil intervention created the clash that nearly stole Sindara's life. That evil must learn such interference will not be tolerated. Take care. That same malevolence will again confront you as it seeks power over Ambracor."

"Your only hope of defeating the evil yearning to rule your world is to cling to one another in solid faith and trust as you defend your homeland and your people," Aminta warned.

Sindara looked into cherished faces, seeing them for the first time as they truly were. Their mystical, angelic beauty was breathtaking. The impact of their warnings was astonishing. "Thehrund was right when he said we will always be thankful for what you've done for us in the name of Creator God. For myself, I can honestly say I always loved you and will always honor you." She paused. "I am saddened that Ambracor faces war, but I will stand by Thehrund's side. Together, we will defend our people against this vile tide threatening our home."

Garen finally smiled. "Sindara, for years we watched the bond of friendship strengthen between you and Kendra. Hers is a powerful spirit, and her abilities will grow even stronger as she continues her studies. The crystals we have given you bear mystical connections that will help shield you from danger. They will also allow you to communicate with one another when times are especially trying. She generously offers to continue helping you maintain blessed light through whatever lies ahead."

"We will need to practice this scrying technique. I know little about it, and I've certainly never tried it," Kendra said to Sindara. Turning to Garen and Aminta, she smiled. "Thank you for honoring me this way. Knowing I can maintain my friendship with Sindara is a gift. The possibility of helping her and her people with this mission exceeds my wildest imaginings."

"We are not the ones to thank," Aminta replied. "Your faith in Creator God and your soul's integrity earn you this opportunity. I believe you have always understood that you and Sindara are sisters in spirit."

Early the following evening, Karan's expression was doubtful as he pulled up a retracting handle on one of the large cases Sindara rolled into the room where the portal hummed a monotonously low note. Aloud, he wondered how they would ever be able to hang onto bundles now secured tightly together.

Unable to resist a high-spirited grin, Thehrund clapped him on the shoulder. "You should have seen this before she put them into bags and attached the tube that removed all the air. I thought we might need one of those huge carriages for everything. Compacting her things was quite an amazing feat to behold."

"It wasn't so much," Sindara chided Thehrund. "This world uses far too much packaging. Once wrappers and boxes were removed, there was little left."

"Little left? My beloved Sindara, one of these two cases by itself weighs twice as much as all of the bags we carried here."

"Who insisted I buy extra garments at the lingerie store? And who insisted that he just had to have extra boxes of chocolates?" she countered with an accusing look.

"Ah, I think I deserve some measure of immediate gratification once we return, as well as some reward to anticipate." Despite the certainty of problems awaiting him at home, the prince was in a jovial mood as they made final preparations to enter the portal.

"Perhaps I shouldn't have taken you to the bookstore to get that book from this world's ancient Chinese warrior Sun-Tzu. The books you bought account for half the weight in one of those suitcases."

Thehrund conceded the point as a hint of solemnity returned to his eyes. "Perhaps you should not have told me about him. Still, if he was such a great warrior that his work has been studied and utilized for centuries, those books may well prove valuable."

Nagrand finally joined the trio. "How soon do you think?"

"Very soon," Thehrund answered, his voice losing earlier levity. "I can manage the largest bag if the two of you handle the rest." He turned his gaze to Sindara. "The journey through the portal will be swift. I want no mistakes or accidents. The currents are very powerful. I want you to put your arms around my neck and lock your hands tightly together."

Temptation to further tease him faded. "I understand. You can be sure. I will not let go."

Observing rising anxiety in her expression and a slight tremor in her hands, he smiled reassuringly. "Do not fear. I will also be holding you."

Drawing in a deep breath, she leaned into him and lifted her lips close to his ear. "As long as you promise to hold me, I will not be afraid."

As the portal's currents swirled faster, flashes of light and color settled into a column with a steady, luminous glow the color of a clear summer sky. The mood of the travelers changed. Karan led them in prayer for divine protection and safe passage home to Ambracor. On Thehrund's signal, Karan and Nagrand each firmly grasped their travel gear and disappeared one after the other into the portal.

Thehrund gingerly stepped sideways as if leading Sindara in a slow, romantic dance. Pausing for just a moment, he dropped a kiss on her forehead. "Remember, my love. Hold tightly. Once we arrive, you will likely feel dizzy. I don't want you to fall."

Apprehension tightened her features as she nodded. "I'm ready. I want to go home."

Thehrund had not exaggerated the sheer velocity of currents within the portal. She was glad for the long strap on the one tote she carried because she had worn it across her body. Swift cyclonic winds could have easily sucked the air from her lungs had she not followed Thehrund's instructions to take a deep breath and hold it. While she focused all her energy on keeping her fingers interlocked behind Thehrund's strong neck, the tightness of his right arm around her waist gave her courage.

Whirling currents challenged her concentration. Her hair whipped around in every direction, catching and tangling with his. What had sounded like a steady hum outside the portal expanded in a growing crescendo until her ears ached from the roar. Frigid cold penetrated her back and legs, her body sensing warmth only where it pressed against his. When she feared her chest might explode with desperate need to expel the deep breath she had taken, what had seemed like eternity abruptly ended.

Her feet hit solid stone floor. Her legs felt as insubstantial as jelly. Her body slumped against Thehrund's as her head swam in dizzy circles. Her ears popped. She heard a loud thud. Awareness slowly penetrated her mind. Both of Thehrund's arms securely encircled her. He was carefully guiding her backward. A new sensation. She felt herself lowering onto a chair. He was kneeling. His hands cradled her face. Even her body was weaving in circles. Together, they rocked in rhythm until the nauseating spinning gradually slowed and stopped altogether.

Raising her head proved impossible. Breathe, she thought to herself. Breathe deeply. Were the thoughts hers, or was it Thehrund's voice prompting her?

"Breathe, Sindara. Breathe deeply." It was his voice after all.

She flexed fingers that were stiff and aching, finally separating her hands and allowing her arms to slide limply to her sides. A pungent scent suddenly assaulted her nose. Her head snapped back. She batted at the source of the vile odor, but her coordination was not yet fully restored. "My God, what is that awful stench?" she demanded, her words sounding like a drunken slur.

Karan chuckled. "Only a restorative elixir meant to clear your mind."

"Clear my mind or make me vomit?" she cried out indignantly. Her speech was quickly becoming normal.

Physically shaking off lingering effects of the portal journey, she carefully controlled her breathing. Despite feeling a little unsteady, she slowly stood. Reaching out, she grabbed Karan's arm for extra support. Her vision was also clearing, and she fixed her eyes on Thehrund's face. "Are we really back?"

The prince again embraced her. "Welcome home to Ambracor, Lady Sindara."

The only light in the darkened corridor shone from a fat candle surrounded by a hurricane glass. Thehrund pulled an ornate iron key from his pocket and inserted it into the lock. When he glanced around, he grinned as her eyes widened in question.

"Yes, I still have the key to your apartment. I also kept everyone away except Marnee. She keeps her bedchamber here and ensures everything stays clean and orderly. During my lowest moments over these past years, this was the only place I could come for any sense of peace."

His revelation surprised Sindara. "Marnee knows?"

He answered with a short nod as he opened the carved door. Lowering his voice to just above a whisper, he said, "Other than Karan and Nagrand, our parents and Marnee are the only ones aware of my search. My parents, however, know nothing of the portal."

Thehrund set down the candle and lit a small oil lamp on a table. Reaching for Sindara, he drew her into his arms. Deep within its core, his body craved union with hers. He literally ached to make love to her. Until he could arrange their wedding, he would satisfy himself with whatever closeness he could achieve. Planting kisses on her hair and then seeking the sweetness of her mouth, he reveled in renewed wholeness that continued to seep into the most remote corners of his being.

Gently pushing her away, he smiled. "I want you to rest. Stay here until I send Karan or Nagrand for you in the morning."

"And you? Do you not also need to rest?"

Concern filling her eyes and lacing her voice delivered unparalleled comfort to his battered psyche. "I do, but I first must learn what has happened during my absence and make arrangements for announcing your return. Please trust my discretion in this matter."

"You have my trust," she murmured before rising on tiptoes to kiss him. "In case good manners have failed me, thank you for all you've done to bring me home."

"Good night, my love."

After he departed, she picked up the oil lamp and gazed at the familiar surroundings of the palace apartment she had used while planning their wedding. In some ways, that time seemed like just yesterday. In other ways, it felt like a lifetime ago. Ironic, that thought. She had indeed lived another life since she left this place.

Sindara pondered lingering questions regarding Garen's incomprehensible explanation of how she could have lived twenty-three years on one Earth-plane while only six years had passed in Ambracor. She marveled that Thehrund had spent those six years pursuing his quest.

Dismissing perplexing concepts related to quantum consciousness and divine intervention, she went straight to Marnee's chamber door and knocked lightly. Hearing no reply, she quietly opened the door, entered, and set the lamp on the nearest night table.

Affection flooded her as she gazed down at her maid's well-remembered face. Soft lines of age had deepened. Her long, thick, nighttime braid was now more white than gray. Her ample bosom rose and fell with each breath. Despite the passage of years, Sindara felt safe just knowing Marnee was near.

Leaning forward, Sindara placed a gentle hand on the older woman's shoulder. "Marnee," she whispered. "Marnee, wake up. Marnee?"

Marnee turned slightly. "Yes, child, what is it you need? What can Marnee get for you?"

Sindara could hardly avoid smiling. "I need a hug, Marnee. It's been so long since last you hugged me."

The older woman lay perfectly still and stared up at beloved features softly illuminated by the lamp's golden flame. She then squeezed her eyelids tightly shut. "It's only a dream, old woman," she told herself. "Wake up so you can see it's only a dream."

Sindara chuckled softly. "Marnee, it's quite safe to open your eyes. I am neither dream nor ghost."

Wrinkled eyelids popped open. Softly creased features showed utter disbelief. "An angel perhaps?"

Sindara sat down on the bed and gathered Marnee into an affectionate embrace. "Not an angel."

Pushing the younger woman away, Marnee gazed into eyes that she had never forgotten. "He found you? He actually found you?" she squeaked.

"He found me, saved my life in the process...in more ways than one, truth be told, and brought me home tonight."

A flood of happy tears burst forth and soaked the old woman's face. "My dear, sweet child! How I have longed to see your face!" She gulped in a shuddering breath. "Prince Thehrund swore you were alive and that he would find you. His parents didn't believe him, but I did. I prayed every day that he would succeed and that you wouldn't turn him away."

"Dear, dear Marnee," Sindara murmured in a trembling voice, "so much do I appreciate every single prayer."

"The prince? Where is he? Is he well?"

Sindara smiled. "He brought me here with orders to rest. He left after saying he needed to learn all that happened during his absence before he could take rest."

Marnee's quivering hand flattened gently against Sindara's cheek. "And the two of you?"

"I fear we shall cause you many headaches. We plan to marry as quickly as we can make suitable arrangements."

"Oh, child, such news brightens my very soul."

Disoriented after awakening from a sound sleep, a servant at the home of Cleotis Tamazor slowly dragged open one of the front doors. Upon seeing Prince Thehrund's commanding figure, he hurriedly apologized and led the prince inside to the private office used by the master of the house. He then rushed upstairs to rouse his employer.

Surprise was evident on Cleotis' face when he entered his office while tightening the belt of his long robe. "Your Highness," he said, concern tightening his features, "what can I do for you at such a late hour?"

Fatigue was beginning to show on the prince's face. "Minister Tamazor, you must forgive me for the unfortunate hour. I've just returned to Bracordia, and I must know the current political situation before asking of you a great favor."

Sindara's uncle shook off vestiges of sleep. "Should you not consult first with your father?"

Thehrund's head dipped slightly. "I prefer not to...not just yet."

Aware that King Hamund had sent a courier to summon the prince home, Cleotis was confused. "Did his dispatch not advise you that the reconvening of provincial governors has been advanced?"

"I have seen no dispatch."

"What? I don't understand. Artrian responded that he would send for you. We expected delays with the storms to the east, but I don't..."

Thehrund held up his hands. "I believe I can clarify any confusion, but I suggest you sit down first."

Fifteen minutes later, Cleotis gazed through his office window at moonlit gardens. Shaking his head, he turned to face the prince. "This is so much to absorb," he said. "You realize that I, too, defended you against rumors that you had gone slightly mad after Sindara...after Articene. I cannot believe my sister kept such a secret from me."

"Lady Liana did so at my bidding. The fewer people who knew meant less likelihood of discovery. Now that Sindara is safely returned, we plan to marry immediately. That alone should placate Father."

"Perhaps you should avoid revealing all the details. There's really no reason he must know everything, especially considering all his opposition. I recommend that you inform him only of your success and your intention to marry. We can then focus on Ambracor's security. Let details of finding her rest until circumstances are more settled."

"Your advice sounds much like what I would expect from Lord Artrian."

"Hmm," Cleotis mumbled thoughtfully. He definitely planned a serious discussion with his sister and her husband when they arrived.

Picking up the conversation, Thehrund explained his plan to have Nagrand escort Cleotis to Sindara's palace apartment the following morning. In the meantime, the prince would approach his father and inform him of her return.

As Thehrund departed the Tamazor home for the palace, one complication severely troubled him. According to Cleotis, Count Brandere was already in Bracordia with his family. Brandere was also pressuring the king to force Thehrund into marrying Breeneth by leveraging support for any proposed preemptive strikes against Breyal. He prayed his father had not already yielded to Brandere's demands.

King Hamund glanced up in stark surprise as his son strode purposefully into the family's private dining room. He might have smiled had it not been for his son's unusual expression. "Welcome home. You're just in time for breakfast."

"Thank you, Father. I must say it feels good to be home. May I speak with you over breakfast?"

Hamund nodded to a servant to set a place for the prince. "Considering the spring storms that hit Arvacon, you have come sooner than we expected. Your early arrival is fortuitous. I have critical matters to discuss with you."

Queen Narlina entered the dining room while apologizing for being late. "Thehrund! Good morning," she greeted, somewhat shocked by his unexpected presence.

Rising from his seat, Thehrund went to his mother and kissed her cheek. "It is a good morning, Mother," he said as he pulled a chair out for her. Retaking his seat, he turned his attention to his father.

"Thehrund," Hamund began, giving his son no chance to speak, "I understand you have again neglected your duties."

Thehrund's eyes darted toward his mother's face. When she only dropped her gaze, he sighed. "Your understanding is flawed. I promised to study plans for the protection of Ambracor, and that I have done."

Hamund was determined to control his temper. "You were searching for a dead woman."

Thehrund stared at his plate. "I also searched for Sindara," he admitted.

"At least you're man enough to admit the truth. I do credit you that."

"Father, please, that point we must discuss."

"Thehrund, I have no desire to hear anything you have to say about this ridiculous obsession of yours."

"Father..."

"Thehrund!" His father's voice sharply rose in anger. "The time is come when you must reconcile yourself with the truth and dedicate yourself to your duties for the sake of this country! That includes protecting Ambracor and ensuring there is a suitable heir to follow you!"

"Father, please listen..."

"You listen! You have nothing to say that I care to hear! Count Brandere has brought his family to Bracordia. He offered to withdraw opposition to any plans for defending Ambracor against Breyal if you will only marry one of his daughters. My son, they are both beautiful, and there is no shame in a marriage arranged to create political stability."

"I assume Brandere favors marriage to Breeneth?"

"He does. I agree with his preference."

"Father, I will not marry that woman or her sister. Neither has any place on the throne of Ambracor. Besides... "

"You know that I can command you to marry her." Hamund's voice sounded full of threat.

Narlina placed a hand on her husband's arm. "Hamund..."

Thehrund ignored his mother's attempt to calm his father. The gruff tones of his voice conveyed angry disdain. "What have you done, Father? Have you already promised I will marry one of Brandere's daughters? Have you?"

"And if I have?" Hamund roared back as his face flushed bright red.

Thehrund's blue eyes darkened with fury. "If that is so, then I refuse. Should you insist, understand me well. I will immediately renounce my claim to the throne. I will leave Bracordia, and Ambracor will have no Cobrandya heir to follow you. Tell me now. What have you done?"

Hamund leaned against the tall back of his chair. "You would never do such a thing," he snarled.

"I warn you, Father. Do not test me in this. You taught me to be a man of my word. Do not force me to demonstrate further proof that I am, especially on a morning when I meant to deliver glad news. Tell me now. I must know. What have you promised Brandere?"

Anger snapped in the king's eyes, but the vehemence in Thehrund's voice and the fiery gleam in his eyes were sure signs that he would live or die by his word. Hamund recognized he was precariously close to building an impassable divide between himself and his son.

"I have told Brandere only that I would consider his proposition and discuss the matter with you upon your return. I am, however, telling you that I expect an end to this damned search of yours. You must do as I deem necessary for the sake of this nation."

Thehrund's chest fell as he exhaled the tense breath he had held. He stared pointedly into his father's eyes. "Then your honor and integrity continue to merit a level of my respect. To a point. Understand well that I will stand by my word. Under no circumstances will I marry either of Brandere's daughters."

"Thehrund..." his father began with renewed threat saturating his voice.

"Father! For once, will you please just listen to what I have to say?"

Narlina cast a warning glance at her husband's hardening features. "Tell us, Thehrund."

The prince paused to take a long drink from a glass of freshly squeezed juice. He drew in a deep, calming breath. "I actually came to seek your advice on how best to proceed with what will surely be a shocking announcement."

Hamund leaned forward, intently studying his son's face. There was definitely an indescribable difference completely removed from their argument. Curiosity alleviated a small degree of stress. "Exactly what sort of announcement do you have in mind?"

"Father, I wish to announce that I shall wed. I also want the ceremony conducted immediately."

Astonished, Hamund gave a single shake of his head. "Do you expect me to believe that, after all this time and our discussion just now, you have finally decided to marry?"

"I decided long ago, Father. I found Sindara and brought her home."

"I don't believe you!" Hamund roared as he slammed his fists on the table. "Impossible!"

Narlina stared at her son. "Is this some sort of bad joke?"

"It seems we return to an old, familiar pattern. Why can the two of you not believe me? I have never before lied to you. I admit that I have, at times, told only half-truths, but never have I told an outright lie. As we speak, Sindara is here, in Bracordia, inside this palace."

Hamund glared intensely as he leaned forward. "How can this be? With my own eyes, I saw the Breyal lance impale her. How could she have possibly survived? Where has she been these past six years? How did you find her?"

"Father, explanations will take hours. With so many provincial governors already here and others arriving soon, I ask that, for just this once, you trust me until we have time to discuss all in detail. Accept that I have brought her home and that we wish to marry immediately."

"If this is true, why the hurry? After years of separation, perhaps you should wait."

Tenderness transformed Thehrund's face. "Mother, you will find Sindara remarkably unchanged. Already too much time has passed. I love her more than ever, and I feel more than blessed to possess both her love and her forgiveness."

Hamund slouched backward in his chair. If Sindara indeed still lived, her return presented a complex set of considerations. A politically advantageous marriage with Breeneth Brandere would no longer be possible. Sindara's return would halt discussions with Count Brandere, making the nobleman unwilling to terminate his vociferous stance that dangers of Breyal invasions were exaggerated. Beyond that, the very notion of Sindara being alive challenged his own accepted reality of what he had witnessed in battle. Still, if true, her startling return could help mend animosities between king and son while reinforcing the foundation of faith that had inspired his people since ancient times.

Wrestling with an unexpected onslaught of ideas, Hamund finally sighed. "A royal wedding might lift the spirits of our people, especially considering current circumstances. Thehrund, our people hold you in high esteem. They look to you with respect and admiration. The Varacor family is much loved throughout most of Ambracor. Sindara's return, when all thought she had died, would be perceived as no less than a miracle. If only I could bring myself to believe she still lives."

"She lives, Father. I told you years ago. Her life depended on my actions. I fulfilled the oath I made. Now, I shall finally carry through on my promises to her."

"When can I see her?" Hamund asked, still struggling to comprehend his son's revelation.

"I escorted her to her apartments last night. She was attacked by criminals two weeks ago, but Nagrand and I were able to fend them off. Karan cared for her injuries. Since then, everything has happened very quickly. She needed rest."

Studying his son, Hamund finally identified the difference he had noted earlier. Despite their bitter exchange, strain no longer lined Thehrund's face. His body was relaxed. A forgotten peacefulness marked his presence. "Karan and Nagrand were with you?"

"Their trust and friendship have been with me from the beginning. They accompanied me each time I left to search for her." Thehrund's rich voice revealed sincere appreciation for the loyalty shown by his friends.

Tears sparkled in Narlina's eyes. She actually felt in Thehrund what Hamund only observed. "Would you object if I go to welcome her home?"

Thehrund smiled for the first time. For a fleeting moment, Narlina wondered how long it had been since she had seen him smile so effortlessly.

"Mother, although her uncle may be with her by now, I'm quite sure Sindara would be delighted to see you."

After Narlina excused herself and left, Hamund inhaled deeply. "If this is all true, I wish with all my heart your marriage could begin without this damned crisis hanging over our heads. New plans must be developed to deal with escalating threats to Ambracor."

"Father, no matter what you may think, I have made time to review old plans and contemplate new strategies. After I left Sindara last night, I met with Cleotis Tamazor. He has already updated me regarding recent developments."

A long, uncomfortable silence ensued. "It is apparent my criticism of you has been more than unfair," Hamund finally admitted with profound regret.

"It has been unfair for a long time, Father; however, when I consider your perspective, I recognize the burdens you carry for Ambracor."

"Not just for Ambracor and our people. My primary concern has been and always will be you. No matter what, you are my son, and I love you. The misery you endured tore at my heart and filled me with fear and guilt."

Eyebrows met questioningly above Thehrund's straight, prominent nose. "I can understand you worried for my well-being, but why guilt?"

"Years ago, I sent you to Bramond despite your protests. I should have heeded the captain of my guard and taken a larger escort with me to Cahmdurn. Then, had I not been thrown from my horse, Sindara never would have dismounted to defend me. Every time you and I argued, I blamed myself for causing both her death and your anguish."

Words eluded Thehrund. So mired in his own guilt and sorrow, he had never considered the complex dimension of his father's emotions. More lessons learned from this ordeal. That was the first clear thought to penetrate his mind.

"Father, not once have I ever blamed you. Not a single time. My own actions that created this predicament remain a mystery to me. The best we can do is learn from what happened and focus on building a secure future for our nation."

"You too readily acquit me of fault. Even knowing your feelings toward Brandere's daughter, I seriously contemplated his offer of cooperation that would have bound you in marriage to someone you loathe. Had I followed through, I now realize that I would have surely lost you."

Thehrund swallowed against tightening in his throat. "I can say only that I am grateful to Creator God that we are spared that ordeal. We both would have lost far too much."

Morning sunlight invaded through sparkling clean glass. Admiring eyes gleamed like polished turquoise. Waving black hair shone with healthy highlights. Thehrund's handsome face, framed by his meticulously trimmed beard, held an expression of utter approval. "You look absolutely beautiful, Sindara."

Her luxuriously thick, light-brown tresses fell in soft curls around her shoulders. Golden-brown eyes glowed. Fair skin looked smooth, the only flaw being discoloration lingering from bruises suffered during the attack he and Nagrand had thwarted. Her gown had been sewn from supple silk the color of claret wine. The scooped neckline created a vibrant contrast of dark red fabric against ivory skin. Long sleeves finished just past slender wrists. The fitted bodice hugged the smooth lines of her body until stopping at her waist. From the wide waistband of woven gold and ruby threads, the long skirt fell in richly shimmering folds. The same fabric used for the waistband accented the hemline. Other than the crystal amulet, her only jewelry included her ruby engagement ring and a pair of ruby earrings received years earlier from Thehrund's parents as an engagement gift.

Masking her delight was impossible. "I remember how much you always liked this wine color. That's why I ordered this gown for our honeymoon."

"An entire barrel of wine could not be as intoxicating as I find you at this moment."

Sindara laughed. "I can hardly believe you just said that."

Approaching her, he gently caressed her cheek with the backs of his fingers. "Do you dislike such compliments?"

"Truthfully?" she asked, her eyes merrily twinkling with golden lights. "I cannot lie. From you, I love them."

His response was a satisfied chuckle. "Good. You must get used to them. Now, are you ready to face Father?"

Her expression softened. "I am, although I do wish my parents were here."

"Father already dispatched a courier requesting them to do all possible to expedite their arrival. He advised their presence is of the utmost urgency."

The prince tightly held Sindara's hand as he escorted her through palace corridors that had been cleared of all staff and guards. King Hamund had decided it best to keep Sindara's miraculous return a secret until her parents' arrival in the capital. Reaching double doors opening to the royal family's private apartments, Karan and Nagrand waited with Cleotis Tamazor. Sindara placed her right hand on Thehrund's arm as the prince escorted her inside, ahead of the other three men.

"Your Majesty," she greeted as she performed an elegant genuflect, "how glad is my heart to see you again, safe and well."

Years of training and practice at mastering his emotions abruptly failed. Tears ran unchecked down the king's face. He took her hands in his. Then, helping her stand, he wrapped his arms around her. "How does a man express the joy filling me at this moment? Welcome home, Sindara. Welcome home."

When Sindara stepped back from his embrace, Queen Narlina kissed her on each cheek. Their earlier reunion had also been one of happy tears. "Your king is thrilled that you are safely returned to us. I say with absolute certainty that no one is happier than our prince."

Blinking back tears, Sindara nodded and smiled tremulously, feeling completely unprepared for the king's reaction. She felt thoroughly relieved when Thehrund's hand gripped hers tightly as they moved to an elegant sitting area to discuss some of the wondrous events that had led to her homecoming.

Hearing Thehrund's parents describe life after her disappearance touched Sindara's heart. She had already heard accounts from both Karan and Nagrand detailing Thehrund's steadfast devotion since the momentous battle near Articene. King Hamund's description of his son during her absence added fresh and poignant observations from a parent's perspective. Those accounts, combined with her own experiences with the prince since their reunion, continued to inspire forgiveness and anticipation of a future they would build together.

Three hours later, palace aides fielded angry demands from Count Brandere regarding the unexplained delay of his scheduled meeting with King Hamund. Experienced in the fine art of tactfully managing visitors wishing audience with the king, aides extended apologies and recommended that the Bramondan governor return to his lodgings. Despite assurances that a carriage would be sent for the count once the king finished with a matter of unexpected urgency, Brandere had stubbornly remained, growing angrier as time passed.

One of the king's top advisors finally appeared in the opulent reception area. The stout, middle-aged aide had already been informed of Brandere's displeasure. "My Lord, King Hamund sends sincere regrets, but he must postpone your meeting until tomorrow morning."

"Tomorrow morning!" the count shouted. "We agreed to meet today! What is so damned important that Hamund would cancel with no warning? I demand an explanation!"

The advisor kept a steady voice and a stern manner despite the count's florid features and incensed posture. "Count Brandere, a serious family matter has arisen that no one could have foreseen. I assure you that the king will meet you tomorrow morning at ten o'clock."

"What sort of family matter? Tell Hamund I want an explanation now."

"Sir, I'm quite sure the king will explain when you meet. Now, if you will excuse me, His Majesty requires my assistance."

The advisor turned and, after instructing palace staff to cancel all other appointments for the day, departed without further comment. Brandere's eyes flashed furiously as he ranted to aides who politely addressed him only when necessary. Even the king's staff was caught off guard by the rare cancelation of an entire day's engagements with the king.

The following morning, Count Brandere arrived a full half hour early for his meeting with King Hamund. His surly demeanor was intended to intimidate aides who had fended him off the day before. He was offered refreshments along with assurances that the king was addressing an earlier obligation before receiving the count. Fortunately for the aides, the king's advisor appeared ten minutes early to escort Brandere to Hamund's private office.

"Count Brandere, good morning." The king stood to greet the nobleman, using his height to full advantage in establishing who was in control of the meeting. "I plead your understanding for the unfortunate cancelation of our appointment yesterday. A matter arose that required my personal, undivided attention. I sincerely apologize for the inconvenience."

Brandere eyed the king suspiciously. "I was under the impression our meeting was one of critical importance to you."

"Indeed," Hamund replied coolly. "That is why I beg your pardon. You know very well that I place high priority on keeping the integrity of my calendar. There are times, however, when one must allow for unforeseen circumstances."

At the king's invitation, Brandere sat in a chair directly in front of Hamund's desk. "I suppose even a monarch encounters occasional difficulties," the count commented, wary of a change in Hamund's bearing. "My disappointment yesterday stemmed from knowing that most of the other governors have arrived. I very much want to finalize our agreement prior to the emergency assembly of the Board of Governors."

"You refer to your offer to withdraw opposition to more aggressive recommendations expected for defending Ambracor's borders."

"Precisely," Brandere answered. Something in the king's manner prompted apprehension. "Breeneth is my oldest child, and she has yet to marry. She fell in love long ago with the prince and refuses to accept any other suitor. I'm certain you can understand a father's desire for his children's happiness."

Hamund propped an elbow on his desk and rested his chin thoughtfully on his closed hand. "Of course, just as I'm sure you understand that I must discuss this with my son. In the end, the choice of a bride should be his."

"With all due respect, our prince must bear in mind his responsibilities to Ambracor. I know that his engagement to Sindara Varacor ended with her tragic death. As the saying goes, life must go on."

"Indeed. Still, Thehrund has just returned to the capital. I wish to explain to him your offer."

Brandere stiffened. Rumors abounded regarding the prince's refusal to consider marriage after his fiancée's death. "You have authority to issue a royal decree commanding him to marry Breeneth."

Hamund remained quiet for several uncomfortable moments. "I do, but I respect my son enough to discuss the matter with him before issuing any such edict."

"I had the distinct impression when last we talked that you were in full accord with my proposal."

"I admit I found your offer most interesting, but I was quite clear that I needed to consider all implications."

"Should not your highest priority be the defense of Ambracor and the welfare of its people?" Brandere countered.

Hamund showed no emotion whatsoever. "Should your highest priority not be the same?"

"My highest priority goes first to my family," the nobleman declared.

"As does mine. Since we apparently agree on what matters most to each of us, we shall meet again before the Board of Governors reconvenes. That will allow me sufficient time to talk with my son. Now, if you will kindly excuse me, I do have other commitments."

Brandere could hardly believe the king's curt dismissal. Something had changed, but the count had no idea what. Facing his daughter would be more than unpleasant. She had accompanied him to Bracordia, confident she would stay and marry Thehrund. Brandere shuddered. Breeneth could be highly unpredictable as well as vengeful. She was also uniquely ingenious when it came to ferreting out information that she showed no qualms about using to coerce others, even her own father, into bending to her will.

Chapter Eleven

ARTRIAN VARACOR, HIS WIFE, AND four members of Arvacon's militia turned their horses onto the short lane leading to the home of Liana's brother. All felt chilled by penetrating dampness and tired from riding horseback for the better part of five days. Most main roads were passable, but some were either washed out or too muddy to travel by coach. The Varacors had already embarked on the remainder of their trip to the capital by horseback when they encountered the king's courier. They quickly hastened their pace to reach Bracordia.

"Liana!" Cleotis Tamazor exclaimed as he met his somewhat bedraggled sister just inside the double doors of his house. Embracing her affectionately, he shook his head at her husband. "Since when did the honorable Count Varacor start imposing forced marches on delicate females?"

Liana sneered good-naturedly at her brother. "Delicate? I may be four years older than you, but I can still outride you on any given day and under any conditions you choose. That, dear brother, you may take as a challenge. You've grown soft with all this fancy city living."

Artrian saluted his brother-in-law with an elegant bow of his head while removing leather riding gloves. "I would not argue if I were you. Your sister possesses all the vitality of a woman half her age. Now, on a different note, we met a king's messenger en route who advised our presence at the palace was urgently required. I hope you have space for unexpected guests. We need baths, a hot meal, and a good night's rest before we meet with Hamund."

Liana gazed at her brother's oddly cheerful face. "Where is your dear wife? And why in the world do you look as if you just stumbled over a pot of gold?"

"Julina went to be with Elsana since our first grandchild is due any day. Which reminds me: how is Erator's little one?"

Artrian laughed. "My grandson is barely three years old and already learning to sit in the saddle. Genuine Arvacon blood runs through that little one's veins."

Cleotis beamed. "That is good news. Now for the bad. I'll send you both upstairs to bathe and change clothes. Hot food will be waiting when you come down. After that, my coachman will drive us directly to the palace."

Artrian scowled. "The governors aren't scheduled to meet for several days yet. I believe Hamund should be quite satisfied that we made the journey as quickly as we did. What could be so urgent that it cannot wait until morning?"

Cleotis carefully controlled his features. "I know how tired you must be, but it is necessary that you go to the palace this evening."

Liana studied her brother's expression. "Could anything honestly be so urgent?"

"Sister, talks with Count Brandere have not gone well. The count even attempted a bit of extortion in exchange for withdrawing his objections to offensive tactics."

Artrian's thick eyebrows lifted. "Extortion? What sort of extortion?"

Cleotis shook his head. "Brandere demanded that Thehrund marry Breeneth. Much has happened, though, and I am bound by my word to leave all explanations to the king. Go now and change. After that, you can eat before we leave."

Upstairs, Artrian sat on a chair and leaned forward while pulling on warm stockings. Shaking his head, he commented on having fresh appreciation for clean, dry clothing. Liana barely smiled as she brushed long hair before tightly twisting it and securing it in a thick circle above the nape of her neck. When her husband stood, he came to her and rested his chin on top of her head.

"What?" he asked as he gazed at her pensive reflection.

"Cleotis is hiding something."

Artrian grinned. "He's just nervous awaiting his first grandchild."

Liana moved away and slid her feet into slippers to go down for a quick bite before leaving again. "Remember. He's my brother. I know him well. What do you think he meant by leaving all explanations to the king?"

Artrian lifted long locks of graying hair up and back over his shoulders. "I prefer waiting to find out. I have worries enough concerning Thehrund. I had hoped to spend the night here and have time in the morning to seek Cleotis' advice on how I might approach Hamund."

Liana's attempted smile fell short as she used her hands to smooth wrinkles from her husband's woolen jacket. "I suppose we should go eat and get this over with. I feel exhausted, and I long for a warm, dry bed."

Reaching Bracordia's royal palace, Artrian and Liana exchanged glances that were both puzzled and concerned. Two of the king's aides already awaited their arrival. Cleotis Tamazor's coachman handed the Varacors' travel bags to a palace servant. When Liana turned to question her brother, he only shrugged and promised to ensure their escort and their horses were properly accommodated. Before climbing back into his coach, he hugged his sister. "I shall return tomorrow. Good night."

Following aides through the palace, the Varacors needed only seconds to realize they were being escorted directly to the royal family's private quarters. Artrian's face drew into a solemn mask. Dread invaded with uncomfortable certainty. Hamund must have finally discovered their deeds in covering for Thehrund. Hamund had long been a good friend. Although respected for being a reasonable man, the king did possess a formidable and occasionally unpredictable temper that Arvacon's count preferred to avoid.

Artrian and Liana were ushered into the spacious foyer of the king's residential apartments. A butler bowed and guided the couple into the formal parlor. He advised that the king would arrive shortly to greet them.

When Hamund appeared, Narlina was at his side, her hand resting formally on his forearm.

"Artrian, how glad I am you have arrived safely. Liana, although you look a bit fatigued, you are as lovely as ever. I understand spring storms to the east have created havoc for travelers. Please sit down."

Artrian forced a smile, uncertain how to respond to Hamund's apparent good mood as they all settled comfortably. "Liana and I decided days ago to pack a few essentials and make the remainder of the trip on horseback. Our coach will follow as soon as the roads are dry enough."

Liana smiled charmingly. "We actually met your courier on the road. We hastened our journey as best we could."

Servants brought in a silver platter with an attractive assortment of hors d'oeuvres and another with stemmed glasses and a bottle of wine. Each tray was placed on a carved table trimmed with elaborate designs in gold leaf.

"You must be exhausted," Narlina commented. "So much has happened of late. Hamund and I regretted learning that you stopped at your brother's house instead of coming directly to the palace. Had matters not been so pressing, we never would have insisted that you come this evening."

Artrian breathed out a heavy sigh. "We planned to stay the night with Cleotis so we might be fresh and rested for a morning meeting."

Hamund stared at his old friend. "No doubt you also wanted to work out ideas with Cleotis as to how to go about explaining all the secrets you've kept regarding my son's...shall we say...obsession."

Caught. Artrian faced Hamund squarely. "Hamund, I sincerely value our friendship. Placing that friendship in jeopardy was not a decision lightly taken. Before you say another word, you must know that I stand by my choice to support Thehrund. He showed great courage coming to me at a time when I was furious with him for what happened to Sindara. Liana and I listened to him when you would not."

Liana gave the king no chance to respond. "My husband has long agonized over how it might eventually affect your opinion of us, but Artrian and I could not turn our backs on Thehrund. We believed he needed to work through whatever it was that drove him for so long. No matter what happened or why, our daughter loved him."

Hamund's penetrating gaze failed to intimidate the Varacors. Few in all of Ambracor would face him with such aplomb. Thoughtfully scratching his temple, the king paused before responding, "Artrian, what happened six years ago has severely tried us all. You and Liana have coped remarkably well with regard to Sindara. Narlina and I have not done so well with our son. Adding to our challenge, Thehrund has now presented his mother and me with an inexplicable conundrum. I've just learned that even Marnee and two of my son's friends, one a priest no less, have also plotted with him to undertake what I deemed pathetically hopeless searches. And for what? A young woman I saw killed right in front of me."

Liana reached for her husband's hand. Stubborn light shone from her eyes. "Your Majesty, we respect you more than we can say. We know how you encouraged Thehrund to shift his attention to issues critical to our nation. We are also well aware of the values you instilled in him."

"Values our son did not always take to heart," Hamund interrupted.

Artrian lifted his head in a prideful gesture of conviction. "He was a young man who made a terrible mistake. That error tormented him more than you were willing to acknowledge. As dear as I've always held our friendship, you must understand. I willingly admit deep regret for the times I misled you, but I have no intention of apologizing."

Hamund glanced at his wife. She had told him to expect exactly such a response from Artrian. For generations, the Varacor family had maintained its reputation for faith and integrity. Such honor was more than virtue, especially in troubled times such as they now faced. Their brand of forthright honesty served as safe harbor for those with sufficient strength of character to respect and appreciate it.

"Artrian, in all honesty, I never expected an apology. You live according to your principles and willingly face any consequences." Hamund stood. Walking to the fireplace, he stared a moment at logs burning brightly. Finally looking back, his face was solemn. "I consider it both good fortune and blessing to have at least one friend like you. I am not immune to making mistakes, and you have perhaps saved me from making the worst mistake of my entire life."

Artrian and his wife exchanged yet another perplexed glance. Artrian also stood. "I am not certain I understand your meaning."

"Perhaps I can clarify matters for you." Thehrund's resonant voice sounded from the arched doorway opposite the fireplace.

Turning, Artrian froze. Attired in a beautiful gown of wine-colored silk, his daughter stood motionless by the prince's side. Her hair, capturing glints of golden light, framed the almost ethereal features of the child for whom he had so sorely grieved. Shapely lips formed a delicate, trembling smile. Those amber eyes, so much like her mother's, glistened with tears.

"Sindara..." Her name spilled forth from both her parents at once.

With arms outstretched, she rushed straight into her father's arms. Tears slid down Artrian's cheeks with joyous abandon as he held her so tightly she could hardly breathe. "Sindara, my sweet baby girl..." he murmured, finally daring to loosen his embrace long enough to gaze into eyes he'd thought never to see again.

Suddenly remembering his wife, he turned to where she now stood in front of the sofa. Tears glazed Liana's eyes as she stared at her daughter in mute shock. Her breathing was rapid and shallow. She had surrendered to nothing more than faith and intuition upon placing her trust in Thehrund's account of voices that had spoken to him. She had given him her support, and she had prayed.

Several steps carried Sindara from her father's embrace to her mother. She raised her hands to cradle her mother's face. "He came for me, Mother. Thehrund found me and brought me home. He told me how you and

Father helped him. I cannot express how much I appreciate all you did for him or how much I love you."

Liana wrapped shaking arms around her daughter. She laughed and cried simultaneously. She reached up and stroked silken hair. She kissed her daughter's cheeks and then her hands. She shook her head back and forth, words lost in an explosion of sheer elation. Fearing she might simply faint, she sat, pulling Sindara to the sofa with her.

"Just let me look at you," she whispered, lifting her daughter's hands to her lips. She inhaled a deep breath. "You are exactly as I remember."

Artrian, feeling weak at the knees, joined them on the sofa. "Your mother is right. It has been six years, yet you look as if not a day has passed...exactly the same as when last we saw you."

Sindara smiled and wiped a stray tear from her cheek. "Thehrund would tell you that I have changed. He made the rather startling observation that his hair is now longer than mine."

Liana gently combed trembling fingers through her daughter's curling tresses. She quietly laughed. "I believe Thehrund might be right about that."

Her mother again embraced her, as did her father. As both held her close between them, Artrian prayed aloud, offering heartfelt thanks for the warm, living, breathing daughter miraculously returned to them. As he prayed, he realized that Thehrund, Hamund, and Narlina knelt around them, joining the prayer of praise, joy, and love.

Dark waves were elegantly arranged and held by golden combs. Smooth skin, the color of fine alabaster, created a perfect canvas for ruby lips, high cheekbones, arched eyebrows, and almond-shaped eyes of darkest brown. Her finely detailed gown accented the fullness of her breasts and the tiny line of her waist. Her beauty was renowned in her home province, where suitors continuously sought her attention, lavishing her with compliments and expensive gifts.

Inside the luxurious suite of rooms occupied by Count Brandere and his entourage, Ingnan Brandere faced his oldest child and hoped to avoid the inevitable eruption of temper whenever events disappointed her. "Breeneth, Hamund did not reject the offer. He said the prince had just returned home and that he would explain our proposal to him. That is far from unreasonable."

Anger seethed from her very presence. "I told you, Father. You were to return yesterday with Hamund's agreement to the wedding between Thehrund and me. You failed yet again."

"I am to meet with Hamund again before the governors reconvene. I will issue my final demand. You must realize that the king has little choice. When he faces the Board of Governors, he knows support from Bramond Province will be essential for any strategy he may champion. The time is exactly right to force him to bend to our will."

Breeneth's cold, stormy expression caused the count to shiver. "Will you attend the reception at the palace?"

"Of course. Hamund will have no chance to ignore me or the offer I've made."

"Good. Since Mother is ill, I shall accompany you. That gives me two days to prepare to see Thehrund again."

"Breeneth..."

"Father, you *will* take me."

He shivered again at her icy stare. Whenever that look crept into her eyes, he could almost believe some of the rumors about wicked behavior that had occasionally reached his ears. Shaking off the thought that was both disturbing and frightening, he sighed. "I scheduled our coach to leave at five." As an afterthought, he added, "Look at the positive side. Perhaps this surprise invitation is a good omen for us."

Inside the palace, the entire roster of servants and staff had been galvanized to welcome nearly eighty guests. The grand affair was announced with little notice. Handwritten invitations were delivered to visiting governors and other officials. Kitchen chefs and assistants rushed to begin preparing the immense variety of appetizers, meats, side dishes, and desserts to be served at the elegant affair. Servants scurried around the spacious banquet hall to ensure tables and chairs shone with fresh polish before arranging exquisite settings of silverware, crystal, and china, all adorned with the royal crest. An ambience of refined elegance would welcome the king's guests.

Inside her apartments, Sindara sat quietly by a window. In her hand, she held the crystal Garen and Aminta had given her. She had gazed at the silver-white circle for several minutes. Finally, a swirl of iridescent colors settled into Kendra's image.

"Sindara, I miss you, but I'm glad you look so well. And happy."

"I am happy, Kendra. Thehrund's father will issue a formal announcement tonight. Thehrund and I will marry tomorrow."

"So soon?" Kendra asked in amazement. "He was serious then, wasn't he?"

"He was."

"I'm glad you sensed my attempt to contact you. You must be especially careful. In meditation, I saw evil very close to you. Although I can't explain, I feel that same evil is connected to the battle where you were hurt."

Sindara nodded. She felt it, too. "My senses seem to be awakening in a new and profound way. I will be watchful. I promise."

Kendra sighed. "This is astonishing. Nothing I've found indicates scrying can be used for two-way communication. I still need to improve on the concentration it requires. I'll meditate and send positive energy to help keep you strong. I love you, Sindara. Stay safe."

Sindara smiled. "I love you, too, dear Kendra."

The image faded from the face of the crystal. Sindara admired the precious gift angels had said to keep close at all times. The gold frame of the amulet had been fashioned to wear as either a brooch or a pendant. She typically wore it on the sturdy gold chain Thehrund had used to carry her engagement ring. At the king's banquet, however, she would pin the crystal to the inside of her petticoats. Prudence seemed wise as she decided to heed Kendra's warning and her own intuition.

"Sindara? Are you almost ready?" her mother asked as she crossed the room and caressed her daughter's cheek.

"I am, Mother. I just need to finish one small detail."

"You're so quiet. Is everything all right? I worry you might have misgivings about marrying so soon after your return."

"This is what I want, Mother, although I confess I wish we didn't have to wait until after the conferences to have a few days to ourselves." Sindara's features were remarkably tranquil. "Mostly, I am still overwhelmed by all that has happened. Home never meant more to me than it does now. I have you and Father again, and Thehrund has quite astounded me with his devotion."

Liana smiled thoughtfully. "I think back on the times your father and I had such conflicting feelings about him."

"Why did you help him?"

"An interesting question." Pausing, Liana considered the array of emotions that had flooded her after Articene. "Part of me wanted to strike out at him. That part was full of pain I thought would never cease. Some part of my heart recognized the truth he told us. Despite every reason to shut him out of our personal lives, instinct refused to allow me that path. There were occasions when doubts crept in, but they were always driven away by one thing. I believed him."

"And Father?"

"He would phrase it differently, but I believe his answer would be much the same."

The tip of her right index finger lightly tracked across the curves of gold holding the ruby in place on her engagement ring. "I am thankful that you lent him such unwavering support."

"Thehrund quickly earned our respect with his mission to find you. With the benefit of hindsight, I believe his ordeal gave him more than the chance to save your life and reconcile with you. Credit intuition again, but I think the trial strengthened his character and personal resolve. It also gave him valuable experience that may well mean survival for Ambracor."

Sindara stood and embraced her mother. "Let us hope that both Thehrund and I will have the courage to face whatever tribulations lie ahead."

Liana blinked against sudden tears. "Trust Creator God and the gifts he has given you. Protect and cherish your love. You will overcome whatever obstacles cross your path."

Carriages drawn by matched teams of horses rolled beneath the porte-cochere and waited while liveried palace attendants assisted guests from their coaches. Gentlemen, attired in long, tailored, formal coats, escorted ladies wearing fashionable gowns in shimmering silks and glistening satins. Guests were guided through towering doors of polished brass where gilded invitations were exchanged for token gifts wrapped in glossy blue paper tied with silver ribbons.

King Hamund rarely entertained on a grand scale. He preferred smaller, more intimate gatherings. The unexpected invitation to this palace banquet had initiated rampant speculation. Had the king decided that pressures over the past few months merited a chance for provincial leaders to gather under less stressful conditions? Did he hope to inspire delegates to mingle and thus promote greater cooperation once emergency meetings began in earnest? Or, as some hinted, could there be a significant announcement in the offing? Whatever the case, the growing crowd hummed with anticipation.

Breeneth Brandere commanded admiring glances from nearly every man and woman waiting in the anteroom to be escorted to reserved tables. Her gown of dark brown satin dipped low to reveal the ample cleavage of her breasts. Despite the early-spring chill, her dress was sleeveless. Ivory silk gloves, delicately embroidered with fine gold threads, created an elegant line that ended just above her elbow. Her tiny waist was accented by the close-fitting bodice of her dress. Its skirts were not overly full. Instead, the narrow bell shape made her petite stature appear taller. A double strand of pearls graced the column of her neck, and drop earrings boasted pearls accented with diamonds.

As she scanned the anteroom where drinks and appetizers were being offered to visitors, her brilliant smile drew attention from the rapid movement of her dark eyes. King Hamund and Queen Narlina stood just beyond granite columns supporting tall arches opening onto the banquet hall. Odd, Breeneth thought. If Thehrund had indeed returned home, why was he not with his parents as they personally greeted guests? When her father led her forward, she wished she had brought her favorite talisman. With that rune-engraved stone in hand to magnify her senses, she could better detect any sign of insincerity or deception in the welcome as well as any compliments from the gracious royal couple.

A short while later, surrounded by opulence she craved for her own, Breeneth sat beside her father near the front table where the king would dine with his family and closest advisors. She noted the king's table was set for nine with chairs on the far side only. Frowning, she dreaded the boring political remarks that would likely precede dinner and probably end the affair.

The drone of numerous voices annoyed her. Constant noise in this unfamiliar place dulled her perceptive abilities. Conversation with her dinner companions was an even greater annoyance, but she responded to inane comments and platitudes with forced grace. She would grant her father one credit. He managed social graces quite well with people she considered boorish and inferior.

In a guarded corridor opposite the hall's main entry, Sindara waited with Thehrund. The prince looked more handsome than ever. The fit of his luxurious velvet coat elegantly outlined broad shoulders and muscular arms. The rich royal blue enhanced the brilliant sapphire hue of eyes shining with renewed vitality. The belt he wore was elaborately crafted from overlapping scales of gleaming gold and silver that accentuated the breadth of his chest and trim line of his waist. Elegant toggle closures of gold punctuated the center line of his coat. Black leggings hugged power-ful, well-defined legs and tucked into the tops of polished black boots.

He held both her hands close to his heart. "Sindara, I'm so sorry. I received word that Breeneth arrived with her father. That is something I neither expected nor wanted. What I do want is for you to be sufficiently confident in my love to face her."

Gazing into his eyes, she smiled reassuringly. Her intuitive awareness was definitely burgeoning in ways she was only beginning to comprehend. She did not simply hear his words of love and reassurance. She actually felt them in a curious, physical way. "Thehrund, do not fret. I'm fine. When you could have had her anytime you wanted, you spent years searching for me. I shall rely on that kind of love to make this a happy evening for us both."

As distress eased, pride beamed from the prince's face. "Sindara, you already make this evening happy for me."

Inside the banquet hall, a captain of the king's guard requested that all stand as His Royal Majesty King Hamund prepared to join the gathering and be seated. Queen Narlina walked at her husband's left side. Behind them followed Count Artrian Varacor, his wife Liana, and State Minister Cleotis Tamazor. The royal entrance was completed by Sir Nagrand Mezden, Reverend Master Karan Mezden, and an honor guard of four uniformed officers. Reaching the table, the king's party was seated, leaving two empty chairs to Hamund's right.

King Hamund stood at his place and jovially smiled at the gathering. His voice, low and pleasant, carried easily throughout the hall designed for excellent acoustics. "Ladies and gentlemen," he began, "I regret the dire circumstances that bring us together this week. Your presence in Bracordia represents significant sacrifice from each of you. I will, however, leave security and defense discussions for the approaching assembly of Ambracor's Board of Governors."

The king smiled thoughtfully as if drawing his audience into personal conversation. "Tonight gives us cause to celebrate the way of life for which we stand. This is a night for us to reflect on life, faith, and even miracles. Although always a man of faith, I have occasionally faltered. Especially tonight, I remind us all that Creator God blesses us in ways beyond measure. Despite the dangers we face, life has a way of marching on. How it marches depends on how we choose to follow its path.

"Continuing that thought of life marching on, I stand before you as a man exceedingly proud of his son. Prince Thehrund has proven himself a man of far greater faith than his father. His courage, devotion, perseverance, and sense of duty deliver great pride to both his parents."

Breeneth glanced questioningly at her father. His eyebrows lifted. Relieved that Hamund had likely demanded his son's agreement to marry, Brandere dared a smile. After all, their assigned seats were directly in front of the king's table. Both father and daughter returned their attention to the king.

Hamund continued, "This very week, my son has introduced me to the existence of miracles in our own day and age. Our hearts are filled with happiness that Queen Narlina and I invite you to share. Please stand and join me as I welcome and congratulate my son, Prince Thehrund, on his upcoming wedding."

Shocked gasps swelled throughout the hall as the stately prince entered the banquet room with his beaming fiancée, her hand placed formally on his arm. To a gathering crescendo of applause, Thehrund escorted Sindara to the front of the king's table, where both bowed first to his father, then to the audience. Nearly everyone present had known Count Varacor's daughter and had immediately recognized her. All had heard of her heroic death at the hands of Breyal raiders. Applause quickly faded as the gathering shared a variety of mixed reactions, including shock, awe, and unrestrained curiosity.

The prince's baritone voice addressed the guests. "Thank you for your welcome. I appear before you as a blessed man. During years of mourning and journeys to faraway places, I searched based on information from a sacred source. My efforts were rewarded when I finally found the miracle of whom my father spoke, my bride-to-be, Sindara Varacor. I humbly ask you to welcome her home and to pray your good blessings for our upcoming marriage."

The prince glanced down at Sindara. "Welcome home, my love." He then lightly kissed her forehead to near-deafening applause.

Later that evening, Sindara stood by a window. Clouds outside were clearing to reveal a full moon. Thehrund sat on the sofa in her apartment and thoughtfully regarded her with admiration. "You were brilliant this evening. Beautiful and elegant. Your poise in the greeting line after dinner was nothing short of astounding."

"You refer to Breeneth?"

Breathing out a heavy sigh, he nodded. "I honestly hoped never to see her again. I would have done anything to protect you from having to meet her."

Sindara crossed the room and knelt in front of him. Taking two of his braids in her hand, she kissed gold bands binding the ends. When she looked up, her gaze was steady. "Thehrund, trust me when I say I'm glad for the chance to finally see her face to face."

"Not just in the reception line, I noticed several times the way she looked at you. Most people were shocked to learn you were alive, but her reaction was intensified by absolute disbelief and stark, cold fury. What I saw causes me great concern."

Making no move to rise from the floor, Sindara considered how to respond. He would need to hear the truth soon. Very soon. She would wait until after their wedding. He deserved time, no matter how short, free of guilt and worry where Breeneth was concerned. A thought popped into her mind. "Wait. I shall be right back."

Knocking at Marnee's door, she was glad to see her maid still up and dressed. "Marnee, please summon Karan. Ask him to come right away. Tell him I will ask him to do something for Thehrund and me, but he is not to question my request. I will find time tomorrow to speak to him alone."

If Marnee thought the request strange, she said nothing and left immediately.

Back in the sitting room, Sindara again knelt before her solemn fiancé. "Tell me you're not having doubts about the wedding tomorrow."

"Doubts? About our wedding? How could you even suggest such a thing?" He reached for her hands, drawing her up to the sofa. "About marrying you, I have no doubts whatsoever. I do, however, think it odd that you asked Father not to announce the actual wedding date. Perhaps you're the one seeking possible escape."

Her features mirrored his earlier solemnity. "Never. You, dear prince of mine, promised to marry me. I have every intention of holding you to your promise."

Her response lightened his mood. "I do love you, Sindara. If only you could know how much I missed you."

She grinned mischievously. "Prove it. Kiss me now because you must leave soon. I need rest for a momentous day tomorrow."

Barely restraining laughter, he caught her in a possessive embrace and covered her mouth with his. He thrilled at her response as she seemingly melted against him. The passion with which she returned his kiss sparked sensations that flowed through his veins with the heat of molten lava. He literally groaned when he heard a knock at the door.

Breaking their embrace, she struggled to catch her breath. Momentarily unable to speak, she held up a finger, signaling him to wait while she got up to greet the late visitor.

Edging the door open, she smiled. "Thank you for coming so quickly. Come in."

"Karan?" Thehrund asked, his voice huskier than usual. "I didn't expect you."

"I sent for him," Sindara said. "I knew you were worried about the encounter with Count Brandere's daughter. I thought it wouldn't hurt to have Karan pray Creator God's protection on both of us."

Thehrund shot a questioning glance at Karan, but his friend smiled and replied, "Prayers for protection are never unwarranted when ill will might be near. Considering the extent of your future wife's religious education, I advise you to accustom yourself to such spontaneous requests."

Masking curiosity, Karan noted fleeting gratitude in Sindara's eyes. He then instructed the couple to sit together on the sofa and hold hands. Placing his hands above theirs, he chanted an ancient prayer requesting Creator God to dispatch his angels to keep the couple safe from all harm or illness and to shield them from all evil intent.

As Marnee later helped her undress and prepare for bed, Sindara carefully unpinned her crystal from the folds of her petticoat. During dinner, she had felt the power embedded in the jewel and silently prayed praise and thanks. Sliding it onto its chain and slipping the chain over her head, she instantly felt the surge of protective energy. Crawling under warm blankets, she whispered more prayers for her family, the king and queen, her people, and, most of all, her beloved prince.

By mid-morning, the palace's chapel entrance had been adorned with colorful sprays of fresh flowers from Bracordia's famed glass gardens. Bright sunshine had chased away a light morning shower. Nature's music of chirps, peeps, and twitters cheerfully floated on light breezes. Fresh air filled Thehrund's lungs as he paused to admire the beauty of the day he had long awaited.

"Good morning, Your Highness," Nagrand greeted as he trotted across thick, greening grasses. "You look to be in high spirits this fine day."

"Nagrand, good morning," the prince returned. "It seems the heavens smile down upon me today."

Falling into step beside the prince, Nagrand grinned. "We found her just when I'd finally grown accustomed to traveling via whirlwind to search for your phantom bride."

Thehrund chuckled. "Are you not satisfied with all of the action and adventure lying before us here in our own world?"

Nagrand gazed at the walkway leading to the chapel. Blond hair streamed down to conceal his profile. "You must admit our journeys through the portal held a different kind of excitement."

"True," Thehrund readily agreed, "but I'm glad to be home. I belonged in none of the worlds we visited."

Nagrand laughed and slapped the prince on the shoulder. "And so we both are glad for home, my friend. Now, let us go make a married man of you."

The interior of the chapel was quiet in advance of the small private ceremony. At the front of the center aisle, Karan spoke with Lord Artrian and Cleotis Tamazor. Behind them, the single granite step up to the altar curved across the width of the chapel. Its center section was padded and covered in supple leather for the comfort of those kneeling for prayer or ceremony. The altar itself had been crafted centuries earlier from light-gray granite. A silver silk runner covered the top and draped down the sides. Behind and high above the altar, sunlight flooded through intricately fitted sections of beveled, leaded glass, creating a veritable shower of rainbows to enliven the sedate, elegant interior of the chapel.

As Nagrand and the prince headed from the narthex to greet the other men, female voices echoed from the corridor that ran along the far right side of the chapel. Thehrund paused close to the passage to listen to Marnee.

"Lady Liana, I told her she has no cause for worry. I'm confident he will not be repulsed by those scars. The prince will love her no less."

"Thank you, Marnee. You know that as well as I, but scars such as those can be troubling. Every woman wishes to look her best for her new husband," Liana said quietly.

Marnee's stronger voice carried further than Lady Liana's. "She wants this day to be perfect for him. She worries that the scars will remind him of the battle at Articene."

Liana sighed. "I'm sure they'll both be fine. Brides are always nervous on their wedding days. Considering all she has overcome already, I pray she might set aside such concerns and enjoy today as she deserves."

Hearing the women approach the end of the corridor where it curved into the narthex, Thehrund turned and hurried to join Karan and the others. He did not want the ladies to know he had overheard them.

Soon, King Hamund and Queen Narlina entered the chapel. The king's personal escort remained outside to safeguard the entrance. Lord Artrian departed the chapel's nave while the intimate gathering settled on thickly padded pews at the front.

Karan had disappeared into the small sacristy for a final personal prayer before beginning the ceremony. Returning to the altar alight with flickering candles, he nodded for Thehrund to take his place at the front of the aisle. Karan then rang an elegant bell cast of gold, its tinkling notes signaling Lord Artrian to escort his daughter into the chapel proper.

When Thehrund raised expectant blue eyes, the image he beheld prompted a quiet, involuntary gasp. As his heart throbbed within his broad chest, he reverently regarded every detail of her appearance. Producing a smile for her was impossible. His long, handsome face revealed pure adoration rising from the depths of his soul.

Sindara's appearance could easily be described as magical...wholly ethereal. The fluid fabric of her golden gown flowed around her figure, enhancing feminine curves with a shimmering cascade of narrow pleats falling from the high waistline just beneath the fullness of her breasts. The bodice and sleeves were fashioned from ivory silk beneath an overlay of intricate gold lace. Her hair was pulled into a cluster of curls at the back of her head and adorned with combs studded with diamonds and rubies.

Amber eyes met and held the prince's gaze. How handsome he looked in his ceremonial uniform jacket tailored in a vivid shade of purple lavishly trimmed with gold braid. He also wore the crown distinguishing him as heir to Ambracor's throne. Her sensually shaped mouth spread into a smile meant for him only. Sindara's breathing quickened in rhythm with her accelerating heartbeat. Each step carried her closer to the man who had not merely spoken words of love. The man awaiting her had spent years proving his devotion despite his family's disapproval. Blood raced through her veins as she anticipated marital bonds now assuming far greater magnitude than the couple would have known without the battle at Articene and Thehrund's years of unwavering quest.

With practiced elegance, Artrian Varacor placed his daughter's hand in Prince Thehrund's. The distinguished nobleman bowed in esteem for his soon-to-be son-in-law. "I deliver into your care my beloved daughter. My wife and I pray Creator God's blessings upon your union."

Thehrund met the count's direct gaze and responded respectfully, "I accept your daughter's hand with profound gratitude for the gift she is to me. I gratefully receive your blessings for the life Sindara and I will share."

When Thehrund's eyes shifted to regard his bride's expression, he felt instantly spellbound. One corner of his mouth lifted slightly. His breath caught at her image before him. Momentarily paralyzed, he could do naught but lose himself in the glorious love glowing from her eyes. He consciously forced himself to breathe again when Karan's voice interrupted his private reverie and bade him face the altar.

Clad in blue and silver vestments, Karan initiated the relatively simple ceremony that would bind the lives of the couple before him. In a solemn voice, he issued brief reminders of all they prepared to undertake. In the eyes of Creator God, their union would make of them a whole, requiring mutual love, honor, and respect until the end of their days. Their marriage would serve as the foundation for them to share the many joys and tribulations to be found on their path through life. At the last, he instructed the couple to face one another.

Sindara lifted gleaming eyes to meet Thehrund's. Soft and steady, her voice held not a single note of reservation. "Thehrund Cobrandya, I pledge to you all that I am in this life as I accept with full heart and soul the blessing of our union according to Creator God's teachings. To you only, I will give my whole self in honor, respect, support, and love throughout the days of our life together. This I most solemnly promise."

Banishing years of sorrowful mourning, her words infused Thehrund with an indescribable rush of energy. Powerless to resist the impulse, he lifted her hands to trembling lips. Drawing a quivering breath, he thought it yet another miracle when he heard the firmness of his own voice. "Sindara Varacor, I pledge to you all that I am in this life as I accept with full heart and soul the great blessing of our union according to Creator God's teachings. To you alone, I will give my whole self in honor, respect, support, and love throughout the days of our life together. This is my most solemn promise."

Together, the couple knelt and lifted their voices in unison. "In the presence of our beloved Creator God, his priest, and those gathered with us as witnesses, we declare our acceptance of vows that now bind us into the sacred union of marriage."

Thehrund stood first and then offered his hands to Sindara. Steadied by his firm grasp, she gracefully rose amid rustling yards of shining silk lamé. Following the priest's instructions, Nagrand stepped forward and held out an engraved tray of crystal with a single prong over which rested two gold bands. Karan stepped from behind the altar and prayed a blessing over the rings to be worn as symbols of the couple's nuptial vows. The newlyweds watched as each reverently slid a golden band into place on the left ring finger of the other.

The rite ended when Karan held one hand above and the other below the couple's joined hands. "In accordance with my authority as Creator God's fervent and humble servant, I pray long life filled with abundant blessings upon Thehrund Cobrandya and Sindara Varacor. From this day forth, may they undertake in joy the privileges now granted through their duly consecrated union."

As Karan stepped away, Thehrund extended his arms to draw his bride into a powerful embrace. He showed no embarrassment when tears escaped the corners of his eyes. Slowly, he brought his face toward hers and captured lips awaiting the kiss that sealed the commitment they had just pledged.

Moments later, King Hamund approached the altar where his son and new daughter-in-law awaited. The looming threat of war had prompted the cautious monarch to break longstanding tradition. A public ceremony would certainly be held according to custom, but Hamund felt great need to formalize all aspects of his son's new status in life. The king smiled with genuine pleasure before bestowing kisses on the cheeks of each newly-wed. He then watched as, with her hand firmly held within Thehrund's possessive grasp, Sindara again knelt.

Continuing his dignified, priestly role, Karan came forth with a thick cushion of violet satin balanced on outstretched hands. Upon the pillow rested a diamond-studded ring of gold filigree, its intricate designs testimony to the skill of the ancient craftsman who had fashioned it.

"Sindara Varacor Cobrandya," Hamund spoke in a firm voice, "you bring to the House of Cobrandya the dignity and integrity long associated with Ambracor's House of Varacor. As wife of Thehrund, prince by birth and duly crowned heir to the throne of Ambracor, do you now accept to share responsibilities that are integral elements of both his heritage and his duty?"

"I do." Her melodious voice held conviction.

"Sindara Varacor Cobrandya, do you swear fealty and service to the king and the citizenry of Ambracor?"

"I do," she again stated firmly.

"Do you willingly extend your oath to do all possible to preserve justice, faith, prosperity, and peace, to the best of your abilities, in your position as royal wife to Prince Thehrund? Do you also extend your pledge to rule and guide our nation in the unlikely event you would survive the deaths of King Hamund and Prince Thehrund with no children born of your union?"

"I do so swear to rule and guide with willing heart, in faith and honor, should I be called upon."

Hamund removed the gold crown from its cushioned resting place and ceremoniously positioned it on his daughter-in-law's head. "With authority vested unto me as King of Ambracor, I crown you, Sindara Varacor Cobrandya, as princess and successor to the throne of Ambracor. I declare you second in line until such time as children might be born of your marriage with Prince Thehrund. May Creator God bless you always."

Following a flurry of warm wishes and affectionate embraces, the few guests gathered with the wedding party in the royal apartments for a sumptuous luncheon. Once grace was said, everyone sat down at the banquet table covered with snowy white linens, adorned with fragrant floral arrangements, and set with gleaming china and silverware. Delectable foods, excellent wines, lively conversation, and good spirits held at bay the worries that lay fomenting outside the great walls surrounding Bracordia's grand palace. For at least a little while, the parents of the newlywed couple were determined to give their children the joy long denied them.

After the meal, Thehrund relented and allowed his new bride to stray from his side. She had insisted on having a few private moments to thank each of those who had made this day particularly special for her. Her tactic had been devised well. She desperately needed to speak to Karan without arousing her husband's concern.

"Sindara, I'm happy beyond words that you and Thehrund are finally reunited," Karan said with sincere affection.

Golden eyes glittered with happiness and humor as she replied, "And now actually united for good. I do hope our prince never suffers regrets."

"A worry to be banished at once," Karan laughed, shaking his head as he glimpsed Thehrund's eyes shift toward his bride.

"Karan," she began, trying to maintain her lighthearted expression while venturing toward the worry uppermost in her mind, "I must tell you something to be kept in confidence for now." She cast a loving smile in Thehrund's direction as he talked with his father and hers. "Thehrund has borne grief far too long. I want this day to be as happy and worry-free as possible for him."

Gray eyes darkened with inquisitive regard. "You know that you can trust me."

"Trust I expect to last a lifetime," she replied in a soft, appreciative voice. "Karan, there is great evil here in Bracordia. It is a force so dark and powerful that even Kendra sensed it and warned me."

With some degree of effort, the priest controlled his own countenance despite the rise of unwelcome apprehension. "So, the crystals actually enable you and Kendra to communicate?"

"They do," she answered with lingering awe. "I'm so thankful the angels gave them to us. In truth, I sensed the presence of this evil, but the crystal is what alerted me to its source. You must not think what I tell you is born of jealousy. I assure you it is not. The crystal vibrated uncomfortably when I was in Breeneth's presence. Hers is a dark, malevolent energy fed by a source that frightens me. We must take great care when she is about. Please, Karan, address this in prayer. Also, send urgent word to Reverend Master Zoman. He must move the original Ambracada from Bramond for safekeeping."

"Ah, Karan, have you not dominated enough of my lovely bride's time?" Thehrund approached with a broad smile lighting his features.

Sindara reached for her husband's hand. "Our dear friend only wished to share final words of advice before we make our daring escape from this glorious party."

Thehrund's sweeping black brows lifted. "A fortunate man am I to hear that my bride also wishes to depart this cheerful gathering."

Karan managed a laugh. "The surprise is that you haven't whisked her away already."

The prince's eyes lowered to meet Sindara's loving gaze. "If you're finished with all of Karan's admonitions, I already made our excuses so that we might take our leave."

A surprisingly tranquil prince led his new bride to the spacious palace apartment reserved for them until life's natural progression would place him on Ambracor's throne. The narrow, arched entry hall opened onto a wide parlor, its walls papered in a subtle pattern of pale blue stripes decorated with twisting vines of gold ivy. The longest wall was to their left and invited an invasion of natural light from two tall windows, one on either side of an enormous fireplace. Above the fireplace was an elaborately carved mantel adorned with only an antique clock. Two more tall windows divided the wall directly in front of them. Sofas and chairs were upholstered in lustrous blue jacquard that contrasted beautifully with ornate gold-leafed frames and matching tables. Elegant valances and draperies of the same jacquard, trimmed with luxurious gold fringe, hung over lace curtains at all the windows. Other than oil lamps and candelabras, there were no other decorations.

To their right, a series of doors opened to rooms on the left side of a wide corridor. Mirrored sconces held candles protected by etched glass globes. Polished wood floors reflected light and contributed a sense of warmth and permanence.

Nervousness created waves of flutters in her stomach as Sindara let her head fall backward when Thehrund's strong arms slid beneath hers to clasp together in front of her waist. Covering his long hands with hers, she smiled as the rich, velvety tones of his voice and the warmth of his breath teased sensitive ears.

"Welcome to our new home, my love. I hope you will find all to your liking."

"I'm sure I will once you show me everything." Golden eyes sparkled as she loosened his embrace and turned to face him. Her hands moved upward to rest against his chest. "I can be happy anywhere so long as we're together."

"This place awaits your artistic touches to make it home. For now, I think the tour can wait till later," Thehrund said as he kissed her forehead.

Since returning to Ambracor, there had been little time for them to be alone together. His smile faded into a gentle line. Humor departed darkening blue eyes, leaving in its place suddenly expectant, smoldering fires that fascinated her. Large hands tightened at her waist as his face lowered. His lips sought hers in a kiss that swiftly bound her to him in an exquisite exchange of ardent sensation.

Without conscious realization, Sindara slid her arms upward to encircle his neck. She marveled at the vibrating tremors traveling throughout her body as his kiss grew deeper and bolder, their tongues meeting with thrilling fervor. She breathlessly moaned in protest when he broke the connection their mouths had formed.

"Thehrund," she gasped, tightly clinging to him. She could scarcely believe the swift transformation from humor to passion overtaking her, leaving her knees weak and her body aching for more of his exhilarating touch.

"My beautiful Sindara," he whispered in low, husky tones. "Come, my love," he murmured as he effortlessly lifted her into his arms and carried her into the spacious bedchamber they would now share.

Inside, Sindara's only awareness of her surroundings encompassed the many tall vases containing fresh, vibrantly colored flowers and the enormous poster bed that dominated the chamber. She hardly noticed the softness of the velvet bedspread beneath her hands where Thehrund gently deposited her before kneeling to remove satin slippers from her feet. It seemed the whole of her being encompassed the striking image of the man now her husband.

With remnants of her sensibilities returning, she straightened and leaned forward. Slender fingers stroked through the length of dark waves that hid his face from her. "How can it be that you love me so?"

His head lifted. Black eyebrows rose, his forehead creasing in response to her question. Standing, he paused to remove the crowns they still wore. Turning, he placed them on a nightstand with scrolled legs. He then removed his boots. Joining her on the bed, he reached for her and lowered her to lie beside him. He tenderly caressed her cheek with sensitive fingertips. He swallowed hard. "Sindara, the greater question would be how I could not love you."

Pensively, she studied the face that had haunted years of her dreams in another place, another life. She affectionately held two of his braids in her hand, her thumb sliding along the silken ropes. "I find it so hard to fathom how you cared enough to search so long for me...or that your quest took you so far from home."

Intuitively, he comprehended that words alone could never adequately express the intensity of his love for her. Slowly, he pulled her closer, breathing in her sweet scent that engulfed him in a massive swell of desire. He allowed himself the freedom of running a hand the length of her arm before gently turning her onto her back. Rising and supporting himself on one elbow, he rested his free palm against her midriff and let it roam upward to cup the fullness of her breasts. Meanwhile, he brought firm lips to move against hers in passionate possession.

Dragging her face away, she softly moaned her frustration. Yards of silk and lace separating them were more than she could bear. "Help me," she pleaded in a tremulous whisper as she stood.

Drawing in rapid breaths, he forced himself to rise and concentrate on undoing the long row of pearlescent buttons down the back of her wedding gown. Meanwhile, she leaned forward to fold back the bed's velvet coverlet before tugging at jeweled combs and pins to free gleaming tresses that cascaded to her shoulders. Closing his eyes, Thehrund nestled his face into flowing locks as trembling fingers completed their task.

Firmly grasping her arms, he turned her around. He had dreamed of her for years. The difference now was that the beauteous image before him was warm and vital flesh and blood, not some ethereal vision to dissipate into shadowed memory. Drawing breath and holding it, he raised his hands to guide golden lace and silk from her shoulders. The sliding fabric gradually revealed the creamy expanse of skin from the column of her graceful neck to just above the cushioned mound of her bosom. Hungering lips moved across her shoulder as he finally pushed the offending barrier of her wedding gown downward until it formed a pool of molten gold around her feet.

Sindara met his scorching gaze with some trepidation. Still, her hands reached out and touched his bearded jaw before dropping to perform their own task of sliding golden toggles through satin loops to remove his formal coat. Pushing it from his body, she admired the breadth of his chest beneath the thin layer of his linen shirt. Her lips curved slightly as she boldly began undoing buttons that gradually revealed smooth skin stretched over the powerful muscles of his shoulders and upper arms.

She recalled the morning in her other world when she had finally gone to him and watched as he slept. Upon his awakening, she had sought comfort within the circle of his embrace. That had been the morning she had promised to accompany him home. She now rediscovered that same comfort and reassurance as she pressed her cheek against his bare chest and once again listened to the steady beat of his heart.

Thehrund's breathing grew ragged. He could scarcely believe she would finally be entirely his as he began to strip away the final barriers of her beribboned undergarments. Holding her slightly away, he felt entranced by the vision of her feminine body's enticing contours newly revealed to him. How captivated he was by the beauty of this woman who was now his wife! Swallowing several times, his voice caressed her name. "Sindara...my precious Sindara. Dare I believe I might finally show you how much I truly love you?"

A tentative smile curved her lips. Words fled. Her sole focus lay within myriad emotions and demanding sensations clamoring for fulfillment. She again touched his cheek. Slowly, languorously, her fingers moved downward, tracking along his neck. Transfixed, she watched her nails lightly trace the line of his shoulder and then graze more firmly across his chest. Shining eyes noted the abrupt rise of his chest as his breath caught.

Lifting one hand to push backward the long locks of his hair, she rose on her toes and leaned forward. Her breasts barely grazed his chest as she whispered against his ear, "Please, Thehrund, now. Show me how much you love me. Please?"

Some scrap of sanity reminded him of her inexperience, her innocence. He pulled her flush against him, reveling in the feel of firm breasts now pressed against the unyielding expanse of his chest. His hands traveled along her back, dropping to pull her hips tightly against him, allowing her to feel the demanding tide of his rising passion. Of its own volition, his right hand swiftly rose beneath the cascade of her hair and cradled her neck as his mouth claimed hers in a desperate, electrifying kiss. He then quickly swept her up into his arms and settled her back on the bed.

His vision hungrily absorbed her stunning feminine beauty while he quickly shed the remainder of his clothing and joined her on the enormous bed. Drawing her close, he guided her hands along the sculpted, firmly muscled lines of his masculine physique. He shuddered with frissons of rapidly mounting desire as she instinctively understood his burgeoning need and freely caressed his arms, his sides, and his hips. He gloried in the sensations racing throughout his being as she either stroked sensitized skin with her hands or drew the tips of her nails lightly along the planes of his hard body.

Again, his mind clutched at fleeting tendrils of sanity. He wanted their first full union to bring her joy as well. Once again, he shifted her onto her back and leaned over her. Long locks of waving hair created a dark curtain around their faces as he kissed her with total abandon, his tongue teasing and tantalizing her to a near frenzy. Then, holding tight control over throbbing passion, he ended their kiss. Her slight whimper gradually transformed into soft moans as he initiated a new quest...that of exploring the smooth curves of her body with marauding lips while his hands glided along in rapturous unison.

Memory abruptly pierced his brain. Moving past the incurve of her waist, he gently drew the tip of his index finger along the length of the faint white line that scarred her lower left side. Raising his head, he noted the invasion of painful recollection and anxiety that suddenly shadowed her gaze. Words would never suffice to convey his acceptance that this scar would forever serve as a reminder of both how he had nearly lost her forever and how he was now bound always to cherish her. With his eyes locked on hers, he tenderly kissed the scar's length before moving to cover her body with his.

"Thehrund!" she gasped, her fingers practically digging into his shoulders.

His swelling passion refused to yield further to his mind's control. Only profound love prevented his violent possession. Still, his body's initial invasion met with momentary stiffening of hers. Whispering a flood of loving words against her ear, he felt gradual easing of her virginal tension. Within the warm sheath that now surrounded him, he carefully began the measured rhythms meant to convey the depths of his love and the power of their sacred union.

Her roving hands inflamed every inch of the masculine body that had become part of hers. Coherent thought drowned in the flood of desire raging through her. She writhed in sweetly torturous appeal for more of his heated touch. Her body arched against his. His name spilled from her lips, and she lost herself in the quickening rhythm of his loving. When he finally released a cry of ecstasy, she passionately clung to him. He now belonged to her as much as she belonged to him.

His pounding heart slowed. His panting abated. With tender concern, he eased away from her and lay on his side, turning her to face him. His lips pressed gentle kisses against her forehead and mouth. He loved her with words of praise and contentment. Tears trickled from the corners of his closed eyes.

Sindara rested her palm against his cheek. Eyes the color of dark honey regarded him with adoring admiration. "I love you, Thehrund Cobrandya. I promise I will always love you."

For several prolonged moments, he remained mute. The corners of his mouth lifted in the slightest of smiles. Never before had he dreamed such overwhelming satisfaction could exist in loving a woman as he had just loved her. How he thanked Creator God for giving him both opportunity and courage to pursue his quest to save her. How much more he would treasure her following those years of fear, guilt, and sorrow, all now banished from his life.

Eyelids, thickly lined with black lashes, lifted at long last to reveal intensely blue eyes regarding her unique radiance with boundless adoration. "My precious Sindara," he murmured, "I swear. I will forever cherish your love."

❋ ❋ ❋

Late afternoon shadows drifted through lacy curtains hanging beneath draperies held open by tasseled silk ropes looped over twisted brass hooks. Sindara stirred from light sleep. Full lips formed a smile at the weight of Thehrund's arm tucked beneath hers and nestled comfortably on the curve of her waist. How comforting...how perfectly natural she felt to awaken with him beside her.

While listening to the steady rhythm of his breathing, she relished quiet moments to reflect on the two times he had made love to her that afternoon. The sheer strength of his body amazed her. Even more astonishing were the fascinating sensations his touch had spawned. Never in her life, here or on her far Earth-plane, could she have imagined the mighty swell of ecstasy that his lovemaking had delivered. Even though hours had passed, she still felt warmth lingering inside her body.

Part of her puzzled over how she had expected to feel. Yes, there had been that initial, painful thrust, but he had swiftly soothed away her discomfort. Then, the second time they had loved, he had guided her until an unexpected surge of shuddering pleasures had flooded her body with a rapture that unleashed torrents of joyful tears.

A sudden grin crossed her face. She wondered what those mired in conventional standards of propriety would think to know how little shyness she had felt with him. Instead, she had openly admired the image of his vigorous masculinity. There had been practically no bashful case of nerves as she had delighted in exploring the firmly defined contours of his body with eyes, hands, and lips. Her heart had filled with bliss at the realization she could give him the pleasures she felt he deserved. Her grin widened, and she exhaled a deep sigh of satisfaction.

Her eyelids slid closed as she felt him stir and nuzzle his face against the back of her neck. His hot breath sent a tide of quivering tingles dancing along her spine.

"Have we slept too long?" he murmured.

"Your father kindly freed our schedule until the day after tomorrow. Go back to sleep if you wish."

He smiled at the humorous lilt in her voice. "How wise Father can be when he so wishes."

"I suppose. At the moment, however, I want food. I don't remember ever feeling so hungry!"

He laughed and sat up. His expression was teasingly playful. "Food!" he exclaimed. "There's an excellent idea when I think of how very busy we've been!"

She rolled out of bed, dragging the light blanket with her to cover her nakedness. Even though she tightly pursed her lips, she couldn't suppress an eruption of giggles at the sight of his exposed nudity. "Your Highness, aren't you supposed to be a bit more...shall we say, dignified?"

He swiftly rolled from bed and dragged her into a rollicking embrace. "Even a royal prince is permitted high spirits on his wedding day!" He suddenly quieted, his eyes roving over every feature of her lovely face. "My soul has never felt so light or so elated as it does at this moment."

"My handsome prince, your words give me such happiness!" She followed her declaration with a tender kiss.

Somewhat reluctantly, he retrieved their wedding finery from the floor and led her into a spacious dressing room to select more comfortable attire for the remainder of their day. After managing to dress between constant interruptions to share caresses and kisses, Thehrund led her to the small dining room and kitchen that she had missed upon their earlier arrival. Pulling a bell rope to summon a servant from the palace kitchens, he then held her arm tightly as they toured their new quarters.

Candlelight later bathed their dining table with a warm glow. Aromatic and delicious, a light supper satisfied appetites whetted by the vibrant lovemaking that had filled their afternoon. Little conversation passed between them. For the time being, words were mere shadows of emotions more accurately expressed through loving glances, gentle smiles, and hands that seemed magically attracted.

Lured outside after dinner by clear skies of midnight blue liberally sprinkled with shimmering stars, Sindara clung to Thehrund's arm as they ambled contentedly along pathways winding through palace grounds.

The prince frequently paused to place kisses on his wife's hair or to stroke sensitive fingertips along her cheek.

Finally stopping, he gently grasped her upper arms while his eyes locked onto hers. "Do you remember this spot?"

A puzzled look crossed her face. "Should I?"

A grin lit his features as he gently spun her around. He was convinced he actually felt the smile that spread shapely lips. Bending slightly, he nuzzled his face into silken tresses and whispered, "What about now?"

Sindara stepped off the edge of the stone path and lightly kissed the forehead of the marble figure she had nearly forgotten. "How appropriate, don't you think?" she asked, turning back to him.

Thehrund shook his head as a shiver began at the base of his neck and radiated throughout his tall body. "I have heard it said there is no such thing as coincidence. This angel witnessed our first kiss...the kiss that awakened me to the realization that I could never love anyone as I had come to love you. Do you not find it just a little ironic that angels would come to save and protect you?"

Sindara cast a thoughtful glance at the marble statue. "My mind still struggles to comprehend what you said about angels speaking to you that day when..." Her throat constricted painfully for several moments before she could continue. "I now think in awe how I lived a whole other life in another world while in the care of angels."

Strong fingers stroked locks of hair fluttering with the light touch of spring breezes. Thehrund shook off a brief tremor in response to the surfacing memory that reminded him of past terror and sorrow. "I believe you and your purity of faith were not fated for death in that battle. Remember what Master Garen and Lady Aminta told us. Evil forces were at work."

Sindara regarded him with invading, unwelcome concern. A heavy sigh accompanied sudden widening of honey-hued eyes. She quickly cast her gaze downward.

Thehrund instantly noted the sheen of tears and her attempt to hide the abrupt change in her expression. Reaching out, he tucked a finger beneath her chin and lifted her face. "What?"

She tried to shake off the disconcerting sense of dread that unfurled tendrils curling into the very core of her being. "Thehrund," she whispered, "hold me. Please. Just hold me."

Drawing her into his embrace, he was caught off guard when her arms tensed around his waist. "Tell me. What troubles you so?"

Pressing her cheek tightly against his chest, she listened to the comforting rhythm of his heart's beat...a sound now permanently etched into her memory. How she wanted to give him more time before duty would force him to face powers threatening their nation and their way of life.

Thehrund again allowed himself a moment to indulge in the fresh, sweet fragrance of her hair. He wished fervently that he could just dismiss her sudden disquiet and return to their earlier lighthearted mood; instinct warned him to trust her. "Sindara," he whispered, "you must tell me. We shall face together whatever trouble you perceive."

She sighed heavily. Reluctantly withdrawing from the precious solace found in his closeness, she met his waiting gaze with resolve. "I intended to wait until tomorrow to tell you." Without another word, she took his hand firmly in hers and led him back to their new apartment.

Once inside, she put Thehrund's coat and her wrap away while he stoked the fire a servant had thoughtfully started in the bedchamber's marble fireplace. When she emerged from the enormous dressing room, her soul ached when he held his arms out to her. Her heart lurched inside her chest as she again considered futile wishes to spare him from worry just a little while longer. Inhaling deeply, she gratefully sought precious extra moments in his arms before trying to explain the exact nature of the menace in their midst.

Chapter Twelve

THE BEAUTY OF ALABASTER SKIN vanished beneath a scarlet blaze. Large brown eyes were mere slits. Red lips pursed in fury. Her usual silken voice snarled and growled words distorted by pure rage. Beyond mere anger, Breeneth Brandere had exchanged her arrogant style of grace for a ferocity that caused her father to recoil from his eldest child in shock.

"How dare you come to me like a cowering mongrel with its tail between its legs!" she shrieked. "How could you fail to detect Hamund's deception? He was stalling all along, and you were too pathetically stupid to see. You've ruined everything! Everything!"

Ingnan Brandere's chest heaved as he confronted his daughter's vicious diatribe. "Breeneth, please. Calm yourself. You know your mother isn't feeling well," the beleaguered count reminded his daughter.

Breeneth's laugh sounded cold and harsh. "Are you really such a complete fool?" she sneered disparagingly.

Brandere stiffened slightly. "What does that mean?"

Breeneth glowered at her father with caustic scorn. "What do you think I meant?"

Her father nearly choked on his next breath. "You've turned on your own mother, haven't you? What have you done to her?"

"Mother will be fine. She suffers only from a mild potion I made to keep her out of my way."

Brandere stared at Breeneth first with incredulity, then with foreboding he rapidly tried to hide. Fearful tremors raced through his body. He knew how his older daughter had always demanded her own way. During her childhood, he had laughed and attributed her behavior to passing phases of development. When she reached her teens, he had been reluctant to acknowledge shameful rumors about her hedonistic conduct. He could hardly believe the maelstrom now before him was his own child.

He watched as she furiously paced across the large sitting room and back again. Her appearance held none of the elegant refinement he typically associated with her. Her shoulders hunched forward. Ebony hair spilled almost to her waist in an untidy mass. Livid anger distorted lovely features and discolored her perfect complexion. Her very posture communicated sheer wrath as her hands flew wildly in all directions to emphasize various points as she raged, seething over news that Thehrund had already married Sindara Varacor in a private ceremony.

"Sindara!" she snarled as her pacing quickened. "This I do not understand! She died! I made it clear that she was to die in that skirmish! She did die! Everyone saw it! Even Thehrund and his impudent father! How is it that she lives? How has she returned? How?" She raged uncontrollably.

Color swiftly drained from Count Brandere's face. His hands clenched into impotent fists. Her words pierced the fabric of the carefully woven cloak of denial he had maintained for more years than he could recall. Rumors did not begin to address the reality before him. This woman...this stranger...his own daughter...manifested an evil that caused his blood to run as rivers of ice through his veins.

As if he had spoken his thoughts aloud, she halted abruptly and fixed her fiery gaze upon him. "Understand well. Your foolish failures spur nothing but my utter contempt. You wield no power over me. Do not even think to defy me in any way."

Brandere winced involuntarily at the unfamiliar, sinister tones of her voice. He cast his glance away, unable to maintain eye contact. Shivers raced down his back and made his skin crawl. His stomach pitched and roiled with revulsion. For brief moments, he flailed in the wake of her malevolence, hoping to awaken from a nightmare.

"What are your intentions?" he asked reluctantly, his voice catching slightly.

She glared at him, her patience completely gone. "Intentions? I intend to possess what is rightfully mine, of course. I *will* have Thehrund! I *will* wear the queen's crown! They both belong to me! Sindara Varacor has no rightful claim to either."

Loath to remind her that Thehrund and Sindara were already married, Count Brandere carefully chose his next words. He needed to know what to expect. "Considering they have wed already, how do you plan to accomplish your goal?"

Her outward anger dissipated somewhat as she pondered how she might possibly use her father's position to her advantage. His membership in the Board of Governors and access to the king could prove useful as she calculated her next moves. She dared not consult with her master from here in Bracordia.

"I must know how Sindara survived the attack outside Articene. I need to know who saved her and how. How Thehrund found her...I must know that, too." She glared at her father. "Do not fail in bringing me this information."

"What will you do then? And what if I'm unable to discover the answer to this mystery?"

Breeneth's face transformed into a mask of unbridled fury. She threw her arms upward. Her palms faced outward with her fingers spread wide apart like branches on a leafless tree. A mighty rush of mephitic air violently swept Brandere off his feet and pinned him against a wall. As his lungs battled for breath within the searing stench of invisible shackles, he glimpsed his daughter's form surrounded by an undulating whirlwind of black mist. Unable to resist her power, he lost consciousness as she let him drop into a heap on the floor.

Thehrund tenderly tucked his index finger beneath his bride's chin and raised her face. Golden irises were wide with black pupils drawn to tiny points in the brightly lit room. His heart contracted upon noting the glimmer of tears glazing those eyes he thoroughly adored. Feeling her need for reassurance, he bent his head and lightly kissed eyelids that suddenly fluttered and closed.

"Sindara," he quietly began, "not for a minute would I ever think you could make up such a story. I recall clearly what Garen told us. The attack at Articene was no random ambush."

Thehrund continued to muse aloud. "Thinking on that and what you just told me, mysteries begin to clarify. The letter from Bramond reached you far too quickly. No rider could have overtaken my party. Of that, I am sure. My waking with Breeneth must have been planned. Your reaction and return to Arvacon were anticipated. The Breyal attack was premeditated."

He sighed heavily, sickened by a truth that set his nerves on edge. "From the beginning, the intent was to murder you. It's also entirely possible that they planned to assassinate Father."

Kendra's voice echoed inside Sindara's mind. "Trust your intuition. If you feel deep stirring inside, *it is then that truth resonates.*"

"I greatly fear for both you and your father." Sindara reached out and placed her hand against his cheek. "I love you far too much to lose you again. I cannot allow that to happen."

He turned his face to place a lingering kiss against her palm. His eyes had darkened to deep sapphire when they met hers. "Perhaps you are now in greater danger than ever. Father had a meeting scheduled late this afternoon with Count Brandere. Brandere likely knows we have wed and has informed Breeneth."

Sindara's expression was grave. "She wants you. She has all along. She covets the power that comes with Ambracor's crown. Her actions far exceed mere immorality. She's not merely a traitor allied with the Breyals.

There is much more...a connection to some vile malevolence that intends to spread its dark dominion across Ambracor."

Thehrund framed her face between his huge hands. His thumbs softly traced small, soothing circles at her temples. "That is precisely why you are in more danger now than ever before. From her perspective, you stand between me and her contemptible plans. I've brought you home to face yet again enormous risk for violent attempts against your life."

Sindara nodded in understanding. "We must not forget the danger to your father. I so wanted at least this one night to belong to you and me alone, but I believe we must hasten to explain everything to him. We cannot delay in advising him of perils so close at hand."

Thehrund drew Sindara into his arms. His most fervent wish had been to find her...to save her life, restore her love, and make her his wife. His hopes had been to build his private world around her even as he devoted his public life to Ambracor. That precious dream had driven him for years. His success now forced him to face new, onerous truth. Desperately clutching her close, he prayed to Creator God to protect and keep her safe from the same evil that again threatened her along with all he cherished most in life.

❈ ❈ ❈

Ingnan Brandere lay on his back. Earlier, as he'd regained consciousness, his body had ached as he slowly pulled himself into a sitting position. Weakly gripping the edge of a table, he dragged himself off the floor. Traces of a putrid smell still hung in the air. Staggering into the suite's main bedchamber, he had lain down beside his ailing wife.

Staring at the ceiling, he wondered where Breeneth had gone. He heard none of the usual chatter typical when his daughters were nearby. A sudden barrage of fearful questions plagued his stunned brain. Was Brenna compelled against her will to do Breeneth's bidding? Worse yet, was she in league with her older sister? What would happen when they returned? What were Breeneth's plans? Why had he never investigated the ugly rumors that had repeatedly surfaced through the years? What was he to do now that he had seen and felt an unconscionable force willing to destroy anything or anyone that might hinder Breeneth's selfish objectives? What was the source of the awesome might that had powered her attack against him? That final question spawned a flood of adrenaline that coursed through his battered body.

"Shush," Brandere whispered to his wife half an hour later. She moaned softly and shivered with chills brought on by whatever potion Breeneth had given her. He tugged her warm dressing gown snugly around her as he cast furtive glances through the small glass window of the door leading to the lobby of their hotel. He breathed his first real prayer in years, thanking Creator God that he had gotten this far without encountering his daughter.

Just as he grasped the door handle, he heard multiple boots marching through the hotel's front entrance. He pinned his wife against the wall, supporting her weak form as he listened to the sharp voice of a military officer. He dared to lean forward and peek into the lobby. At least two dozen of the king's elite guards had spilled into the hotel. Brandere feared the worst...that his wayward daughter had already made an attempt on the life of the prince's new bride.

He must act quickly. He would gladly forfeit his own life, but his wife did not deserve to suffer. Besides, he would rather face Hamund's soldiers than confront Breeneth again. Reaching out, he grasped the door handle and shoved it downward. Clutching his wife close, he stumbled into the lobby.

Nagrand Mezden's head jerked up. He signaled four soldiers to rush to Brandere's side. One lifted the petite countess into his arms while another helped the weakened count. The remaining two stood careful watch.

"Count Brandere, what happened?" Nagrand demanded.

Tears of shame and relief suddenly coursed down Brandere's face. "My daughter..."

"What has she done? Where is she?" Nagrand gruffly inquired.

Brandere shook his head as he fought a rising sob. "My wife suffers from some potion my daughter gave her. Breeneth also attacked me. Perhaps an hour or two ago. I can't recall exactly. I don't know where she is. All I can tell you is that she plans to murder the prince's bride. I've no idea how to stop her."

Nagrand's blond hair briefly swung in front of his face, momentarily shielding his look of dread. He barked orders to half a dozen guards, reminding them of Prince Thehrund's warning to avoid crossing paths with Breeneth Brandere. Their objective was to ensure word reached the palace should she be found at the hotel and then to monitor her movements. He turned to meet Brandere's ashen, tear-stained face. "We shall leave immediately and take you and your wife to the palace."

Hamund paced the length of the throne room in agitation. His mind faltered as he tried to grasp details of all Thehrund and Sindara had related. In his youth, he had actually held the original Ambracada in his hands and felt its power radiating from within. He readily accepted the existence of Ambracor's invisible Creator God, but whole worlds existing in other dimensions? Angels? Portals? The tale told by his son and daughter-in-law sounded far too fantastic to be true.

His pacing stopped as he finally leaned heavily against the side of his throne. His head shook back and forth, long gray hair and royal braids swaying from side to side. He looked up, blue eyes reflecting his mighty struggle to absorb startling revelations from a priest and four of the people he most trusted in the world. Insidious threads of apprehension wove themselves into the fabric of his thoughts. He was a king who surrounded himself with brilliant minds and wise friends. Together, they could surely devise strategies to confound and defeat any ordinary enemy. Dismayed, he quickly realized that the foe now threatening his nation, his people, and his family was thoroughly extraordinary.

"Your Majesty," Karan began cautiously, "I can appreciate how impossible this all must sound. Should I be in your shoes, I'm sure I would feel much the same. While I heard no angel voices, nor did I meet any angels, all Thehrund told me about the portal and the search that would eventually lead to Sindara proved accurate. I traveled the portal. I also witnessed the awakening of memories Sindara could not have known had she been another person."

Hamund raised his eyes to meet those of his son. How he had doubted Thehrund. How he now regretted those doubts.

"Karan," he finally said, nodding toward the priest, his son, his daughter-in-law, and her parents, "I do not doubt the veracity of all you have revealed to me. What troubles me at this moment is how we move forward. I have many questions that require answers. How extensive is the information provided to Breyal leadership concerning our strategies and defenses? Are there traitors and spies in our midst? If so, how deep does their infiltration go? How do we ensure the safety of our people? Where do we begin?"

Freeing her hand from her husband's, Sindara approached Hamund. "Father, we must draw strength from faith and pray for protection while we determine the extent of Breeneth's treachery. We must protect you as our king and leader. Then? We prepare ourselves for severe hardships because it seems we are being forced onto the path of war."

Hamund lifted his hands to frame Sindara's face. His eyes beheld hers with heartfelt affection. "My beloved friend Artrian and I now share honor having you as our daughter. There is no way to express my happiness that you're returned to us, but I am also exceedingly afraid. Your life, Sindara, is also in great danger...perhaps the greatest danger of all. That you must not forget. Not one of us here can face losing you again."

The king's face lifted sharply as one of the towering doors to the throne room opened. Erect and purposeful, Nagrand Mezden strode forward. Bowing, he excused himself to the king before addressing Thehrund. "I apologize for the interruption, but Count Brandere has returned with us. He asks to speak to you and your father. The information he wishes to relate is critical."

Instantly aware of Nagrand's sense of urgency, Thehrund turned to his father. "I sent Nagrand to the hotel to verify Breeneth's presence there."

Hamund guided Sindara into Lord Artrian's care and then took his seat on the massive throne that had been carved centuries earlier from a single oak tree. Once Thehrund advanced to stand by his father's right side, Hamund visibly exchanged his image of concerned parent for the authoritative demeanor of reigning monarch. "Sir Mezden, escort Count Brandere before the throne."

If the king and his son were surprised, their expressions remained implacable as two soldiers physically helped Brandere limp forward. Sandwiched between her parents, Sindara stood erect and attentive. Remaining with the Varacors, Karan noticed when the princess placed her hand over the pendant suspended from the gold chain around her neck.

"Your Majesty," Brandere murmured as his head dipped low in a gesture of respect.

"Sir Mezden advises that you wish to speak to us." The king's voice held steady despite anxiety roused by the nobleman's disheveled, feeble appearance. The man before him bore little resemblance to the intractable nobleman who, just days earlier, had bullied palace staff and arrogantly demanded a royal decree mandating that Prince Thehrund marry Breeneth Brandere.

Leaning heavily against one of the guards, Brandere forced himself to face his king. "Your Majesty, your life is in jeopardy, as is the life of the prince's new bride. My daughter..." He coughed several times before continuing in a hoarse croak, "Breeneth is not the person I thought she was. She has made her mother ill with some vile concoction and..."

He paused again, his vision fixed fearfully on the memory of the confrontation with his eldest child. Drawing a trembling breath, he continued, "Breeneth attacked me. She has powers...powers no normal person could possess. She is overtaken by some dark entity. I saw it, Sire! I swear! I saw the black essence of evil erupt from her! It lifted me from the floor and flung me against the wall of our suite! Never..." A sob erupted as a fit of violent coughing overcame him.

Surprising her parents, Sindara quickly stepped forward and grasped the count's upper arms. She shuddered upon perceiving vestiges of pure evil still torturing the injured man. "Tell me honestly," she sternly demanded. "Did Breeneth plan the Breyal attack that nearly claimed King Hamund's life and mine?"

Tears coursed down the man's cheeks. "She said so. She claimed Breyals were ordered to kill you."

"Calm yourself," she told him, her voice revealing no emotion.

"How can I?" he exclaimed as a fresh round of sobs wracked his body. "She threatened me should I defy her in any way! My wife is ill. I have no idea where my younger daughter is! I do not know if Breeneth has harmed her or plots with her!"

"Calm yourself," Sindara repeated. "Lord Ingnan, trust me. Close your eyes." She tilted her head, signaling the guards to release their hold on the count and move aside.

Too drained to resist her gentle insistence, the count obeyed and let his head droop forward. Sindara firmly grasped her pendant and pressed it tightly against Brandere's chest, just above his heart. The man's body abruptly straightened, stiffening before being overtaken by a surge of tremors.

As others in the throne room watched in abject horror, Sindara's hair and clothes were whipped about by forceful gusts of air erupting from the count's presence. With her feet planted in a wide stance, she leaned into the burst of air until a flurry of shadowy wisps spewed from Brandere's body and clothes. As murky traces of black dissipated like puffs of smoke, the air calmed around the nobleman, and his powerful quaking subsided. Limp and languid, he would have collapsed to the floor had the soldiers not caught him.

"Karan?"

White-faced, Karan approached Sindara. "What do you wish me to do?"

Recalling passages from a rare and ancient book her grandfather had given her, Sindara answered, "We need your most fervent prayer for Creator God's protection. After that, someone must quickly remove every scrap of clothing and jewelry from the Branderes. You must see to the blessing of a place where all can be burned. Also, ensure that a cedar log is burned separately. Mix its ashes with the ashes of their belongings and then bury them deep in the consecrated ground. Reserve a portion of cedar ashes to mix with blessed oils. Anoint the count and his wife first to help shield them from further attack. Later, anoint all of us here tonight and anyone who has come into immediate contact with the Branderes."

Karan dipped his face in respectful acknowledgment of her instructions. Then, gathering everyone in a circle around him, he initiated the ancient prayer for protection. Calling each person by name, he prayed for Creator God to protect them all from the dark force that had been manifest in the mist driven from the count's body and its source. His chanted prayer complete, Karan led the soldiers carrying Count Brandere from the throne room to complete the tasks Sindara had assigned him.

All was tranquil as Sindara's heavy eyelids slowly lifted. She smiled into early morning's velvety gray shadows. Her head rested comfortably on a down-stuffed pillow. A warm blanket had been carefully tucked around her bare shoulders. The only sound she heard was that of Thehrund's steady breathing as he slept soundly with his arm draped protectively across her midriff.

Turning carefully onto her side to face her husband, she freed her right arm. Catching the gold-bound end of one long braid, she indulgently rubbed it between her sensitive index finger and thumb. Barely making out his features in the bedchamber's dim light, she admired the distinctive arch of his eyebrows and the thick fringe of lashes edging his closed eyelids. His nostrils flared slightly on the sides of his narrow, straight nose. The usual precise line of his black beard blended into the night's shorter growth. She silently marveled at the mobility of pliant lips that, with their distinctive shape, added so much extra dimension to his expressions. How peaceful he looked in sleep and how utterly handsome.

Sindara placed the braid against her lips while appreciatively breathing in the masculine scent she always associated with his presence. An odd memory flickered inside her mind. He had just picked her up off the cold, damp street. Barely conscious, she recalled noticing that scent. Even more than the strength of his arms cradling her body against his chest, she suddenly realized that fragrance had been the real beginning of her awakening to her true identity. She again smiled to herself.

Suddenly, a long hand emerged from beneath the covers to grasp hers. Dragging it across his pillow, he brought it to his mouth for a tender kiss. "My beautiful princess bride," he murmured, his lips moving sensually against the back of her hand. "Such a joy it is to awaken to your loving gaze."

She laughed softly. "And what makes you think I was gazing at you? You were asleep with your eyes closed."

"Hmm," he sighed drowsily. "I feel your eyes upon me, my love, and wonder in astonishment that such a woman could behold me as you do."

Gently freeing her hand, she drew her fingers across his forehead and along his cheekbone. Releasing a shaky sigh, she felt the tickling caress of teardrops sliding along her face. "How I do love you, Thehrund."

His blue eyes slowly opened and wandered from the tumble of her curling hair to her lovely features. Dwelling several moments on the vision of luminous, expressive eyes and soft, inviting lips, he moved to partake of his first kiss on this first full day of their marriage. He delighted in her resistance when he ended the tender kiss.

Gently pushing aside the blanket, he revealed more of sleek, silken skin that appeared softer than ever in the slowly brightening room. Beginning with the backs of his fingers caressing her cheek, he allowed his hand glorious freedom to slide from her neck to her shoulder. Growing bolder, he drew the full length of his hand from her shoulders to the firm swelling of her breast. Pausing over the swiftly sensitized mound, he returned his gaze to her face, noting with satisfaction the expression of rapidly heightening desire in her eyes.

When his hand resumed its deliberately languorous journey, his fingers splayed over the firm, velvety flesh of her midriff and continued its path, finally resting his palm near the scar on her side. Once again, his eyes traveled unhurriedly toward the face now flushed with desire rising from his intimate caresses. Treasuring beauty reserved solely for him to love, Thehrund moved to lean over her. As he had done the day before when first he made love to her, he paused in adoration. He then drew his lips in loving salute along her body and across the scar she bore as evidence of all they had endured in the failed plot to end her life.

"Thehrund, please..." The tremor in her hushed, pleading tones called his awareness to tension in the body now appealing for the relief only he could bestow. Reaching for him with both hands, she laced her fingers into the length of his hair, pulling his face back to lips hungering for the deep kisses that so thoroughly inflamed her senses.

"Sindara," he whispered as he dropped a flurry of light kisses on waiting lips. His own desires were clamoring for the pure delight created by her touch. Curving one hand behind her head as his mouth welded to hers, he used his other hand to guide hers to the chiseled contours of his powerfully muscled body. Closing his eyes, he reveled yet again in her instinctive comprehension of his need. Her fingers traced erotic paths across his chest, along the sculpted definition of his upper arms, and over the hard plane of his abdomen. He suddenly gasped, breaking the bond of their kiss to catch his breath. Her fingers had dared more intimate exploration that generated a surge of excitement impossible to control.

Within seconds, Thehrund changed positions and reclaimed profound union with the woman now his wife. With every touch and every stroke, he sought to regale her with the pleasures and joys of his love. At the same time, her soft moans and whimpers combined with the frenetic movement of her hands along his back and hips, stirring his desires to a pinnacle entirely new to him.

"Thehrund!" she gasped, her fingertips raking across the rippling muscles of his back as her entire body quaked beneath his. Recognizing her enraptured exclamation, his movements intensified until he swiftly joined her in sharing their ultimate satisfaction.

Panting breaths slowed. Bodies relaxed. Gently, he moved to lie beside her, holding her snugly against him. His eyes closed. Resting his chin atop her head, he gloried in the way she had loved him. Her love had proven its power to raise his soul above the growing turmoil beyond palace walls and the boundaries of Bracordia. Merciless dangers awaited him. He would think of that later. For the moment, he wanted nothing more than to cherish his precious bride.

❈ ❈ ❈

King Hamund exuded all one might expect from a monarch determined to defend the nation he ruled. Wisdom tempered profound anger. Courage ascended from the depths of his soul as he willingly accepted the role as his people's protector. Ambracor's governors responsible for security and defense would look to him for stability and guidance. From childhood, he had been carefully groomed, coached, and educated to meet such challenges. He sat in the king's chair at the head of the conference table and watched his only son greet each of the gathering committee members. Hamund silently acknowledged the most painful challenge of all. He must suppress profound regret that his son must forego the pleasures of his first days of marriage so as to address the magnitude of the crisis at hand.

Once all committee members had arrived and stood behind their assigned seats, Prince Thehrund approached his father. Bowing his head in respect, he formally announced, "Sire, the assembly is complete. We are ready to begin."

Hamund stood, his posture erect, his gaze steady. Although not as deeply intoned as his son's, the king's rich voice addressed the committee. "Ladies and gentlemen, I called this emergency session after learning of threats beyond any I ever expected to endanger our nation. I have asked Reverend Master Mezden to pray a blessing over us before we begin."

Clad in simple robes of white linen with a magenta cincture at the waist, Karan approached the king and the prince. At Hamund's signal, the priest stretched his arms high above his head. In a clear, melodious chant, he called upon Creator God to bestow wisdom, courage, and resolve on those assembled to protect Ambracor's people and their way of life. Then, raising many a curious brow, he initiated the traditional prayer for divine protection that had been rarely invoked during recent generations.

Hamund eschewed his royal seat for a time to expel nervous energy born of anxiety. Stepping toward a window, he paused to look over the city he loved so dearly. Despite all former hopes, he realized that he would need to exercise his most convincing arguments ever. Resigned that he would indeed be the first king in centuries to lead Ambracor into war, he sighed before facing waiting governors.

Countess Esmina Lamal later shook her head. "This is so hard to comprehend, but it helps explain Bramond Province's recent resistance to strengthening existing fortifications and expanding our armies. Are you absolutely sure that Count Brandere's loyalty to the crown is not compromised?"

Thehrund gave one shake of his head. "Due to his current physical condition, I cannot say with total certainty. It is entirely possible Breeneth somehow controlled him. He is too weakened by the attack to answer all our questions, but I believe what he did reveal indicates the treachery is his daughter's, not his."

Hamund shoved from his mind haunting thoughts of his near acquiescence to Brandere's demands to command Thehrund to marry Breeneth. "Initially, Count Brandere's goal was to secure agreement for my son to marry his older daughter Breeneth. I am convinced Lord Ingnan acted primarily to appease her. Connecting his family's bloodlines to the House of Cobrandya was secondary."

"His shock and fear last night were not at all feigned," Artrian Varacor commented. "His distress over his daughter's connivance with Breyals to stage the ambush at Articene was genuine. He plainly stated that they planned to murder my daughter and that Breeneth still pursues that end."

"Considering the circumstances, Lord Artrian, you are remarkably calm."

Artrian met the gaze of Count Delgaro, his longtime ally in securing stronger defenses for provinces bordering Breyal. "Our prince saved my older son's life six years ago at Articene. Creator God saw fit to spare my daughter's life and return her years after I had resigned myself to her death. It was Thehrund who persisted with uncommon faith in the search that brought her safely home. No one knows better than I how noble and how capable Prince Thehrund is. I have complete confidence in his abilities to command our armies."

"To command armies against invading Breyals is one thing," Lady Esmina replied. "I do not doubt the prince's courage or skill in facing Breyal warriors. What I do question is how we prepare to face such an enemy as Brandere described before he collapsed."

Hamund frowned as he shook his head. "Preparing to confront the kind of dark force I witnessed last night is unthinkable, yet it is the reality we face. Initial action has already been taken to implement that process. Thehrund?"

For the first time since the meeting convened, Prince Thehrund stood to address the committee. "As you all know, Father announced Sindara Varacor's return to Ambracor two days ago and that she and I would wed. We married yesterday in a private ceremony here at the palace."

Surprised, Count Delgaro stared at the prince. "You circumvented all traditions for a royal wedding?"

Thehrund dipped his head respectfully toward the elderly governor. "We did, Lord Jepro. Tradition would have required us to travel to Bramond Province for final counseling and blessings at the Sacred Halls of Faith. Although we had no idea of the real dangers in Bramond before last night, Father and I had already consulted with Count Artrian and his wife on the matter. We all felt uneasy about taking Sindara there. Sindara was especially anxious that such a trip could prove disastrous." He paused, tilting his head to emphasize his next words. "You knew her for many years."

"Yes," Lord Jepro replied thoughtfully, "I did. Her faith was inspirational and her intuition formidable, but she often discounted her abilities. Now?"

Thehrund's mouth formed a thoughtful smile. "Sindara now acknowledges her gifts and seeks to strengthen and use them to aid us through this critical time."

The governor of Zelcon Province spoke up. "Is it not foolhardy to risk sending you to command our military forces, Prince Thehrund? You have just wed. Should unspeakable disaster occur, there is no heir to Ambracor's throne."

"You make an astute observation, Count Zelban," King Hamund responded. "Although I never dreamed it would be necessary, I have already utilized my authority as established in ancient laws."

The balding count's forehead drew into deep furrows. "You have named Sindara Varacor as heir to the throne should you or your son not survive this catastrophe?"

"Sindara is now Cobrandya through consummation of our wedded union," Thehrund stated firmly. "She is strong, well educated, and fully capable of assuming rule should tragedy befall us. Father has already designated her second in line to the throne should the worst happen and we have no children to assume that responsibility."

King Hamund cast his eyes around the room, capturing the attention of all members. "There is no longer reason to remain secretive about the prince's marriage to Sindara. They were betrothed many years ago and would have wed long since had the Articene attack never occurred. They are finally married according to our nation's faith practices and with full blessings from their parents. For the information of those present only, I also conducted her official coronation yesterday in private. Although we shall say nothing of the latter ceremony for now, we will announce a public ceremony for the encouragement and benefit of our people. With that said, the time is at hand to cast votes in favor of plans now set forth by this committee."

❈ ❈ ❈

"How I yearn for more than your image in this crystal," Sindara said longingly. "I would feel much more confident with you here."

Kendra smiled reassuringly. "You always worry too much. You must trust yourself."

Sindara's face brightened for mere seconds. "I do trust myself, now so much more than ever before. If only I could banish from my mind what I saw last night. The mist that fled Count Brandere's body was so foul. I pray for strength and insight to meet our future here. We face attack by something few of us understand." She paused. "Kendra, I so fear losing Thehrund."

Kendra nodded, feeling in the pit of her own stomach the sense of dread Sindara's expression conveyed. "We will both continue to pray for his protection and surround him with white light." An idea crept into her mind. "Sindara, do you still trust me?"

"Completely," Sindara swiftly replied. "Why such a question?"

"I'll tell you another time. I need to go now, but I have an idea. Let me work on it. Okay?"

"Of course. I'll try to avoid falling into a well of curiosity."

Kendra giggled. "I assume there's some sort of Ambracor anecdote that goes with that saying."

Sindara finally smiled. "Your Earth-plane's fables and sayings make more sense."

"We'll talk soon. I promise. In the meantime, stay out of wells and away from trouble. Agreed?"

Sindara nodded and watched as Kendra's image faded in gleaming swirls of color that quickly settled into the ordinary appearance of her crystal pendant. Gazing at the precious gift, she jumped when her husband's hands gently slipped beneath the shining length of her hair. Twisting in her chair, she shook her head and looked up. "Must you startle me that way?"

Thehrund bent and lightly brushed her lips with his. "I've been here for a while," he told her as he rounded the chair and crouched low in front of her.

She gave him a sheepish smile. "You're too quiet. No one else has ever been able to sneak up on me that way."

"I pray no one else ever does," he said, half-serious. Piercing blue eyes met golden-hued mirrors to her soul. His smile faded as his features assumed a solemn expression. "Of everyone I know, you are the one I most need to believe in me. You must also understand something you said yourself. Life has never been more precious."

She realized he had overheard her comments to Kendra. Reaching out, she held his face between her hands. "How could I not believe in you after all you did to bring me home? I have every confidence in you, but what we face...the evil that woman dares to bring into our midst... It is danger we can regard with nothing less than total awareness of every step we take. I will not rest peacefully until we can defeat whatever this is before it claims too many lives. Especially yours, Thehrund. My life will hold little meaning if I lose you."

Dropping his knees to the floor, he leaned forward and rested his head on her lap. Prolonged moments passed in silence as memories of bleak, lonely desolation swept through his soul. For six long years, grief and guilt had wrapped him in chill blankets of self-doubt and self-deprecation. He had borne personal shame, and he had suffered his beloved father's ceaseless reproach and scorn. Adrift in private oceans of sorrow, he had clung tenaciously to promises from strange voices heard only inside his mind. He had vowed to pursue whatever course they set before him. Despite aching loneliness...despite his father's disapproval and ridicule...he had remained true to his word. The voices had then delivered on their promise.

Thehrund now relished inner calm long denied him. Events over the past few days had brought redemption in his father's eyes and the return of his own self-respect. However, neither compared with the bliss of having Sindara bound to him in marriage.

Lost for the moment in the sensation of her fingers floating through his hair, he thrilled at tingling shivers of delight traveling the length of his neck and across his shoulders. How glorious her sweet and loving caresses! How blessed he felt now that she was his wife! Pushing from his mind all thought of what might lie ahead as Ambracor faced turbulent descent into war, he raised his face to accept her freely given kisses. He then stood, lifted her into his arms, and carried her to the private retreat of their bedchamber.

Chapter Thirteen

Huddled in a damp corner, Brenna waited. Her shelter for the moment had only two walls. The roof above her head protected several small coaches for hire. The parked carriages did little to break the chilling breeze of yet another cool, misty night. Her stomach rumbled with hunger pangs. She clutched her woolen shawl more tightly around her, grimacing at the pointless effort.

"Brenna! Wake up!"

Rousing slowly from sleep-induced stupor, Brenna's eyelids fluttered. "Breeneth," she mumbled weakly, "I can't do this anymore. Please…"

The toe of Breeneth's shoe jabbed painfully into Brenna's side. "Get up," came the hissing response. "Hurry! We're leaving!"

Brenna grabbed her side. Exhaustion subsided as anger flared. "Don't do that again."

Breeneth shook her head impatiently. "I said get up! Hurry! Follow me!"

Scowling indignantly, Brenna staggered to her feet and followed her sister. Tense minutes marked their cautious path between the carriages. Finally, they darted around the corner and behind the stable where Breeneth had two horses hitched to a travel coach.

"Are you stealing this?" Brenna asked, her temper rising as quickly as her patience dwindled.

"Would you prefer to walk home?" Breeneth sarcastically mocked in an angry whisper. "Get in. Now."

Brenna knew better than to argue. She obediently climbed into the coach and settled inside its drafty cab. Glancing around as the carriage lurched into motion, she noticed a horsehair blanket that she wrapped around herself. Although hunger continued to gnaw sharply at her insides, at least she had the comfort of extra warmth.

Clad in stolen livery, Breeneth sat on the driver's seat and forced herself to keep the horses at an unhurried, steady pace. In the hour just before dawn, few people were outside to take notice. With her senses in a state of heightened alert, she drove through deserted city streets. Glimpsing an increased number of military patrols about, she quickly turned corners or stopped the carriage to avoid attracting unwanted attention. Beneath her breath, she cursed and promised retribution to her father for his betrayal.

Just above tiled rooftops near the city's edge, night skies brightened with the earliest hints of light heralding a new day. A patrol of four soldiers appeared ahead at a junction where several outlying roads converged on a primary entry to Bracordia. There was no side street where Breeneth could turn to avoid them. Retaining outward calm as two started toward her, she decided that a slow forward pace was her most prudent course of action.

"Halt!" The lead officer approached and threw up his hand as a visible signal affirming his shouted command.

Sucking in her breath, Breeneth stared at the young man whose horse now carried him closer. Carefully maintaining her composure, she tipped her head forward in acknowledgment and waited for the officer to speak.

"Driver, what is your purpose? Why are you out so early when the city lies under curfew?"

The words that emerged from Breeneth's throat sounded little like her usual voice. "With my master's permission, I take my sister to visit our parents just outside the city. Our mother has fallen gravely ill."

A second soldier guided his mount close enough to the carriage to rap sharply on the window. When a wan face peered out at him, he tossed his head backward. "There's one passenger inside," he said. "A woman."

The officer in charge scrutinized the driver before deciding to dismount. "I apologize for any inconvenience. Would you mind climbing down? I need to speak further with you and your sister."

Carefully controlling her features, Breeneth merely nodded before doing as the soldier instructed. She then walked around the side to open the carriage door. "Sister, the soldiers wish to speak with us. We mustn't keep them waiting."

Nervously clutching the blanket around her, Brenna pushed the door open and stepped outside. The young officer immediately observed her damp, straggling hair and the crinkled, dirty hem of expensive skirts. He looked to Breeneth and instantly noticed the contrast. Her maroon uniform was neatly pressed and spotlessly clean. The hat she wore sat at an odd angle on her head. A downward glance revealed feet clad in expensive dress shoes. Instantly sensing something seriously amiss, he felt a rush of apprehension.

"Please excuse the delay, but we must escort you to our commanding officer. It's just a formality while we properly iden..." The officer's words dissolved into a breathless scream of agony as a churning cloud of shadowy mist enveloped him. Lifting his body into the air, massive black swirls hurled him against a wall across the street. The other soldier called out a warning before twisting coils of mist shot out and swept him from his startled mount and onto the brick road in a motionless mound.

"Quick!" Breeneth yelled at her sister before turning to leap onto the skittish horse. "Take the other horse! Ride!" Digging her heels into the stolen horse's sides, she then raced off without checking to see if her sister followed.

Waiting near the junction ahead, the remaining soldiers started at the unexpected sounds of their comrade's shrieks. Tightly gripping reins and swiftly pivoting, they urged their horses toward the now driverless coach. A rush of foul, reeking air hit them with stunning force, causing the animals to stagger awkwardly. The soldiers, gasping for breath while attempting to control panicked mounts, glimpsed a petite figure racing across their path on the back of the stolen military horse. Trailing behind was a billowing cloud of black that obscured the escaping rider's course.

Quickly realizing they had no idea which road the thief had taken, the remainder of the patrol cautiously approached the carriage. Lights suddenly illuminated windows inside homes up and down the street where occupants had been shocked awake by screams from the street below. Drowsy citizens, spilling through their doorways to investigate the unusual commotion, were assaulted by a vile stench worse than decaying flesh hanging in hot summer air. Scalding tears stung eyes. Coughs emerged from burning throats. Stomachs pitched in reaction to the ungodly odor. A few covered their noses and mouths with sleeves or handkerchiefs and then ran toward the fallen soldiers.

An elderly man knelt beside the body of the first man attacked by Breeneth. He glanced upward at the face of the youthful guard who reached his comrade first. Neither could believe the mottled gray mask of death that had replaced the handsome features of a vital young officer. More disconcerting were his features, frozen in a state of permanent terror. In the meantime, faint moans came from the guard who had been flung from his mount. Several men hurried to his aid.

One soldier roughly grabbed a shaking, sobbing Brenna by the shoulder, hauling her to her feet. Anger flared in his eyes as he glared at her. "What is your name?" he demanded gruffly.

Brenna's eyelids drooped in exhausted despair. Her voice trembled. "I am Brenna Brandere. Please don't hurt me. I'm so sorry this all happened. My sister...she forced me to help her. You...don't know her as do I."

With the fetid odor in the air slowly dissipating, the crowd continued to grow. Many apprehensively watched those attending the victims while others murmured frightened conjectures about what had occurred on their calm streets. Some broke through the edges of the crowd to carry blankets for the downed soldiers. Several men carefully wrapped the injured soldier in one blanket and used another as a makeshift stretcher. Placing the unconscious guard inside the stolen coach, two civilians volunteered to accompany him inside while two others climbed onto the driver's seat to drive him to the military hospital.

The elderly man first on the scene took another proffered blanket from someone's hands and respectfully covered the body of the slain officer. While one of the remaining soldiers secured Brenna Brandere, the other stood reverent watch over the corpse and solemnly awaited the arrival of additional officers summoned by a volunteer resident.

"Will he live?" Nagrand Mezden tersely asked the physician on duty at the small hospital serving the army's compound in Bracordia.

Bushy white eyebrows knit tightly together as the doctor shook his head and expelled a frustrated sigh. "How can I possibly say when I have no idea what caused his condition? He shows minor injuries consistent with being thrown from a horse; however, I see nothing that enables accurate diagnosis."

Muttering a curse under his breath, Nagrand quickly turned at the sound of a door opening. "Brother! How glad I am you are come."

"What happened?" Karan asked without greeting or preamble.

Nagrand's handsome face was flushed florid with fury. "It seems this soldier suffered an encounter with Count Brandere's missing daughter. I have one dead lieutenant and this man who is severely ill after being hit by what two surviving soldiers described as a fetid black cloud that almost seemed alive."

"Doctor Orman," Karan acknowledged the attending physician with a nod of his head. "What do you think?"

"His condition is serious. There is no fever, nor is there any sign of internal injury. I gave him a light sedative because he demonstrated signs of panic, extreme agitation, and irrational terror. I feared he might hurt himself or someone else. Examine him yourself. I welcome your opinion."

Clenching his jaw, Karan approached the patient whose eyelids twitched erratically. Gray pallor had replaced the victim's ruddy complexion. The soldier's skin felt cold and unusually dry. There was little reaction to the gentle prodding of the priest's examination.

"Should we summon Sindara?" Nagrand asked in a hushed voice.

Karan shook his head in frustration. How he hated the tumultuous beginning Thehrund and Sindara had already been forced to deal with in these first days of their marriage. To expose them to yet another crisis rocked him with regret. He gave his brother a solemn nod. "She may well be his only chance for survival."

The velvet blanket of peaceful meditation extended its gentle flow through every inch of Kendra's lithe, elegant body. Her soul felt awash in gentle ripples of soothing rhythms drawn from the furthest corners of the universe, its softly pulsating light and subdued hum lulling her into a state of complete relaxation and total receptivity.

"Kendra."

She heard her name clearly enunciated by a voice as smooth and clear as the ring of a perfectly cast bell. She smiled. Her lips mouthed words audible to no one but those who had come to her upon currents emanating from the universal source to which her soul had gravitated. She trusted that God would answer the prayerful entreaty for protection she had whispered before initiating her meditation.

The voice spoke again. "Kendra, you seek guidance. To one whose heart is so filled with trust, we gladly wish to help. Tell us."

Again, Kendra's generously full lips moved to shape silent, voiceless words. "My sister-in-spirit confronts powers that endanger her life and the lives of those she loves. I wish to help her, but she now lives where I cannot go. I have ideas, but I must know my direction is safe for her. My heart would break to bring her harm or more danger than she already faces."

For prolonged moments, Kendra waited and listened to musical measures emanated by the infinite universe. All sense of time had disappeared the second she entered the depths of her meditative state. She knew no sort of impatience. Her body and mind swayed in rhythm to the timeless song of the cosmos. Her lips curved upward as the distant voices again reached into her mind.

"Kendra, you have once already sought counsel from one older and more experienced than you. Trust your inner perceptions. Your intuition is blessed with clarity you must never doubt. Follow where it leads."

Kendra's expression changed. "I still have so much to learn. Wisdom comes to me slowly."

"You are far wiser than you realize. That is part of your gift. Cling to your wisdom. Trust your instincts. They will serve you well. Be warned that your forward path may carry you beyond what your mind has ever conceived, but we will always be near. We will always watch over you."

An hour later, Kendra felt unusual tranquility as she logged onto her computer. Her direction was clear. She glanced at the book beside her and entered the website name on her browser. A site with soft music and restful artwork welcomed her. She clicked on the link to contact the website's owner while hoping to be remembered as she typed in her request. Having taken the initial step, she breathed a sigh of satisfaction before resuming her studies.

Two days later, Kendra sat down to a light breakfast of fresh fruit and cereal while perusing her email. Her spoon stopped halfway to her mouth. Quickly putting it back in the bowl and shoving the dish aside, she opened the message that had caught her attention and eagerly read its contents. Tears brimmed in her eyes as she read the response a second time. Beyond mere knowledge, she literally felt the aid ready and waiting for her call.

Kendra forced herself to finish breakfast slowly, to enjoy nature's sweetness meant to nourish her body. A tempered joy filled her thoughts. Diana had stepped forth from shadows to defend her. She had then stood by her side through the years as both matured into womanhood. Diana had refused to let Kendra wallow in grief after the deaths of her parents. Taking charge of setting up a sound financial base with life insurance monies, Diana had encouraged her grieving friend to remember that her life was the greatest gift her parents had ever given her. Not only should she honor their memory, she should also honor her parents' lives and her own by fulfilling all the promises and dreams the Porter family had shared.

Kendra's hand lifted to fondle the crystal worn around her neck. Aside from memories, the precious pendant was the only remaining link to the real persona of her beloved friend. Kendra thought back to the many times the two had sat on Diana's bed, seeking reasons behind the bewildering dreams haunting her friend. Kendra's intuition had risen to new heights as she sensed forces far beyond their small apartment. Not once had she imagined the far reach of those forces.

Sitting at the breakfast table, she suddenly recognized an odd truth. Kendra understood that some remote part of her soul had always known that Diana was not as she appeared...that she was far more than a young woman delving into the world of banking. She had never belonged in that career any more than she had belonged in Kendra's world. Yes, Kendra affirmed to herself. She had always known that. When Diana began to awaken to her identity as Sindara, Kendra's innate wisdom had helped guide her friend to a quicker, more peaceful recovery of the life she was born to live.

The next week passed more quickly than Kendra expected. Work on final assignments proceeded smoothly and successfully. She would soon receive her coveted master's degree. She visited her parents' graves to pray and share her news. She meditated daily. Sacred energy streamed through her being. Those who took notice saw her walk alone, but Kendra knew that she was always loved, always protected. Although not yet sure where her path would lead, she looked ahead with quiet confidence.

Saturday morning. The coffeemaker gurgled its magic while creating an aromatic brew. A glass tray arranged with pastries, berries, grapes, and white cubes of mild cheese sat in the center of the kitchen table. While adding finishing touches to the settings, Kendra looked up at the sound of knocking at the door. Her heart leapt. Her glowing smile also shone from her eyes as she went to greet her anxiously awaited visitor.

An hour later, Kendra's gaze was thoughtful. Features the color of smooth milk chocolate were patiently expectant as she silently considered how glad she was to have ignored initial reservations. Dark brown eyes now fixed on the face of her visitor who appeared lost in deep thought.

Seated in the corner of the sofa, Madalyn Amador had listened to Kendra's account with rapt attention. Her memory returned to her first meeting with Kendra at the local expo. She recalled the moment she had touched Kendra and felt the surprising surge of energy from the young woman. Her mind's eye also swiftly recaptured the perplexing image of Diana Lorenz's aura that had fluctuated continuously in both breadth and color. Since their unusual discussion that day, Madalyn had often wondered if they had uncovered the mysterious source of Diana's dreams. One thing her guides had not prepared her for was that Diana had been a transplant from an entirely separate Earth-plane.

Madalyn's brown eyes finally left the realm of visualized memories to rejoin her hostess. She expelled a long breath. "I often wondered what happened to the two of you after I did your friend's reading. What you tell me goes far beyond anything I might have imagined or expected."

"I miss Sindara more than I can say," Kendra remarked, somewhat awed by newfound confidence. "I know very few sisters as close as we are."

A gentle smile lit Madalyn's face. "How much I admire you, Kendra, for speaking so firmly in the present when the person closest to you now dwells in another dimension."

The corner of Kendra's mouth twitched until a small smile lit her features. "Sindara and I are still able to talk with one another."

A puzzled frown crossed Madalyn's face. "Telepathically?"

Loose curls bounced as Kendra's head shook. "No, we actually see and speak to one another."

The older lady's head tilted to the left for several seconds. "My guides say you were given a rare gift. Precious few of the sacred crystals from the Guild of Angelic Guardians were ever permitted leave of the Repository of the Guardians. The amulet you wear is far more powerful than any simple tool for scrying."

"Fear not, Kendra," came the familiar voice inside her head. "Madalyn fills herself with light for the good of all and the harm of none. She comes only to serve her higher purpose and to offer you the benefit of her experience."

Rising from her chair, Kendra crossed the living room and knelt on the floor by the sofa. She drew in a deep breath and reached inside her blouse to withdraw the gold-framed crystal that had become her constant companion. Holding it on the palm of her hand, she showed Madalyn the precious pendant. Looking up, she noticed glistening tears brimming in the woman's eyes.

"Never in this lifetime did I expect to lay eyes on such an extraordinary treasure. Such a crystal serves so many purposes. Beyond the interdimensional communications you have with Sindara, these particular crystals offer protection to their bearers and repel sinister spirits seeking to spread chaos. My own guardian angel says that they can even be used for healing and to restore life to those at death's door."

Kendra swallowed several times before finding her voice. "That clarifies some things for me. I tried, but I found nothing to explain how Sindara and I see and speak with one another using the pendants."

Madalyn reached out and affectionately stroked Kendra's cheek. "You are especially blessed, Kendra Porter. I know you realize how important it is to protect this great gift. I would advise you to meditate on how best to utilize the many powers of your amulet. Your path is not yet revealed to me, but I sense your friend Sindara faces perhaps the worst of the dark entities. She will have great need of your help. This crystal will afford unique capability to fulfill your own higher purpose while helping her and, indeed, humanity on more than just her Earth-plane."

The magnitude of Madalyn's advice settled inside Kendra's mind as she prepared for bed that night. Her senses mulled over myriad aspects of all she and Madalyn had discussed. She decided to rest for the night and linger at church the next day to pray for continued divine guidance. After that, she would come home to meditate. Then, she would try to contact Sindara. Lying in the comfort of her own bed, she felt enveloped by the love of her angels, guides, and most of all, her loving God.

Thehrund's lips fervently plied those of his bride. He felt her mouth spread slowly into a smile before opening to the rapidly growing pressure of his kiss. Meanwhile, his hands began to roam the length of her feminine form, the silken smoothness of her skin feeling heavenly beneath the questing sweep of sensitive fingertips. Having roused her from deep slumber, he gloried in her responsiveness to his desire to love her.

Suddenly lifting his face from hers, he shook his head once in frustration before returning his full attention to his wife. Her eyes, still heavy with sleep, gazed at him with sensual regard. Just as he lowered his face to resume the possessive kiss he had used to awaken her, he heard what had been a tentative knock surge into urgent pounding.

His eyes met hers with exasperation and regret as he rolled over her body and slid off the bed. Shrugging into his robe and tugging it closed, he quickly tied the belt as he padded from the bedchamber. Shaking his head as he went, he finally reached the door and opened it.

"Nagrand," he growled in a low voice, "your timing could hardly be worse."

Nagrand's expression revealed guilt at disturbing his friend. "You know I never would have..."

"What happened?" Thehrund brusquely interrupted him.

"A patrol encountered Breeneth a short while ago near the southeastern edge of the city." Nagrand swallowed uncomfortably. "One soldier is dead. Another lies near death at the central military infirmary. Dr. Orman is attending him. Karan is there, too. Karan thinks Sindara may be the soldier's only chance for survival."

Squeezing his eyes tightly shut and grimacing, Thehrund shook his head. "So it begins," he muttered angrily. "Come inside and wait."

Returning to his bedchamber, Thehrund beheld his bride, his expression at once apologetic and appreciative. In the time it had taken him to answer the door and speak with Nagrand, she had risen and laid out a clean uniform for him and was already dressing herself. He still struggled to subdue the unfulfilled passion of their early morn awakening. As he started to change, he tamped down the woeful sense that he might never be able to share with her the time and attention she so deserved and that he so deeply craved.

Sindara deftly buttoned her cream-colored silk blouse and stepped into a burgundy riding skirt, quickly hooking the fasteners on the embroidered waistband. Padding across blue and gold carpet, she stretched out her right hand and gently grasped her husband's bearded chin, turning his face to meet her gaze. "Thehrund, do not fret. This great need is why I still live...and why we're now together."

"It's all so unfair, especially to you," he quietly remarked. Long hands spanned her waist, drawing her closer. Shadows darkened blue irises as he looked into her eyes and considered her selfless response. He realized with abrupt clarity that he could never face the violent and uncertain future ahead without her.

Rising on tiptoes, she brushed his lips with a gentle kiss. "Hurry, my husband. We are needed." She then backed away from his grasp to pull on riding boots and the jacket matching her skirt.

A half hour later, Sindara looked up at Karan with fresh appreciation for both his skill and his foresight. She dipped two fingers into a small jar of blessed oil and then into a carved box of cedar ashes he held for her. She drew a line with the mix across the forehead of the soldier now peacefully asleep. Minutes earlier, violent spasms had wracked his body as murky remnants of evil were expelled by the touch of Sindara's amulet. Silently, as Karan prayed for protection on those who had carried or treated the soldier, she marked everyone present with the sacred blend.

Leaving the patient under Dr. Orman's watchful eye, she and Karan left to join Thehrund in the office of the compound's commander. A young man in a crisply pressed uniform courteously opened the door for the priest and the princess to enter the comfortably furnished command office. Captain Modrun instantly rose to his feet and acknowledged them both with an elegant bow.

Sindara nodded at the captain before moving to stand beside her husband. Seeing questions in everyone's eyes, she managed a faint smile. "Your soldier rests. Dark remnants of Breeneth's attack have been driven from him. What have you learned about the incident?"

Nagrand spoke up in response to the prince's nod. "A patrol noticed a carriage approaching the southeast convergence leading to and from the city. Two soldiers went to investigate because of the current curfew. The officer in charge dismounted, apparently to speak to the driver and passenger. We're not exactly sure what happened after that, but it appears the lieutenant was hurled against a wall and killed. The other was forcibly thrown from his horse. As two remaining soldiers started toward the disturbance, Breeneth mounted a horse and fled the scene. Their report states they were unable to determine which road she took because of a billowing black cloud that engulfed her and sent a reeking wave that physically prevented pursuit."

Sindara shook her head. "I suspect they live to tell the account because the cloud stopped them from following." She sighed heavily. "Were there any other witnesses closer to the attack?"

278

Thehrund solemnly faced his bride. "One." Firmly grasping his wife's arms, he looked intensely into her eyes. "Brenna Brandere."

Sindara could not restrain the shocked gasp that followed his revelation. "Brenna?"

"Sindara," Thehrund began, noticing the instantaneous blanching of her face, "she has been taken to an office where she's being held under heavy guard."

"Has anyone questioned her?"

Captain Modrun shook his head. "After speaking to Sir Mezden, I thought it best to consult with the prince before undertaking any interrogation."

Thehrund's features revealed both anger and anxiety. "I thought it wise to discuss the matter with you first. You have the best insight regarding the nemesis we face."

Breathing in deeply, Sindara sifted through memories from years past when she attended school with Brenna. Silent for long moments, she turned her focus inward. There was no choice. Brenna must be questioned. With no knowledge regarding the extent of the prisoner's involvement with her sister, such interrogation might prove dangerous.

Sindara's eyelids closed as the men anxiously observed. Thehrund watched his wife's hand rise to cover the pendant he knew was tucked inside her blouse. He cast a troubled glance toward the others. Karan tilted his head to one side, signaling the need for patience. The prince's breath caught painfully in his chest as he watched and waited.

When she opened her eyes at last, resolve was evident. "I will speak with Brenna."

Thehrund shook his head. "We already know Breeneth planned the Articene incident six years ago. We also know she wields a sinister and deadly power. We have no idea how deeply her sister might be involved. I cannot allow you to expose yourself to such danger."

Taking no notice of those in the office with them, Sindara grasped his arms reassuringly. "It is imperative that we learn as much as possible about the extent of Breeneth's treachery. If Brenna is embroiled in this, there is less danger to me than anyone else."

Fearful anguish drew harsh lines into her husband's face. His voice dropped to barely more than a whisper as he echoed his father's words of days earlier. "I cannot bear even to think of losing you again."

Observing the exchange, Karan comprehended the depth of Thehrund's concern. "I will stay with her. Before we go in to speak with Brenna, I will pray protection on both of us and again anoint us with the cedar and oil." He paused and gave his friend a pointed look. "Remember. Sindara is better protected than any of us."

Ignoring everyone else, Thehrund drew his wife into his embrace. Gazing into her eyes, he confronted his most dreaded fear. He had lost her once. Losing her again would destroy him. This was burning truth he could not deny. He swallowed hard. "You are as my life's blood, Sindara... my heart and my soul. Are you sure?"

Her lips formed a smile. "I don't know what to expect, but I trust those who watch over me. You, my husband, must learn to believe in them. You also must remember to trust them. They did not fail you in the past. They will not fail you now."

When a sentry opened the heavy oaken door, Sindara swept into the office with Karan following close behind. The solid sound of the door closing finally stirred Brenna to faint awareness. She had dozed on and off ever since the soldiers had left her in the stark office containing only a battered desk and a chair covered in cracked leather. She had not cried out once or attempted to make any demands of her captors. Her appreciation for warm, dry shelter was too great.

Rousing herself, she looked up at a face that struck her as impossibly out of place. That familiar countenance was one she had thought never to see again. "Sindara," she croaked, her throat sore from several nights spent outside in dank, cold air.

Sindara's face remained impassive as she addressed her former class-mate. "Are you thirsty? Would you like water?"

Tears brimmed in dark eyes as Brenna lowered her face in shame. "I am thirsty...and hungry."

Sindara nodded her head sideways toward Karan. "Have someone bring her something to eat and drink."

Brenna rallied sufficiently to sit straighter in the old chair. Clutching the rough horsehair blanket more tightly, she attempted to smile. She had always been uneasy in Sindara's presence and had often conducted herself in an excessively ebullient manner to disguise how she and many others felt whenever Sindara was near.

Once a soldier delivered a tray holding a small pot of hot tea, a cup, and a plate of fruit and biscuits, Sindara spoke while Brenna started to eat. "Brenna, I am unsure you realize the gravity of your current circumstances. I have much to ask of you. I will accept nothing less than the truth in your responses."

Terror flashed in Brenna's eyes and then quickly faded as she swallowed hot tea. Her face dropped. The older sister she once adulated had changed, using fear and threats to coerce Brenna into acts far exceeding juvenile plots and pranks. Involuntary shivers raced through her body as her skin crawled with gooseflesh. Facing Sindara's stern expression suddenly seemed much less intimidating than dealing with Breeneth.

Brenna spoke haltingly as she slowly drank the soothing tea and nibbled a crisp biscuit. "Breeneth told me you were dead. She constantly gloated about how she planned with the Breyals to murder you. She never hesitated to remind me that she could do the same to me if I refused to help her. She set her mind long ago on marrying Prince Thehrund. She doesn't care a bit about him. I honestly doubt she loves anyone but herself. Her goal is to rule Ambracor."

While Karan leaned against a wall to observe, Sindara paced thoughtfully. "What is the source of power she uses? Do you know?"

Blood drained from Brenna's already pale face. "She will kill me if I tell you."

Sindara's head tilted sharply backward, and her eyes appraised the prisoner with fiery sparks of gold. "Your life could be forfeit already. You conspire with a traitor who has already killed an officer of His Majesty's army."

Brenna's chin quivered. Tears slid from the corners of her eyes. "Execution at the king's command would be mercifully quick. I have seen how my sister kills when she is angry. That is death no person should ever endure."

Sindara drew an impatient breath. "Brenna, your sister has given noxious drugs to your mother and has attacked your father. No one in her path is safe from the evil she employs. Understand what I say. No one in all of Ambracor is safe from her. You must tell me what you know. I must understand the source of her powers if we are to have any chance of stopping the spread of her malevolent plague."

Brenna shuddered yet again. When her hands trembled so violently that she could not even pick up the teapot, Sindara stepped closer to replenish the cup, which the beleaguered girl took up with both hands. Drinking slowly, she dared to meet the princess's gaze.

Stammering nervously, she replied, "My sister answers to an evil master. I saw them together only once. She doesn't know what I saw." A sob wrenched from the depths of her breast. "His image drove fear into the very core of my heart. His is a demonic presence, exactly like something I once read in the Ambracada. My sister delivers live victims to him."

Her eyes closed, and her jaw clenched. The very thought of the scene she had inadvertently witnessed still sickened her. "They kill the victim and then drink the blood. Then, he...Breeneth... They... They are...lovers of a most vile nature."

Sindara's eyes swiftly shifted to Karan, who had just straightened in shocked dismay. They had expected to learn Breeneth was a conjurer of dark spells and perhaps in collusion with others devoted to serving ne-farious entities. Her union with a master demon far exceeded any threat they might have anticipated. Sindara's right hand lifted involuntarily to rest above the pendant tucked inside her blouse.

"Sindara?" Brenna murmured fearfully as tears streaked pale cheeks. "Papa? Mamma? Are they dead? Did she kill them? I've been so afraid for them. She was furious when she forced me to go with her after she attacked Papa. When we returned to the hotel, we had to hide and then flee because of all the soldiers there."

Sudden sympathy filled Sindara. The crystal vibrating against the sensitive skin of her chest assured her of the truth of Brenna's revelations. Disregarding rapidly expanding abilities to discern the significance of the crystal's messages for later contemplation, Sindara shook her head. "Your parents are weak, but they are recovering. I cannot promise you complete protection, Brenna, but you must tell us everything you know. I need to understand the black cloud and the traces it leaves in its victims following an attack. Every shred of information you reveal provides us a better chance of preventing others from being hurt and stopping the spread of Breeneth's wicked intentions."

A fleeting spark of trust flashed in Brenna's eyes. When she had at-tended school with Sindara, most students had kept discreet distance from the girl from Arvacon. Rumors, gossip, and speculation abounded. Every-one recognized how different she was. Even teachers treated her with exceptional deference. Some had thought she was an angelic incarnation. Others suspected she might be one of the faith guardians described in some of the earliest accounts of Ambracor's history. Watching her carefully and noticing the slightest shimmer of light surrounding her, Brenna wondered if she might be both.

"I will help you in every way I can. I only ask that you try to protect my parents and my brother."

"And you?" Sindara asked.

"I will accept with a grateful heart any help you can give, but I have done much wrong because of my sister. Guilt now rests heavily upon me. I did not resist her demands when I could have. It may be too late for me... but not so for others."

Chapter Fourteen

KING HAMUND'S BEARING WAS TALL and stately as he conducted a final inspection of troops gathered in the large square outside the gated walls of the royal palace. Broad shoulders squared as his hands firmly clasped behind his back. Long gray hair fluttered in light breezes as the braids he wore on either side of his bearded face reinforced the regal image his soldiers expected of him. Blue eyes surveyed men standing by their horses, all prepared for the hastily organized journey to Arvacon Province. While stern features conveyed proud approval, his heart dreaded the very real possibility that many of these fine soldiers might never return to their homes and families in Bracordia.

The king's farewell address had been forthright. He had told his army that, although Ambracor was not yet fully engaged in active war, they faced a most appalling enemy. That enemy was aggressively inciting barbaric Breyals to invade and destroy the peace and prosperity their nation had enjoyed for centuries. Within Ambracor's borders lay a growing menace that intended to bring the savagery of Breyal warriors into the heart of this peaceful haven. Hamund had urged his army to cling to courage, faith, and prayer. His expression had been grim, his mood somber, his voice grave. The king finally dropped to one knee and prayed for Creator God to guide his people through whatever chaos war might bring.

Hamund barely concealed burgeoning worry as he faced his only child. As he assessed Thehrund from head to toe, his chest swelled with pride at the fearsome warrior image projected by the tall, powerful man his son had become. Grasping Thehrund's forearms, he thoughtfully inspected thick leather bracers reinforced with bands of steel. Despite feeling immense esteem for this young prince, his stomach pitched uncomfortably as his son prepared to lead the heavily armed battalion to Arvacon.

"Father," Thehrund began as he held his father's attention, "this excursion is not an army marching off to war. Not yet anyway. You mustn't worry so. It's not good for you or Mother."

Hamund briskly shook his head. "I know, Thehrund. Most of these men will remain at the fort in Articene to reinforce Artrian's militia. That means fewer guards will accompany you to Cahmdurn. When you have children of your own, you'll better understand our feelings. It's especially worrisome knowing that Sindara travels with you."

Thehrund nodded. "You cannot blame her for desiring a reunion with her family. You know how close they are."

"I know, just as I know how close your trip will carry you to our borders with Breyal when your route turns toward Articene..."

"We're prepared this time, Father. I cannot guarantee there will be no clashes, but you know the extent of precautions I've taken. I'm confident all will go well."

Hamund forced a smile. Raising his right hand, he tightly gripped his son's shoulder. "Thehrund, I know I've said it far too little, but I am exceedingly proud of you. Ride well, my son. May Creator God's blessings shine upon you throughout your journey."

Sindara hugged a tearful Queen Narlina a final time before joining her husband and father-in-law. Her countenance was gentle as she looked up into Hamund's face. "Father, I remind you. We go because there are things we must do to ensure Ambracor's survival in the event full-scale war erupts. Thehrund prepares the military side. I must address matters of faith that will sustain us all. While we're gone, we must rely on your unique skills to unite all of Ambracor's provinces to stand as one."

As he often did, Hamund held her face between his hands. He tamped down reviving memories and gazed affectionately at the young woman who had saved his life. "Sindara, I finally have a daughter in you. My pride in you and my son is beyond measure. Take care...great care..." His voice broke as he hugged her tightly.

Queen Narlina walked to her husband's side and clutched his arm as they watched Thehrund help Sindara mount her horse before he returned long enough to kiss his mother's cheek. Then, swinging neatly up onto his tall, majestic, Arvacon-bred stallion, he cast his parents a farewell smile before signaling the company of soldiers to begin their expedition to the southeast.

On the third night of their trek, Thehrund silently observed his new wife as she quickly and efficiently organized the inside of the large tent erected for the royal couple's use. His mouth twitched with a suppressed grin. He had always admired the formidable equestrian skills that seemed bred into Arvacon men. Until this trip, he had often doubted tales about Arvacon noblewomen being just as well suited to riding horseback. Keeping a watchful eye on his wife as they traveled, he could only admire the way she sat in the saddle hour after hour without complaint or appearing overly weary.

"There. Our bed is made," she pronounced as she turned to her husband. "Are you ready to retire, or will you go out once more to check the camp?"

Thehrund rose from the bench where he sat and approached his wife. "I'm quite content to rest tonight." He reached out and tucked her hair behind one ear. "Do you have any idea how much you amaze me?"

"In what way?" she asked curiously as his fingers gently pushed away her hands to take over the task of unbuttoning her blouse.

For a long moment, he ignored her question and concentrated on opening her blouse. Bending forward, he brushed heated kisses along the base of her throat. She reacted with an involuntary gasp and tilted her head to invite more of his tantalizing attentions. Checking himself, he took a single step backward and regarded her with an intense gaze.

"You, my beloved princess, have kept unwavering pace with an army for three solid days of riding. Next, you ensure our comfort in this tent. Then, you respond to a kiss that invites your tired husband to forget his weariness and make love to you in a bivouac surrounded by a full battalion of the king's finest troops. I find that quite amazing."

Pursing her lips in a sad attempt to avoid grinning, Sindara snaked her arms upward, gently sliding her hands beneath his hair and clasping them behind his neck. "Even as Diana, I grew up loving horses and riding as often as a city girl could." Her eyes suddenly darkened, and her voice lowered to sultry tones. "As for the rest, Your Highness, I am inspired by the handsome prince who sought me out and claimed me for his own. Should I not take full advantage of every moment we now share?"

She followed her question by rising on her toes and tugging gently on his earlobe with her lips while allowing her warm breath to fill his ear. The erotic gesture launched a veritable explosion of tremors that swiftly rippled along every nerve of his spine and then spread tingling waves throughout his body. He lowered his face to capture her lips in a demanding kiss that all too quickly flared into passionate flames only she could quench.

Quickly discarding their clothes, Thehrund carefully lowered her to the thick pad laid out on the ground. Kneeling over her, he swept a languorous gaze along the length of her body as light and shadows cast by a small lantern highlighted the gracious contours of her feminine beauty. How captivated he felt by her presence as she gently stroked the well-defined lines of his muscular arms and chest.

"Sindara," he whispered, his low-pitched voice sounding even deeper as flaming desire sent hot blood roaring through his veins.

Firmly grasping his braids in her hands, Sindara drew his face closer. She literally ached for his touch. Her lips parted, begging from him the ardent kisses that kindled her own fiery pleasures. The moment he responded to her unspoken request, she wrapped her arms tightly around him, pulling him until his weight pressed her into their sleeping mat. Long, elegant hands caressed his arms, his back, and his hips, eliciting occasional gasps as he momentarily broke the union of their kiss.

The warmth of her skin against his quickly overwhelmed him until he was helpless to resist. Dragging his lips from hers, Thehrund initiated fresh exploration of the body he was coming to know so well. He freely bestowed kiss after kiss, lingering in those special places that he now knew drove her into impassioned frenzy. Never forgetting the conversation he overheard just before their wedding, he again made certain to pay homage to the narrow white scar low on her side. He then retraced the blazing trail of kisses until his mouth once again reclaimed hers.

From the first moment of their bonding, his impassioned possession filled her with the heated sensations that often drew fervent moans of ecstasy. Faintly aware of the army beyond the tent's canvas walls, he planted kiss after kiss on her mouth to quiet her as he sought to give her the ultimate pleasure of their union. Feeling her shuddering responses inspired him until he surrendered to his own driving need. Breathlessly, they held one another, limbs entangled, breathing ragged...each thoroughly satisfied with their loving.

Reluctantly, Thehrund slowly forced himself to rise from their sleeping mat. Behind an adoring smile lay acute awareness that, despite an army of soldiers surrounding them, they were still vulnerable to attack. In dim lamplight, he located hastily discarded clothing and donned tunic and trousers.

"Thehrund? Is something wrong?"

Sindara had raised up, supporting herself on one elbow. Dark tresses draped over her shoulders and clung to her cheeks. Illuminated by the lantern's dim light, he could see features soft and glowing in the aftermath of their lovemaking. How he wished for the freedom to lie with her in peace and to hold her body close to his in tranquil slumber.

"There's nothing wrong," he replied after a prolonged pause, finding speech surprisingly difficult. Perhaps it was because he almost regretted the sense of duty forcing him to leave her side. "I'm glad the night is cool. I'm not overly fond of sleeping fully clothed, but considering how close we are to the border, being prepared for unexpected visitors seems a wise precaution."

She understood his explanation as matter-of-fact. Extending her hand, she accepted his help in rising from their bed. Quickly pulling on lace-embellished pantalets, she then put on one of the lace and satin bras she had brought with her through the portal and slipped a camisole and shirt over that. Quickly organizing shoes, stockings, riding skirt, jacket, and her sheathed sword on the bench, she ensured that essentials would be ready in case of urgent need.

Thehrund's forehead crinkled as his eyebrows rose impossibly high. His mouth spread into a wide grin as he again shook his head, his tousled hair creating that wild, leonine appearance she found so seductive. He then chuckled while admiring her quick efficiency in preparing for un-welcome contingencies. "I remain more amazed than ever," he remarked sincerely.

Laughing softly, she kissed her index finger and then placed it gently against his lips. "It's time to sleep, my husband. Tomorrow will be another long day of travel."

Settling into place on the makeshift bed, he stilled an oath born of anger at the threat posed by marauding Breyals and Breeneth Brandere. Resting his arm beneath Sindara's, he tucked her close, clothes notwith-standing, and chose prayer to usher him into sleep. He prayed for his wife's continued safety now that she was home in Ambracor and thanked Creator God for the immeasurable blessing that they were now wed. His last prayerful entreaty was to help him and his people through whatever dangers and hostilities might lie ahead.

Four days later, the battalion approached Fort Articene. During the years following the Breyal attack against the king's escort, Count Varacor invested heavily in reinforcing the fort's perimeter with thick walls of stone. Watchtowers, spaced at strategic intervals, provided sentries with excellent vantage points for monitoring the surrounding territory. Towers on the east side of the fort were higher to enable sentinels to view a broad expanse of terrain beyond Arvacon's border with Breyal. Stonemasons had laid huge stones and placed openings at irregular intervals for use by archers in case of all-out assault. Meticulous design and construction would make scaling the high walls difficult. Tall iron fencing, topped with sharpened spikes, lined outer edges of the upper ramparts. Soldiers on walkways could more easily defend against enemy fighters in the unlikely event some might successfully reach the top of the wall.

Sentries alerted the fort's commander to the imminent arrival of nearly a thousand troops flying the king's colors. Colonel Erator Varacor called for his horse and rode out with several aides to welcome the massive force. Nearing the advancing body of mounted soldiers, he murmured silent thanks to Creator God. A lead soldier carried a banner signaling they rode under the command of Prince Thehrund, prompting a flood of relief as Erator realized his father must have successfully convinced King Hamund of Arvacon's desperate need for reinforcements.

A high-stepping black stallion broke through the front ranks. Impressively tall in the saddle, Thehrund urged his steed forward to meet the greeting party. Quickly dismounting, Erator strode forward to greet the prince who had just gotten off his horse and handed the reins over to a junior officer.

"Your Highness," Erator bowed in greeting. "Welcome to Articene. You cannot imagine how much your arrival is appreciated." Propriety fell victim to their long friendship as Erator then greeted the prince with a hearty embrace and a grin. "After just returning from an excursion to monitor Breyal movements, I must say the sight of all these soldiers is certainly a surprise. How I hope our fathers have finally agreed to augment our provincial militia with some of these troops."

Thehrund tugged leather riding gloves from his hands and nodded. "I bring four hundred troops plus a convoy of supplies to reinforce your position here. Another four hundred are to be stationed at strategic points along Arvacon's borders. Your father is most persuasive when the need arises."

Erator chuckled. "Father is exceptionally convincing when it comes to protecting Arvacon's welfare. Tell me. How are your parents?"

"They are quite well, thank you. I admit, however, that Father was quite worried about my leading these regiments here with all that threatens your borders."

Erator's expression settled into a grave mask. "Patrols are constantly routing small raiding parties. We're convinced the Breyal intent is to assess our strengths and weaknesses. I think they may even be trying to draw sufficient troops from the fort to leave it more vulnerable to attack."

"No doubt," Thehrund replied with a curt shake of his head. "On another note, I apologize no advance notice of our arrival was sent. Unsettling events in Bracordia have caused us to implement extreme caution with dispatches to provinces bordering Breyal. You must have your staff start organizing encampment for the regiments to remain here and then prepare their assignments. Regimental commanders will cooperate in every way possible."

Erator's golden brown hair rippled with the shake of his head. "Such news goes beyond simple relief. You can brief me on those unsettling events over dinner. Meila will be delighted to see you." Pausing, he continued, "And you, Thehrund...you look remarkably well. Certainly better than you've looked for quite some time."

Thehrund met Erator's appraisal with a nod. "Fortunately for me, recent events in Bracordia have not been all bad. Once things are settled here and remaining troops move out to their assignments, I will travel with an escort to Cahmdurn to meet your parents. They're headed home via the road through Carlester. I plan to stay with them several days. Your presence in Cahmdurn will be required for at least two days."

Erator's forehead furrowed. "I don't understand. I can't imagine Father wanting me to leave my post if the situation is severe enough to merit stationing so many soldiers here."

"We have many plans to discuss, and I have much to explain. The privacy of your home in Cahmdurn will be far more suitable. Your father has also kindly offered me the use of the Varacor country estate for a few days before I return to Bracordia. Recent affairs have given me hardly a moment's peace with my new bride."

"New bride? You've finally married?" The startling news prompted stunned disbelief that plainly showed on Erator's face.

"I have," Thehrund replied. "She travels with me and should reach the front ranks any minute now. I do hope we might impose upon your hospitality for a night or two before we leave."

Before Erator could question Thehrund further, the sound of hooves against the packed dirt road caused both men to turn. Flanked by guards on either side, the center rider wore a fawn-colored riding habit typical of styles long preferred by Arvacon noblewomen. The broad brim of her hat shaded her face from bright afternoon sunlight. Her body moved in fluid rhythm with her horse's pace as it trotted forward.

Guiding her mount toward the soldier holding the reins of the prince's horse, she prepared to dismount. Thehrund hurried to place strong hands around her waist as she seemingly floated down from the saddle. Murmuring thanks for her husband's help, she reached up, swept the hat from her head with a flourish, and then turned an excited expression toward her older brother. Her shapely lips spread into an impossibly wide smile as tears suddenly filled her eyes.

Paralyzed momentarily by shock, Erator stared at the beaming face he had long since relegated to memory. When he saw her arms stretch out and heard her well-remembered voice call his name, he launched himself forward. The length of his stride carried him to her in seconds. Enfolding her in an exultant embrace, he lifted her off her feet. "Sindara!" he cried out. "How can this be? Is it really you? I thought..."

Once he set her back on the ground and tightly grasped her arms, tears of joy streamed down his cheeks, creating jewel-like sparkles as they caught in his sable-brown beard. Scanning every feature, he could scarcely believe hers was the same face he had last seen in combat six years earlier. Leaning forward, he kissed her cheeks and then pulled her into a tight hug.

Thehrund firmly grasped his brother-in-law's shoulder. His voice held a tremor that conveyed empathy. "Perhaps now you better understand why I said we have much to discuss."

That evening, spacious quarters assigned to the fort's commanding officer were alight with candles casting a mellow glow over faces celebrating the miraculous return of Erator's sister and her marriage to Ambracor's prince. Over a dinner of simple but satisfying fare, Sindara much preferred hearing how Erator had met his wife and their subsequent courtship and marriage. With the upcoming trip to Cahmdurn, they all agreed it would be easier to discuss details of Thehrund's search for Sindara and their reunion once the entire family gathered together.

Meila, Erator's wife, had met her husband only months after the skirmish that had marked what everyone thought was Sindara's death. Since then, she had heard many stories about Erator's sister. Watching the close bond between brother and sister, she better understood the somber mood that overtook the Varacor family each year when they observed the anniversary of the Articene attack.

After dinner, Sindara sat happily on a woven rug to play with Graden, her precocious nephew. Thehrund watched in wonder as his wife connected with the youngest Varacor. Exchanging occasional glances with Erator and Meila, the prince found himself thoroughly entertained by the antics between aunt and nephew as they invented games with a ball and other colorful toys.

Rarely had Thehrund interacted with young children, but he eventually joined the fun with Sindara and little Graden. The ball often rolled in a direction past Sindara's reach, causing the prince to stretch across the floor to retrieve the toy. When play turned to softer animals stitched from colorful fabrics, Graden made sure to place an extra toy beside Sindara.

The child's delightful laughter soon quieted as he began to yawn. Toddling over to his new uncle, Graden grasped one of Thehrund's braids and tugged gently. "Unca," he murmured, "I'm tired. Time for bed. Will you come?"

"No, Graden, Deiria will take you to bed," Meila told her son as she picked him up and handed him to the child's nursemaid. "Say goodnight to Uncle Thehrund and Aunt Sindara."

Graden vigorously shook his head, golden curls bouncing. "No, Mama. I want Unca."

Thehrund's broad smile held newfound affection. "Graden, let your nurse get you ready for bed. I'll come in to say goodnight before you go to sleep. Is that all right?"

The child's pleading blue-gray eyes regarded his uncle. "You won't forget?"

"I promise. I won't forget."

When the nursemaid advised the child waited in bed, Thehrund followed Erator and Meila into the baby's room. Once the parents had kissed their son and said goodnight, Thehrund leaned far over the edge of the bed to caress the child's velvety cheek. "Goodnight, Graden."

A chubby hand once again reached for one of Thehrund's braids. "Unca, I like Aunt Sindara's angel. It's so pretty." The little boy yawned. "G'night."

Thehrund swallowed hard and watched until the boy's eyelids slowly closed. Never had he seen such an expression of pure peace as when he noted the soft, round features of the sleeping child's face. Little Graden's words lingered in his mind, filtering through thoughts and feelings but failing to find a place to settle. What had the child seen? Why had he told only Thehrund?

Late the following morning, Prince Thehrund found himself thoroughly impressed with his brother-in-law's tactical thinking and organizational skills. Following Count Varacor's detailed planning and Erator's subsequent implementation of those plans, Articene had become a key fortification because of its size and strategic location. With the arrival of additional troops plus quartermaster support and supplies to augment the large provincial militia garrisoned there, the fort was more secure than ever.

Analysis of defense readiness led the two men to discuss additional possibilities for addressing the Breyal threat. Somewhat restless, Thehrund rose from a wooden chair and paced over to stare through the window of Erator's office. Erator watched with complete comprehension of the kinds of questions and concerns that must fill the prince's mind.

"You may disagree," Erator began in a voice accustomed to command, "but I urged Father to approach the Governors' Security Council with a recommendation to undertake offensive actions. No one hates the idea of war more than I. I've witnessed too many instances of the brutality upon which Breyals thrive. To allow them to continue gathering warriors in ever larger numbers strikes me as folly...an open invitation for full-scale invasion. Do you know if he broached the subject?"

Thehrund exhaled a heavy sigh. "He did." Returning to his chair, he firmly grasped the back and leaned forward. "I had planned to discuss this after we arrived Cahmdurn, but perhaps now is as good a time as any."

Erator's eyes reflected questions. "Does your father continue to oppose such action?"

Penetrating blue eyes gazed steadily at Erator. "When I left Bracordia, Father still detested the idea of war. He was, however, working with provincial governors from the north and west to better organize militias and to recruit and train as many new federal troops as possible. He finally comprehends the need for tactical offense. Speed, cunning, and faultless planning are crucial. There is, however, another factor that casts a dangerous shadow over all we might hope to accomplish."

"What might that be?" Erator asked cautiously, noting growing strain on the prince's face.

Thehrund straightened before sitting down. "Not so much what as who...Breeneth Brandere."

Erator responded with a brisk shake of his head. "Count Brandere's daughter? The one..."

Thehrund quickly interrupted him before he could finish. "The same. The ambush at Articene where Sindara disappeared was no random attack. Breeneth is a traitor and involved with the Breyals. The attack was planned to murder Sindara so that Breeneth could plot circumstances that would force me to marry her."

"Count Brandere's daughter a traitor?" Erator questioned incredulously. "I'm not sure what to say. For six years, it surely seemed she was successful. We all accepted Sindara's death. Now..."

Thehrund smiled wryly. "Not all of us. It's too complicated to go into at the moment. I promise that Sindara and I will explain when we meet with your parents. For now, the most frightening issue is one of an utterly sordid nature. Breeneth's family is being held in protective custody at a secret location. She drugged her mother and attacked her father. She also threatened to kill her entire family. If she finds them, she's fully capable of carrying out any threats. She has already murdered one officer in Bracordia and critically injured another as she fled the city."

Erator's eyes widened. He felt a sickening hollowness in his stomach. "Dare I ask how?"

Thehrund swallowed against the knot in his throat. "According to her sister, Breeneth has become consort to a master demon. She also commands unusual powers he has given her. They already exert strong influence over Breyal. Their sights are now firmly set on conquering Ambracor."

Erator's quick mind assessed Thehrund's revelation. "I find it more imperative than ever to prevent the enemy from amassing an even greater army intent on invasion. It will be much easier to catch them unaware and eliminate smaller tribal groups traveling toward Barachal. Surprise can prove an effective weapon. My concern is that our militia and our army are trained well to fight Breyal warriors. That obviously isn't our greatest problem. How are we to face demonic forces such as you describe?"

Heaving a sigh, Thehrund leaned forward. "Before we leave for Cahmdurn, we must summon all local priests and other avowed religious. When they meet with Sindara, she will instruct them on what we know and how to address the threats. Beyond that, every man, woman, and child will need to understand that Creator God is our greatest strength. Our collective faith must serve as our best defense."

❈ ❈ ❈

The warmth of a bright spring day quickly diminished as evening's cooler air slowly descended on the peaceful city of Cahmdurn. Broad avenues, constructed of cobblestones or bricks, crisscrossed Arvacon's capital. The city's central district boasted elaborate architecture with sturdy brick walls lending an air of durable stability. Stucco walls in residential areas, gleaming brightly in the afternoon sun, began to blush with rose-colored hues. Brilliant reds, blues, yellows, and greens on neatly painted doors, window frames, shutters, and trim assumed softened tones beneath waning sunshine.

Notices posted early that morning had announced Prince Thehrund's impending arrival in Cahmdurn. He was bringing his new wife, the daughter of Arvacon's beloved Count Varacor whose life was being openly declared a miracle of their age. The prospect of witnessing Sindara Varacor's return to Cahmdurn gave rise to an unparalleled mood of celebration. Main streets crowded just after noon with citizens anxious to catch a glimpse of their prince and his bride.

Enthusiasm stirred the gathered throng into a state of throbbing exultation. Tears streaked many faces. Flowers of every color rained down on the newlyweds and their dignified escort. As Sindara's horse proudly pranced alongside her husband's stallion, a great roar sounded when the prince deftly snatched a white rose from the air, kissed it, and then offered it to his wife. Cheers of "Long live Prince Thehrund!" and "Long live Princess Sindara!" came from hundreds upon hundreds who had spilled onto the streets to welcome their future king and queen.

Sindara Varacor was fondly remembered for her kind attentiveness to the sick and elderly during her holidays from school so many years before. Those who saw her were dumbstruck by beauty untouched in the years that had passed. Although no details had been released, a simple statement drew the crowd's adulation to their handsome prince. He had risked his very life persevering in the search for the woman he loved. Unwavering faith in Creator God had inspired him to undertake a perilous quest that had finally led to the couple's triumphant return home.

Outside the stately governor's mansion, citizens filed respectfully along well-kept lawns and walks beneath the golden glow of dozens of lanterns suspended from scrolled, wrought-iron posts. Cahmdurn's residents left small gifts, heartfelt notes, and bouquets of flowers in reverent tribute to the couple whose beaming smiles had accompanied their waves to the city's affectionate welcome.

Inside the house, lights shone from every window. Servants who had worked years for the Varacor family had been treated to tearful greetings from the new princess whom they remembered so affectionately. Sindara felt overjoyed to receive enthusiastic hugs from Rezda, the younger brother who had delighted in teasing her unmercifully during their childhood. Greeting Rezda's new wife had thrilled Sindara as she shared memories that brought embarrassed color to her brother's cheeks and prompted comical, lighthearted defense.

Dinnertime found the entire family gathered at the long dining table lit with flickering candles that glinted light off porcelain dinnerware, hand-blown crystal, and gold-trimmed silverware. No effort had been spared in the preparation of Sindara's favorite foods. Heavily laden serving trays were set on wooden stands by smiling servants attired in white jackets. Count Varacor stood at the head of the table and invited his wife and his sons, daughters-in-law, daughter, and son-in-law to stand and join hands. Noting aloud how the circle of family had grown, he prayed they would always be bound by sacred familial love and loyalty. He offered intense gratitude to Creator God for the gift of their lives and prayed for continued blessings upon each and the nation they were bound to serve.

As the bounteous repast moved from delicate soup, hearty main courses, colorful vegetables, and freshly baked bread, Thehrund undertook a daunting task. He described his tale of angel voices, frozen time, and wanderings that had frequently taken him far from Ambracor to worlds very different from their own. He described enormous vessels that gleamed with metal skins and sailed through the air. He talked about slender rectangles that showed moving pictures complete with music and voices. He spoke of great chests that kept food icy cold and carriages needing no horses to pull wagons larger than average houses in their own world.

His description of Sindara driving a smaller coach into which Karan, Nagrand, and he had barely fit was one that elicited laughter from all around the table. Thehrund told how he had squeezed his eyes tightly shut while she drove the strange vehicle. With sweeping gestures, he described being terrified that she would surely crash into one of hundreds of such carriages speeding haphazardly in every direction or smash them into some great wall. In the end, he humorously conceded that her skills with the motorized coach had been impressive, delivering them safely from one side of the city to the other, then back again.

As a luscious, creamy dessert garnished with fresh fruit was finished and tea served, the mood in the dining room assumed a more thoughtful tone. Rezda, generally the most extroverted of the three Varacor siblings, cast an adoring glance in his sister's direction. Intense eyes, blue-gray like his father's, caught her gaze. "Sindara, you've been so quiet. What was this like for you? How does it feel to live another life in another world and then suddenly learn you actually belong somewhere else?"

Solemnity replaced her merry expression. "I think words cannot possibly express the array of emotions I've experienced since Thehrund and Nagrand rescued me from a band of assailants." She paused, then reached for the reassuring grasp of her husband's hand.

"At times, it seemed as if I lived two lives at once. There was the couple I thought of as my parents who tended to my every need. They provided me a home, affection, religious guidance, and education...all I could have wanted. Much like here, I knew many people, but I called few friends. In fact, for many years, I had only one really close friend." She blinked back tears as she thought how much she missed Kendra.

"Sindara?" Thehrund's quiet voice gently encouraged her.

Drawing in a shaky breath, she glanced appreciatively at Thehrund before meeting her brother's waiting gaze. "For many years, my nights were filled with dreams so real and vivid that I often awoke laughing or crying. I saw faces and heard voices." She glanced around the table. "I saw *your* faces and heard *your* voices, but I couldn't imagine it being anything more than images from an overworked imagination. Once I became close to my friend Kendra, their intensity increased. I remembered sorrow and piercing pain."

She looked down at her hand wrapped securely in Thehrund's. Her lower lip quivered. "That's when I started thinking of the dreams as nightmares. As the frequency grew, so did my fears. During the last few years, I saw eyes staring at me whenever I dreamed. The face was always hidden in shadows, but the eyes terrified me. Someone was watching me, but I had no idea who."

"Sindara, you can stop if you wish. You don't need to relive this now," Artrian told his daughter in a tender, soothing voice.

She braved a smile. "Father, it isn't easy, but sharing this is like clearing weeds from an overgrown flowerbed. I'm clearing away shadows of fear with the help of everyone I love most. It is a good thing to release the memories."

She looked back at Rezda. "For the longest time, I sensed deep inside that I was somehow in the wrong place. Not only did I feel it, I somehow *knew* it. I had been told that I was abandoned as a newborn and adopted by Master Garen and Lady Aminta, who turned out to be angelic guardians.

"When the face in the shadows of my dreams grew closer and more intense during the last year of my other life, I actually developed physical symptoms. As far as I knew, I already had two scars on my left side when I was adopted. Suddenly, my side often hurt after I woke from the nightmares, and those scars began to bleed. I saw several doctors. Not one could explain the bleeding."

Thehrund's forehead creased as he turned questioning eyes to his bride. "Was it the same pain you mentioned that morning in the park?"

Somewhat surprised that he recalled her remark, she slowly nodded. "How can I possibly explain the confusion related to the nightmares and unexplained bleeding? When Thehrund rescued me, I didn't recognize him or the others at first. I do vaguely recall Thehrund picking me up off the street. The faintest scent he uses caught my attention before I lost consciousness. I think that may have been the first tangible link to my life here. Still, it took days for my memory to return. Kendra was the first to realize that the face in my dreams that frightened me so much was actually Thehrund's. She told me with absolute certainty that his were the eyes I saw as he searched for me."

Tears streaked Liana's cheeks as she reached across the table for her daughter's hand. Her eyes briefly darted to her son-in-law's face. "His heart never faltered, Sindara. Never have I known a man to cling so tenaciously to faith as he did while he searched for you." To Thehrund, she said, "You cannot know how much I love you for your courage in bringing our daughter home."

Thehrund's face fell. His own lashes restrained unbidden tears. His voice wavered when he finally looked up. "Creator God blessed my quest. Now, I have all of you as my family and Sindara as the wife I always needed."

Sindara leaned against Thehrund's arm. Her expression was tranquil. Her eyes shone with love. "Because my husband received Creator God's blessings, I am reunited with the family I love. I praise Creator God daily in prayer for each of you and for finally allowing me the joy of having Thehrund as my husband."

Chapter Fifteen

THE LEAFY CANOPY ALLOWED ONLY random patches of sunlight to penetrate the dense forest. Scattered across damp ground were soggy leaves, swollen pine needles, and broken branches. Tall, straggly stems abounded, their stiff, prickly thorns snagging clothing and scratching delicate skin. Stretched from tree to tree, sticky, silvery threads were woven into intricate webs nearly impossible to see unless a ray of sunlight hit at just the right angle.

Birds scolded the intruder who dared to disrupt the peace of their lush forest abode. Insects buzzed the head of the lone figure tramping along with a large stick to knock offending brush out of the way. Trunks of tall, sturdy trees grew close together, making passage difficult while their thick roots protruded from the ground in an apparent conspiracy to trip the invader.

Tired, bruised, and frustrated, Breeneth finally felt she could continue no longer. She needed to stop, to rest. So far, she congratulated herself on her resourcefulness. She had stolen food and clothing from unwary farmhouses during her solitary trek southward. How she desired a bath and a dry bed. Dreading the thought of a shower coming in the guise of cold rain, she spotted a possible bed ahead of her. Reaching a grove of thick pines, she gratefully clambered beneath their sweeping boughs and nestled into the soft depths of pine needles covering the ground.

Sleep quickly claimed her. Hers was a dreamless slumber. After committing herself to her master, she had gladly forsaken a life of simplistic wishes and hopes. She took no satisfaction in the happiness of those around her. Her life did have purpose...purpose centered on accomplishing personal comfort, grandeur, and whatever or whoever might fulfill her fancy at any given moment. People standing in her way meant no more than scraps of useless garbage to be kicked aside or burned to ashes. No longer did dreams visit her sleep. Her waking obsessions were more than sufficient to merit her full attention.

Awakened by the tickle of a tiny spider trekking across her cheek, she irritably swiped the offending creature from her face. Her arms and legs felt chilled and stiff, the hideous-looking farmer's jacket too short to cover her completely. She hissed aloud at the monotonous chirruping of crickets. The chirping ceased instantly, replaced by eerie pre-dawn silence. She sat up, angered anew that she had not tethered her stolen horse tightly enough two nights earlier, giving the cursed animal its chance to escape.

Getting up, she yawned and stretched. Glancing downward, she rued the fact that her shoes were hardly sturdy enough to withstand the rough path she followed through forest and glen as she forged her way toward safe haven. On the other hand, her stolen livery proved much more practical than the snugly fitted bodices and full skirts of her luxurious gowns. The woolen jacket and linen shirt gave her ease of movement while trousers, rolled up at the hems, allowed more efficient progress through thick brush. Leather driving gloves provided little warmth but helped protect small hands unaccustomed to harsh activity.

Carefully walking beneath dark skies yielding to a determined sunrise, Breeneth stared upward. Master had told her to watch the heavens for a particular constellation that appeared in the shape of a hexagon. An unusually bright star would look much larger than the others. Should she ever lose her way, she could turn in the direction of that brilliant morning star and head toward home in Bramond Province.

Spotting the welcome formation, she removed a chunk of stale bread and a piece of bruised fruit from a stolen rucksack. She ate quickly and then started out in the direction of the star. Obstinate determination drove her toward her master. Once reunited with him, she would work on strengthening her powers and focus all her cunning on gaining revenge on Ambracor in general and against Sindara Varacor in particular. Sindara would pay for her audacity in surviving the Breyal attack and then returning to Ambracor to marry Thehrund.

Breeneth kept sight of the distant mountain that had aligned with the star she had seen before sunrise chased away night's darkness. She carefully listened should the forest's ordinary sounds be interrupted by approaching people. There was little doubt that patrols would have been dispatched to search for her. She did not fear them. Already killing during her escape from Bracordia weighed not at all on her mind. She would not hesitate to kill again.

Doggedly picking up her pace, she cynically smiled to herself. For the moment, her greatest care was reaching home quickly. From the familiar comforts of her own home, she would assume control over Bramond Province, employ means to demoralize Ambracor's citizens, and embark on avenging herself against those who had failed or defied her. She would also bring Master into her father's house. Master would be pleased and would richly reward her efforts in expanding his supremacy and reign over the richest nation in their world. Images of ending Sindara's life and forcing Thehrund to his knees in surrender drove her footsteps ever faster.

A slight smile lifted one corner of Thehrund's mouth. Inside the small drawing room attached to his wife's private suite at her family's country estate, he sat at her desk while she relaxed in the luxury of a warm bath. A neat collection of leather-bound journals stood between heavy bookends carved from white marble into detailed images of rearing horses. One at a time, he tipped journals toward him and noted her grandfather's neatly embossed initials. Yes, he recalled thoughtfully, those books were filled with hand-drawn star charts sand detailed astronomical notations that he and Sindara had frequently discussed.

His vision drifted to a stack of bound journals on the right corner of her desk. Choosing the book second from the top, he opened the blue-dyed cover. On the first page of thick ivory paper, his wife's name was written in the center. Each page was dated, the final entry being just before they first met.

In an unusually nostalgic mood, he began turning pages, noting the precise lettering of her script and wishing his own handwriting could be half as elegant and free of errors. His eyes occasionally fell to dated entries. Some early notations referred to the state of her final preparations to join the abbey after an extended visit with her parents. Her words excitedly conveyed her desire to be home, to wander through spring gardens, and to take time for meditation and prayers atop the hillock she had frequently visited with her grandfather. The final page of the diary caught his attention. He read the words twice through before closing his eyes.

> *Prayer has again filled me with a sense that I may not be suited for life here at the abbey. I ask myself how that can be when I so love the peace I find here. Precious are the people who share my desire to tend those in need. I doubt for not a moment my faith in Creator God, yet I reluctantly face a kind of uncertainty that this is truly where I belong. If I readily accept I'm so filled with faith, then why do I find myself struggling with this strange emptiness? What is this longing that aches within my soul? Home. I must go home. My heart tells me that is where I must be. I must not wait, for it is there where I will put to rest these questions that stubbornly resist answers.*

Thehrund closed the journal and put it back in place. Never would he forget the evening he had asked her to become his wife. The passage he just read echoed words she had spoken that night. She had mentioned the empty feeling that had assailed her at Berancor and caused her to return to Arvacon much sooner than planned. The thought crossed his mind that she had prayed, seeking whatever was missing from her soul. His heart swelled with gratitude because the Divine One had sent her home at precisely the right time for them to meet.

Standing, he walked to a window and looked out over moonlit gardens. Moonbeams created a magical scene of light and shadow as faint breezes swayed lengthening flower stems and the branches of trees and bushes bedecked with spring leaves. He smiled to himself, recalling the night he had proposed. She had told him that he had filled the empty space in her soul. Irony lay in how empty he had felt until she burst into his life. Duty and responsibilities had indeed filled his daily existence. He had also loved his parents and valued his friends. Real fulfillment had been absent until Sindara's love had made him feel whole.

His head turned slightly. Something inside the bathroom had prompted melodic notes of her laughter. His smile faded, but his expression exuded the tranquility he had savored during the respite of these past few days at her family's summer home. Pushing aside the burdensome cloak of command that would descend upon him far too soon, he had determined to cherish their time in Arvacon's peaceful countryside.

Hearing voices and realizing it would be a while before she would be ready for bed, he again sat at her desk and reached for the top journal. Slowly turning stiff pages of rag paper, he occasionally stopped to read an entry. Toward the center of the diary, her words spoke more and more of her changing feelings. He realized her initial disdain had been born of confusion linked to tales told by Brenna Brandere. He read how she questioned herself as her emotions grew more complex. Her words began to reflect change. Dates in the diary ended just before she left Arvacon to prepare for their wedding. One particular passage, although filled with the sweetness of her love, struck him as nearly prophetic.

I ask myself how I ever doubted him. When those mag-nificent blue eyes look my way, I can hardly believe the love I see shining in them. I must cling to necessary pro-priety when I find myself wishing to stroke the length of his dark braids and touch my lips to his. During those rare moments when we can escape the scrutiny of others, I find myself quite happily melting into his embrace. When he tightens his arms around me, I have the sense that there is no calamity great enough to bring me harm or sadness. I now have but one fear in life... that of losing him. Should I ever lose his love, I believe death would swoop down upon me on the dark wings of a bird of prey. All would be lost.

Slowly, Thehrund put the journal back in its place. Rising, he again started toward the window but stopped and turned. His breath caught as he watched her enter and close the door behind her.

Her image was enthralling as she greeted him with a smile. The gauzy fabric of her rose-colored robe revealed the silken nightgown of magenta that dipped daringly low at the neckline and clung alluringly to feminine curves. Freshly washed hair, gleaming after a maid's vigorous brushing, floated around her face and shoulders. High cheekbones, delicately shaped nose, and smiling lips highlighted the distinctive beauty of her face. Thick lashes framed large, luminous eyes shimmering with flecks of gold. He felt dumbstruck by her unique loveliness.

Noting something odd in his expression and posture, Sindara crossed the room and reached for his hands. Mesmerized as he was by the sheer splendor of her appearance, the touch of her exquisitely soft hands spawned quivering waves that rushed throughout every inch of his body. The subtle floral fragrance surrounding her teased his nostrils with intox-icating effect. Spellbound, he could only watch as her eyebrows rose in question.

"Thehrund?" she asked, her voice a velvet whisper.

Some part of his sanity parted clouds of wonder long enough for him to catch his breath. "Sindara," he murmured, "there are times when I am simply struck wordless by your beauty."

Her gaze dropped, and her cheeks flushed. She gave him a shy smile. "I've never seen myself in such light, but I must admit one thing. You always make me feel beautiful."

Producing even the slightest smile was impossible. His eyes, brilliantly blue and expressive, studied every detail of her face. Strong hands were remarkably gentle as they moved from her grasp to untie the braided ribbon just above her gown's lace-trimmed décolletage. Slowly sliding the frothy robe to the floor, he bent his head forward to place a kiss at the base of her throat. Eagerness filled him when he felt her tremble as her head fell sideways in silent supplication for more of his rapturous touch.

A chuckle rose from his throat as he playfully caught her sensitive earlobe with his teeth, causing her to shake with the intensity of rapidly burgeoning desire. "Come, my beautiful Sindara," he whispered, leading her by the hand through the suite to the bedchamber.

Golden eyes fixed on him as he began to undress with what seemed like agonizing slowness. As he shed elegant coat, linen tunic, and trousers, her breathing grew rapid and shallow. She questioned if he could possibly understand how hard it was to wait for him. Her heightening need for his loving literally made her sway dizzily.

With deliberate languor, Thehrund turned to lay his discarded garments over the arm of a chair. When his eyes finally met those of his wife, he barely smiled. He actually felt the sudden swell of his chest as he breathed in the fragrance of her presence. His heart drummed a quicker beat. All thoughts escaped except the soulful elation and physical ecstasy he anticipated in making love to her.

Moments later, after watching her remove her nightgown to drape over the bed's footboard, he lay by her side on the plush mattress. He indulged himself with the pleasure of trailing his fingers along every smooth, scented curve of her body. Sensitive fingertips luxuriated in the velvety softness of her skin. He grasped her hand that reached to touch him and held it prisoner against his lips while his free hand continued its quest across her body.

Gently, he turned her onto her stomach. His mouth embarked on fresh exploration as his lips touched kisses along her shoulder blades and slowly forged a sensuous trail down the center of her back. Reaching her waist, he detoured, kissing the inward curves and then raking fuller flesh with just the edges of his teeth. Truly noticing for perhaps the first time the scar low on her hip, he blinked against the memory of how that mark had come to be and saluted it with a rain of tender kisses.

Feeling her body's intensifying shudders and hearing his own name within her pleading murmurs, he turned her again. He paused long enough to kiss the front scar before rising above her. His own passion throbbed through his veins. No longer could he resist his body's demands. Joining with her in a triumphant thrust, he gloried in the shared ardor that bound them. Lost as they both were in their precious union, all sense of time vanished. Their reality had consolidated into a private dimension all their own until each cried out in blissful exultation.

Well after midnight, Sindara bolted upright in bed. Thehrund woke instantly and sat up beside her. "Sindara?" he questioned in a voice husky with sleep, "What's wrong? Are you all right?"

She glanced toward the window. Moonlight created a narrow column of light drifting through draperies left partially open. Taking a deep breath and holding it, she tilted her head to one side. "I heard something," she answered, sliding her legs around and leaving the bed. Grabbing a robe, she put it on and headed for the door.

Quickly donning trousers but not bothering with robe or shirt, Thehrund hurriedly followed his wife into the broad corridor and down the main staircase. Although his senses had immediately snapped into a state of alert, he noticed nothing amiss. The manor was completely quiet except for the soft padding of his wife's rapid footsteps. Reaching the set of double doors that opened to gardens behind the house, she stopped and placed her ear against the glass.

Before Thehrund could reach her, she shoved polished brass handles downward and rushed outside. Alarmed, he broke into a run as he watched Sindara also running, her hair and light summer robe flowing behind her. He called out to guards he knew were stationed around the grounds.

Upon finally reaching the cherry orchard, Sindara's pace slowed. Quickly shifting her head from side to side, she was definitely listening for something. Upon reaching her, Thehrund grasped her shoulders. "What? What is it?" he whispered breathlessly into her ear.

"Shush," she answered, tipping her head slightly to one side. She gulped in a deep breath and listened. Suddenly, ignoring sticks and rocks beneath bare feet, she rushed through the orchard. Stopping quickly and falling to her knees, she gathered a prone body into her arms and gently lifted the hooded head against her shoulder.

Thehrund quickly glanced behind him at the sounds of boots hitting the ground as soldiers approached in response to their prince's beckoning call. Kneeling beside Sindara, he glanced at the face shadowed by the hood and then noted his wife's worried features. "Who is it?"

Ignoring her husband, she cradled the face against her shoulder. "Master Zoman? Can you hear me?" Her voice grew more insistent. "Master Zoman!"

Moonbeams scattered light through tree branches, lending an eerie effect to the scene. The man lying in Sindara's arms moved slowly, his labored breathing slowing to a more natural pace. With one hand, he reached for hers. "Dear Sindara," he whispered hoarsely, "it's true. All thanks be to Creator God that you still live."

Her countenance was grave, yet curiously peaceful. "Rest a moment, Master. Our prince is here, and we are surrounded by king's soldiers."

Master Zoman gladly obeyed. His chest ached. Muscles in his legs burned with uncommon ferocity. His flight had been driven not by fear of death, for he was a man filled with trust and faith. What had propelled him was dogged determination to protect the treasure securely strapped to his back. For the sake of his people, he had risked his life to deliver the original Ambracada from danger. The last four nights of travel had forced him to run, to hide, and to push his aging body to its limits. He had successfully evaded pursuers intent on destroying the revered symbol of faith that would sustain Ambracor's people through whatever grim times might lie ahead.

Finally summoning sufficient strength, he raised his head. "The sacred book...it's strapped to my back. I left as soon as I received...Karan Mezden's...message. Ten of us departed together. Later, we divided into groups. Three accompanied me. The others left in different directions... hoping to distract attention should the danger be real. My companions were all murdered. I would not have escaped our pursuers had it not been for them."

Noticing his sorrowful expression, Sindara smiled comfortingly. Her firm voice was soothing. "You are safe now. The Ambracada is safe, too. We will take you inside to rest."

Thehrund signaled two soldiers to help Master Zoman inside. To another, he gave orders to summon additional guards with instructions to patrol the grounds in groups of four. With all on high alert, he intended to minimize risks of any enemy reaching the house.

Inside, Thehrund's long legs easily took stairs two at a time. Rushing to dress, he returned to the family's drawing room dimly lit by candles reflecting light from several wall sconces. Soldiers stood watch outside the room's double doors while two others guarded the entrance on the inside. Sindara had already helped Master Zoman unstrap the pack in which he had carried the heavy Ambracada. She had also summoned servants. One had brought a blanket to cover the exhausted master while another set about lighting fires in the kitchen to brew tea.

On her knees, Sindara lightly stroked the forehead of the religious leader who had so patiently mentored her throughout her years at school. "I must go upstairs for a warmer robe. I want you to rest until I return."

When she stood, she paused briefly, grasping Thehrund's arm. "I'll return as quickly as I can," she said. "Guard the book. Don't allow him to move yet."

A short time later, Master Zoman sat upright with the blanket draped around his shoulders. He slowly sipped hot tea while studying Sindara, who sat across from him in a tall, elegant, wing-backed chair. Standing behind her, the prince rested his hands on her shoulders.

"How grateful I am that you had the presence of mind to send word to move the Ambracada. On our third day of travel, a rider informed us that the Sacred Halls had been invaded. The violators apparently tore apart everything in search of the sacred book. That's when our party decided to split up lest we draw unwanted attention to ourselves."

Thehrund sighed. "It is a miracle you got here safely. How were you able to travel by night without becoming lost?"

Master Zoman's expression reflected appreciation. "A former pupil of mine had a fascination with astronomy. She gave me copies of charts she had drawn with her grandfather and explained how they could be used for navigation. The pupil's lessons likely saved the teacher's life."

"And our nation's most precious relic," Thehrund added as he recalled his very first venture to the nearby hillock where he and Sindara had gone stargazing on his initial visit to the Varacor country manor.

Sindara reached up and covered her husband's right hand with her own. "Master Zoman, the Ambracada is safe here for the time being. I want you to go upstairs to sleep. In the meantime, Thehrund and I will rest. In the morning, we'll discuss what must be done to secure the book and decide our next course of action."

Immensely relieved to have reached safe refuge, Zoman gratefully accepted Sindara's reassurance and rose from the sofa. Pausing behind the servant leading him upstairs to a guest bedchamber, he turned to Thehrund and Sindara. "Ambracor faces much turmoil. Our nation is blessed that you two are united to protect our home."

By mid-morning, the prince had his escort ready a full day ahead of their intended departure. Couriers were dispatched to alert Count Varacor and nearby encampments that unidentified invaders had crossed into Arvacon from Bramond Province. Thehrund also instructed servants at the Varacor manor to quickly lock down the house and prepare to remove themselves to Cahmdurn. He would leave a military escort to accompany them.

Heeding his own intuition, he had eaten an early breakfast with Sindara and Master Zoman. He instructed his wife's former teacher to travel with the party headed to Arvacon's capital. The prince, however, trusted no one but his most elite guards to escort him and his bride back to Bracordia. They would carry with them the precious Ambracada for which at least nine had died to ensure its delivery for safekeeping. The relic and Sindara would be safest in Bracordia, the prince reasoned as he pulled a padded gambeson over a thin tunic. He then allowed a junior officer to assist him in donning the protective hauberk of fine metal mesh.

Carefully tightening studded battle bracers on his forearms, Thehrund turned at the sound of his wife entering her childhood suite. Swallowing against invading anxiety, he forced a smile. Her hair had been braided and looped at the nape of her neck and then covered with a restraining net of silk. Seeing her attired in trousers, tall riding boots, and a young man's training habergeon provided grim reminder that the trip home could very well be dangerous. He exhaled a breath fraught with frustration. "Even in armor you look beautiful."

She met his dour expression with a smile. "I'm confident our trip home will be safe. What most worries me at the moment is how soon our people must face war. I'm sure it looms close at hand, and many will suffer grievous injuries. We've just lost many skilled healers. Our people...our armies...they will need physicians at the ready."

Thehrund reached out to stroke her cheek. "We must rely on you and Karan to quickly train more in the basic arts of healing."

"Thehrund..." She choked briefly before moving into his arms. "I love you. Wherever this infernal struggle takes you, always remember that my love goes with you."

Chapter Sixteen

CURRENTS OF CONTINUOUS ENERGY SWIRLED inside the tunnel.
Although she traveled within the circular motion of the universe's pulse,
she felt no dizziness or other ill effect. To the contrary, soothed by extraordinary gentleness, her soul reveled in exquisite peace as awareness of her
body encompassed naught but the rhythm of her heart's beating and the
ebb and flow of her breathing. With all sense of time lost, she had no idea
how long her journey had lasted.

Her vision focused on an image rarely seen by human eyes…an elaborate pagoda fashioned from pillars of perfectly clear crystal. Embellished
scrollwork, also cut from crystal, adorned corners where the supports met
the structure at both top and bottom. Seven steps led up to the platform
supporting the pillars. The roof rested on the elegant columns and also
rose seven levels. Each level was graduated until the uppermost formed a
small peak above which hovered a blue-white, iridescent globe that rotated
continuously, casting sparkling rays of light all around.

Perfectly centered on the pagoda's base was a rounded crystal dais.
A tall, slender figure stood to one side. Clad in long, glistening robes, the
figure glowed with the same blue-white iridescence as the globe above
the roof. Although wondrous radiance prohibited discernment of gender
or features, she sensed the welcoming smile and approving expression.
There was no doubt. This figure was angelic, a guardian of truth and light.
Deep meditation had transported Kendra to the sacred Repository of the
Guardians.

A subtle nod of the angelic head caused Kendra to glance to her
right. She felt herself smiling. By her side stood the one whom angels

had described as her sister-in-spirit. Without conscious intent, her hands reached out and clasped those of Sindara. Concepts formed inside Kendra's mind and filtered through the very fibers of her soul. Were they words spoken by the glistening guardian? Were they entreaties from her beloved friend?

Kendra's only true certainty existed in deep, fresh awareness. The source of all creation had constructed multiple planes of existence within the incomprehensible infinity of the universe...so unfathomable that one might even describe the different planes themselves as parts of distinctly different universes, all connected by light to the original source, the original Creator God.

The generosity of Creator God had been vast, allowing newly created beings freedoms to explore and experience the glories of love and harmony along with the scintillating energies inherent in the interconnection of all creation. Discord insinuated itself into Creator God's perfection when some began to desire control of the light. The progression of that dissension evolved into a craving for Creator God's power. The dire objective became to eliminate precious illumination and overtake selfless harmony with a shadowed existence fueled by violence and destruction.

Kendra's vision fixed on the face of her sister-in-spirit. They were as human as all of the precious humanity designed by Creator God. All were gifted with that original ability to explore and experience the universe's great glories of life. The two sisters-in-spirit, however, possessed awareness that differed because their souls had consciously retained the original essence infused with sacred light. Their paths crossed because their spirits had willingly accepted special purpose. In this hallowed place, no spoken words passed between them. They simply understood one another.

Realization came to Kendra that her own willingness to support Sindara's imminent struggles might hold universal ramifications. Expansion of darkness encroached on many Earth-planes and would require time and effort to contain. Those who had chosen wicked paths, defying the source of creation, must be converted back to light or brought to an end. The destructive nature of those clinging to evil must be prevented from spreading their plague.

Others, like Kendra and Sindara, accepted the battle against darkness and would face severe trials. As such, they were entrusted with exceptional strength necessary to confront the rebels and force them to recede. Creator God had also appointed angelic guardians who would intercede only when absolutely necessary. Beings given gifts of life must vanquish evil to fully restore the light granted to their kind.

Kendra shook herself hard. Her alarm clock blared its announcement of the new day. Sitting up in bed, she consciously wiggled her toes, bent her knees, and flexed her feet and ankles. Shaking her head again, she curled and then stretched her fingers, rotated her wrists, bent her elbows. She shrugged her shoulders and tilted her head forward and backward, then side to side. She opened her mouth wide until her jaw felt like popping. Blinking her eyes, she finally squeezed one eyelid tightly closed and glanced around.

Rising from bed, she crossed her room. Peering through the window, she saw that a few people were already walking outside. The sun was shining. Shrubs and trees surrounding the apartment complex appeared healthy and green in early summer's finery. Her world seemed unchanged. How could everything look so completely ordinary considering all the awareness now saturating her being?

She sighed heavily. A shower should quickly revive her physically. Glad for the weekend, she planned a quick trip to church for some serious prayer. She couldn't remember if she had shared a farewell with Sindara, but she better understood the immense danger facing Ambracor. What Kendra comprehended on a higher plane was that she would support Sindara's fight against one of the most powerful of evil entities. Prayer must continue unabated to maintain her own strength and to keep Sindara surrounded with sacred light.

Refusing to cower like some sniveling, whipped animal, Breeneth Brandere defiantly met Master's gaze. He raged at her. With every step and every word, murky, writhing wisps emanated from his body. Their smoky, contorted fingers filled the air with vile odor. His voice echoed throughout the stone chamber where he had been forced to dwell. Finally pausing his tirade, he turned fiery eyes toward his servant. Needing to further vent his ire, he drew back his hand to strike her.

Alert and aware of his intent, she stepped backward. "Do not dare to strike me. Kill me if you so desire, but remember this. I will return to claim vengeance."

Master glared at her. The sheer audacity that filled this young servant was fueled by a loathsome energy even he could not ignore. Stalemate. They glared at each other. Though not yet his equal, he perceived power in her that was growing...power that already commanded caution.

"What happened to prevent your marriage to Thehrund Cobrandya?" he growled, his swarthy complexion darkening, his gaze glowering. "How did you fail?"

"The failure began with your assurance that the Breyal war party would kill Sindara Varacor," Breeneth informed him, her voice laced with malice. "She survived the attack and disappeared. Thehrund somehow found her and brought her back to Ambracor. Before Father could con-clude an agreement with King Hamund for my marriage to the prince, Sindara's return was revealed. She and Thehrund then married immedi-ately in an unannounced ceremony."

Master stared at uneven chinks in the gray stone of the cave's floor. "This should not be. I felt the glorious moment the lance pierced her body. Since then, I have had no sense whatsoever of her life force. All who knew her mourned. I felt their exquisite pain. Its intensity pleasured me greatly." He grunted angrily. "This should not be!"

Breeneth's lips drew into an ugly line. "It matters not that it should not be. The fact is that she lives. I saw her with my own eyes. What matters now is how we proceed."

Curious, Master glanced at Breeneth's hate-filled expression. Inwardly, he realized he must take care. Although her power was intensifying, she did not yet possess sufficient self-control to address problems at hand. Her outward calm masked volatility that he clearly sensed. Her lack of patience was currently managed, but he had no doubt it could explode and ruin plans to draw this world fully into his dark domain.

"We must proceed with caution. To do so, we can no longer remain here. I will become much stronger beyond the confines of this cavern. You will also gain greater control over your powers."

Breeneth nodded agreement, anxious to free herself from the musty cave chambers. "I cannot communicate with my spies from here. Except for my brother who's away at school, my family is in Bracordia, so they pose no interference. If you're ready and willing to exercise your powers, we can easily enter my father's mansion and begin to assert our control from there."

Master subdued the inclination to chastise her for her arrogant insolence. She was not the only one capable of concealing innermost thoughts. Zimda had grown overly confident with her constant successes. The demonic master would not be so foolish.

"Let us prepare immediately. Your human form requires more care. We both can enjoy the luxury of your home while we plan our strategies against Ambracor."

Breeneth lifted her chin high, her expression bold. "Do not forget. Thehrund belongs to me."

Master cocked his head sideways, indicating outward accord with her declaration. He would find her useful, but in the end, all would belong to the darkness. All would be his alone.

With hands clasped behind him, Artrian Varacor stood with his back to those gathered in his office. His mind raced through the many plans covered when governors responsible for Ambracor's security met in Bracordia. More recent discussions with Thehrund and Erator had severely heightened his concern. When he finally turned around, his expression revealed the grim nature of his thoughts.

"Father," Erator began, "Articene is now well fortified and supplied. Extra troops garrisoned there should definitely discourage Breyal attacks in the surrounding regions. Are you convinced we should stretch reserve troops to guard Arvacon's boundaries with Bramond Province?"

The count nodded his head. "We have no idea what to expect from Bramond. I'm sure its people are not in league with Breeneth Brandere. On the other hand, my heart aches for the calamity Bramond's citizens doubtlessly face. She will surely open their borders and give free passage to Breyal war parties. Of Ambracor's four provinces that face this threat, ours alone shares long borders with both Bramond Province and Breyal. It is only logical to surmise that Arvacon faces enormous risk."

Erator's face dropped as he sighed heavily. "Thehrund's most recent dispatch advised that additional regiments will arrive within a fortnight. Do you wish to await their arrival, or can we begin the surprise attacks we discussed when he was here?"

Artrian turned his attention to Nagrand Mezden. "What is your opinion? Are your assault squads ready?"

Nagrand drew in a deep breath. "Our personnel are trained well and adequately armed. Maps have been studied and memorized. My commanders understand the crisis we face. Volunteers are fully aware of the risks at hand. I agree with Erator. We cannot afford to postpone offensive actions. To do so only allows Breeneth and her master more time to organize Breyal tribes."

"Erator," Artrian told his son, "consult with your officers. Determine how best to distribute troops already in Arvacon so that all borders have some degree of scrutiny. I recommend evacuating smaller villages and towns closest to Bramond border points from which attacks might be launched. I will have Cahmdurn's administrators begin organizing housing and supplies to accommodate evacuees. I won't have our people caught unaware of this present danger. Preparedness is the best defense for ordinary citizens."

Erator stood and gravely nodded agreement. "I will depart immediately for Articene. Meila and Graden I will leave here with you and Mother."

"Of course," Artrian replied with a solemn expression. "Nagrand, proceed with offensive tactics according to your discretion. You have Thehrund's full confidence. Know that you also have mine. Please convey to your officers and men that they will be kept in our people's most fervent prayers."

Minutes later, alone in his office, Artrian Varacor sat down. With elbows on top of his desk, he buried his face in his hands. He wanted to pray. No one knew better than he that even the most impossible of prayers could be answered. His own daughter was living proof. His spirit, however, reeled under the crushing burden he prepared to bear as governor of his beloved Arvacon. He dreaded the impending specter of death and devastation. How he wished Creator God would spare his nation this ordeal. How he wanted to know why his people...a kind, industrious, and peaceful race...must be subjected to this coming conflict. Why? Why?

Gentle hands came to rest on his hunched shoulders. He hadn't even heard her enter.

"Artrian, you must not torment yourself. None of us understands this terrible calamity lying at our doorstep. The Ambracada speaks of those who chose to defy Creator God. All who are truly part of the light must unite lest darkness encroaches to overtake all. Those lost in such battles will most assuredly be restored to share in the glories of Creator God. We dare not lose faith."

When Artrian finally lifted his face, wet streaks of gray hair clung to his cheeks. "Did we not cry enough tears of sorrow when we thought our own daughter lost? How, Liana? How do I face our people when I cannot promise them a return of their sons or daughters, brothers or sisters, fathers or mothers, husbands or wives, the way Sindara was restored to us? How do I ask of them the great sacrifices that we both know lie ahead? How, Liana? How am I to do this?"

Liana pulled her husband's distraught face to rest against the cushioned swell of her bosom. Her heart sorrowed with the same questions. How unfair this all seemed. She lowered her face to kiss the top of his head and stroked her fingers through his long hair.

"I wish I had answers to your questions. I do not comprehend this path ahead of us. What I do know is that, as long as this terrible darkness freely stalks people of light, it will continue to employ its power against us. Only through alliance of all who cleave to Creator God's light will we be able to free ourselves from the shadows of war and its terrible destruction."

❖ ❖ ❖

King Hamund leaned against the high back of his chair. Ambracor's provincial leaders had responded in outstanding fashion to his call for reinforcements for the nation's armies. There had been minimal dissent from provinces situated far northwest of Breyal or Bramond Province. New recruits were volunteering in droves and being trained and outfitted for battle. Taking counsel from the writings of Sun-Tzu, the prince was selecting officers who would command soldiers in the dire circumstances of all-out war. Maintaining morale was a concept Thehrund repeatedly emphasized to them. He needed to know that they would show respect while also requiring strict discipline.

Smithies across the nation busied themselves forging weapons, armor, and other materiel to meet the demands of swelling army ranks. Tailors and seamstresses spent seemingly endless hours cutting and sewing padded gambesons, coifs, and gorgets to be worn under protective chainmail, metal breastplates, helmets, greaves, and bracers. Cobblers worked from dawn to dusk cutting leather for sturdy boots while other leather workers fashioned bracers reinforced with steel bands or spikes. Warehouses stockpiled foodstuffs. The sheer volume of supplies necessary for Ambracor's burgeoning army could have been overwhelming. Hamund noted with pride the way his people were responding to their country's time of need.

"Father?"

Hamund looked up. His sense of pride swelled even as it threatened to choke him. "Do you still plan to leave tomorrow?"

Thehrund nodded. "I received word from Lord Artrian. They were too late reaching two villages near the borders where Bramond Province and Breyal meet Arvacon's southernmost corner. Other towns and villages are being evacuated. Evacuees are converging on Cahmdurn and other cities in central Arvacon."

"Is there news from Bramond Province?"

Thehrund's eyes turned icy blue as he met his father's waiting gaze. "Refugees are fleeing by the hundreds. Many escape with only the clothes they wear. They carry stories of entire towns being transformed into labor camps guarded by Breyal warriors. Tales of atrocities are sickening. Breeneth has made the Brandere mansion her headquarters. There are rumors of a man who lives there and commands Breyal tribes amassing for invasion."

King Hamund shook his head in disgust. "How one so lovely to look upon could have such an evil soul defies my comprehension."

Thehrund declined comment. He saw no need to remind his father that he had warned him as much.

"There are positive reports. The most recent reinforcements arrived and are marching to secure borders with Bramond. Nagrand's assault squads have proven effective in stopping many war parties advancing toward Barachal. His guerilla teams have attacked camps at night and significantly reduced enemy ranks. If we can decrease the number of warriors directly east of Arvacon, we can possibly diminish the number of fronts that will require buildups of our own troops."

Hamund's jaw clenched. "How disgusting it is to speak aloud in terms of reducing warrior ranks when such declarations equate to wholesale slaughter of other human beings."

Thehrund remained silent for several tense moments. "Father, if I had any sort of viable alternative, I would not hesitate to change our strategy. If we don't seize the initiative, Breyal warriors will invade and place us at the mercy of Breeneth Brandere and her demonic ally. At the moment, several of our governors have wisely exercised foresight to strengthen their own provincial militias and stockpile war materiel. Our people labor to ensure additional necessities will be readily available if and when needed."

"Beyond basic supplies, refresh my memory on the other plans you have in mind," Hamund said, needing reassurance that his son had clearly thought through his plans.

Thehrund paced across the room with restless energy. "Safe and timely drayage of supplies will be crucial. The quickest, safest routes have been determined and will be continuously monitored by mobile patrols for potential hazards or attacks. With this being early summer, we should not be hampered by extended inclement weather for several months yet."

"Have you considered how costly this war might be?"

Thehrund's eyebrows lifted, and his forehead creased. "If you refer to the national treasury, careful, frugal management by you and your father have kept it sound. There's no way to avoid the drain on reserves, but much has already been paid for by wealthy provinces such as Arvacon and Gorandro where governors were already preparing for such contingencies.

"I would recommend a royal decree making it criminal to artificially raise prices for food staples and other provisions that general citizenry will need. Our people need to see that we are doing everything in our power to prevent internal ruin while still protecting lives and property. We must not tolerate those who would seek undue benefit from the expected chaos.

"We must also be forthright. The treasury is not bottomless. We may need to find additional revenue...taxes, if you will...to ensure the effectiveness of our armies. Our people are clever. They will weigh the risks and recognize bitter truth. Gold in hand means little to a dead man."

King Hamund finally rose from his chair. Approaching his son, he rested a hand on each of Thehrund's broad shoulders. "I'm impressed with your summary of our current situation. I have no doubt you've already considered the many consequences likely to result from this impending struggle. My greatest hope is that this war might yet be avoided. If that is not to be, then I pray your strategies will minimize loss of life and avoid protracted hostilities."

"Father, you must accept that we're already at war. I hope to assess the enemy's strengths and weaknesses and to anticipate their plans. My goal is to utilize all combined intelligence to seek victory as quickly as possible."

Still gripping his son's shoulders, Hamund gazed into his son's eyes. "You must exercise great care, Thehrund. It will surely be the end of your mother and me should we lose you in battle."

Thehrund forced a meager smile. "Father, there is much I hope yet to learn from you. I will be careful."

Hamund finally let his arms drop. "You now have a wife who loves you as much as any woman has ever loved a man. Let her love strengthen you during the difficult times ahead."

The king then watched his son turn and leave. His heart throbbed with fear. Silently, he prayed his son's life might be spared.

Sindara meditated in the small chapel outside the palace. She had gone there immediately after an unusually quiet breakfast with Thehrund. Her hands clutched the precious amulet she had received from Master Garen and Lady Aminta. The crystal had stirred her from slumber just after midnight.

Waking had brought memories of a great journey. Streaking trails of light marked the walls of the swiftly spinning passageway in which she traveled. Neither time nor distance could be measured as she made her journey. Fear did not enter her mind. She felt secure within the power that moved her with such apparent speed.

Awareness. All was suddenly still around her. Her eyes lifted to drink in the magnificent beauty of flawless crystal crafted into a shining pagoda. Warmth. She turned toward it and felt her hands enfolded in the familiar grasp of her beloved Kendra. She thought they exchanged smiles. They had been summoned by Creator God's most fervently loyal angels, those assigned as guardians to watch over countless levels of sacred creation. The sisters-in-spirit listened with their souls.

Initially, the dark entities had been created as shining beings filled with the energetic beauty and power of light. When some saw the greater power of Creator God, shadows of envy had crept into them, corrupting the glow of their original brilliance. Corrupted light faded, leaving voids that filled with invading shadows. Darkness inundated the traitors, driving them to defy the one who had created them.

Malevolent entities joined forces, retaining their energetic power and outward beauty. As their inner darkness grew, their unity disintegrated into the same chaos they eventually spread throughout Creator God's universe. Each entity sought to build its own sphere of power in order to shift all light to darkness.

Kendra and Sindara learned that such darkness could reach a point where it might recall the perfection of its original creation. Lost beings could seek reunification with the light. Some saw the chaos, suffered the void, and chose restoration. Others clung to their defiance, claiming its strength as their own path to ultimate power. Those entities were forcibly divested of their angelic state, thereby finding themselves cast into obscure places where they sought to spread the contagion of their demonic influence.

Karan walked into the chapel and stopped. His eyes fell upon Sindara as she knelt on the padded, curved step leading to the altar. Her head bowed low. Between hands held close to her heart, she clutched the crystal pendant. Rays of light escaped from between her fingers. He sensed the power of Creator God's presence within the confines of the chapel's walls. Without thought, he dropped to his knees. He, too, bowed his head. Drawn into an inexplicable cocoon of light, he joined his prayers to hers. Never before had he experienced such power in combined prayer.

Finally rising from her knees, Sindara neared the altar itself and leaned forward to kiss cool, smooth stone. The top had been replaced with a slab of granite practically identical to the original. The difference was that this altarpiece had been carefully designed with a chamber accessible only from underneath. Within that chamber rested the Ambracada, its location and means to access its safe place a secret from all but a precious few. Except Sindara, even the royal family did not know the precise location of the holy relic.

Karan completed his prayer and went to her. Sadness in her eyes touched him deeply. "I volunteered to go with him, but he insisted I stay to help you train additional healers to address expected medical needs."

Her smile lasted only a fleeting moment. "I would feel better if you were with him, but I know his decisions are for the benefit of our people."

"You know that many prayers will be lifted daily for his safety." Karan wanted so much to ease the desolation in her eyes.

"That I also know, Karan. What troubles me is the future I cannot see. The master demon with Breeneth is one of the most powerful and evil of all. Many will die as the demon unleashes his powers. As much as I love Creator God, I cannot escape my fears that Thehrund will be taken from me."

Karan thought back over the years he and his brother had journeyed through the portal with the prince. Success had finally come to them when they consciously changed their mental approach. "Sindara, look at me."

Amber eyes lifted, the sheen of tears enhancing the effect of liquid gold in the depths of her waiting gaze.

"During the years we searched for you, I prayed as a priest would be expected to pray. Toward the end, Thehrund struggled to retain hope. Finally, after I reminded him of something you once told him, he also turned to daily prayer. Before we entered the portal on our final journey, prayer had changed Thehrund's outlook. He told us we must banish from our minds any concept of *if* we would find you. He insisted that we think in positive terms of *when* we would find you. Maintaining that concept occasionally proved difficult. We sometimes had to remind ourselves, but we clung to it with absolute faith that there would be a *when*."

"And that's when you found me," she murmured. She turned, placing her palms flat upon the altar stone. Even through the thick layer of granite, she felt energy emanating from the Ambracada. She raised her face and watched the invasion of brilliant sunshine streaming through leaded glass windows.

"I shall try to think in terms of *when* he will return home in peace." Seeking comfort and reassurance, she turned into the circle of Karan's arms. His whispered words delved into the most remote reaches of her being.

"Sindara, cast out all thought of believing in Creator God and believing that he will bring Thehrund home. Do not believe in God and the good things he will bring you. Exchange belief for knowledge. *Know* that Creator God *is*. Also, *know* that he *will* bring Thehrund safely home."

Dinner inside the king's quarters was quiet. Both Hamund and his son deliberately avoided talk regarding the current crisis and Thehrund's imminent departure from Bracordia. Sindara tried to follow her husband's lighter example but found herself continually lapsing into silence. Her hand repeatedly drifted to the side, affectionately stroking her husband's sleeve or casting a glance at his beloved profile. The somber look and brimming tears in Narlina's eyes reflected a mother's fears.

Finally, Thehrund looked up from his plate. "Mother, try to smile. Please? I don't know how long I'll be away. Let my memory of this dinner be a glad one."

Narlina stared at her plate a moment and then dabbed the corners of her mouth with a napkin. "Your father and I..." She bravely blinked back tears. "We will miss you so much."

"As I will miss you. I promise to write whenever possible." His smile was warm, his voice remarkably steady. Without shifting his gaze from his mother's face, he reached sideways to gently clasp Sindara's hand. "I leave reassured in the knowledge that you and Father are safer here in Bracordia. I also leave my wife in your care."

Barely able to contain threatening tears, Narlina glanced toward her husband. "You can rest assured we'll take good care of her, won't we?"

Hamund nodded. His heartache over his son's departure was compounded by the fear and sadness in his wife's eyes. "We will most assuredly take care of her."

Sindara smiled for the sake of all gathered at the table and quipped, "I promise to be on my best behavior."

Following dinner, Sindara excused herself to allow Thehrund extra time alone with his parents. As much as she craved every possible second with him, she thought of how her own parents had described their sense of loss after Articene. They had said the worst had been having no chance to say goodbye. Understanding the nature of their fears, she thought to give Hamund and Narlina the kind of consolation her parents never had. If Thehrund should be lost, she wanted his parents to have this opportunity to bid loving farewell to their only child.

Hearing the door to their apartment open, Sindara rose from the desk where she sat writing in her journal. Marnee had already helped her change from her formal dinner dress into a lovely gossamer nightgown and had brushed her hair until it shone with lustrous highlights. Slowly turning, she watched as Thehrund quietly entered their bedchamber.

He stopped just inside the doorway. Worry was evident in his expression. His eyes locked onto the lovely features that regarded him with such tenderness. Pursing his lips tightly, his face dropped for several moments before he could lift his gaze again to convey appreciation for her beauty in both appearance and spirit.

"How, Sindara, do I thank you for allowing me to indulge my parents' need for private farewells?"

Gliding into his arms, she rested her cheek against his shoulder. "You gave my own parents comfort and hope while I was gone. How could I be so selfish as to deny your parents similar consideration?"

Her murmured words reminded him of the kindness and compassion that had ignited sparks of growing attraction into the fiery love that now inspired him. He slid his hand slowly up her back until it reached her nape. Long fingers delved into silky hair. Resting his chin on the crown of her head, he breathed in the subtle scent he would always associate with her presence. Leaving her was something he dreaded, yet he knew their very lives were already at risk. He would gladly face death if it meant protecting the woman now his wife.

His voice was low, almost a whisper, when he said, "The night outside is warm and the skies clear. May I fetch a light cloak for you so that we might walk a while before we go to bed?"

Later, he clutched her close to his side as they strolled through palace gardens. Early summer blossoms bobbed with gentle caresses from soft evening breezes. Lush foliage rustled like silk as the air wafted floral perfumes across the brick paths they followed. Stars twinkled merrily against infinite heavens. The full moon, brilliant and silvery white, cast its beams upon the two lovers.

Glancing upward, Thehrund pointed out a falling star in the cloudless sky. "It seems Creator God gives us a most beautiful and magical display of light this night."

Sindara stopped and watched in silence. Suddenly, she realized they were only steps away from the angel that had witnessed their first kiss. Freeing herself from Thehrund's grasp, she went to the stone statue. Drawing her fingertip along its smooth cheek, she leaned forward and placed a kiss on the curls that topped its finely sculpted head.

When she turned back to her husband, her features appeared surprisingly tranquil. His dread of leaving drilled painfully into her awareness, but she refused to send him off with more burdens than he already carried. She would draw upon every ounce of strength she possessed to make their parting more bearable for him.

"I think we should go back inside now," she told him quietly. "My husband begins an arduous journey tomorrow. Since we have no idea how long he'll be away, I should like to love him this last night so that he well remembers who will anxiously await his homecoming."

When they reached the seclusion of their bedchamber, Sindara began to undo the fastenings of his formal coat with shaking fingers. Folding the garment and laying it on a chair, she then helped him unbutton his linen shirt. She paused to plant a reverent kiss above the heart beating faster and faster as her attentions set every nerve in his body ablaze.

Quickly stepping out of shoes, stockings, and trousers, Thehrund pulled Sindara flush against him. His body reacted with a jolt to enticing curves covered by the smooth silk of her gown. His mouth sought connection to hers with desperation stemming from their upcoming separation. As one hand supported the back of her head for the kiss growing deeper and more frenzied, his other hand pulled and tugged at the fabric barrier between them until it fell to the floor.

Guiding her toward the huge canopied bed they had shared since their wedding, he forced himself to lower her gently. His eyes hungered for the glorious vision of beauty promising him irresistible pleasures. He stroked silken tresses from her face. A trembling fingertip traced the full line of her lips. His great, powerful body humbly bent forward, paying respect and homage yet again to the scars on her side.

Reaching for his hands, her fingers interlaced with his. "Thehrund," she pleaded, "hold me. Hold me close."

Lips, hands, and bodies bound the frantic lovers as one, their feverish union driven by events over which they had little control and by fear they might be forever parted. The rapture they drew from their love rose in expansive surges that exploded and receded, then rose again until their shared ecstasy subsided in total gratification and sweet exhaustion.

Dawn's first rays peeked through lacy curtains. Sindara's eyelids fluttered open. She had not wanted the heavy drapes drawn the night before. Moonlight had cast such fascinating light on her husband's handsome face. Turning slowly to avoid disturbing him, she looked at his sleeping features. Smiling to herself, she noted the narrow width of his nose and the flare of his nostrils. She studied the curve of his black eyebrows and the contour of his cheekbones. In morning's quiet, she committed to memory the shape of his mouth. She felt a stirring deep within as she recalled the way those lips opened to bestow intoxicating, fiery caresses.

Noting the line of his beard and the wild tumble of his long locks, she took a deep breath. The complex notes of exotic oils in the soap he used teased her senses. His breath, quiet and rhythmic, created the softest of sounds that often lulled her back to sleep whenever she awoke in the night. In slumber, his expression was calm and peaceful. Tamping down invading thoughts of the warrior's life upon which he would embark this day, she indulged herself in the appeal of his sleeping image until the risen sun would force them from their private retreat.

Hours later, Sindara Varacor Cobrandya leaned against a flag post rising from the highest walkway of the palace's outer walls. All that remained as evidence of Thehrund's departing army was a faint cloud of dust in the distance and the memory of the last moments before his departure. She had watched the king embrace his son and then firmly support the queen as Narlina nearly swooned following a final, tearful embrace.

As she stared into the distance, Sindara's awareness encompassed only the memory of the tender smile on her husband's face and the richly vibrating tones of his voice. His palm had felt warm against her cheek as he smiled into the golden eyes he adored. "Thank you, beloved, for giving me the gift of your smile to treasure while I'm away."

She had lifted her lips to capture his in the briefest of kisses. "If you must go, I want you to leave with the secure feeling that I remain to support our cause in every way possible. I want you to remember the happiness you are to me and never forget the woman whose love anxiously awaits your safe return."

Thehrund had then embraced her, his arms tightening possessively. She had felt the violent shudder course through his body. Her whispered words of love had prompted a lingering kiss that abruptly ended when he released her to mount his waiting stallion.

When she finally turned to descend stone steps to the palace complex's ground level, her jaws ached with suppressed tension. She crossed brick walkways leading to the main palace. Each step felt leaden. Her stomach pitched and roiled like a deserted ship tossed helplessly on stormy seas. She felt as though an enormous, gaping void had supplanted her heart. Her outer expression revealed none of the inner turmoil.

After what seemed forever, she reached the apartment she shared with Thehrund. She staggered as she headed toward her maid's quarters. Some mysterious source gave her strength to lift her hand, to knock lightly at Marnee's door. Leaning her head against smooth, polished wood, she waited. When she felt every vestige of strength fading, she heard the door handle move.

"Oh, child, come," Marnee said, her voice filled with compassion. The maid's sturdy arm encircled Sindara's waist as the two crossed the room to a small couch.

If Sindara had thought herself emotionally drained, she quickly realized the error in her thoughts. Caught in the protective embrace she had known since childhood, she finally surrendered to anguish she had so carefully subdued. Tears burst forth in a flood. Great sobs wracked her body.

Marnee held her firmly, cooing soft words of praise and encouragement. The servant had never been more proud of her charge than that morning as she watched the lovers' farewell. While bestowing comforting caresses, Marnee silently prayed she would live to see Sindara happy again.

Chapter Seventeen

Breeneth Brandere sat at an elegantly carved vanity in what was once her parents' suite. The reflection in the mirror pleased her. Dark eyes were bright and surrounded by lush lashes that lent a wide, sensuous flair to her expression. Ebony locks were tamed into a mass of curls secured at the back of her head. Alabaster skin was flawless. Standing, she twisted from side to side. Her figure was as voluptuous as ever, her full bosom and tiny waist emphasized by the cut of her form-fitting gown. Nodding self-approval, she left to go downstairs to attend her master.

The demon Thafalos had converted the spacious, formal dining room of the Brandere mansion into his private court, complete with a newly carved throne. Walls had been covered with dark wood panels and windows adorned with heavy draperies sewn from black velvet. Sunlight disturbed the master demon after the ages he had spent in obscure chambers hiding from angels assigned to search for rebellious entities. Benches lined opposite walls of the long room. Tapestry runners began at the massive doorway and extended to a spot that ended in front of the throne. On one side of the throne stood a gold-leaf table, always ready for service to the master. On the opposite side, a small chaise, upholstered in silk damask, waited for the master's chosen consort.

Seeking to enhance his darkly handsome features and finely proportioned body, he had ordered a new wardrobe. His new apparel consisted of colorful robes and vestments, all embellished with gold or silver embroidery and clasps and fastenings of precious metals. Many garments glittered with sparkling gemstones. Soft leather had been crafted into comfortable slippers. Adorning his fingers were jeweled rings offered by wealthy merchants in exchange for their lives or appropriated from Bramondans killed for their defiance.

Upon entering the master's presence, Breeneth performed an elegant genuflect while carefully balancing a golden tray laden with matching pitcher and two goblets of engraved gold. When Thafalos bade her approach, she glided forward and placed the tray on the table beside him.

"May I serve you, Master?"

Determined that she remain aware of her lower position, Thafalos gazed upon his servant with mild condescension. "What have we this morning?"

Breeneth dipped her head respectfully. "A defiant militiaman kindly offered himself as source for your morning's pleasure."

The spread of Thafalos's dark lips could hardly be considered a smile, but Breeneth accepted his approval. Carefully, so as to waste not a single drop, she poured the still-warm scarlet fluid into the larger of the two goblets and offered it to the master. Upon receiving his nod, she poured a small quantity for herself and sipped the intoxicating liquid.

"You choose well," Thafalos praised his willing minion after tipping the goblet and draining it. "The life force was especially strong in this one."

She only smiled before respectfully nodding again.

"Please, Breeneth, sit. We must talk."

Once she had lowered herself to the chaise and arranged the folds of her voluminous skirts, she watched and waited as Thafalos left the throne to walk around, his robes rustling and swishing with every step. "Have Kicchak's couriers returned with news from the borders?"

"Only one as of this morning. Warriors from several northern tribes have not yet reached Barachal. Survivors from two tribes, some grievously wounded, straggled in with tales of attacks during the night as they slept. They claimed to have heard no sounds whatsoever."

The expression on Master's face turned ferocious. "How can this be? Does Kicchak have so little control over his tribes? Do they already fight among themselves?"

Breeneth tilted her head to the side. "There are rumors that Ambracor has taken offensive action."

Master Thafalos spun on his heel and glared at her. "Hamund hasn't the stomach for such strategy! He's a coward who would fear defending himself if Kicchak marched directly into the palace at Bracordia."

Breeneth breathed in slowly. Already the air around her master was turning murky with swirling mist, a sure sign of his rising fury. "Master, King Hamund may be reluctant to take up arms, but I think Prince Thehrund is fully capable and willing to meet any threat head on. He will also have support from those damnable Varacors and their provincial allies."

"You have heard nothing from your spies?"

"Nothing, although I do expect my scouts to return by day's end."

"Let us hope they do not fail. Your sister certainly did you no good."

Breeneth scowled. "Brenna was weak. That I admit. You, however, were the one who delayed her initiation."

Thafalos spat in Breeneth's direction, his spittle rising in a plume of steam from the cold tiles. "Careful, my beauty. You pleasure me well, but not so well that I will ignore impudence."

"Master," she responded in a contrite voice, "I agreed with you that Brenna proved useless. My intent was not to sound impudent, only to remind you that I knew my family well. I have no greater desire than to advise you on points you may be too occupied to notice."

The handsome demon grimly smiled at her quick acquiescence. "Summon Kicchak. If Ambracor's prince has decided to bring war to defy me, then he and his armies will taste the bitterness of my vengeance."

By afternoon, only three of Breeneth's scouts had returned. Recruited from Breyal ranks when she had first approached them at her master's bidding, they brought news of vast armies moving through Arvacon. Besides reinforcements already encamped near Articene, borders along both Breyal and Bramond Province were being fortified with additional soldiers. One scout reported that several towns close to Bramond had been evacuated and converted into bases occupied by Ambracor's armies.

Attacks unleashed against Ambracor had been the beginning of a campaign to terrorize and demoralize citizens with no taste for violence, no desire to face death. The master's plan had seemed perfect...utilize the primitive viciousness of newly allied Breyal tribes to launch their deadly aggression against Ambracor. Breeneth had expected the nation's leadership to posture, threaten, and display a show of force beneath which lay no real substance. She had also schemed to wed Thehrund and be in a position to end Hamund's reign so she could exert her own influence over the new king by whatever means at her disposal. That had been the plan... one that would have forced Ambracor to join Breyal under the ruthless domination of Master Thafalos.

Crossly dismissing the scouts, Breeneth fumed. Sindara Varacor's inexplicable return had wrecked well-devised plans. None of her spies had yet learned how Sindara had survived her injuries at Articene or where she had been for six long years. Neither had anyone discovered where Thehrund had traveled to bring her back. What secrets did the new princess conceal? How could Breeneth possibly learn those secrets and use them to her own advantage?

For the moment, Breeneth considered how she would inform Thafalos of unexpected offensives. Delaying the inevitable would only provoke his ire. She was uncertain how he would react. Deciding there was no way to temper the truth, she prepared herself to return to the master's throne room and give him the information with as much calm as she could muster.

Thehrund sat inside the muggy confines of his tent. The canvas tent he had called home for weeks provided little relief from the sweltering heat of a cloudy afternoon promising summer thunderstorms. His left hand closed around the earthenware mug at his side. Tossing his head back, he gulped down half of the fresh water in a single go. Setting the cup aside, he bent forward and scanned the paper lying flat on the table's surface. He had read the letter twice already, but his eyes were irresistibly drawn to carefully penned words.

My dear husband,

I am sure you will be relieved to know that staunch support comes in fresh waves to Ambracor's capital district. Bracordia throbs with activity. The protection of our way of life is just and worthy, but I so wish this cooperative vitality was for a more peaceful cause. There is naught I can do to change the deplorable circumstances at hand. Please, my love, take reassurance from the extensive efforts of all provinces to care for displaced citizenry who sincerely appreciate the consideration given to their plight. Although our people have always respected the Cobrandya royal family, they now perceive their king and their prince with far greater devotion and reverence than has been seen for generations.

Your father is well. He is masterful at working with politicians who present themselves in never-ending processions. I caution him daily to take more time for rest. I remind him that a rested mind performs its waking tasks more efficiently. He resisted my counsel at first, but he now smiles and accepts my gentle rebukes with good favor.

Your mother, too, is in good health. A daunting task it was to encourage her to rise from her state of depression. While she doesn't possess the same energy I always associated with her, she is improving and has set about making a cause of her own. When not at your father's side, she spends many hours with children, especially those among the refugees from Gorandro and Zelcon Provinces. The children quite adore her.

As for your wife, I must report that she works hard during the mornings with Karan and other priests and physicians. We mix the many compounds, wound binders, and elixirs needed by our soldiers in the field. In the afternoons, she stubbornly visits the palace chapel for prayer before rejoining other physicians to conduct training classes for those who will serve our wounded.

Promise you won't laugh too hard at the silly woman your bride becomes at night. Once Marnee helps me dress for bed and brushes out my hair, I go to our dressing room. It has become my habit to choose one of your shirts or tunics and hang it on your valet stand. I then turn my back to the garment. Taking hold of the cuffs, I pull them so that I am surrounded by the sleeves. I stand with my eyes closed and allow my memory to recall the times your arms held me so tenderly. I think tonight that I may change this ridiculous habit. I may take one of your jackets and lay it on the bed by my side so that I might rest my head on its shoulder and dream it is really you beside me. There. I have confessed.

Thehrund, I do miss you. I pray for you daily and surround your remembered image with silver light at night. With all I do to occupy my time, I still fail to keep at bay constant thoughts of you. I love you, Thehrund. I always will.

Yours forever,
Sindara

His head fell backward, long hair reaching halfway down his back. With eyes tightly closed, he indulged himself with comforting memories of home. There was no way to suppress the broad grin and quiet laugh as he tried to picture his wife with her head lying upon an empty shirt. Her humor and unique way of addressing life's events never failed to charm him. Especially now, those charms soothed the spirit longing for home.

With the day's unusual heat and approaching storms, he enjoyed brief respite from the saddle and increasingly frequent skirmishes with Breyal invaders. Reaching for pen and paper, he decided to answer his wife's letter.

My beloved Sindara,

I've always believed in the solidarity of our people. Their joint actions during this crisis far exceed my expectations. The courage and tenacity of our soldiers are astonishing as they face Breyal brutality. I am overwhelmed with respect and admiration for these troops who defend the essence of our nation with their very lives.

I'm glad to know that Father is learning to accept counsel as well as give it. He had no choice, of course. The princess who advises him is extremely persuasive and brooks no arguments. His initial resistance was destined to fail. As for Mother, I think of her with concern. Hers is such a gentle soul, but I warn you. She can stand as firmly as anyone when she so chooses.

Storms are approaching, so I have unusual opportunity to reflect on your letter. Ah...my silly bride conjures up images that most certainly chase shadows of war from her husband's weary face. How jealous I am of my shirts and jackets. How unfair that their empty fabric takes rest at your side when my shoulder aches to feel the softness of your cheek at rest upon it. Remind me to scold them most soundly when I return home for their audacity in trying to take my place.

Seriously, Sindara, my heart often wanders to the hillock where we watched the stars at night and talked of science and dreams and love. It is only with strictest discipline that I plot and plan to defeat the Breyals and the carnage they inflict. I so want to come home and hold you again. I am filled with worry. Breyal warriors gather in ever greater numbers. I sense they will bring the full wrath of Breeneth's demon lover upon us very soon. Keep your prayers strong, beloved. Breyal warriors I can manage despite the havoc wrought on battlefields. I am not so confident about what will happen when the evil ones actively enter the fray. I feel in my bones that time is close.

Your love keeps me strong. Knowing that you are helping our nation prepare and cope eases my burden. Most of all, I long to hold you and love you. I remember our last night together when you said you wanted me to comprehend the love that would await my return. I cling to that memory, determined to ask of you further proof.

I send you my love,
Thehrund

Hours dragged. Glancing at the clock, she wondered if time had stopped. Apparently not. When she looked closely for long enough, she could actually see the hands moving. Kendra shook her head impatiently. Her stomach felt totally off kilter. Her shoulders tensed. Her head throbbed. Gathering strained wits about her, she prepared for her final appointment of the day. Immersing herself in the young wife's concerns, she asked questions, listened to responses, and offered suggestions that might help resolve some of the problems her client faced.

Deciding that cooking dinner definitely did not fit her mood, she left the office and stopped at a nearby specialty market to get something already prepared to take home. Standing at a glass case while deciding what she was in the mood to eat, she heard her name and turned, her mouth opening in surprise.

"It's been some time since I last saw you. How are you?"

Kendra managed what passed for a friendly smile. "Busy with work. How about you?"

Jennie Clarke smiled wryly. "The same. These past months have been an eye-opener for me. I probably shouldn't admit this, especially to you, but I never realized how much I depended on Diana. We really miss her at the bank."

Kendra's eyebrows rose involuntarily as she resisted temptation to make a snide remark. "She loved working at the bank."

"Have you heard from her? I've often wondered how well she recovered from that horrible attack."

"We spoke not long ago. She made a full recovery."

"Even though you might not believe me, I'm really glad."

Kendra's forehead creased. Jennie's manner seemed sincerely remorseful. "Thehrund made good on his promise to make the very best care available to her."

Jennie looked around when the clerk behind the counter offered assistance. "I'm still trying to decide." Returning her attention to Kendra, Jennie appeared to be dealing with some inner struggle. "Have they gotten married yet?"

Kendra smiled warmly. "They did, not long after they left. Sin...Diana is extremely happy with Thehrund."

"I've never met anyone like him. He was quite..." She searched for words.

"Impressive? Imposing? Handsome? Striking?" Kendra offered.

Jennie chuckled nervously. "All of the above...and a whole lot more. Was it true what Diana said about him being a prince?"

"It was. It feels odd now when I think of my best friend being a real, live princess." Kendra gave the clerk her order and turned back to Jennie. "Is everything all right with you?"

Jennie's face dropped. "I suppose I feel guilty about how I treated Diana. I'm not saying I've changed my feelings about everything, but I was wrong in the way I approached her. I've worked hard with counselors, but I know I've lost management's respect. They're not altogether sure that Diana's leaving wasn't precipitated by our relationship. I was recently passed over for a big promotion that should have been mine. It made me think about a lot of things."

Kendra hid her truest feelings. "Guilt has both good and bad aspects. We can do great good for ourselves if we channel it properly."

"Kendra, I really want to apologize to Diana. Is there any way I could call her and talk to her?"

How to answer that one, Kendra thought. "I don't get to speak to her often, but I'll be glad to give her your message the next time I do. At the moment, she's facing some extremely difficult circumstances. To be honest, I'm worried about her safety." Kendra stopped abruptly, appalled she had let that bit of information slip.

"I hope it's not a problem with her husband."

"No, not that. One thing's for sure. Someone would have to kill Thehrund before they could hurt Diana. It's a different kind of danger. The very best thing you can do is to pray hard for her safety and the safety of her family. The more prayers said, the better."

Jennie gazed at Kendra and wondered what lay behind the poignant expression that sparked a glaze of tears in dark brown eyes. The two women quietly waited for the clerk to assemble and pack their orders. Before parting company, Jennie reached out and touched Kendra's arm.

"It sounds crazy, but I dreamed last night that she might be in some sort of trouble. Then, I see you here. How odd is that? Please tell Diana that I'll pray for her and her family every single day. That's a promise."

When Kendra finally sat down at her kitchen table, the food in the Styrofoam container suddenly lost all appeal. She hadn't heard from Sindara in several weeks. She knew Thehrund had left Bracordia to lead Ambracor's armies. Kendra abruptly shook with a frigid shiver that raced through her body. Psychic senses droned with the solemn weight of a dirge. The encounter with Jennie had been no coincidence. Jennie's dream had been a sign Kendra could not ignore. Closing the lid of her food container, she got up and went to her room where she could immerse herself in meditation.

Kendra carefully set several candles in a semi-circle in front of her. Just as she started to light them, she heard a knock at the door. It seemed her evening would be more unsettled than her day. She so rarely had visitors anymore. Of course, she wasn't home much. Rising from the floor, she went to the door and peered through the peephole. Her heart thudded heavily just as something crashed in the pit of her stomach. Undoing chains and deadbolt, she opened the door and invited her visitor inside.

Kendra's mouth opened and closed soundlessly. Unable to force words past her constricted throat, she pointed to the sofa. The silence in the living room was nearly unbearable. Finally, Kendra caught a deep breath and freed her voice. "Is it really as bad as I think?"

Madalyn Amador responded with a shake of her head. "Not yet, but sheer catastrophe is near at hand if Ambracor's enemies cannot be stopped. Demons could get stronger and cross into our dimension. Disaster there could easily spill over here. We have more than enough violence and war already."

Kendra drew in several deep cleansing breaths. Her mind revisited her trip to the altar now known to her as the Repository of the Guardians.

She had held Sindara's hands. Their sisterly bond she accepted as a sacred gift. She consciously returned to the present. "I will do whatever I can to help her."

Later, Kendra picked up each glass jar holding a burning candle. Gazing at each flickering flame, she murmured a prayer that its light be returned to God before extinguishing the candle. With each prayer, she attached a heartfelt request for peace.

Standing and stretching several times, she switched on the lamp on her nightstand. Soft light illuminated familiar possessions, family photographs, and walls protectively surrounding her nighttime retreat. For the moment, she relished a sense of peace and safety.

After a trip to the bathroom to finish getting ready for bed, she piled cushions and pillows against the antique headboard that had belonged to her grandmother. Settling herself into cushioned comfort, she pulled the gold chain from around her neck and fixed her gaze on the precious pendant she always wore. Barely a minute passed before entrancing color dominated the silver-white crystal's face.

"Kendra." Sindara's voice sounded weary.

"Are you working too hard again?" Kendra asked, her voice holding a gentle tease meant to ease tired lines from her friend's face.

"Always it seems. There's so much to do. Every day, I help prepare medicines for transport to the battlefields and then spend hours teaching others how to administer medical care to wounded soldiers. We're also setting up hospitals here in Bracordia for severely injured arriving."

Kendra's sigh held deep sadness. "War is in full swing."

Sindara nodded. "It is. Thehrund has been gone nearly four months. I rarely receive even a short message from him." She paused. "Kendra, I fear our advantage is fading. Our people remain brave and steadfast. We all recognize the evil we face. What I cannot dismiss is the feeling that this master demon of Breeneth's will soon summon other dark entities to serve him. Our troops have fought exceedingly well against Breyal tribesmen, and they've won many victories. Especially with winter approaching, my intuition prods me to consider different options."

Kendra's eyes briefly closed. "By different options, you mean taking personal action."

"Yes."

Kendra had expected the reply. What surprised her most was that she did not feel a resulting flood of dread. "Remember what I always told you. Trust your intuition. Sindara, your whole world is in danger. I had an unexpected visitor earlier."

Watching her amulet resume its gleaming silver-white, Sindara breathed in and out as Kendra's words settled. Disarray in her thoughts was something she dared not permit. Neither could she allow an invasion of fear. Another deep breath. The sudden flash of Thehrund's face before her mind's eye. Sindara tucked her amulet back inside the bodice of her gown. She reached over to a bell rope.

Minutes later, Marnee appeared inside Sindara's bedchamber. The elder woman's expression immediately noted stubborn sparks in honey-hued eyes.

"I must be prepared when the time is right. Pack the very basics I'll need for travel by horseback. Also, please be sure to include the pants I brought when I came home. See if you can locate a hauberk and gambeson that will fit me, along with anything else you think necessary. Everything must be ready at a moment's notice."

Marnee assessed Sindara's composure with a discerning eye. "I assume you'll also need weapons."

Sindara nodded. "Marnee," she said as the maid started to leave, "not a word to anyone. And thank you...for understanding."

The corners of Marnee's eyes crinkled as she forced a smile. "Dear child, I am thankful for the honor of serving you."

Chapter Eighteen

Two days later, Sindara returned from the chapel after helping Karan prepare fresh supplies of the blessed oil and cedar-ash blend. Reaching the palace's back entry, she was met by four armed sentries. Their demeanor immediately sparked alarm.

"Your Highness," one said, "we were just coming for you. It seems King Hamund and the queen have disappeared. Servants and guards are searching every corner within the palace walls."

Sindara's right hand instantly rose to cover the amulet resting against her chest. "They are near. I feel them. Keep searching. Summon Karan immediately. I may need his help." As a sentry headed toward the chapel, she stopped him. "Tell him to bring some of the mix we just made."

Accompanied by the remaining sentries, Sindara raced through the long corridors of the palace until she reached the massive staircase leading to the upper floors. Lifting her skirts, she ran up the stairs to her own apartments. "Please, gentlemen, wait here for me. I'll only be a minute."

Having heard the apartment door slam, Marnee appeared almost immediately. "You know?"

"Yes, Marnee. Help me get out of this gown and into pants and a tunic. Hurry. I fear for the king's life."

What followed was an astonishing display of balance and agility. While Marnee quickly unlaced the back of Sindara's gown, the princess swiftly stepped out of pantalets and petticoats and into a pair of well-worn jeans, her deft fingers zipping and snapping them closed. Turning, she bent forward while her servant tugged the dress over her head and tossed the garment aside. Donning a long-sleeved tunic over her lace camisole,

Sindara loosely tied ribbons at the neck while Marnee secured long hair in the loop her mistress had called a rubber band.

Just as Sindara headed out the door, Marnee called her back. "You forgot something, child," she said as she held out a sheathed sword.

Snatching the weapon, she quickly ran through the door, calling out, "I love you, Marnee."

Hurrying down hallways with her guards, she encountered the captain of the palace guard at the top of the main staircase. The captain's eyes noted and summarily dismissed the princess's unusual appearance. "Your Highness," he said with a bow of his head, "you should stay with sufficient soldiers for safety's sake."

"Captain," Sindara replied brusquely, "at this moment, no one in this palace is safe."

Two officers bounded up the stairwell, nodding toward the princess before facing their captain. "Sir, we just received word that sentries at Taramor House have been murdered."

Captain Modrun stared at his subordinates. "The Branderes?"

One officer's face fell while the other tersely responded, "Dead. All in a bloodbath such as cannot be imagined."

"Captain," Sindara said with an air of uncompromising command, "escort me to His Majesty's throne room."

"Your..."

"Immediately!" she snapped, sidling between him and the two officers to rush down the stairway.

Reaching the king's throne room, Sindara ran to the wooden throne. Breathlessly grasping an ornately carved arm with one hand, she yanked open the neckline of her tunic and reached for her amulet. Clutching the crystal, she struggled to catch her breath while focusing full attention on vibrations emanating from the pendant.

The terrifying image that flashed through her mind prompted an agonized cry. Pivoting, she ran back to the open doorway. "Karan! Thanks be to Creator God! The kitchen cellars! Hurry! Captain! Send more guards to defend all entrances to the cellars!"

With Karan at her side, Sindara wove her way at a dead run through the maze of corridors until she reached the palace kitchens. Staff had all been removed from the area for questioning. The pendant lay close above her heart, its vibrations guiding her as she chose one of several doors leading to cellars filled with wines, cheeses, and other provisions. Pausing to quiet her frantic breathing, she eased open the massive door and descended stone steps.

As she reached the bottom step, two horrific screams echoed through stone passageways. Instantly, she turned right and headed down a corridor where meats were prepared for the kitchen. Without hesitation, she reached a door and kicked it open. The sight that met her eyes flared into fury she had never before known. Her father-in-law lay on a stone slab, blood spurting from where the bone had been hacked, leaving only glistening, bloody strands of skin and muscle connecting the motionless, mutilated section of his severed leg.

"You!" Breeneth shrieked upon turning to see Sindara. "You're too late! I will kill him just as I destroyed my own worthless family!"

Before Breeneth could again raise the cleaver, Sindara let out a senseless cry and leapt forward. She slammed the other woman so violently against a stone wall that the enormous, bloody blade clattered across the floor.

"You will do no more harm here today!" Sindara shouted, grabbing the woman's arms and holding them with all her might.

Breeneth jerked sideways but was unprepared for the kick that sent her flailing to the floor. She had never anticipated such resistance from the reserved girl who had devoted herself to religious pursuits. "I will kill you, too!" she cried out as she pushed herself off the floor to attack her rival.

Words shafted through Sindara's mind as her voice called out an echoing demand. "In the name of Creator God, I command you to stop! Stop now, Breeneth Brandere!"

Power from Sindara's amulet shot forward in a stream of light that scorched through her tunic. Before the beam of light could strike Breeneth, she disappeared within the sound of a loud, prolonged hiss and a cloud of black mist.

Spinning around, Sindara saw that Karan had already removed his sash to create a tourniquet around the king's bleeding stump. Narlina ripped away her underskirts to use as temporary bandages to help stanch the flow of blood. Spotting the tin Karan had dropped to tend the injured king, Sindara snatched up the container, opened it, and immediately dunked her fingers inside. Fervently whispering prayers, she drew lines of oily ash across Hamund's forehead and along an exposed part of his injured leg. She also dabbed the mix on the faces of Karan and the queen.

Karan glanced upward, his expression grave. "He's lost a great deal of blood, but I think we came in time to save him. We need to get him upstairs where we can better tend the injury."

Ignoring her mother-in-law for the moment, Sindara rushed to the door and shouted desperate orders to waiting guards. "Hurry! We need a stretcher and men to carry it! The king is hurt!"

The sound of boots rapidly thumping down stone stairways sent chilling echoes through cellar corridors. Sindara looked around the room and placed her hand over the hole burned through her tunic. For the time being, evil had fled. She turned her attention to Narlina. "Mother?"

Narlina lifted her pale face, blue eyes brimming with tears. "I will never forget. She just suddenly appeared in our drawing room. A cloud of glowing black surrounded her. The stench was nauseating. The next thing I knew, we were here. Sindara, I watched as she lifted Hamund off the floor and then laid him on the cutting slab. She never touched him. Not even once. When I saw her raise that huge cleaver, I tried to stop her. I wasn't strong enough."

Sindara embraced her mother-in-law. "She's in league with demons, Mother. You were brave to even try."

"Hamund…" Narlina whispered her husband's name as she watched soldiers gently lift his limp body onto a stretcher. "He refused to tell her how or where Thehrund found you. She threatened to cut off our limbs one by one until we told her. She also wanted to know the location of the Ambracada. We knew she had every intention of killing us, so we told her nothing." Squaring her shoulders and tightly clutching her daughter-in-law's hand, Narlina then led the way as the two women followed the stretcher being carried from the room.

When they reached the king's apartments and settled him on a bed, Sindara drew Karan aside. "Summon all the priests still on palace grounds. We must mark every window and door with the oil and cedar-ash blend. We must also pour lines of sea salt around the walls, top and bottom. That will prevent any further invasion by those of her ilk."

"You didn't destroy her?"

Gritting her teeth, Sindara gave a somber shake of her head. "Before the crystal's light struck her, Breeneth sensed something beyond what she could manage. She used some evil incantation to escape. I'm sure that's also how she entered the palace."

That evening, Sindara witnessed what Thehrund meant when he wrote of his mother's inner strength. The queen had waited until her husband's condition stabilized before going to wash and change clothes. She had then ordered a large chaise carried into the heavily guarded bedchamber where the king slept under the effect of drugs administered by the physician who had taken over from an exhausted Karan Mezden.

Narlina gazed at Sindara, who held her mother-in-law's hand in a comforting grasp. "My husband is a strong, healthy man. He will live and be more determined than ever to vanquish this enemy."

Sindara responded with a nod. "I'm certain he will." She hesitated before continuing. "Mother, there's something I must tell you."

Narlina blinked several times and gave Sindara no chance to continue. "I understand. I will never comprehend all that I witnessed today. When she just disappeared after you..." She swallowed a sob and forced herself to continue. "You, Sindara, are our only hope. You are my *only* hope. She must not get to Thehrund."

Sindara gently squeezed Narlina's hand. "I've already instructed the captain to organize an escort and supplies so we can leave once I'm sure of Father's recovery. I must know that I can rely on you to oversee matters here."

Narlina nodded. "I shall ask Cleotis to help me until Hamund improves. Your uncle is a wise man."

Sindara stood and went to her father-in-law's side. Bending forward, she kissed his forehead and then placed her dangling pendant over his heart. "Be well, Father. I intend to end this madness."

Chapter Nineteen

Atop his stallion, Thehrund visually tracked widespread pandemonium extending as far as he could see. Dust billowed in massive, rolling clouds as innumerable hooves pounded against dry earth. His eyes watered as bits of dirt flew into his face. Falling tears created puddles beneath his lower lashes that rapidly mixed with grime and sweat to slide down his cheeks in muddy rivulets. His heart pounded a furious beat. His loud, resonant voice, hoarse with all the dust drawn into throat and lungs, called out command after command as battle-hardened troops responded and fought savage invaders from the east.

Shrill war cries from Breyal warriors rose in frenzied calls for attack. Lengths of bone and stone beads dangled from their battle garb and rattled loudly in accompaniment to their continuous yelps and bellows. Arrows swooshed through the air. Steel rang out against steel as brandished swords forcibly collided with opposing blades. Sounds of combat settled into a sickening drone.

Officers and soldiers on horseback raced into the fray, slashing and thrusting at Breyal warriors clad only in thick leather battledress that offered minimal protection from weaponry of finely forged steel wielded by Ambracor defenders. Groans of men generated an almost steady roar as they exerted every bit of strength to swing weapons with deadly impact. Agonized screams punctuated the bedlam when sharp, pointed blades struck their targets with brutal force. Moans of injured and dying swelled into an unending wave as those still engaged in battle kicked them aside or horses trod over them.

Casting his glance to the right, the warrior prince motioned with a sharp nod of his head for mounted troops to initiate a fresh charge as Breyal ranks began to scatter and retreat. Raising his broadsword and digging his knees into his horse's sides, he raced toward one band of enemy warriors stubbornly holding their position. With swift, powerful strokes, he struck down man after man with grim determination. So concentrated on the attack, Thehrund didn't even notice an arrow catching in one of the links of his hauberk.

His peripheral vision barely caught sight of a Breyal leaping toward his left side. Swinging his arm out with all the force he could muster, he caught the attacker in the face with the steel spikes embedded in the bracer protecting his arm. Deafened by the din of the ferocious battle, he didn't even hear the scream as one of the spikes caught the attacker directly in one eye.

Ambracor's army staunchly defended its flanks until the Breyal war party was forced to retreat. The courageous prince had lost count of the hours he and his troops fought on the battlefield that day. As fighting subsided, dust settled on bodies strewn across the open plain where the Breyals had confidently marched. Patches of ground not littered with battle debris and bodies oozed with pools of dull scarlet mud.

Near exhaustion, Thehrund scanned the gruesome scene. Dismounting, he glanced to his left as one of his officers tugged an arrow dangling from the protective mail of his hauberk. Grunting what passed as thanks, he started mental assessment of the most vicious battle yet. His stomach pitched as he watched soldiers searching for wounded survivors. The sickening sweet scent of exposed flesh and spilled blood assaulted his nostrils and made him feel like gagging. Shaking his head, he could hardly fathom the number of limbs and even heads lying alongside bodies from which they had been severed.

The prince carefully picked his way across the macabre field. He praised courageous soldiers and uttered words of encouragement to those whose expressions were stricken with the shocking sight of so much death. He occasionally stopped to help lift injured men onto stretchers. Every moan of pain pierced his soul as surely as the sharp point of a sword or lance.

As he continued walking, he spotted a fallen horse, its golden hide splashed with drying blood. His heart lurched when he heard a faint cry and hurried toward the dead beast. Calling for help, he spoke soothing words of encouragement until several soldiers managed to shift the horse's body enough for Thehrund to pull its rider free. Gently, he cradled the officer's head against his chest.

"Rezda, help is coming," he choked out. "We'll take care of you. I promise."

Rezda's pain-glazed eyes fixed on the prince's face. "You mustn't give up. You mustn't let them destroy our land or our people."

"Shush, brother. Save your strength."

"Tell my parents not to grieve. I did...what was...necessary. Tell...my wife...I love her." Rezda's eyes, so like his father's, then froze into the cold, fixed stare of death.

Thehrund's face dropped as he feared he might finally succumb to tears. How would he ever tell the Varacors that their youngest son had been slain in battle? What comfort could he offer Rezda's pregnant wife? Where would he ever find words to tell his own wife that he had ordered Rezda into combat and then held her younger brother in his arms and watched him die?

When he finally stood and straightened his back, he watched solemnly as Rezda Varacor was borne away by equally somber soldiers. They had been ordered to prepare the young officer's body for transport home. Because of his string of recent victories, Thehrund was convinced Breyal tribes would require time to regroup. He expected more of what seemed an unending source of fighters for whom life seemingly held little value and war was an exhilarating occupation. He would, however, make time to accompany his brother-in-law's body home.

The coolness of an autumn afternoon claimed the prince's attention. His padded gambeson was soaked with sweat from his exertion during battle. Waning sunlight and a sudden breeze prompted shivers as he started to feel the cold. His throat felt sore. His head pounded. The fact he had led his troops to yet another victory left him with a hollow sense of achievement.

Liana Varacor sat on a sofa and stared into the roaring fire easing the evening's cool embrace. Her heart suffered anxiety. She had awakened that morning with tightness in her breast and tension in her neck. With two sons actively fighting the Breyal invasion, she had lived for months fearing news that one or both might be killed. The morning had dawned with an ache that would not cease, a foreboding that would not loosen its clutching tendrils.

"Liana, you've hardly eaten a bite today. Will you not have something light before you go to bed?"

She looked up at her husband with solemn eyes. Lines in his handsome face had deepened noticeably since full-scale war had begun. His eyes reflected his weary state of mind. As governor of Arvacon Province, he bore demanding burdens while coordinating the care of refugees and staying abreast of the needs of the Arvacon militia now under the command of Ambracor's prince. Artrian worked tirelessly to manage administrative duties and make time to visit injured soldiers receiving medical care in Cahmdurn.

Liana knew beyond any doubt that tragic news was imminent, but she would relieve her husband of undue concern for her. "Perhaps some fruit and cheese would do well," she responded agreeably, rising from the sofa and meeting her husband as he crossed the spacious drawing room. Surrounding his waist with her arms, she rested her head against his shoulder.

The clatter of hooves on the brick drive in front of the governor's mansion captured their attention. A footman hurried to advise them that a group of soldiers was approaching. For one swiftly passing moment, Liana felt faint. Artrian drew in a ragged breath. Riders arriving so late could not be good. He steeled himself for yet more bad news. Drawing in a sustaining breath, he headed to the entrance to meet the new arrivals.

Double doors were opened wide. At least a dozen soldiers in full armor had dismounted and held the reins of their horses. Wearing a captain's insignia on his flowing cape, an officer stood beside a chestnut horse. Count Varacor watched curiously as the officer stretched his arms upward to assist the final rider down from the saddle. Once solidly on the ground, the rider tipped back the helmet's visor and strode purposefully past the captain.

"Father!"

Artrian Varacor quickly raced down the steps. "Sindara! I can't believe it! What in the name of Creator God brings you here?"

Sindara lifted her face to kiss her father's cheek. "I needed to talk with you and Mother. Before I go inside, is there space here to accommodate my guards? We passed the encampment northwest of the city and left the rest of our regiment there. I promised the king I would go nowhere without the special escort."

"Sindara!" Liana rushed toward her daughter, her slender hands barely able to cradle her daughter's face because of the steel helmet. "It's so good to see you...I think. I never imagined you clad in soldier's armor."

Count Varacor instructed house servants to summon grooms to care for the horses and then to organize proper accommodations for his daughter's escort in the mansion's many guest suites. He then grasped his daughter's hand and guided her inside.

Once doors were closed, bolted, and barred, an unusual precaution Sindara had never before seen, she removed leather gauntlets and helmet. "Such a relief as cannot be described," she said, shaking her head and freeing rippling waves of hair. Sindara unfastened the brooch holding her cloak. Her mother's personal maid then helped remove her chainmail hauberk by pulling it up from her knees, over her torso, and finally over her head. When at last she unlaced the gambeson and removed the weighty garment, she breathed out a sigh, stretched, and twisted before smiling at her parents.

"Now, for a proper greeting," she said, affectionately embracing each of them and kissing their cheeks multiple times.

A while later, Sindara gladly shared with her mother a tray of crisply toasted flatbread, chunks of farmer's cheese, and sweet apples. Noting her parents' continuing appraisal of her appearance, she actually grinned. "I know how strange I must look. I brought several pairs of these with me from the other Earth-plane. They're comfortable and durable. I had hoped the long tunic might soften the look."

Artrian shook his head. "It matters not. You look beautiful regardless of what you wear. What worries me is that you've been riding through the countryside while our province is embroiled in this damned war."

Sindara popped a small piece of cheese into her mouth and then reclined wearily against the high back of a comfortable side chair. "We traveled via the Carlester route. It lies further from the battlegrounds. I've kept abreast of courier reports. Gorandro and Zelcon have seen serious action, but not nearly as much as we've had here considering they border only Breyal. As I understand, our militia and armies have fought with remarkable success and valor."

Artrian nodded. "Arvacon suffers the dual curse of long borders with both Breyal and Bramond. Since Breeneth established her base of command there, we find ourselves on constant alert. That's partly why I'm utterly astonished that Hamund allowed you to travel so far from Bracordia."

"What?" Liana asked, immediately noting anger snapping in her daughter's eyes.

"He had little choice. In fact, he had no other viable alternative."

Artrian settled himself on the sofa beside his wife. "What happened?"

"Breeneth's alliance is with possibly the most powerful and dangerous of master demons. Somehow, she has developed powers no ordinary human possesses. She simply appeared one day inside the king's apartments. Using strange powers, she transported them to the cellars where she tried to force them to reveal how and where Thehrund found me. Before we reached them, she hacked off one of the king's legs."

Liana clamped her hand over her mouth in horror as Artrian gasped in shock. "Hamund? How is he?"

Sadness and wrath mingled with pride when she replied, "Physically, he is recovering quickly and remarkably well. Mentally, I'm not certain I've ever seen anyone so resolute when it comes to bringing this war to an end. His fury knows no bounds."

"And Breeneth?" Liana hesitantly asked.

"Karan and I found her in time to prevent her from doing more harm to the king and queen. I shoved her away from Hamund. Before I was able to subdue her, she just vanished in one of those misty black clouds."

"What are we to do if she possesses such powers?"

Sindara went to lean against the fireplace mantel and stared into dancing flames. "I believe time is short before her master is able to augment Breyal forces with whole armies of lesser demons. Our only hope is to confront them both and put an end to the evil they have brought to Ambracor."

Artrian's mind raced through the possibilities. Each question entering his mind led to a single conclusion. "That is your mission?"

Sindara did not look up. "I am the only one who has any chance of success. Father, you and Mother are also in danger. She brazenly located and slaughtered her own family. She will not hesitate to come after you to strike at me. I brought a supply of a particular blend of blessed oils and cedar ashes along with sea salt. Karan remained at the barracks with the rest of my escort to begin anointing soldiers there. I have some with me tonight to anoint the two of you and to mark openings to the house to deter entry from the dark ones."

"But you, Sindara, what about you?"

Finally looking up, Sindara's expression was grave. "I'm convinced that the salvation of Ambracor rests on the love Thehrund and I share. Our love must be strong enough to defeat this evil. My life was saved for this mission. I was born to help Thehrund defend the light of our world."

❊ ❊ ❊

Wispy clouds boasted magenta shadows cast by dawn's earliest rays of sunlight. Sindara sat under a tree where she had spent many childhood hours with her grandfather whenever the family was in Cahmdurn. Her mind turned backward in time. Her grandfather's image filled her memory and brought a faint smile to her face.

"Sindara, you mustn't think of fall as a time when everything starts to die. Life fades in autumn, and most of our world sleeps to escape the bitter cold of winter. You might think of winter as a time for the whole of nature to rest."

"But, Grandfather, winter is so disagreeable. I like the flowers and the birdsongs when spring comes."

Her grandfather's blue-gray eyes twinkled. His long mane of snow-white hair fluttered in the breeze. His countenance, a mass of wrinkles, spread wide with the smile formed by his thin lips. His hand, soft and permanently curled with advanced age, held hers in a grasp that was remarkably firm, infinitely comforting. "Child, we all have our time to live and our time to die. The blessing for those of us who believe in Creator God is that we know our spirits do not perish. They return to the Creator where they brighten his light and wait to serve should they be needed again."

"What do they do while they wait?"

Her grandfather's patience never wavered with her unending questions. "They enjoy the peace and love found in Creator God's presence. They commune with other spirits."

"Will you see Grandmother again?"

The old man smiled thoughtfully. "Your grandmother was a kind, beautiful lady. I'm quite sure she waits for me. We loved each other very much. I pray that someday you might find a love just as great."

Sindara's gaze dropped. "Grandfather, I know you miss her, but I shall miss you if you leave me."

An age-gnarled hand gently patted her cheek and then stroked her hair. "My darling Sindara, I shall always watch over you. I already have everything planned. When I reach Creator God's presence, I plan to ask him immediately for the job of being your guardian angel."

She looked puzzled. "Do you mean I don't have one yet?"

Grandfather Varacor chuckled. "Of course you do. I just have the feeling my independent little granddaughter may need at least two guardian angels...perhaps even an entire legion of guardian angels! Not one, however, will guard you as bravely as your grandfather."

Her grandfather had died soon afterward, but she always recalled that conversation with particular affection and curiosity. Had he merely tried to soothe her childish concerns, or had he foreseen the dangers her future would bring?

"Your Highness..."

Sindara reluctantly tucked away precious memories and glanced up at the captain of her guard. "Yes?"

"Your Highness, you should not be outside alone and unarmed," the captain quietly chastised.

Sindara looked up at him. "I thank you for your concern. Here, I feel safe. I have a very stubborn angel watching over me at this very moment." Noting the captain's puzzled look, she cast him a smile of contrition. "I apologize for causing any undue concern. I promise to be more careful."

Throughout the morning, Sindara wandered the confined grounds of the family's home in Cahmdurn, remembering to be considerate of the captain's admonition by keeping an escort nearby. She savored moments alone with her thoughts. How she wished she could go to the country estate. That was the one place where she felt most at peace and most capable of marshaling her thoughts into a logical plan of action.

Returning to the enormous oak where she had talked so often with her grandfather, she put her arms around the centuries-old tree. In her mind, her grandfather's voice sounded near. Freeing her imagination, she pretended he was the tree so she could listen to him. "My sweet Sindara, I always watch over you. Believe in yourself, little one, and never let anyone challenge your faith in Creator God."

Karan arrived shortly after the family's lunch. Following introductions to Meila, Graden, and Rezda's wife, discussion naturally turned to the crisis dominating everyone's mind. Lord Artrian updated his daughter and Karan on the many battles that had occurred and lamented the staggering death toll. Karan expressed his appreciation that Master Zoman had agreed to oversee preparations for blessing additional oils to blend with cedar ashes. Many would be saved by the special anointing should Breeneth meet their expectations of drawing demonic servants into the conflict.

Midafternoon brought a lull in conversation. Lord Artrian invited Karan to accompany him to a nearby refugee camp while Meila took Graden upstairs to rest. The idea of a nap also appealed to Rezda's wife, who was approaching the eighth month of her pregnancy. Alone together in the family drawing room, Sindara noted her mother's poorly disguised anxiety.

Going to the sofa and kneeling down, she took her mother's hands and lifted them to her lips. "Will you tell me what troubles you?"

Liana looked away. "I'm afraid, Sindara. So afraid. Beyond my worries for you, my heart tells me something is very wrong."

Sindara's thumbs gently stroked her mother's hands. "Mother, our whole way of life is at risk. I do not question your fear or your intuition. If tragedy befalls our family, we must bear the grief and remain faithful to Creator God."

Liana's eyes dropped to hands joined with her daughter's. "How can you be so brave?"

"Mother, how were you so brave when you thought me dead? Your faith kept you strong. Families across Ambracor are mourning lost loved ones. I fear for Erator and Rezda more than I can say. The thought of losing Thehrund terrifies me. For now, all any of us can do is to entrust the spirits of lost loved ones to Creator God and continue this fight. We must cling to Creator God's light if we are to drive this evil from our world."

Tears glazed Liana's eyes. "I feel the loss already."

Gazing into her mother's eyes, Sindara felt a frisson of fear shaft downward along her spine. Without a doubt, her mother was right. "News will come quickly enough. Don't lose sight of Meila and Dalina or your grandchildren. You have extraordinary strength, Mother. Of that I am sure. Whatever has happened, your faith and your wisdom will be sorely needed. I expect we will all cry until we can cry no more, but we must not let any sacrifice be a step that will raise Breeneth and her master above us."

Liana could not hide her sadness, but she reached out to lay her palm against her daughter's face. "You have always been so strong. That must be why Creator God sent you to us at this moment."

Sindara shook her head. "I suffer my own moments of weakness, Mother. You have no idea of the despair I felt when I thought Thehrund had callously betrayed my love." Her thoughts drifted back to her morning reflections. "I thought of Grandfather Varacor this morning. He once told me that, because we believe in Creator God, we can always trust that our spirits will return to his holy light. We must let Grandfather's wisdom remind us to be strong during these sorrowful trials."

Her mother slowly nodded. "I'll try to remember." Smiling weakly, Liana continued, "Your grandfather said trying times would likely come within our generation. He said he had read it in the Ambracada. He also said those times would be full of grief. They would not end until two supremely bright lights would appear to banish the darkness."

Not knowing what more to say, Sindara rose from the floor. "Mother, I'm going to rest a while. We plan to leave tomorrow, and I'm sure the journey won't be easy." She paused. "Always remember I love you."

The next morning, Sindara arose early. Before dressing, she raised her amulet to her lips and kissed it. "Lady Aminta and Master Garen, please watch over my family." She closed her eyes and sighed. "Kendra, please keep your prayers strong." She then pulled on tall socks, denim jeans, and a tunic falling to mid-thigh. Tucking the crystal pendant beneath her top, she went downstairs to join her family for breakfast.

Dawdling over tea, Sindara finally decided she should wait no longer. "Mother, would you help me get ready?"

The two women climbed the staircase. Inside Sindara's bedchamber, they began the tedious task of securing fastenings on the thick, quilted gambeson that fell just above the hem of her long tunic. Bending over, Sindara pushed her arms through the long sleeves of her hauberk. Then, while her mother held the tunic fashioned from riveted rings of metal, Sindara wiggled into the awkward garment until her mother could tug it neatly into place. At the last, they tightened the fastenings of a blue brigandine made of thick leather reinforced with protective metal rings.

Lady Liana cast a doubtful gaze at a steel gorget, padded coif, helmet, and long cape lying on the bed. "How did you ride here wearing all of that?"

"I only used those when we traveled roads closer to the battlefields. They're miserable to wear, but Captain Zimaron insisted. Wearing them was easier than listening to him complain."

"His concern is for your safety."

"I know," Sindara sighed. "I just need more freedom of movement. The helmet I shall wear, but the rest I'll carry for now. I feel more secure if I can reach the pendant."

Entering the foyer, Count Varacor gazed at his daughter with a curious mix of pride and melancholy upon seeing her clad in battle garb and armed for combat. His heart revolted at the idea of her riding toward Bramond Province for the express purpose of challenging the evil entities that had incited war. Still, he respected her courage as well as her conviction. How much he had wanted her to live a peaceful, happy life. Instead, he smiled resolutely as he linked her arm with his and led her outside to her waiting horse.

Once mounted, she gazed down at both her parents. "Do not worry about me. My purpose is clear, and I will find a way to accomplish my task. I love you both."

Captain Zimaron raised his hand for the small escort to advance to join the regiment awaiting them. Reaching tall gates that opened to Cahmdurn's main street, the captain signaled a halt. Approaching from the north was a column of soldiers flying mourning flags of black and gold and accompanying a funeral coach. Holding his guards in place, he was surprised when the column paused, waiting for the captain's unit to ride out so they could turn onto the circular drive.

Sindara's breath caught painfully in her breast. She signaled her guards to move far to the side to allow the coach and its escort to pass. Once the way was clear, she quickly turned her horse back toward the house. Frozen in place, she watched as soldiers dismounted in unison.

Their lead rider was the last down. She instantly recognized her husband's tall, imposing figure even before he removed his helmet and freed his long black hair. She watched her mother slump sideways against her father. Sharp pain pierced her heart with the realization that the funeral coach bore the body of one of her brothers.

Carefully edging her horse past the ranks of her escort, she approached broad front steps where her parents' expressions reflected shock as Thehrund delivered news her mother had expected. Reaching the side of the coach, she reined in her mount but sat fixed to the saddle, dreading to learn which of her brothers had lost his life.

Lord Artrian looked up at her, his eyes filled with pain. Thehrund turned, suddenly wondering why his father's special escort was in Cahmdurn and why Artrian's attention was so fixed on the soldier whose hands had dropped the reins and reached out to him. Confused, he started to question the rider when shifting breezes carried the faintest hint of a fragrance forever imprinted on his consciousness.

He reached her in an instant and helped her down. "Sindara," he rasped, the rich tones of his voice revealing an indescribable mix of emotions.

Lifting her helmet's visor, she questioned him with her eyes only.

"Rezda," Thehrund murmured before drawing her into aching arms.

Sindara's guards all dismounted and joined the soldiers who had accompanied Rezda's body home. House servants appeared and removed the stand that would be assembled quickly inside a large reception area used for official functions. While the military escort stood at respectful attention, eight of the king's guards gave battle-weary soldiers welcome moments of relief. They solemnly withdrew the simple wooden coffin from the funeral coach. Carefully lifting and balancing it on strong shoulders, they followed their prince and his wife in a somber procession into the governor's home.

Holding each other in a trembling, fearful embrace, Meila and Dalina stood at the foot of the formal staircase. Tears streaked both their faces. Sindara clasped her husband's upper arm, giving him much-needed encouragement as he delivered the news of Rezda's death to the young, pregnant widow. When Dalina swayed in a grief-stricken swoon, Thehrund alertly caught her. Lifting her into strong arms, he followed Sindara into the family drawing room and carefully laid Dalina on one of the sofas. The remainder of the day passed in a blur.

Lord Artrian's foresight yet again proved its value. Praying he would never need them, he had prepared advance plans should one of his sons die in combat. His chief aide immediately issued the announcement that Captain Rezda Varacor had been killed defending Ambracor at the Battle of Torandor. The public would have an opportunity to pay respects two days hence, but in the meantime, the family would appreciate prayers on behalf of their fallen son, their grieving family, and their beleaguered country. The announcement concluded with an entreaty that citizens make time to visit and encourage soldiers currently hospitalized with battle injuries and to comfort families already suffering losses inflicted by war. Arvacon Province must lead Ambracor in showing appreciation to everyone enduring sacrifices for the greater benefit of their people.

Lady Liana Varacor drew heavily on her core of faith as she knelt beside her son's wife. In a gentle voice, she continuously reminded the young woman that Rezda would want her to take care of herself for the sake of their unborn child. She patiently wiped the unending stream of tears from her daughter-in-law's cheeks and encouraged her to sit and sip tea to calm herself. Relief came when Karan arrived and pulled up a chair. His softly chanted prayers finally eased Dalina's immediate distress until, exhausted, she dozed off.

Upstairs, Meila attempted to help Graden's nursemaid console the boy whose childlike senses absorbed the sorrow around him. The child fussed and cried, clinging to his mother and refusing Deiria's efforts to distract his attention from all the commotion downstairs.

Inside the privacy of Artrian's study, the distinguished count shed his image of the calm, thoughtful, and controlled governor. Sobs shook his tall body as his daughter held him in a firm embrace. Some part of his soul was beyond grateful for her comforting presence. He had mourned her death for years while guarding fragile shreds of hope that her life might be restored. He could harbor no such hopes for his youngest child. Grasping at shards of a newly broken heart, he reminded himself that he would have Rezda's babe to guide and protect.

Late that evening, Sindara made rounds within the quiet house. Dalina dozed fitfully after crying herself to sleep, the cumbersome state of her pregnancy adding to her unrest. Graden's nursemaid rested on a chaise to keep a watchful eye on her. Peeking into Meila's bedchamber, she smiled as she saw her sister-in-law fast asleep with little Graden cuddled snugly in her arms. Lights in her parents' suite were extinguished, but she was certain they were awake, finding comfort in their shared love.

Pausing in the upstairs hallway, she clasped her hand over her amulet. For just a moment, she wondered if she had traveled the closer route if she might have been able to alleviate the destruction at Torandor, perhaps even saving her brother's life. As much as she already missed Rezda's teasing and pranks, she hoped his spirit had found its right time to return to Creator God.

Light steps carried her down to the first floor. The hall where her brother's body lay was lit by several tall candelabras. Members of his militia unit were taking turns to provide a continuous honor guard for their slain comrade. Each bowed his head in respect. Neither spoke. The wooden coffin had been exchanged for a more ornate casket, its stand draped in black and gold silk. Sindara calmly gazed at pale features. She felt sure Rezda's spirit was at peace. To honor his memory, she would do everything in her power to destroy the scourge that had ended his life and others now mounting into the thousands.

She didn't even blink when strong hands came to rest firmly at her waist. The comfort in those beloved hands gave her cause to offer a brief, silent prayer of thanks as she leaned backward against her husband's firm, muscular form.

"You should rest," he whispered softly against her hair. "Let me take you upstairs. Your family will need your strength tomorrow."

Yielding to her husband's advice, she leaned against his arm as they slowly turned and went upstairs to the suite that had always been hers in Cahmdurn. Once inside, she was glad a servant had thoughtfully started a fire in the small, ornate, square stove used both to warm the room and heat water for washing. A lamp had also been lit, its golden light soothing.

Turning to face Thehrund, she raised her hands and framed his face between them. "My dear husband," she whispered, "how I have missed those magnificent blue eyes of yours."

He tenderly kissed her forehead. "How have you faced this day with such grace and tranquility?"

Shaking her head, she moved closer to rest her cheek against his shoulder. "For now, I don't want to think about it. I wish only to know the joy of your arms around me, yet there's so much I must tell you."

With one hand snugly at her waist and the other gently pressing her face against his chest, Thehrund closed his eyes and savored the exquisite solace of holding her. "I already know something drastic must have happened for you to be here, dressed for battle and accompanied by Father's guard. Is there anything so important that telling me tonight will change what has already happened or the situation we face beyond this house?"

Tears threatened to fill her eyes. "I don't think so," she whispered almost inaudibly. Pulling slightly away, she studied every feature of his darkly handsome face. "Thehrund, may I ask a question?"

He responded with only a nod, his eyes locked on hers.

"With all the grief filling this house just now, would you think me a terrible person if I told you how much I want you to make love to me?"

The pleading tone in her voice swept throughout his being. How well he understood the source of her plaintive inquiry. He realized how much he also needed her to revitalize energy sapped by haunting images and suffering wrought by war. "How can you imagine I'd ever think such a thing? Our union...our love...that is what gives us strength to deal with this awful nightmare."

Sliding her arms upward around his neck, she sought lips that quickly melded to hers. Their mouths opened to intoxicating sensations only hinting at the impending union where, at least for a brief time, they could escape the emptiness endured throughout their long separation and the tragedy borne by their people.

Chapter Twenty

Blaring horns startled Kendra from her lapse of attention. Glancing quickly to each side, she proceeded through the intersection, determined to focus on her driving until she reached the turn-off to the cemetery. Upon arriving, she quickly found a space near the entrance. After parking the car, turning off the engine, and shoving the key into a coat pocket, she sat quietly for several moments.

Getting out, she opened the back door to retrieve her purse and two baskets of flowers. Balancing her awkward load, she closed the door with a shove of her hip and left the car under the scrutiny of protective angels. She just didn't have a free hand to reach into her pocket for the key to lock the car.

Strolling along a peaceful path lined with trees, she remembered her first visit to this place. Childhood stories had conditioned her to think of graveyards as spooky places where ghosts hid behind tombstones, lying in wait to jump up and frighten the wits out of unwary visitors. Those tales had puzzled her that beautiful spring day when her parents had held her hand as they walked to a tree-shaded area.

She remembered studying the tent, its scalloped edging fluttering in the breeze. Bronze supports held the closed casket she had seen earlier that morning at church. There, it had been open, the gray-haired head of her beloved granny resting on its satin pillow. A kneeler had been placed beside it. Family and friends had paused to pray for the peaceful repose of Jane Mae Porter.

Jane Mae, whose husband had died fighting a war in a foreign land days after the birth of his only child, never remarried. Instead, she concentrated on rearing her son to the same standards so important to her husband: love for God, honesty, integrity, and hard work. She toiled for years in a dirty factory, earning a living so her son could grow up in a clean, decent environment. She always found time to spend with him so he would never feel the need to look beyond his home and good neighbors for guidance and friendship. Teaching him by example to help others in need and to value family, she watched him grow into a fine man who married a loving woman. Together, husband and wife later cared for Jane Mae when she fell ill with inoperable cancer.

The mixed perfume of hundreds of flowers had smelled so sweet as little Kendra listened to the priest's final prayers over her grandmother's coffin. A dear friend sang a touching hymn. All the while, the little girl, dressed in her Sunday finest, wondered why everyone at the gravesite looked so sad. Granny had promised Kendra that she and the angels would always watch over her so long as she kept goodness in her thoughts. At the end, she was certain she had heard Granny whisper in her ears, "I'll never leave you, Granny's baby."

A cool breeze again lifted the scent of fresh flowers to Kendra's nose just as she reached the plots where her parents were buried next to Granny. Kneeling, she carefully placed flowers at the double headstone belonging to her parents and then set the second arrangement by her grandmother's marker. She reached out, slowly drew her finger along the smooth edge of gray stone, and read out loud, "Jane Mae Porter, loving wife of Cpl. James T. Porter, who lies a hero in Arlington, VA, their spirits finally reunited." She remembered holding Daddy's hand when he had told the man that was what Granny wanted on the tombstone. When she looked up, she had seen tears streaming down his dark cheeks and again wondered why he felt so sad.

"Granny," Kendra said aloud, "I miss you. I know you're watching over me because I always feel you close. I'm sure you remember Diana, my friend who sometimes came with me to bring flowers. She's in a very dangerous place now...and really far away. Granny, you always told me how our spirits are eternal, but you also said we needed to cherish the lives God gives us and the lives of those who love us. Diana loves me, and I love her. She needs my help, but I don't know what to do. Angels told us that we are sisters-in-spirit. Please ask your angels to guide me so I can help her."

Kendra exuded an aura of tranquility as she crossed herself before and after reciting a precious prayer. Rising from grasses starting to wilt beneath fall's chill, she smiled at the stone bearing her parents' names. "Daddy, I love you and Mommy. I wish you both peace."

The very air inside the Brandere mansion reeked. Thafalos watched with an angry sneer as Breeneth paced back and forth in an agitated frenzy of frustration. She muttered incomprehensible obscenities as her state of irritation mushroomed. Their careful plans had yet again been thwarted, and both were sorely vexed by continuing successes against the Breyal warriors as well as Breeneth's failed invasion of the royal palace.

Thafalos finally cocked his head to the side. "You must control yourself, Breeneth. Your storming temper only aggravates the situation and prevents calm assessment of the difficulties at hand."

Breeneth stopped and glared at her master. "The strength I gained from my family's horror and then partaking of their blood should have been more than enough to accomplish my plans to kill Hamund and his wife. How did she find us? What was the light I saw as I departed?"

"Sit and be quiet," Master Thafalos ordered, pointing to her place beside his throne. "We must calmly examine and understand this mystery if we are to claim victory over Ambracor. You also need to recover your energy."

Breeneth's expression remained surly, but she obeyed without protest.

Thafalos lifted his chin high, which added to his haughty, disdainful bearing. "For the moment, we shall disregard the failure of the Breyals in battle. Kicchak will soon have many more warriors aimed at Arvacon borders."

Breeneth snorted in disgust. "Kicchak is a fool. He is no match for Thehrund Cobrandya."

"You forget. Kicchak is but a pawn. He whittles down Cobrandya's armies in number and morale. His primitive warriors live only to die. With every death, I grow stronger. Once we achieve sufficient power to summon lesser demons, Ambracor's armies can no longer succeed in combat."

Breeneth lifted scornful eyes to her master. "You said you would not be strong enough to summon sufficient members of your kind or to fully dominate Ambracor until the original Ambracada is destroyed. Have you forgotten that it has disappeared?"

Tawny skin darkened ominously. Shimmering black mist emitted flurries of undulating spirals from the demon's entire body. His voice thundered in rage. Chandeliers rocked from their ceiling anchors, and windows rattled. "Do not insult me, girl! Your fate lies in my hands now, and I will tolerate none of your contemptuous insolence! Do you understand?"

"How have I insulted you?" she asked, carefully modulating her voice with a sound of contrition she did not feel.

"There are none like me. Those I would summon to our cause are lowly spirits who do not begin to compare with the powers I possess," he responded with a roar. "Remember that!"

"I would never even think to suggest any might equal you," she said in a conciliatory tone as she lowered her face in a show of deference.

"So long as that is very clear," he stated, somewhat pacified. "Now, we must define issues that require resolution. The Ambracada is missing. There are two possibilities. Someone at the faith center had already hidden it and died before revealing its hiding place. Otherwise, someone escaped with it. The next question is this. Why did they move it?"

Breeneth breathed in deeply as her chin twitched from side to side. "They suspected the book was in danger. I think it no coincidence that the book disappeared shortly after Sindara Varacor's return to Ambracor."

Leaning backward, Thafalos gazed upward at molded plaster ceilings. "Yes. Sindara Varacor. She continues to be our most mysterious dilemma. I still question how she survived and how she returned without my sensing her. Where was she all those years? Those questions intrigue me."

"Her body was never recovered," Breeneth mused thoughtfully, "but how could she have escaped?"

Master's ebony eyes stared straight ahead. "Breyals often take slain bodies as trophies, but I heard nothing of her body reaching Breyal camps. We must solve this mystery."

"Thehrund knows. When his father announced her return, he mentioned that Thehrund never faltered in faith. Thehrund said he had searched until he found her and brought her back."

Thafalos shook his head in rising apprehension. "Back from where? This information is crucial to hastening our victory. I tire of being so restricted when I should be able to walk about freely in the glory I deserve."

Breeneth's hatred for Sindara seethed with ever greater vehemence. Blaming Sindara for stealing Thehrund and plaguing plans unknown even by Thafalos, she vowed to find a way to force the enigmatic princess into submission. She considered anew the pleasure she would know upon discovering Sindara's secrets and then killing her. She would then deal with Thafalos and claim Thehrund as her own personal slave.

Turning an admiring gaze toward her master, she smiled. "I shall dedicate my every effort to supporting you, Master, as you defeat Ambracor and acquire the great glory that is rightfully yours."

Placated to a certain degree, Thafalos reached for her hand. He gave her the searing gaze and subtle smile that told her they would retire for a while to the comfort of the master suite where they might indulge their shared lust.

Morning skies brightened with the rising sun, its rays streaking clouds with glowing pinks and gold. Slight winds carried a nip that portended cooler temperatures and rain. Geese flew in formation overhead, their honking loud and raucous compared to the sweet harmony of spring's songbirds. Still, neither their noisy calls nor the bite of morning air failed to stir Sindara from deep contemplation.

Inside, Thehrund had felt her leave the warmth of their bed. He had also felt her light, tender kiss against his temple, but he had been unable to rouse himself from the comfortable mantle of slumber that held him prisoner. For months, he had traveled war-torn border regions of Ambracor and Breyal. He had killed enemy warriors and ordered his own soldiers to fight in full knowledge many would die. After months of sleeping in tents or on hard ground beneath open skies, his body rebelled at leaving the pleasure of a clean, soft bed.

The night before, he had made love to his wife as a man possessed. Leaving his new bride months earlier had been heartrending. Not a day passed without him stealing a few moments from his armies to close his eyes and picture her. He recalled the brilliance of her smile, the golden hue of her eyes, and the sweetness of her kisses. He often missed her to the point of physical pain. Finding her in Cahmdurn the morning before had been an unexpected shock. Helping her tend to her grieving family had been an honor. When she expressed misgivings about wanting him to love her, he had kissed away her doubts. He had reminded her that they were now a whole, together facing tragic circumstances with love best fortified by the fullness of their union.

Finally mustering sufficient effort to leave bed, he dressed quickly and headed downstairs. A bleary-eyed maid suggested he look for his wife outside. Finding her took little time. He stood in silence, watching as she sat on a pile of leaves beneath a towering tree with a broad trunk. Her knees were bent, providing a perch for her elbows. In her hands, she held the crystal pendant given to her by her angelic caregivers. He caught glimpses of her solemn face only when her hair, floating loose around her shoulders, lifted with the breeze's invisible fingers. How unreal...how utterly ethereal she appeared. He almost feared disturbing her.

Finally approaching, he alerted her with a gentle greeting. "My beloved Sindara, you left me alone inside."

Turning, she cast him a thoughtful look. "You needed the rest."

"May I join you?" he asked. He quickly went to her when she smiled and nodded. He was surprised how dry the leaves were as they crunched beneath him when he sat facing her. Leaning forward, he lightly kissed rose-colored lips. "I have sorely missed my morning kisses."

"As have I."

He swallowed regretfully, but he knew this time together was likely measured by the toll of lives. "You said you had much to tell me." His heart faltered at the distress that quickly tensed her features.

"Thehrund, I'm not sure where to begin. First of all, before I left, I moved the Ambracada again. Only one other person knows where, and no one here can reveal its location to Breeneth."

"You believe it to be in danger," he remarked flatly. "You must have had good reason. Is that why you left Bracordia with Father's elite guard?"

"In part. Breeneth is gaining abilities far stronger than before. I'm sure she's being empowered by this demon lover of hers. Thehrund, she returned to Bracordia."

His black eyebrows drew together in consternation. "She actually made it past all the soldiers? Where did she go? What has she done now?"

Sindara winced at the harshness in his deep voice, although she knew it was not directed at her. "She somehow discovered where her family was staying. She killed several guards. What she did to her family is almost unspeakable. Their bodies were ripped to pieces. Blood was spattered everywhere. She left a crystal glass on a table. It contained blood...and the bloody print of her lips around its rim. Thehrund, she actually drank their blood."

Color drained from Thehrund's face. "Her parents? Brenna, too? They were all anointed with oil and cedar ash."

She nodded sadly. "Lack of real faith made them vulnerable. Before I left, I told the priests to keep precious oils and ashes blessed as deterrents. I also gave instructions for palace walls, doors, and windows to be lined with sea salt for extra protection. They will be effective against any lesser demons that may attack, but against Breeneth and her lover, I know they will not."

His insides twisted in knots. "You know that how?"

She dropped her face and stared at hands trembling more from the memory of that day than from morning's chilly temperatures. "She also invaded the palace. She attacked your parents."

Abruptly leaning forward, Thehrund grabbed her arms, holding so tightly that she flinched with pain. "How did she get past palace guards? Mother? Father?" He gulped in a breath. "My parents! What did she do to them?"

"Thehrund, you're hurting me."

Instantly loosening his bruising grip, he gave her a pained look. "I'm so sorry. You know I'd never intentionally hurt you." He steeled himself for the worst possible news. "What happened?"

"I was returning from the chapel when sentries came to tell me they were missing. Everyone was searching. The crystal guided me to the kitchen cellars. Luckily, Karan came with me. As we reached the cellars, we heard horrible screams."

She paused and tightly grasped her husband's hands. "By the time we got to the butcher's chamber, Breeneth had hacked off one of your father's legs. Your mother was lying on the floor after grappling with Breeneth. I shoved Breeneth into the wall and temporarily subdued her. Suddenly, she just vanished in a cloud of mist and stink."

Thehrund swayed as images tormented his mind. "Father? Mother?" he croaked.

"Karan instantly went to your father's aid. He applied a tourniquet to control the bleeding. Your mother scrambled to her feet and ripped her skirts to make bandages to bind the wound. Her courage bought extra seconds that likely gave Karan time to stop your father from bleeding to death." Pausing again, she swallowed several times. "There was no possibility of saving the leg. The bone was completely severed. Tendons, muscles, and ligaments were mangled."

"How..." Thehrund's voice trembled and cracked, words trapped deep in his throat.

Sindara managed the slightest of smiles. "Physically, he's recovering more quickly than anyone expected. Mentally and emotionally? He's furious because he now sees firsthand how truly evil this threat is. He's determined to conquer it and restore peace. Within two days of the attack, he accepted little in the way of medicines to control his pain, insisting his suffering was minor compared to what his soldiers face in battle. Uncle Cleotis is staying at the palace to help your mother manage matters of state."

Tears eased from the corners of the prince's eyes. "Sindara, what am I to do? This all started with me. How do I live with that?"

She pulled him toward her until his head rested in her lap. Her fingers combed through thick waves. "Thehrund, you cannot bear blame for Breeneth's evil character. Your relationship with her didn't cause this."

Blue eyes filled with tears. "I should have had better self-control. I never should have..."

"Listen to me carefully," she murmured as she wiped tears from his anguished face. "Long ago, while I still questioned my feelings for you, I had a long talk with Father. He certainly didn't condone your affair, but he also admitted he had behaved similarly as a young man. He spoke of it with regret and even a sense of shame, but he attributed it to a lack of maturity typical of young men. On my other Earth-plane, such behaviors are typical for both men and women."

"You did not indulge yourself...here or there. As prince, I should have set a better example. Look at the cost. You nearly died. Soldiers fight and die every day. All because Breeneth decided our affair would lead her to Ambracor's throne."

"Thehrund, stop it! Now! Breeneth's nature has been evil since long before you knew her. I have no doubt she would have plotted and connived to advance her position regardless of any relationship you had with her."

He closed his eyes. Her fingers tenderly caressed his forehead, easing his tortured thoughts. Suddenly, a terrifying thought burst into his mind. Abruptly sitting up, he stared at his bride. "That's why you left Bracordia. You're here because you intend to seek out Breeneth."

"I must."

"No!" he literally shouted as he jumped to his feet. "No, Sindara! I forbid it! I will not see you put your life at risk by confronting her!"

Sindara rose to face him. Her expression was stern. "Thehrund, there is no other way. There is not another person in Ambracor with a better chance of ending her reign of terror."

"And this demon lover of hers? What about him? How do you face him?" Thehrund's face flushed bright red with a rising blend of fury and horror. "No, this I cannot allow! *I will not allow it!*"

Sindara met his flash of temper with her chin held high and an obstinate glare in her eyes. "You cannot stop me."

"You're wrong. I'll order Zimaron to escort you back to Bracordia immediately after Rezda's funeral." Blue eyes blazed at her. "I lost you once. I refuse to let you endanger your life knowing what I now know."

"If you send Zimaron back to the capital, then he goes with the escort only. I will not go with him. Understand me well, Thehrund. This fight is not just yours. It belongs to all of us, and I'm the one with the best chance to succeed against both Breeneth and her demon."

"No," Thehrund growled, "I refuse to let you take such a risk."

"The decision is not yours to make. It is one I have made already. I will not allow you or anyone else to interfere. This is something I must do. Both your parents and mine, loath that they are to face the truth, comprehend why I'm the one who must pursue her."

Turning his back to her, he stared blankly at fallen leaves shuffling about in the breeze. His stomach pitched rebelliously. His chest hurt with each breath. His soul heaved in vehement resistance to her plans. Images of fields and meadows strewn with lifeless bodies flooded his mind. His memory replayed its brutal recollection of watching the Breyal lance as it impaled her near Articene. He staggered drunkenly before violently shaking his head and storming off. "No! This I cannot bear! Not this!"

Sindara watched him stalk back to the house. Rising from the ground, she inhaled a sustaining breath, held it a moment, then blew out her tension. Brushing clinging leaves and twigs from her clothes, she headed back inside. She would allow him some time to let the import of her words settle. His reaction hadn't surprised her. She also expected additional resistance, but her decision was irrevocable. With or without the king's escort, she would depart on the morrow for Bramond Province.

Nagrand Mezden reviewed the latest reports from his scouts. His stomach felt uncomfortably hollow. It seemed all of Breyal's far eastern tribes were converging on Barachal. The earlier slash-and-dash attacks would be of little use now that larger tribal groups traveled together. Absorbed in contemplation of fresh strategies, he was surprised by the sound of his name.

Erator Varacor, recently given a field promotion to general, had a grim expression that prompted immediate knots in Nagrand's stomach. "A courier just arrived with news from the southern fronts."

Almost against his will, Nagrand asked, "What?"

"Thehrund is in Cahmdurn. My brother Rezda was killed in battle near Torandor."

Nagrand's eyes clouded with immediate sympathy. "Erator, I am so sorry. Do you wish to leave to be with your family?"

Erator shook his head once. "My heart is with them. Of that they are sure. As much as I want to be there, Rezda would insist that I remain here. No, I stay. We must end this madness."

Nagrand nodded. "I've been considering different tactics. Scouts have reported the approach of much larger concentrations of warriors converging on western Breyal. Small guerilla attacks would most likely become suicide missions. We must devise a plan to lure them into position where we can contain and attack them."

"I will send a messenger to Cahmdurn with a reply to Thehrund and my father. Thehrund's message also suggested we meet at Lexalor before he turns back south. Circumstances are dire enough to merit such a meeting as soon as possible."

"I agree. Your second-in-command can take over Articene while you and I travel to meet Thehrund." Nagrand paused. "You do have my most sincere sympathy for the loss of your brother."

Erator nodded and turned to leave. Stopping, he shook his head. "I nearly forgot. Father's dispatch also instructed us to have priests prepare as much oil as possible for blessing and to mix it with ashes of burnt cedar. Each soldier should be anointed with the mix and given something Father called a medicine bag containing a small quantity of the mix soaked into a bit of fabric."

"A medicine bag?" Nagrand asked, puzzled.

Reaching into his pocket, Erator produced two. "He sent one for each of us. They're simple leather pouches attached to long pieces of rawhide. We can carry them or wear them as amulets. He also suggested using the blend to mark gates, doors, and windows here again at the fort."

Taking the small leather pouch into his hand, Nagrand curiously gazed at the bag. An odd thought entered his mind. "Sindara...is she in Cahmdurn?"

Erator grimaced. "It would appear so." Serious eyes met those of Nagrand. "Knowing my sister as I do, that causes me great concern."

Nagrand's lips turned upward, barely hinting at a smile. "I would take it more as reason for hope."

⁂

"Father, I hate to disturb you, especially now," Sindara spoke softly, "but may I ask your advice about something?"

Artrian Varacor turned from where he had been staring mournfully through a window in his study. Seeing his daughter's pained expression, he nodded slightly before approaching her. Caressing her cheek, he gave her a gentle smile. "May I assume you and Thehrund are in the midst of some terrible disagreement?"

"Is it so obvious?"

"Sit," he said, guiding her to a small leather-upholstered sofa set against one wall. "First, whatever the circumstances, never hesitate to come to me if you feel the need. Second, yes, it was obvious at the breakfast table. Years have passed since I last saw you so aloof with Thehrund. I presume he opposes your plans to confront Breeneth."

Sindara's wobbly smile confirmed his assumption. "Father, I don't know what to do. While I understand his stance, I also know that no one else in all of Ambracor has a better chance of defeating her than I do."

Artrian reached for his daughter's hands and grasped them firmly. "He loves you, Sindara, and he lost you once already. You did not see his suffering as we did."

Her face fell. "In a way, I did. That aside, I'm convinced this is part of the reason I was saved. He refuses to accept that I have duties and responsibilities just as he does. Father, watching him leave Bracordia...knowing he was going to war...was likely the worst thing I've ever faced in my entire life. Although I thoroughly understood his reasons, it still required every ounce of self-control I possessed to send him away without collapsing beneath the weight of my own sorrow and terror. How, Father? How do I make him understand I need that same support from him?"

Artrian sighed heavily. "Changing Thehrund's mind can be nearly impossible once he settles on a decision."

"I know, Father, but I must go to Bramond. Breeneth and her master grow stronger with each battle. Fear and violence actually feed them. The sooner I reach them, the better my chances are of ending their influence over the Breyals. I have every confidence that our armies can defeat Breyal warriors and end a general war. The problem is that Breeneth and her master prepare to summon an army of lesser demons."

Her father gazed into his daughter's beautiful eyes. Sadness mingled with resolve. "You intend to go with or without his approval, do you not?"

"Yes, Father. I have no choice. What do I tell Thehrund? How do I convince him that I would never take this risk if it weren't absolutely necessary? If I don't go..."

"If you don't?"

"Father, our armies cannot fare well against a demonic onslaught combined with Breyals. That is undeniable fact. Worse, Breeneth will come for Thehrund. She's determined to have him. Her reasons are many, I'm sure. She desires official claim to the crown of Ambracor. I have no doubt she also wishes to punish him for rejecting her. She has no conscience and will destroy anything she perceives as a barrier to her plans. I have long been the one standing in her way. Sooner or later, she will come for me. I prefer the advantage of being the hunter rather than the hunted."

The grieving nobleman rested his palm against his beloved daughter's face. How beautiful and how brave he saw her. How he feared losing her a second time, especially now that he prepared to bury a son. "I suffer to think of you undertaking such a task, yet my heart tells me you are our best hope. Are you really so confident in your ability to fight her?"

"I resumed training in the fighting arts after Thehrund left Bracordia. My other life gave me opportunities to learn new skills. My faith is unshakeable, and it will sustain me. Thehrund's love is a gift from Creator God and a potent source of strength and inspiration. What I fear is weakness...that I might falter if I take with me his angry disapproval."

Tears suddenly streaked her cheeks. Luminous eyes fixed on her father's face. "What do I say to him, Father? The one thing sure to destroy me would be losing Thehrund, and Breeneth will do everything she can to make that happen. How do I convince him to love me enough to believe in me? What do I say to convince him of how much I need his blessing so I can help save both Ambracor and our own lives?"

Her father nodded toward the open door. "I think you may have just done that."

Glancing around, Sindara saw her husband's somber figure standing in the doorway. Unable to move from the sofa, she remained mute, silently staring at him. Her father rose, kissed the top of his daughter's head, and excused himself to tend other matters.

Thehrund quietly closed the door before approaching his wife. Taking her hands, he pulled her up from the sofa and held her with quiet desperation. He had overheard most of the conversation with her father and wondered how he had been blessed with the love of such a woman. Moments slowly passed as he breathed in her scent and drew much-needed solace from the fiercely protective embrace of her arms around him.

"Sindara, I...I...don't..." he whispered brokenly, "I don't know how to apologize for this morning. I love you so much. Your intentions of going to Bramond terrify me."

Unable to find the right words, she rested her face against his chest. There was no better place for her than within the circle of his arms. Her hands clasped securely together behind him as she pressed herself tightly against the firmness of his body. With the passing of each second, she felt the intensity of his love strengthen her resolve.

Reluctantly, they loosened their embrace. Thehrund raised his hands to her face. "I heard what you told your father. Must you do this? Really?"

She cupped her hands over his. "It's the only way, Thehrund. If I don't go, there is little chance we will achieve final victory. She wants me dead so she can have you. Let me dictate the terms of how I meet her next."

"My sweet, courageous Sindara, do you forget the power of her lover?" Thehrund's blue eyes shone with dread.

She shook her head. "I haven't forgotten. I will take special precautions."

"Can you promise you'll come back to me?" he asked, his eyes desperately noting every tiny detail of her features.

Her eyes closed. "I cannot promise that any more than you could promise you would return when last you left Bracordia." She paused and drew in a deep, shaky breath. "What I can promise is that your life will never be without my love."

Thehrund again clutched her tightly. "I need you, Sindara. My heart breaks knowing you intend to undertake this task, but I trust you as I trust no one else. Go with my blessing, but know that I will surely perish without you. You must come back to me."

Chapter Twenty-One

With head held arrogantly high and black eyes flashing, the wary man stood in front of the throne. His face was darkly tanned from hours spent beneath daytime's blazing sun. Shaggy hair barely grazed his shoulders. His feet were clad in soft leather boots. Beneath his leather jacket, wide straps crisscrossed his torso over a long-sleeved shirt of gray muslin. Side seams of brown leather pants bore studs counting the number slain by his sword. Accenting full battle regalia, the broad belt around his waist was adorned with dangling strands of ivory bone and colored beads.

"Kicchak, you are late arriving. I hope you have good news to temper my displeasure," Thafalos stated in a supercilious voice that carried its own echo.

The Breyal chieftain showed no hint of fear, no sign of subservience. "My warriors fight bravely and kill many of your enemy's soldiers. You have failed on your promise to send us reinforcements. Why?"

Thafalos laughed cynically. "I admire your directness, Kicchak. No niceties. No cordiality."

"I have neither need nor desire to waste time for the benefit of your entertainment. What happened to the reinforcements you promised if I gathered our tribes to fight your war?"

Thafalos leaned forward, his posture both condescending and threatening. "I told you in the beginning. I need fear and death to summon the legions waiting to serve me. Your warriors have failed in delivering sufficient quantities of both. We are close, Kicchak. You must increase your efforts to stir deeper terror into the hearts of those Ambracor dogs who dare resist. My legions will then rise, and you and I shall glory in victory."

Kicchak quietly subdued animal instincts that smelled deception in the stench permeating the room where he stood. His outward expression reflected none of his distrust of the tawny-skinned figure wearing opulent robes adorned with precious gemstones.

"Since you claim to be master of fear and death, what brilliant strategy do you suggest I utilize to deliver this level of destruction you desire?"

Thafalos lifted his right hand. The warrior chieftain shot upward and hovered above the floor, imprisoned by roiling, cloudy mists emitted by the demon's anger. "Do not presume the right to address me so insolently, Breyal. I have no tolerance for insults from any of your kind. Do you understand?"

Kicchak gave a sharp nod. The black mist vanished, and the Breyal chief fell to the floor. Stunned, he breathed in, the room's foul air burning his throat and lungs. His immediate concern was to regain his senses and rise from the floor. Peculiar weakness subsided from his limbs, and he finally recovered enough to stand. Facing the demon, he bowed his head. "I ask your pardon. I will not forget or slight your power again."

Thafalos sat back and resumed his intimidating posture. "That is wise on your part, Breyal."

Reclining comfortably on her chaise, Breeneth cast a glance at her master in an unspoken request to speak. Receiving permission in the form of a faint twist of his head, she looked at Kicchak with a humorless smile. "There are two keys to unlock the doors to victory. The first is the death of Sindara Varacor."

"Is she not Prince Thehrund's woman?"

Breeneth's lips curled with unbridled disgust. "She is. Not only did your brother's war party fail to kill her, your warriors allowed her to escape. That's why your brother conveniently died so you could take his place as Grand Chieftain over the allied tribes of Breyal. Sindara Varacor must die.

"The second key is to deliver Prince Thehrund to me here. I might suggest an appeal to his honor and loyalties. If you are unable to capture him, take someone close to him and bring me the prisoner. I have no doubt that Ambracor's brave and noble prince will do whatever is necessary to save one of his friends. He will come. Once here, he will fall under our control, and you will gain your victory over Ambracor."

Kicchak gazed thoughtfully at the demon's consort. She was a stunningly beautiful female, but instinct warned him that her heart was quite possibly blacker than that of Thafalos. Such combined evil was a force to be respected. He bowed his head. "I shall consult our most cunning chiefs and devise plans to hasten the victory over Ambracor."

Thafalos gave the Breyal a satisfied grin. "You know what is expected of you. Go now." As the Breyal chieftain turned to leave, the demon master called out once more. "Before you depart, I suggest you not forget your brother's unpleasant demise that made you Grand Chieftain."

Liana Varacor finished brushing her daughter's damp hair into some semblance of order. Her thoughts collided while she carefully arranged trimmed locks into a bundle that she wrapped securely in a length of white cloth stained red with blood. The sight of Sindara's shorn tresses wrapped in gauze colored by her daughter's blood shook Liana's sensitivities.

Tomorrow would bring lines of Arvacon citizens through the governor's mansion to pay final respects to her youngest child who had been killed in battle. In the midst of her mourning, she would secretly bid farewell to her only daughter who would depart Cahmdurn for the living hell Bramond Province had become. Following Rezda's funeral, she would say goodbye to a fearless young woman who had volunteered to masquerade as the princess. The impostor would don full battledress and then depart for Bracordia with the king's escort. Liana questioned if such a ruse could possibly succeed. Her sorrowing heart wondered if her faith was strong enough to sustain her through such an uncertain future.

Sindara placed the silver-framed hand mirror on the vanity and looked around at her mother. "It really isn't so very short," she said with a wan smile. "It almost reaches my shoulders."

Liana forced a smile. "Do you think this really has a chance to work?"

"We can only hope. The scent of my blood and hair should help the deception. The cut on my leg is healing already from the wound binder Karan applied. The binding with the thick layer of the cedar-oil mix should further mask the smell of blood. I worry more for Irlini than myself."

"She sees this as a chance to save others from the grief she suffered when her husband died in battle. Her fighting skills exceed those of many of the men," Liana remarked.

Sindara's eyelids closed. "Few in Arvacon have been spared the loss of a loved one. Other provinces suffer, too. No matter the outcome of my mission or the battles won, Ambracor faces many years filled with the sorrow war brings."

"Irlini will at least have the benefit of a military escort. What worries me most is that you go alone."

"Mother," Sindara said softly as she took Liana's hand, "you must believe me when I say I do not go alone."

Just as her mother started to reply, a knock interrupted them. Edging the door open, Thehrund peeked inside. "May I see the damage?"

"Come in, Thehrund," Liana said as she picked up strands of bundled hair. "I was just leaving to check on Dalina. Good night."

Sindara grimaced under her husband's scrutiny. "My hair grows quickly."

Crossing the room, he ran his fingers through her shortened locks. "It doesn't matter. You're still the most beautiful woman I've ever known."

She rose from her chair to embrace him. "Irlini's suggestion is brilliant. I pray she lives if they do attack the escort."

Thehrund ran his hand slowly up and down his wife's back. Every second with her was more precious than all the gold and jewels in the kingdom. "I pray we all survive this war. Selfish it may be, but I dream of time with you...time to walk and talk without fear. Time to love you. Time to have children with you. Sindara, I pray daily for the blessing of a life for us to be together. Is that so wrong?"

She leaned back slightly, gazing up into eyes as blue as a cloudless summer day. "That is the sort of life Creator God offers each of us. Why some choose to oppose such generosity exceeds my comprehension. For the moment, I leave the future to Creator God. Right now, I choose to treasure every second we have until we part ways tomorrow."

Thehrund nodded. Closing his eyes, he savored the feel of her fingers sliding along the braids of his hair, gently tugging them to pull his face downward to share the sweet bond of a kiss. Within moments, passions between them blazed, fueled by dread of this newest separation and the very real possibility this might be their final night together.

With desires hotly flaring, Thehrund groaned and gathered his wife into his arms. Carrying her to bed, he watched her every motion as she removed her dressing gown to expose the smoothness of ivory flesh that had been hidden from him. At the same time, he frantically tugged at laces and ties, removing his clothing and revealing his desperation to initiate yet again the ecstasy granted them through their marriage.

Their full union was sudden and forceful, a reflection of their anguished anticipation of parting again. Thehrund loved her thoroughly, conveying his adoration with every stroke, every caress, and every nuanced sound. Sindara encouraged him with hands sweeping along his shoulders, arms, back, and hips. Her voice called out his name, and tiny moans inspired him to greater heights of passion. Once their loving reached a shared peak, they lay close, sated physically and satisfied to share the night wrapped snugly in their abundant love.

❊ ❊ ❊

Glad the week was over, Kendra locked her office door. Saturday morning would find her at the airport for a flight to Vegas. After arriving, she would pick up a rental car, drive to Sedona, and check into a quaint bed and breakfast. When Madalyn Amador had made her surprise visit, the two had agreed to meet in Arizona. Natural energies there were uniquely concentrated. Each believed shared meditation would help them focus on ideas to help Sindara.

Early the next morning, she boarded her plane and quickly located her seat. Stashing her carry-on in the bin above, she excused herself to the elderly gentleman sitting along the aisle and squeezed past him to her window seat. Settling in, she pushed her large purse under the seat in front and fastened her seatbelt. Sitting back, she stared absently through the small window as baggage handlers rolled gear around and started loading the plane's belly with luggage and general cargo. A short while later, she didn't bother with the safety card as flight attendants began the requisite miming of instructions over a sound system playing recordings nearly impossible to understand.

Her traveling companion glanced at her with an amused grin. "Do you always ignore safety directions?"

Kendra gave him an odd look. "I'm usually overly compliant. I've flown this kind of plane a couple of times, so I know the routine."

"I see," the gentleman said, his blue-gray eyes sparkling. "You do realize circumstances can change very quickly, don't you?"

Kendra nodded patiently. He meant well. "No one knows better than I how fast whole lives can change."

"Or even entire worlds?"

Kendra's forehead creased as she met his kindly gaze. "Excuse me?"

He only smiled as he tilted his head toward the front of the plane's cabin. "I like to listen. One can never be too prepared for emergencies."

Shaking her head, Kendra settled back and found herself watching the attendants. All the while, she tried to tune into the odd feeling starting to niggle its way into her mind. Engines began to roar, and the plane started negotiating runways. Upon taking off, her thoughts shifted toward her meeting with Madalyn. Mulling over the purpose of her trip to Sedona, she lifted her hand and flattened her palm over the pendant tucked inside her light blue sweater.

Her aisle partner turned and grinned. "There's no need for concern. This plane will arrive safely. I imagine your real worries won't begin until after you reach Las Vegas." He then sat back and opened a magazine.

Kendra carefully released her breath. What was it about her travel mate that prompted her senses to begin their familiar, distinctive hum? She reclined her seat and gazed out at puffy clouds floating freely across turquoise skies. Closing her eyes, she attempted to push distractions from her mind and think in positive terms of what she and Madalyn Amador might accomplish with their combined meditations in Sedona's sacred spaces.

Looking up suddenly, she smiled at the flight attendant. "Excuse me?"

The young man smiled and repeated his offer of a beverage. She grinned apologetically and requested a cup and a bottle of water. Lowering her tray, she twisted off the cap and poured some water. Taking a sip, she glanced upward at her seatmate. She hadn't even noticed him getting up.

"You missed your chance for something to drink," she remarked in a friendly tone. "You're welcome to the bottle if you like. I only drank from the cup."

"I'm fine, thank you. It won't be much longer before we land," he replied as he sat and buckled his seat belt. "You seemed very far away."

Kendra nodded, her smile holding a tinge of sadness. "I was thinking of someone very far away."

He nodded with a sympathetic expression. "You miss that someone very much."

"I do," Kendra said quietly, finishing her water and handing the cup and bottle to the passing attendant.

The man's eyes assumed a distant gaze. "There are people I miss, but life's rhythms often give us chances to reconnect in surprising ways."

"I wish that were possible in my case."

They quieted as instructions came over the speakers, and everyone prepared for landing. The process was quick, their flight on time, and their gate access efficiently completed. Kendra bent forward to get her purse and then turned a smiling face to her travel partner.

Kind eyes caught her attention. "I can tell you're a woman of faith. Take some advice freely given by an old man."

She smiled patiently. "And that advice would be?"

He stood. Letting her exit in front of him, he whispered over her shoulder. "Always be prepared. Let your heart know comfort. When you see your friend again, hug her first for yourself. Then, hug her twice for me. Remind her always to look to the stars and never to fear because her guardian angel is as stubborn as ever. He always watches over her."

Kendra laughed softly as she headed forward, carried through the plane's cabin by the momentum of fellow passengers anxious to disembark in search of entertainment and fortune. Reaching the end of the exit tunnel, she turned to bid farewell to her odd companion. He was nowhere to be seen.

Three days later, Madalyn Amador watched Kendra's peaceful features as she sat, her vision transfixed by a brilliantly colored sunset stretched across the desert landscape. "This place soothes your spirit."

Kendra lifted her face to reveal a tranquil expression. "I feel the energies flowing through me. I arrived with questions that perplexed me. Although I'm still puzzled, I no longer feel troubled."

"Questions such as?" Madalyn asked curiously.

In a spontaneous gesture, Kendra reached out and grasped the older lady's hands. As her eyes roamed over her companion's wise face, she noted the kind smile, high cheekbones, graying hair at the temples, and complexion the color of cinnamon. All features were indicative of Madalyn's mixed black and Native American heritage. So much wisdom and so much compassion, Kendra thought. "I've mostly questioned how best to help Sindara now that she plans to take more direct action. I dread the idea of her forging ahead on her own."

"Do you honestly think she'll proceed alone?"

Memory teased her with the enigmatic smile of the elderly man on her flight to Las Vegas. "I've been told she has a very stubborn guardian angel."

"Ah," Madalyn sighed with a grin, "I suspect someone may have delivered a message for you both."

Kendra started to question Madalyn, but she suddenly realized it wasn't necessary. She already knew the answer.

Breeneth left the large bed she often shared with her master. His lascivious nature occasionally left her with scratches on the outside and bruises inside. While he continued to loll in bed, she went to wash and apply ointment to soothe burning scratches on her arms and breasts.

Wordless, she pulled clean underclothes and black gown from the enormous dressing room attached to the mansion's master suite. As she dressed without help from any servants, she considered the recent meeting with Kicchak. His arrogance impressed her. Glad for Master's show of force to the Breyal leader, she was more than satisfied to let the chieftain wear down Ambracor armies. Her heart was set on a greater prize. One way or the other, she would bring Thehrund to Bramond. He would bow to her superior power and submit to her demands for marriage, thus giving her official rights to rule Ambracor.

"You smile, my lovely one," Thafalos said, rising from bed without bothering to cover his naked form.

Breeneth gave him a steady gaze. "I always smile after sharing your bed."

He nodded, his ego reveling in praise. "Is that your only reason for smiling?"

"It is the most important reason," she replied, "but I also smile at plans to glorify your position for all to acknowledge."

"You are indeed a loyal servant, Breeneth."

He held out his arms as she began to dress him in the opulent silks and velvets he now relished. Caressing him as she smoothed fabric, Breeneth focused her thoughts on ensuring he was well pleased with her attentiveness.

"What are your plans?" he asked as she finished with the last fastening on his robe.

"I wish to seek out Sindara Varacor. She stands as the most significant obstacle to your final victory. It is time to crush her."

"Have your spies learned how she returned to Ambracor?"

She shook her head. "That matters little to me. I will know once we hold Thehrund captive. Sindara must be eliminated. I will tolerate no more of her interference."

"Take care, my dear, that your jealousy does not cloud your actions. Danger most often lurks in the unknown."

She carefully controlled her expression and replied confidently, "I have faced far worse danger than that weak-minded religious zealot."

With an air of arrogant possessiveness, Thafalos caressed Breeneth's cheek with the backs of his curved fingers. "Caution is never ill-advised."

Horses breathing out heavy grunts only added to the mayhem of the attack against soldiers returning to the southern battlefields after military leaders met with Prince Thehrund at Lexalor. Tightly drawn bows pinged. Arrows swooshed through the air as Ambracoran archers took careful aim from a high point above the battlefield. Battleaxes and swords clashed with resounding rings as armored soldiers exchanged heavy blows with nimble-footed invaders. Shouted commands mixed with cries, screams, moans, groans, and pounding hooves, all blending into the cacophony of deadly bedlam.

Thehrund yanked back on the reins of his stallion. Leaping to the ground, he pivoted swiftly, slashing a Breyal warrior with his sword. Flanked by dozens of Arvacon militiamen, the prince advanced with one thought in mind...drop as many enemy fighters as he could while avoiding their blows. His troops rallied, fighting with determined ferocity. Thehrund's booming voice shouted commands, directing the defensive effort with tenacity while urging his soldiers to hold their ground. When enemy warriors finally turned to retreat, the prince hoarsely roared at archers to take fresh aim. Breyals fell, leaving few survivors to disperse and flee the bloody aftermath of their attack.

Thehrund dragged off his helmet and slowly turned around in the center of the battleground. His chest heaved as he fought to slow his rapid breathing. Sweeping his eyes over the bloody scene, he noted with grim satisfaction that few of his soldiers had been killed, although perhaps a dozen were seriously injured.

He called for his officers to gather and assess the attack, determine losses, and decide their next course of action. His forehead creased as he looked around. Two officers were slightly wounded. His heart thudded heavily. One of his top commanders was missing.

"Sir Nagrand. Has anyone seen him?"

During their meeting at Lexalor, Thehrund had agreed that Erator and his seasoned officers were more than capable of defending the border region around Articene. The prince was in need of experienced leaders at the southern fronts bordering Bramond Province. Nagrand had immediately volunteered to join the trek south.

Soldiers already securing the battleground's perimeter were ordered to stay vigilant in case the enemy should regroup and return. In the meantime, Thehrund personally walked the site, growing angrier with every second that passed. Each dead body heightened his level of anger. Foregoing his usual encouragement to the wounded, his eyes scanned the surroundings in search of his longtime friend. A fatigued officer approached the prince.

Carrying Nagrand's cloak, he shook his head and shrugged his shoulders. He had found the cape but no other sign of Nagrand Mezden.

Later that evening, Thehrund stared morosely at a campfire. He questioned why the band of Breyals had attacked a substantially larger, better-armed force. His thoughts continuously veered toward one disheartening conclusion. They had intended to take a prisoner. Capturing the prince would have been ideal, but taking his closest friend might do just as well.

Accepting a plate of food and mechanically beginning to eat, Thehrund's mind raced through possible options. With Breyal camps constantly on the move, there would be little chance of choosing the right one to follow. Supper landed with a leaden thud inside his stomach. Setting his plate aside, he closed his eyes against a sickening realization. Nagrand was undoubtedly being taken to Bramond Province as bait to lure him into a trap.

Midnight chill caused Thehrund to pull his woolen blanket more tightly around him as he rested on a mat next to a bonfire. Sword and daggers lay within easy reach. His mind refused to surrender to sleep he badly needed. Reaching for the medicine bag he wore around his neck, he pulled from it the thick pad Sindara had soaked in oily cedar ash. He then caught the narrow braid he had added. One side of his mouth curved slightly. After cutting her hair, she had saved some and braided it, securing each end with rubber bands she had brought through the portal. This tiny snippet of hair was all he had of her. Reverently kissing it, he tucked everything back into the bag she had sewn with her own hands.

His vision dimmed as exhaustion conquered his will. His last thoughts were more like a prayer, begging for the safety of his loyal friend and his beloved wife.

❈ ❈ ❈

King Hamund stood as straight as possible. Despite using crutches, he emanated an air of authority more compelling than ever. Slowly moving back and forth in front of his throne, he addressed governors who had responded to his summons. "Your help to date is appreciated more than you can possibly know. Many of you are fortunate that your provinces have not yet borne direct attacks from Breyal warriors or conscripts forced into battle by Bramond's current leadership. I asked you here because more aid is required. We need additional provisions to feed and clothe troops already on the front lines. We also need more soldiers."

Count Jepro Delgaro spoke up. "Your Majesty, Zebrador Province has already recruited and trained more than a thousand fresh troops. By the end of the week, they will join regiments from Metacan Province and then travel immediately to Arvacon."

Hamund's face reflected sincere gratitude. "Count Delgaro, you cannot fathom the depth of my appreciation for your initiative in coordinating aid with Metacan. My son bravely leads soldiers from all of our nation's provinces, but with Breyal and Bramond united, Arvacon Province naturally bears the greatest threat and burden."

Count Zelban of Zelcon Province respectfully addressed the king. "Your Majesty, our northern farm districts enjoyed an unusually bountiful harvest this past season. Provisions are being prepared for transport. We are coordinating with Gorandro Province to assemble and protect supply caravans moving to fronts in Arvacon. I can also confirm Dardron Province resists Bramond with assistance from both Cazol and Lafrindor militias. We all recognize the strains facing Arvacon. Ambracor's governors are united in this fight, but we feel it necessary to ask. Do we honestly have a chance to defeat this enemy?"

Hamund huffed a frustrated sigh. "Regretfully, I cannot read the future. However, if we lay down arms in surrender, there can be no hope of regaining the way of life we treasure."

He paused, glancing downward at empty space once filled by his right leg. "You see in me a man broken in body, but I can assure you that I will ride into battle for the sake of my people. My spirit remains unconquered, and my arms grow stronger than ever. I will not hesitate to swing my sword in defense of this country."

His gaze drifted toward a window where sunlight streamed into the throne room. Brilliant light sharply contrasted with the dark, somber mood of those gathered in his court. "My heart breaks to think of all Thehrund faces as he commands our armies. I imagine his heart suffers far more than mine. His bride's return to Ambracor was indeed a miracle. She confronted Breeneth Brandere here in the palace, saving my life in the process. Then, filled with resolve, she journeyed back to Arvacon. Count Varacor just buried a son killed in battle. Meanwhile, his surviving children willingly face immeasurable risks."

Hamund turned again to the men and women governors. "I have faith in all of them. That same confidence extends to the citizens of your provinces. I prefer death fighting for the salvation of Ambracor rather than death through surrender to the evil Breeneth Brandere has delivered into our lives."

Queen Narlina rose from the queen's throne. It seemed impossible to imagine that one as delicate as she had physically scuffled with Breeneth Brandere while defending the king. Emerging essentially unscathed, she had then watched over her husband while simultaneously managing critical affairs until Hamund was sufficiently recovered. Well aware that her story had reached far corners of the kingdom, she added her voice. "I have learned valuable lessons since my son returned to Bracordia with Sindara Varacor. Even one as small as I can find strength to defend those I most love."

She glanced at her husband and smiled. "Against all odds, Thehrund found the woman we all thought had died. He brought her home and married her. I challenged Breeneth Brandere, demonic spawn that she is, and fought her long enough for help to come and save my husband's life. From those two events, I learned that miracles from Creator God still occur among us."

Artrian Varacor, attired in formal mourning tunic of black and gold, sat on bare ground beside his son's grave. Hours had passed since the graveside service ended. Sending everyone home, he had stayed behind and asked that the grave be left uncovered for a time. Tears formed constant rivers along chafed cheeks as sorrow poured from his soul. Fear for Erator and Sindara accentuated his grief over Rezda's death. His heart ached with indescribable pain. His children represented the greatest joys in his life. Never had he expected to bury one.

His mind retrieved memories from years earlier. He recalled his pride and exultation when each had entered the light of life. He had gazed at perfect, healthy babies, marveling that they had been conceived and born of the love he shared with Liana. Despite burdensome responsibilities for the management of Arvacon Province, he had always reserved time to spend with his children as they grew up. He wondered if they ever understood how much he truly cherished them.

"Artrian," Liana's gently insistent voice roused him from his depressed state, "they knew. From the very beginning, they always knew how much you loved them. The work you did for the betterment of Arvacon was more for them than for our fellow citizens. Your children understood that, and they loved and respected your constant devotion."

Artrian admired his wife more than ever in this time of hardship and tragedy. He took the hand she offered and stood. Welcoming her arms as they slid around his waist, he tilted his face upward. The warmth of afternoon sun seemed at odds with the icy chill pervading his soul.

Liana held her husband for several long moments before she led him to their waiting coach. In a soft voice, she told cemetery attendants they could finally close her son's grave. The countess entered the spacious carriage with the assistance of a coachman. When her husband finally settled himself on the seat beside her, she guided him downward to rest his head in her lap. Their trip home was made in silence as both contemplated their tremendous loss and sought solace and purpose in the coming gift of Rezda's child.

Arriving home, Liana guided her husband up the curving marble staircase to their suite. She insisted that he rest and then watched as he settled his head into a thick, soft pillow. "Artrian, as hard as it may seem, we must stay strong. Especially now. We must not fail in our prayers or our efforts to console others who suffer as do we. We still have two children confronting this hateful scourge. Our son-in-law leads the fight against the Breyals. Unfair it is, but for now, we must direct our energies toward helping end this wickedness. There will be more than enough time later to cry and mourn."

Artrian nodded weakly. Physical and mental exhaustion were quickly draining him of all conscious resolve. As swollen eyelids slowly closed, he murmured softly, "I love you, Liana. I know Creator God lives because he sent you to be my wife."

She bent and kissed his forehead. By the time she straightened, he was already asleep. She drew in a ragged breath. Closing the door quietly behind her, she went to check on Dalina. Her household suffered in throes of mourning yet again, but she would cling to something Sindara had said in farewell. Miracles could only achieve reality if one steadfastly maintained faith.

❋ ❋ ❋

Karan shivered despite the heavily padded gambeson and thick wool coat he wore. Sindara glanced at him with a wry grin. "Be happy. This is as far as you go. You can return to Cahmdurn and enjoy a warm hearth and hot food."

There was no humor in the look he gave her. "I'm not so sure about going back."

She stopped inspecting her knapsack and aimed a penetrating gaze in his direction. "I only reluctantly agreed for you to accompany me to the border. You promised to go back with my horse."

Karan returned her gaze with solemn directness. "Leaving you feels wrong. You must admit that two sets of eyes and ears are a safer option. You'll need time to rest. If I go with you, we can take turns on watch."

Sindara sighed. "The logic I cannot deny, but this is far too dangerous to risk your life. Traveling on foot into Bramond will not be easy. In fact, I expect it to be severely trying considering changing weather and the challenge of avoiding discovery."

"I accompanied Thehrund every time he journeyed through the portal. We faced unknown risks each time we entered it. I at least have the advantage of knowing the dangers here if I stay with you."

Sindara looked up at afternoon skies burdened with dark clouds. What to do? The question sifted through her mind and spirit. She did not relish the idea of traipsing alone through Bramond's forests. Neither did the idea of endangering Karan's life appeal to her.

Karan came closer and gently rested his hand on her shoulder. "Sindara, I appreciate your concern, and I love you for it. I love Thehrund, too. He's like a brother to me. I can't imagine what will happen to him if you get killed. He can't lose you again."

Sindara forced a smile. "Karan, he and Nagrand would both grieve over losing you..."

"Yes," he interrupted, "and at any minute, we could lose one or both of them. The reality is too painful to consider, yet its truth is just so. Please, Sindara, let me come with you."

She leaned against her horse. Concentrating her thoughts, she focused her inner vision on the light contained in the crystal. "Guide me," she pleaded silently. "I must have help with this decision."

Karan waited patiently. He understood Sindara's nature and would not think of pushing her against her will. He raised a hand to his chest and felt the small mound of the medicine bag she had sewn by hand for him. His lips moved in silent prayer. He was afraid. That he could freely admit, but profound convictions dominated his fears.

Sudden winds rushed through nearly bare tree branches. Sindara glanced up and saw dark clouds beginning to cross the sky toward Iglarm, the capital of Bramond Province. She felt faint vibrations from the crystal. The sign was given.

"A storm is moving in. We must unsaddle both horses. We'll leave their halters on. Shayla will lead your horse back to Cahmdurn. We must find a place to hide the saddles and take cover before the storm hits. You also must promise one thing. If something happens and I send you back, you must not hesitate to return."

Karan nodded his agreement as he quickly removed travel bags and saddle from his mount. As soon as he finished, Sindara lovingly stroked the face of the golden mare she had trained years earlier. "Home, Shayla. Go home."

Proceeding cautiously through sparse woods, Sindara spotted a small stream and tipped her head forward. Karan followed close behind. Not far ahead, there was a long, rocky surface formed by several slab-like layers of stone near steep descents to the water. Reaching the rocks, Sindara knelt and leaned over to search for possible places to shelter from the storm. Getting up, she went a little farther and pointed at a spot where they could climb down and huddle underneath an overhang that would offer protection.

Hours later, winds howled above them. From beneath their rocky roof, they watched rain turn to sleet and then to light snow until darkness made it impossible to see anything. Although the cavity under the overhang was cramped, they were able to rest against their lightweight saddles. Huddled close and sharing woolen blankets and an oilcloth cape Sindara had brought, they stayed relatively warm and dry despite dropping temperatures and chilling dampness. They dozed lightly. Although neither expected unwelcome company in such blustery conditions, their swords they kept at the ready. The storm eventually vented its fury. The light layer of snow on the ground created unusually tranquil silence broken only by the faint rush of water flowing downstream.

As Karan opened his eyes, he tugged at the oilcloth that had begun to slide away. Staring into the night, he thought that skies must have cleared. Shiny sparkles of moonlight reflected off rippling waters. With Sindara's weight against his side, there was no hope of retrieving his pocket watch without disturbing her. With a twinge of regret, he quickly realized that he would be unable to fall back asleep.

Acknowledging uneasiness in the pit of his stomach, he escaped thoughts of the present by reflecting on the years he had spent in formal studies of theology and healing arts. His memory probed for long forgotten tales from tradition as well as accounts from the Ambracada. He searched his mind for something Sindara had asked about.

How had that story gone? His breath caught for a moment. The Ambracada said that those of faith who carried the spark of Creator God's divinity would meet opposition. The light defining their souls would be challenged by shadows rising from the cavernous depths of greed and selfish desire. Evil would cast itself over the land, its aim to destroy Creator God's good people. His creation would rise against the threat, but despair would mark the passing of time. His people would need to cling to faith as they braved the onslaught of wicked ones who coveted the power of the one who had created all. Creator God would send holy relief in the form of bright stars with light so brilliant that it would defeat and destroy the menace that endangered sacred creation.

Questions flitted through Karan's mind. If the story was told as a metaphor, then it seemed obvious to him that Sindara might be one of those stars. Did that mean Kendra was the other? Did it refer to the amulets that angels gave to Kendra and Sindara? Was it possible that each was a star for her own Earth-plane and that another might appear in each dimension? Might Sindara be one of the faith guardians promised in ancient times? Each question sparked additional questions until he decided to shove the entire matter to the back of his mind. He could bear no more for the moment.

Minutes later, Sindara stirred and awoke. Shaking off a shiver, she greeted Karan in a voice thick with sleep. Glancing outward, she saw that night skies were slowly taking on the dull gray of the coming dawn. Carefully pushing blankets aside, she eased out from beneath the overhang after checking ahead and to each side for possible travelers. Feeling all was safe, she stood, stretched, and then went to relieve herself behind some thick bushes.

After eating a light breakfast, they filled canteens with fresh water and rolled blankets and supplies into tight bundles to pack inside their knapsacks. Shoving their saddles as far back under the overhang as possible, they concealed them by stuffing in piles of twigs and leaves. With a final look at maps Sindara carried, they assessed their bearings. Sunshine had already melted the light layer of snow, relieving them of worries about tracks left behind. If the weather cooperated and they avoided the enemy, they should reach Iglarm in little more than a week.

Karan was satisfied to allow Sindara the lead. She had lived many years in Bramond Province and was even more familiar with the region than he. Their route would carry them past the town of Tuutla, the site of a bloody attack on civilians. Sindara knew the village well after working for weeks with healers caring for survivors. Altogether, she had spent eight years studying at the private school in Berancor that lay between Tuutla and Bramond's capital. Starting their long trek on foot, Karan prayed for safe passage and relief from the nagging sensation that something was seriously amiss.

Chapter Twenty-Two

NAGRAND MEZDEN FELL TO HIS knees after being shoved forward by two burly Breyals. Filthy and disheveled, he felt weak from lack of food. His captors had given him only sufficient sustenance to keep him strong enough to travel on his own. He had no doubt that he had been treated with a certain level of restraint during the trip. Dread seeped into his thoughts as he prepared to face Breeneth Brandere and her master.

A man with hunched shoulders quietly entered the gloomy, dark room. Quietly, he lit black candlesticks stretching up like ghostly fingers from silver sconces that had provided bright, cheerful light in the once lovely, formal dining hall of Bramond's governor's mansion. Elegant banquet table and carved chairs were gone. At the far end of the room stood a wooden throne carved with frightening gargoyles and other fabled creatures from terrifying tales of old. An ornate, upholstered chaise stood beside the throne.

The servant limped in front of the prisoner to light candles on the opposite side of the room. The face that glanced around with a flash of sympathy showed scars that matched the poor soul's painful gait. Nagrand clenched his jaw. Ill-treatment from the Breyals had likely been gentle compared to whatever lay ahead. For the moment, he remained quiet and waited, head drooping and hands bound in front of him.

He listened as his captors departed the throne room. A short time passed before he heard footsteps approach. Garbed in rustling black satin fashioned into an extravagant gown, Breeneth Brandere sauntered toward him and walked around him with arrogant regard. "It would seem I have the honor of welcoming the respected Sir Nagrand Mezden back to Iglarm. I trust your trip was satisfactory."

His nose twitched at the faint, unpleasant scent that drifted from her full skirts as he nodded acknowledgment of her sarcastic greeting. For the moment, he thought it best to offer no sign of resistance. "Brisk weather was not so pleasant, but the journey was otherwise uneventful."

She tucked her fingers beneath Nagrand's growing beard and roughly tilted his head upward. Her harsh gaze revealed noticeable discomfort. "I remember you as being so fastidious about your appearance, Sir Nagrand. You are filthy as a dog." Her shoulders twitched with an involuntary shudder. "What is it that makes your presence so repulsive?"

"I offer my sincere apologies, My Lady," he replied evenly. "I've traveled many days with no opportunity to bathe or change into clean clothing."

"You play well, Nagrand," she said with a sardonic sneer. "Will you be so agreeable when we discuss matters of state and the problems posed by Prince Thehrund?"

Nagrand suppressed shivering along his spine as he briefly met her gaze. Never had he seen eyes so filled with contempt and hatred. He held tightly to what wits remained in his state of fatigue. "My Lady, since I am unaware of matters to which you refer, I suppose I must wait until you clarify your question."

Breeneth laughed, the sound hollow and mirthless. "You think you're so clever, Nagrand. You consider yourself Thehrund's friend, but he has used you to no end. You were never the wiser. In truth, he has never seen you as more than a loyal dog, scampering around his feet and hoping he might spare you some discarded scraps. You have an opportunity now to correct that situation and raise yourself to a key position in the new order my master and I will bring to Ambracor."

Nagrand breathed in, the foul air irritating both his throat and lungs. "I know nothing of the new order you propose. What I do know is that Prince Thehrund has been my friend and will always remain so."

Breeneth scowled and slapped her prisoner hard in the face. Snatching her hand back and pressing it to her midriff, she glared at him. His face was red with her handprint, but her palm burned from the blow. Refusing to show any sign of weakness, she lifted her head contemptuously.

"Perhaps a bit of kindness is in order. With a little rest, you'll be better prepared to meet with Master. I'm confident he will make you see the truth of your relationship with the prince and the many rewards for joining our new order."

Nagrand refused to be drawn into further discussion with her, at least for the time being. He nodded respectfully. "I shall look forward to learning more about this new order."

Her smile was a sharp contrast to the tone of her voice. "While you rest, consider well what awaits you should you refuse Master's generosity."

Traveling mostly by night, Thehrund rode his magnificent stallion through dense forest. He had left one of his most competent and experienced officers to command troops heading toward Ambracor's southern border. Breeneth had judged Thehrund's character well enough to know he would never remain idle and ignore the danger to Nagrand's life.

Pausing to stare at the sky, Thehrund noted positions of various constellations. He breathed silent gratitude to his wife. Her fascination with astronomy had been early inspiration for their love. Notes and charts from journals kept by her and her grandfather, combined with the prince's astute memory, were proving their worth as he navigated dark countryside with stars as his guides. His sharp mind also raced through remembered images of Iglarm and the lavish mansion the Branderes had occupied. He prayed memory would help him succeed in his mission to rescue Nagrand.

Resuming his pace, Thehrund reconciled himself to the fact he was heading directly into a trap. Perhaps the best strategy would have been to go straight to Iglarm in the first place. Much bloodshed and destruction might have been avoided had he decided on such a tactic from the very beginning. Breyals, who had been attacking for decades, had undoubtedly been incited to escalating levels of violence by Breeneth and her demon. Had she and her lover been confronted at the outset, things might have been different.

Thehrund shook his head…hard. Thinking on how they might have reacted was useless. He needed to discard all thought of what might have been or what could have been. He consciously decided to concentrate on the very real risks ahead and how he might rescue Nagrand.

Thehrund took slight comfort in two thoughts. Breeneth would not kill Nagrand. She needed him as bait. If time, weather, and Creator God smiled kindly upon him, the prince would rely on Sindara's great faith and strength so that they both might reach Iglarm in time to prevent further personal tragedy.

Sindara pressed her index finger to her lips. With Karan close behind, she crouched low as they moved alongside overgrown shrubs and bushes surrounding the quiet village of Tuutla. Dull twilight cast peculiar shadows in what remained of the town. Many homes and small businesses had never been rebuilt after the savage Breyal attack years earlier. Their fire-scarred skeletons stood eerie watch over the village. Odd, glowing orbs occasionally darted back and forth along deserted streets. Dim lights shone from the windows of a few humble dwellings.

Tuutla's stone chapel remained intact. Sindara recalled the weeks she had spent there while nursing the wounded and comforting the dying. Placing her hand over her sacred crystal, she sensed no danger nearby.

"Karan, at the rear of the chapel, a door leads to the cellar," she whispered softly. "The chapel looks deserted, so I doubt it's locked. We can rest there for the night. Let's wait until dark before crossing the meadow."

After darkness descended, they hurried across the field. Stealthily, Karan tested the door. His sigh of relief dissipated when rusty hinges creaked in protest. The two huddled tightly against the wall, hardly daring to breathe. Continuing quiet encouraged them as Sindara once again focused on her amulet. She turned and entered, slowly descending stone steps to the shelter of the cellar.

Trusting watchful angels, she dared to light a small candle from her coat pocket. Glancing around, she noted boards now covering the cellar's small windows. A little table held a lantern. She was relieved to discover the lamp contained both oil and wick to light. Breathing in deeply, she touched her candle's flame to the wick. She then snuffed out the small votive to save for future use.

Karan took Sindara's heavy knapsack and quietly lowered it to the floor. After removing his own, he sat cross-legged on cold stone to remove rations for their meager dinner. Abruptly, he froze.

"Is someone down there?"

Karan and Sindara held their breath, remaining still and silent.

Footsteps sounded slow and cautious on creaky wood stairs leading from the chapel's sacristy. "I know someone's here. Who is it?"

Karan looked up as a figure attired in priest's robes finally reached the bottom of the steps. The man's balding head tilted from one side to the other as he listened for any trace of intruders. It was obvious the elderly priest could not see; his eyelids were closed over sunken sockets. He had been deliberately blinded.

Karan suddenly rose to his feet. "Master Agnos? I am Karan Mezden. Do you remember me?"

The older man's scarred face revealed shock as well as recognition. "Karan? The blond rascal who settled to live a godly life in Bracordia?" Feeble arms reached toward the sound of Karan's voice. "Come closer. Let me reacquaint myself with you."

Approaching his one-time teacher, Karan grasped the man's outstretched hands. Agnos lifted trembling fingers to slide along Karan's handsome features, now scruffy with several days' growth of beard.

"You've grown into a fine man. What madness brings you to this cursed place?"

Karan swallowed against the knot in his throat and led Agnos to a spindly chair near the table. "There's desperate work to be done to end the evil now residing in Bramond."

Agnos shook his head. "The evil now occupying Iglarm is extraordinary, my son. Many have perished at the hands of the wicked ones who dwell there. Others, like myself, have been maimed and crippled to provide living examples of the punishment resistance brings. " He stopped suddenly. "You are not alone. Who travels with you?"

Sindara had already risen to her feet. Her voice was subdued. "Another of your former pupils, Master Agnos."

"That voice! No! This old man must finally be losing his sanity! That voice belongs to one long dead!"

Sindara walked to her former teacher and knelt before him. "You're not insane, Master. I am very much alive."

"Sindara Varacor? How is this possible? Breyals killed you at Articene. I remember visiting your parents with Reverend Master Zoman to offer prayers and encouragement after their loss."

Sindara wrapped her hands around those of the old priest. "The attack near Articene was indeed meant to murder me. By the blessings of Creator God, I was rescued and kept away from Ambracor until the time I would be most needed."

Agnos shook his head in disbelief. "I remember your voice so well. How sad I was when I heard of your death. Does Ambracor's prince know of your return? Never have I seen any man more consumed by grief."

Without thinking, she wrapped her arms around his frail shoulders in a snug embrace. "He knows, Master Agnos. He searched for me and then brought me home. We are now married."

A tranquil smile spread the aged man's lips once she released him. He settled against the hard back of the chair. "Until now, I expected to spend my final days in despair. This terrible darkness nearly robbed me of faith, but it seems Creator God does not forsake us."

"Creator God will never forsake us, dear Master," Sindara replied. "We are hiking to Iglarm to stand against the enemy."

"I remember you so well, Sindara. At Berancor, we all knew you were different, but this level of courage I never expected. It is a very dangerous thing you do. Are you sure you should not go back and return to safety?"

"Master Agnos," Karan responded, "if Breeneth Brandere and her demon master are not stopped soon, they will gain too much power. No part of Ambracor will be safe again."

Agnos nodded understanding. "Please forgive my lack of manners. You say you've been hiking. You must be tired...and hungry, too. I have a pot of stew on the stove upstairs. Come. Eat with me."

Sindara's eyes questioned Karan, but before he could respond, Agnos sensed their hesitation. "It is safe...as safe as any place in Bramond can be. Breyals avoid our small town. Others from Bramond travel around us. We live quietly as best we can."

A shiver suddenly traveled the length of Sindara's back. Her breathing quickened, and her heart beat a faster rhythm. "I understand the quiet now. And the orbs."

Karan turned his gaze to her. "What?"

"Restless spirits dwell here among the living who remained because they either had no place to go or could not bear to leave departed loved ones behind."

"Come," Agnos said again, motioning for them to follow him up the rickety stairs. "We shall pray and break bread together. You can then rest. I'm quite sure the ghosts who remain will stand fierce guard over you, Sindara. They will recall your labors that saved many of their family members and the comfort you gave others as their lives faded."

In a simply furnished room upstairs, Karan offered grace as he and Sindara joined hands with Agnos. Hot food and fresh bread were welcome relief from cold field provisions. Conversation was slow and reminiscent of more peaceful times. The elderly priest took pleasure in the company of rare visitors. He felt his spirit refreshed and his faith revitalized. Following their meal, he contentedly accepted Sindara's offer to clean up while he sat and talked at length with Karan.

A single knock sounded. Lifting a finger to his lips, the elderly priest motioned Karan and Sindara toward the cellar. Once they were out of sight, he slowly opened a side door of the chapel. A middle-aged townswoman waited outside and asked if she might speak to Agnos. Once inside, she wrung her hands worriedly.

"Master Agnos, forgive me for interrupting your evening. While I was at the markets in Soruma, I heard it said that Breyal warriors dragged a prisoner through the streets early yesterday. They said he was an officer from King Hamund's army and that he wore a nobleman's coat of arms on his brigandine. Rumors say he was being taken to the governor's mansion. I know you have recently faltered in faith, but I will not let them take mine. That man will need the benefit of every prayer if he is to face the evil ones in Iglarm."

Agnos reached for his visitor's arm. With a reassuring squeeze, he said, "Losha, my faith is restored this night. I promise prayers for the prisoner. You go home now and pray hard."

Before Losha turned to leave, she paused and gazed sadly at the blind priest. "It is good to hear your faith has returned. I believe we have cause for hope."

"And why is that?" Agnos asked curiously.

"The ghosts are active tonight. Their glowing spheres have settled all around the town. It's as if they guard us against harm. They must have a reason."

"I'm sure they must," Agnos agreed. "You go home now. I shall go inside and pray for the prisoner. You do the same before you sleep."

Agnos stepped outside and listened until Losha's footsteps faded into the distance. Detecting no other sounds, he returned to the chapel and bolted the door. He then beckoned to his visitors. "Will you join me in prayer for one who is in great need?"

Sindara and Karan had left the cellar door slightly ajar and listened to the exchange between the priest and his visitor. Agnos tipped his head from side to side. "Karan, you are deeply troubled. What is wrong?"

A tear slid down Karan's cheek. "I cannot explain how I know, but with all my heart, I believe that prisoner was Nagrand."

"Your brother?" The old priest's forehead furrowed into deeper lines. "Then our prayers must be offered with great fervor. Come."

Sindara firmly clasped Karan's hand. They followed Agnos to the altar of the ancient chapel where all three knelt, joining prayers to Creator God and beseeching protection for Nagrand from whatever vile fate awaited him in Iglarm.

The chinking of metal keys accompanied sounds of heavy boots thumping against dusty rock floors in the cellar beneath the Brandere mansion. Part of the cellar had been partitioned and set with iron bars to create cramped cells for prisoners. Nagrand sat in semi-darkness with his back to the cold wall. He looked up and watched as jailers passed him yet again to take some poor soul to meet an unspeakable fate. Another jailer came and shoved through the door a wooden cup of water, a chunk of dry bread, and a bowl containing some grayish-green lump meant to pass as food.

Determined to retain whatever strength he could, Nagrand thanked the jailer, who laughed shrilly at the prize caged under his watchful eye. Once the foul-smelling keeper disappeared from sight, Nagrand took the food and forced himself to eat what was in the bowl. The bread and water helped rid him of the sour taste of the main meal. How he hoped his stomach would tolerate the mysterious ration.

Time passed with agonizing slowness. He tried to calculate how long he had spent in the narrow cell. He estimated it had been two days since he had faced Breeneth. He recalled her smirk as she told him he might appreciate time to rest. Her aim was clear. She wanted to wear him down physically and mentally before revealing her real intentions.

Not daring to dwell on what lay ahead, Nagrand reached inside his grimy shirt for the medicine pouch. An odd thought occurred to him. Breeneth had looked decidedly uncomfortable when she touched his beard. She had actually snatched her hand back in pain after slapping him. He was certain he hadn't imagined her reactions. Opening the tiny bag, he withdrew the pad saturated with the oily cedar blend. He wiped it across his forehead and above his heart. Absorbing as much as possible into his skin, he returned the pad to its pouch before tucking it back inside his shirt. He then prayed that he would be granted deliverance from the worst Breeneth and her lover might inflict on him. Realizing full well his capture was a ploy to draw Thehrund to Iglarm, his prayer continued as he pleaded for his best friend's safety.

He must have fallen deeply asleep on top of his thin bed of scratchy straw. He hadn't heard the jailer's approach or the opening of his cell door. Roughly grabbing his arms, two guards dragged him off the floor. Groggy and disoriented, he struggled for steady footing. Shaking himself awake, he straightened his back and attempted to match their pace. He consciously breathed in air that was surely fresher than inside the throne room where he expected to be taken.

Wary surprise seeped into his mind when he was guided up two sets of stairs to a small room. Inside, a wide porcelain bowl nestled into the carved wooden pedestal. Beside it was a table holding clean towels, grooming tools, and a pitcher of fresh, warm water. Over a chair in the corner lay a clean shirt and knitted sweater of the type used by fishermen. Another small stand held a covered plate. Escaping steam carried with it the mouthwatering aroma of hot, freshly prepared food.

Nagrand pondered what to do. Did he dare refuse the comforts offered? Would stubborn refusal earn harsher treatment? Would accepting it strengthen him against abuse that undoubtedly lay in the offing? Carefully, he picked up the heavy pitcher with shaking hands and poured water into the bowl. He washed hands and face, carefully avoiding his forehead where he had stroked the oil-soaked pad. Finding a comb, he tugged it through bedraggled locks until they hung in neat, limp strands. Deciding against shaving, he attempted to smooth his unkempt beard.

Removing the filthy shirt that smelled sour, he washed his body, again carefully avoiding places where he had rubbed the sacred mix of ash and oil. He shook out his soiled garment and put it back on. He rubbed the sweet-smelling cake of soap over sweat-stained fabric to mask some of the disagreeable odor. Making sure his medicine bag was tucked securely beneath, he donned the clean shirt. He had been cold. He thought two layers would help him stay warmer. He then pulled the generously sized sweater over his head. If nothing else, the extra layers might soften blows he expected to endure.

Sitting at the table, he lifted the cover from the plate to reveal eggs whipped into a fluffy omelet, herbed sausages, dried fruit, and toasted bread. Although ravenous, he hesitated. He remembered how Breeneth had drugged her own mother. After days with so little to eat, he also feared his stomach might rebel even if the food held no poisons or drugs. Finally, slowly, he nibbled the edges of the bread. Detecting no offending flavors, he continued to eat it until naught was left but crumbs.

He stared hungrily at the sausages and eggs. He lifted a forkful of the omelet to his mouth and touched the tip of his tongue to its buttery firmness. He set the bite back on the plate. His was a sensitive palate. Something tasted slightly bitter. He dared eat no more. He turned his attention to the sausages and cut them into small chunks. He risked a taste. He slowly chewed one piece, hoping it contained none of Breeneth's potions. Placing the cover back over the plate, he pushed it aside.

Standing, he chose to avoid the pot filled with hot tea. Instead, he picked up the empty cup from the table. He rinsed it with water from the pitcher and wiped it out. He then poured a small amount of clean water into the cup to rinse his mouth. Spitting it into the used wash water, he took a few sips before setting the cup aside. He distrusted everything about the offerings in this room, although he wondered if his precautions were worth the effort.

Sitting again on the padded chair, he leaned over to rest his head on folded arms. He felt exceedingly tired while consciously assessing every part of his body. So far, he felt no ill effects from either the food or the water.

He decided Breeneth probably wanted him at his best so that she and her demon could more thoroughly enjoy whatever punishment they would inflict. Resting while he could, he turned his heart and soul toward home, family, and friends. A faint echo inside his mind carried words of his last conversation with Sindara. She had instructed him to call upon the angels for help should he be forced to face any of Breeneth's demons. He must not forget that advice.

Dozing lightly, he raised his head at sounds just outside the room. A guard stood watch in the hallway while the scar-faced servant he had seen in the throne room entered and closed the door behind him. The servant frowned upon checking how much food remained on the plate.

"Mistress Breeneth will not be happy that you did not eat," he mumbled nervously.

Nagrand breathed a sigh. "I fear my stomach was not ready for so much food."

The servant frowned. "We mustn't waste food."

Nagrand noticed the man's gaunt cheeks. "Perhaps you could help me finish," he suggested, recognizing both uneasiness and hunger in the servant's manner.

"I dare not. If the mistress finds out..."

"How would she know? I'll never tell her. Will you?"

Cautiously, the servant accepted a portion of the omelet and a sausage and gobbled it down. Nagrand slowly ate the remainder. Finished, he looked into the servant's face and observed the defeated look in the young man's eyes. "There. The food is gone, and no one will know. Take some water and rinse your mouth so no smell of food lingers to betray you."

The servant glanced around, gratitude for the scraps of extra food clearly showing in brown eyes. "The shirt you wore. Where is it? I was to take it for washing."

Nagrand could hardly bear his curiosity. "I was cold. I cleaned it as best I could and put the clean clothes over it."

"A word of advice," the servant offered as he loudly clattered dishes onto a tray to avoid drawing the guard's unwanted attention. "Do not anger the mistress. Her temper is quick and her punishment swift. If you face her master, I suggest you do naught to challenge or insult him. His power exceeds your imagination."

Nagrand bit his tongue. Although he dared say nothing, experiences traveling the portal had expanded the scope of his ability to grasp the vast possibilities in Creator God's universe. "I accept your advice with thanks. By the way, what is your name?"

The servant glanced up fearfully as he picked up the tray and prepared to leave. "I am Berdran."

"Berdran?" Nagrand asked incredulously. "Breeneth's brother?"

"I was away at school when Father and Mother departed for Bracordia. I tried to resist my sister when I came home. As you can see, her power was too great. I must go now."

Nagrand had little time to reflect on the startling revelation. Two guards arrived to escort him to the throne room for his audience with Breeneth and her master.

Erator Varacor looked up when a courier requested permission to enter the busy command office at Articene. Accepting a sealed document from Bracordia, he didn't bother to excuse himself to officers consulting with him. The message piqued Erator's curiosity, so he read it immediately.

Captain Zimaron's coded dispatch stated that his soldiers had fought off a band of Breyals who had apparently tracked them some distance after their departure from Cahmdurn. Several escaped, but their chief had been captured. Hostile and defiant, he had hurled insults at the princess under Zimaron's protection. He had shouted that she would be better off killing herself than waiting for the death Bramond Province's rulers planned for her. The captain had maintained his deception until his escort reached Bracordia and locked away the captive. The Breyals were convinced that Irlini was the princess. According to the arrogant prisoner, Breeneth Brandere had detected the scent of Sindara's blood and dispatched the band to capture her.

Quickly completing his meeting and dismissing his officers, Erator reread Zimaron's dispatch. He was relieved to know Irlini was safe in Bracordia. Zimaron had played the game smartly. He had defended his decoy, captured a prisoner only too happy to boast threats, and made certain enough warriors escaped to inform Breeneth of the princess's retreat to Ambracor's capital.

Erator sighed heavily. For the time being, the weight of command over all of Ambracor's armies rested on his shoulders. Nagrand Mezden had been captured. The general had shaken his head in dismay to learn Thehrund had departed alone for Iglarm. His heart and mind reeled as he thought of his sister also en route to Iglarm. A pervading madness seemed to be driving everyone he loved toward death and despair brought on by malevolent entities that had already claimed Bramond Province.

Glancing through the window of his office, he watched a fresh patrol gathering to leave and monitor movements of Breyal tribesmen skirting Arvacon borders. Drawing into his lungs a deep breath, Erator released the air in a shuddering sigh. Steeling himself for whatever lay ahead, he wrote two identical messages. He congratulated Captain Zimaron for safely delivering the princess to Bracordia and ordered him to keep constant guard over his sister. He then gave the dispatches to two couriers who would depart separately. One would head straight to the palace via a rarely utilized trail. The other would suffer a staged attack on the regular route and conveniently lose his dispatch. Erator had no doubt the lost message would reach Iglarm.

Turning and gazing at a large map, Erator smiled grimly. For the moment at least, Breeneth would think Sindara was in Bracordia. That should provide his sister extra time. Those words echoed hollowly through his mind. Extra time for what? To reach Iglarm? To confront Breeneth and her demon master? Closing his eyes, Erator offered brief, earnest prayer. He could not bear the thought of his sister dying a second time.

Chapter Twenty-Three

Major Lohrdrend, commanding forces near Arvacon's southern front during Prince Thehrund's absence, reviewed reports from scouts. He warned troops to expect the enemy to launch an offensive to thrust further into Arvacon's southern region. Citizens were advised to evacuate. Families with children gathered what belongings they could and fled northward. Many able-bodied men and women chose to remain behind. Armed with whatever they could use as weapons, they decided they would all defy the invaders and defend their homeland.

Faith practitioners carefully rationed dwindling supplies of the sacred blend of oil and cedar ash so that each person might have some protection against the onslaught of demon reinforcements expected to augment Breyal forces. All had been cautioned to ignore the fear that demons fed upon. Focus on the human invaders. Call upon Creator God's angels for aid.

The enemy's assault finally began. They were intent on pushing further into Arvacon Province. As Lohrdrend scanned mayhem on the battlefield, he swerved his horse around. He had observed a large contingent of enemy soldiers heading north. With a grave expression, he nodded to a bugler. The signal sounded. Ambracor defenders would converge and then shift right to appear as if they were chasing the invaders. In truth, they were driving them toward a trap.

The narrow valley ahead was split by a broad river crossed by two bridges. What the Breyal army did not know was that the river had been dammed and both bridges intentionally destabilized. Troops stood ready with teams of draft animals waiting to drag away dam supports. Enemy warriors crossing the weakened bridges would be swept away by coursing waters freed when the dam collapsed.

Lohrdrend followed Thehrund's plan to the letter. From his vantage point, he watched both invasion and pursuit. He frowned when demon warriors swooped down within their stinking black mist. Recalling his instructions, he shouted out above the battle's deafening clamor, "Sacred angels of Creator God! I beg you hear me! Bring your light to defeat these evil ones who would destroy our people of faith!"

His eyes darted in every direction. The reverberating clang of metal and harsh cries of fighting men and women were suddenly muffled by mighty roars. Advancing enemy soldiers shrieked as the bridges gave way, unable to withstand the rumbling force of the rolling wall of water and debris unleashed by the collapsed dam. The heavens simultaneously opened. Angels, spurred by righteous wrath, pursued demons who dared to rise against a people who had only ever desired lives of peace.

Lohrdrend breathed a prayer of intense gratitude. He could leave the band of demons to the angels. In the meantime, Ambracor would rely on this patched army to defeat human warriors and soldiers who escaped the flood. How he hoped he would never again have to face another army such as he witnessed that day.

❈ ❈ ❈

King Hamund read Major Lohrdrend's dispatch thoroughly for the third time. Without conscious realization, he nervously rubbed the stub of his amputated leg. He felt as if his whole heart had just crashed into his stomach. Blinding pain shot through his brain, and severe tension tightened his jaw.

What was now hailed as the Battle of Two Bridges had been a resounding success for the armies of Ambracor. Bramond's evil leadership had done exactly what Thehrund had predicted. They had gathered their armies and marched toward the heart of Arvacon Province. Demonic entities had joined the effort to break through the king's defenses. Hamund sat back in his chair in his private office. He swallowed several times, failing to dislodge the growing lump in his throat.

His daughter-in-law had warned that it was only a matter of time before Breeneth's lover would be strong enough to summon lesser demons to fight alongside Breyal warriors. She had also introduced means to help protect their people by warding off those inferior servants. His own son's military strategy had successfully met the inevitable offensive action intended to drive a wedge dividing Arvacon in two. The bridges had been destroyed, carrying hundreds of enemy fighters into the raging river. Ambracor's army, joined by local citizenry, had suffered relatively low casualties compared to heavy losses sustained by their adversaries. Bramond's first demonic attack had suffered angelic decimation.

Such excellent news should have been received with relief; however, clutched in Hamund's other hand was the dispatch that had spawned a spiral of fear that saturated his entire being. Nagrand Mezden had been captured, and Prince Thehrund had gone after him. The conclusion was simultaneously glaringly simple and utterly terrifying. Thehrund would try to rescue Nagrand, and both would face the fury of Breeneth Brandere and her demon master in their own lair.

Queen Narlina knocked and entered. Observing her husband's slouched shoulders and desolate expression, she caught her breath as her heart leapt within her breast. "Hamund, tell me. What's wrong?"

Blue eyes held fear only a parent could ever know. "Lohrdrend has secured a crucial victory in the south of Arvacon."

"And?" she asked, fearful of the tremor in Hamund's voice.

He could think of no way to soften the blow. "News is that Nagrand Mezden was taken prisoner and that Thehrund has gone after him."

Narlina gasped in horror. Breathing heavily, she moved away from her husband's desk and stood with her back against the wall. Closing her eyes, she forcefully willed herself to remain calm. "When?"

Hamund blinked at his wife's odd question. "Both courier dispatches are only days old."

Narlina straightened. "Sindara will save them. I know she will."

Hamund reached for his crutches and stood. "Narlina, we must resign ourselves to the truth. Our son may already be dead."

Narlina shook her head adamantly. "He's not dead. I would know." She then turned, fleeing his office for the sanctuary of the palace chapel.

The next day, Hamund gritted his teeth against the discomfort of his stump pressed into the padded cup of the wooden leg crafted by one of Bracordia's finest carpenters. The wound, treated with the best herbal medicines available in Ambracor, had healed quickly with no sign of infection. Despite the injury remaining sensitive to pressure, the king had stubbornly ignored the pain and practiced walking on the prosthetic at every chance.

Narlina watched her husband with immense respect. The man she had married exhibited uncommon determination. He prepared to leave for Articene to discuss current strategies with Erator Varacor. After that, he planned to meet with Lord Artrian in Cahmdurn. Hamund had decided his rightful place was closer to the battlefields. There, his people could see him as an example of perseverance in the face of adversity.

He had promised Narlina to travel most of the distance inside his coach and to use crutches whenever possible. Still, he would ride into the fort at Articene. That was their compromise when she had counseled him to conserve his strength. Remaining in Bracordia, the queen would oversee administrative and diplomatic duties with assistance from Cleotis Tamazor and other top ministers. The king had also prepared alternative succession plans to be implemented if the worst happened in the field. He trusted his wife to ensure Ambracor would remain in wise hands should Thehrund be captured and killed, thus ending the Cobrandya line.

As Hamund donned hauberk over a lightweight gambeson, he smiled at his wife's affectionate efforts to ensure all was smooth and neat. "I shall miss your attentions while I'm away," he said gently.

Narlina glanced up at him with tear-glazed eyes and a quivering smile. "I shall miss my husband while he's away." Despite the cold chainmail, she rested her face against his broad chest. "Hamund, I love you with all my heart. Please be careful."

Dropping a kiss on her hair, the king was glad she couldn't see the involuntary grimace on his face. "I can promise only to remain alert, Narlina. In war, careful is rarely possible."

She nodded silently, reluctantly acknowledging the truth in his words. "There is nothing I want more than to have my family home with me."

"I know," Hamund said, holding her away so he could gaze at her face in case it might be the last time. "That is my most solemn wish, but I also know that sorrow already fills many homes in Ambracor. Each of us must do whatever we can to restore peace for those left behind and for those yet to be born to our people."

With the slightest of nods, she agreed. "Do not worry about me. I shall honor you and our son by doing all I can from here."

Long fingers tenderly stroked his wife's cheek. "Narlina, I've always known you were stronger than you ever knew yourself. Never have I needed that strength more than now. I love you."

He bent his head to kiss her. Then, with her hand gently resting against his back, she accompanied him as he walked on crutches to his waiting coach.

Hours spent inside the coach were tedious. Occasionally sliding down a window to breathe in crisp and refreshing autumn air, Hamund paused from pondering tactical ideas to let his mind wander into fields of memory. Without conscious realization, he smiled to himself as he recalled meeting Narlina and courting her. Even now, these many years later, he savored images and sensations they had shared on their wedding day.

Continuing to smile, he remembered climbing the steps of the bell tower and dragging on the thick rope with all his weight to ring the bell himself the day Narlina had told him she was with child. He had done

428

the same when his son was born. Rarely had he regretted burdensome responsibilities that were his by right of birth. He had cherished the joys and love found with his wife and his son. He had nurtured friendships and done all possible to ensure peace and prosperity for his people. His life had been good.

Just before arriving in Articene, Hamund left the relative comfort of his coach. Assisted by one of his officers, he mounted his horse and settled into the saddle with regal posture. Surrounded by royal guardsmen, he proudly rode the final hours of the journey.

When massive gates opened, King Hamund maneuvered his horse to the front of his guard and entered the fort first. Stunned by the sight of their monarch appearing without notice or fanfare, soldiers bowed low before snapping to attention. Summoned by an aide, General Varacor hurried outside to welcome the king.

Grimacing with discomfort, Hamund refused help dismounting. A guard brought crutches that permitted him to walk with minimal pressure on his prosthetic leg. Turning in surprise, Hamund bowed his head respectfully. Soldiers were heartily cheering their king who, recently crippled as he was by an encounter with their enemy, had taken the considerable risk of riding into one of Arvacon's key defense zones.

Sindara awakened early. Before rising, she mouthed fervent prayers for an unimpeded journey to Iglarm and for the safety of Nagrand and Thehrund. Hearing her stir, Karan also dragged himself from the hard floor that had been the warmest bed he had known since leaving Cahmdurn. Both he and Sindara had stretched out on their blankets in front of the fireplace in the priest's quarters while Master Agnos slept on his small bed in the corner.

Agnos had risen even earlier than Sindara and was busy in the kitchen of his personal quarters. Water steamed in a kettle on the iron stove, ready to brew strong tea. A small pitcher of fresh, creamy milk waited to be combined with flour, leavening, and sugar to make batter for crisp pancakes that would be served with syrup made by boiling dried fruit. Humble fare to be sure, but the elderly priest was offering his guests the best available in his humble abode.

While they ate, discussion turned to the fastest, safest way to continue their trek. News from the previous night's visitor heightened the sense of urgency Sindara and Karan both felt. As the two discussed possibilities, the priest remained quietly thoughtful. "I do have a suggestion that might reduce your trip by a day, perhaps even two," he finally said.

"Master Agnos, we gladly welcome any advice," Sindara responded hopefully.

"Losha's son was left lame after the Breyal attack here, so he was never conscripted. He has a wagon and is permitted to travel the roads because he transports supplies that are transferred to Iglarm or to Breeneth's soldiers in the field. I believe he's taking a load to Soruma today."

"Berancor is only a few hours' hike from Soruma," Karan mused aloud. "Traveling on foot, I'd say we're perhaps two days from the faith center."

"Master," Sindara began, "do you know if they've cut down the forest?"

"I can ask. I am sure of one thing. Habron is trustworthy. I'm confident he would not betray you for any reason. If the forest hasn't been cut, it will provide excellent cover from the road to whatever remains of Berancor."

Karan shook his head. "The risk of retaliation and punishment is too high. Breeneth would not hesitate to murder his family in front of him if she should discover he aided us."

"If Habron took us close enough to the center, could he return right away without delivering his load today?"

A puzzled expression crossed Agnos's face. "I'm not sure. May I inquire why you pose such a question?"

Sindara smiled pensively as her hand yet again rested above her sacred amulet. "Master, if he returns home, the orbs of light from last night will take on the task of protecting all who dwell here in Tuutla. They remained not because their spirits were restless or otherwise trapped by the horror of the Breyal massacre. They stayed to fulfill a role as mystical guardians. They accepted the bidding of Creator God. If Karan and I succeed in our quest, those orbs will carry their spirits back into Creator God's presence where they'll finally find rest."

Agnos shook his head back and forth. "How can you possibly know such a thing, Sindara?"

"Master Agnos," she said in a firm voice, "give me your hand."

Standing and bending forward, she pulled her amulet from inside her tunic. Gently grasping his hand, she placed the amulet against his palm. She and Karan both watched as tiny beams of brilliant light shone from the crystal. Straightening and sliding the pendant back inside her tunic, she carefully observed the priest's awestruck expression.

Several long moments passed before Agnos recovered sufficiently to speak. "Dear Sindara, you commune with Creator God's most powerful angels. How blessed I am to have the opportunity to help you."

Although he could not see, she smiled at him. "I was the one blessed with teachers like you and Master Zoman. You both patiently guided me onto my proper path of faith." She leaned over and kissed each of his cheeks. "Please speak with Habron while Karan and I prepare to leave. Every moment we save is strength we reserve for a battle we cannot lose."

Grappling with an assailant who had jumped on his back, Thehrund toppled from his horse and landed hard on uneven ground bulging with broad tree roots. The attacker had dropped from a sturdy tree branch. Rolling against the tree's stocky trunk, the foe took full advantage of the surprise assault as he pummeled the prince. With the wind knocked out of him by the unexpected fall, Thehrund's strength was no match when the attacker was quickly joined by several other men. Wearing no helmet or coif, he lost consciousness when something struck his head.

Wakefulness came some time later. Dazed and hurting, Thehrund blinked against an invasion of sunshine and blood rushing into his dangling, aching head. With growing awareness, he struggled against thick ropes binding his hands and ankles. The rhythmic plodding of his stallion's hooves finally penetrated his brain enough for him to realize he was draped over his saddle. The sounds of multiple hooves against the road brought him to the unwelcome conclusion that he had been taken prisoner.

Lifting his eyelids partially, his eyes gradually adjusted to daylight. Raising his head somewhat, he saw at least five mounted Breyal warriors behind him. He stifled a groan, wondering how he could have grown so careless. In his desperate push to reach Iglarm, he had decided to chance riding a little farther after sunrise. It was too late to rue his error. If nothing else, he thought cynically, his arrival in Iglarm should prove more expeditious.

The pace of the horses soon slowed to a stop. He listened as his captors dismounted and then watched a pair of fringed boots approach. He felt the rough pull on his hair as the Breyal yanked his head upward. The warrior sniggered when he saw the prisoner was awake. Thehrund felt harsh hands grab his legs. Following a sharp jerk, he landed with a bone-jarring jolt flat on his back.

Shaking off effects of the rough landing, Thehrund rolled to his side and pushed his bound hands against the ground to sit up. Despite the abrupt dismount, his head was clearing as he silently observed his captors, especially the one who rapidly strode toward the warriors who had dragged him from his horse. Without comment or preamble, the party's apparent leader threw a violent punch that knocked one laughing Breyal to the ground.

Turning toward the prisoner, the shaggy-haired chief crouched and leaned forward, stopping when his swarthy face was only inches from Thehrund's. "I will free the bindings on your ankles and legs. You will not try to escape. Do you understand?"

Thehrund only nodded. He watched the Breyal chief tug the ropes free. Surprised when the man grabbed his arm and roughly hauled him to his feet, Thehrund swayed a moment before gaining his balance. Uncertain what to expect, he waited for directions.

"I assume you need to relieve yourself. Two of my men will guide you to the bushes and stay with you until you finish. I warn you again. Do not try to escape."

Dipping his head in acknowledgment, Thehrund staggered slightly as his two guards, one on each side clutching an arm, led him. Using the opportunity to assess his situation, Thehrund took his time fumbling with his clothes to take full advantage of the needed break. Returning to the dozen or so captors, he did not resist when ordered to sit on the grassy side of the road. Neither did he reject a drink from the canteen of water nor the spicy strip of jerky handed to him. Chewing on a bite, he watched the Breyal chief sit directly in front of him.

"You will excuse my warriors for their rude treatment. They are not accustomed to handling prisoners as valuable as you."

Swallowing a bite, Thehrund met the chieftain's direct stare. "I am but a soldier in the king's army."

The Breyal smiled sarcastically. "Let us show no disrespect to one another. You are no ordinary soldier. You lead the king's army. You are Thehrund, his son, and the one who commands great interest from those who rule Bramond."

"Do they also rule Breyal?" Thehrund asked bluntly.

The chieftain scowled as his features twisted and flushed in response. "No one rules over Breyal except Breyals."

Thehrund did not lower his gaze. He decided to meet authority with directness. "I am at a disadvantage. I do not know you."

The Breyal tipped his head backward and drank from a leather canteen before returning his gaze to the prisoner. "I am Kicchak, Grand Chieftain of the Breyal tribes."

Thehrund responded with a respectful nod. "Then I offer you my regards and my respect. You have proven yourself a very effective leader in this war we fight."

"Do you mock me?" Kicchak demanded, bristling at Thehrund's words.

Thehrund shook his head, wincing at the slight pounding. "Mock you? Such a thought would not occur to me considering the skill and tenaciousness of your warriors. Men fight the way your warriors do only when they have skilled leadership. I have witnessed their ferocity in battle. Seeing their actions in combat clearly shows the respect due their leaders."

Kicchak studied the prince's expression and saw no hint of deception or mockery. "Your armies, too, fight with courage and fortitude," the chieftain admitted grudgingly.

"We fight to preserve our homes and our way of life. Would you do otherwise?"

Kicchak offered no reply and waited for Thehrund to finish his food. The captive then gratefully accepted the canteen his captor placed between hands still tightly bound at the wrists. Taking a long drink to wash down the worst of the lingering, spicy aftertaste of the jerky, he handed the canteen back to Kicchak.

"I assume you're taking me to Iglarm," Thehrund ventured to say.

Kicchak tilted his head sharply. "Master Thafalos and his consort offer reward for you that is even more than they paid for your yellow-haired officer."

Thehrund knew he did not dare give freedom to his inner feelings. He also mentally noted the demon's name. According to Karan, knowledge of a demon's name could be valuable in a confrontation. "I assume you refer to Sir Mezden."

"I heard the woman call him Nagrand." Kicchak studied every nuance of the prisoner's expression. "He is your friend?"

"He is a respected officer in our ranks," Thehrund replied without emotion.

Kicchak grunted. "I think he is more than that; otherwise, the Bramond leaders would not have been willing to pay such a high price for him."

"You are a strong leader," Thehrund responded. "Do you not value those with uncommon courage and loyalty who follow you?"

Kicchak merely stared at his prisoner. His demeanor commanded respect. He had also fiercely resisted the attack that morning. The Breyal leader had sternly reprimanded his warriors because it had taken four of them to subdue a single man knocked from his horse. Recalling the prince's remarkable strength, the chieftain noted Thehrund's unusual height and build. What a waste, he thought, that such a man would be delivered to the likes of the dark ones in Bramond.

Standing up, Kicchak signaled one of his troops with a sharp jerk of his head. The warrior dragged Thehrund to his feet. The chieftain observed that his prisoner stood fully a head higher than the tallest of his own warriors. "I will grant you the respect of riding your horse like a man, but your hands will remain bound. My men will help you mount. If you should be foolish enough to try to escape, you will suffer swift consequences."

Thehrund nodded in understanding. Although certainly nothing like the many plans he had considered for rescuing Nagrand, he was headed to Iglarm. There was nothing more he could do for the moment beyond observing his Breyal captors and learning as much about Kicchak as possible. He was sure he had detected disapproval in the chief's voice when he mentioned the demon and the demon's lover.

By nightfall, Thehrund was nearing exhaustion. He had ridden through the past few nights. During the days, he had tried to rest in the depths of the forest while worries marched relentlessly through his mind. He was confident in troops under Erator's command. He hoped the southern fronts would retain their advantage over joint forces from both Breyal and Bramond Province. He dreaded to think of the ordeal Nagrand must be facing as Breeneth's prisoner. He wondered how successful Irlini's ruse had been in diverting Breeneth's attention from Sindara. Mere thought of

Sindara delivered a tortured ache to his heart as he thought of her trekking alone toward the infernal nightmare in Iglarm.

When Kicchak called a halt to the day's journey, Thehrund had barely enough strength to grip the pommel of his saddle and dismount between two surly Breyals. Swaying slightly, he was again guided to a place where he could relieve physical needs before sitting on a mat Kicchak himself removed from Thehrund's saddle bag.

Well within Bramond's borders, the Breyals showed no concern over starting a roaring campfire. The fire's heat provided welcome comfort as it warded off the coolness of an autumn night. Kicchak again offered Thehrund food and drink. If nothing else, the Breyal chieftain showed his captive a measure of respect. While one of the warriors took first watch, Kicchak tossed a blanket over Thehrund's shoulder and watched pensively as his prisoner wearily stretched out by the fire and fell asleep.

Sindara caressed the face of the hefty draft horse, soothing it with the softest of whispers to keep it quiet until they were certain the party of Bramond militiamen was well beyond earshot. She tilted her head forward and followed Karan deeper into the protective cover of thick forest. In the distance, tall spires rose from the Sacred Halls of Faith. They planned a cautious approach, hoping Habron had been right about the worship center being deserted by Bramondans and avoided by Breyals.

Remounting the horse, she listened carefully as heavy hooves trudged between stout trees and past crackling pockets of newly dormant undergrowth. Upon reaching the outskirts of the once thriving center, all appeared eerily quiet. Tying the horses near a patch of grass but still keeping them well concealed, Karan turned one way while Sindara set off in the opposite direction. If all went well, they would walk a circle around the center, cross at the far side, and then meet where Habron's horses waited.

As Sindara carefully crossed a narrow brook, she praised Creator God for their encounter with Agnos and his neighbor Habron. The stocky farmer had insisted that no one would miss him if he didn't show up at the market. His most recent trip had carried little in the way of supplies needed by Breeneth's forces. Fields were exhausted of summer's bounty, and no one would willingly venture to Tuutla to find out if any provisions had been withheld.

Sindara had told him she could not guarantee the return of the draft animals the farmer relied on for farming and transportation. Still, he had firmly gripped her shoulder, insisting he would rather pull his spring plow with his one good leg than let her go further on foot. His eyes had gleamed brightly when he expressed pride at finally being able to serve his king in the fight to defend Ambracor. She had offered no further protests. Her need was great, and she graciously accepted his help.

Lifting her gaze, she was surprised to see Karan approaching her. She could hardly believe they had skirted the edges of the center so quickly. Saying nothing, they continued until each had surveyed the entire perimeter. When they met back where they had started, both were relieved. There was no sign of life other than a few animals skittering across the plaza now littered with piles of blowing leaves. The once-busy square was otherwise deserted except for tall, mute statues that represented key events in the faith history so vividly detailed within the pages of the sacred Ambracada.

Leading the horses past the shrine that once housed the holy book, Karan and Sindara both felt grateful for the darkening skies of an early twilight. The evening's fading light revealed shattered glass on brick streets and walkways. Some doors swung precariously on loosened hinges while others had been knocked completely off their frames. Sturdy stone buildings had resisted destruction on the outside. Both priest and princess preferred not to look inside at whatever damage might have been wrought on beautifully carved woods, paintings, and vast libraries.

Sindara led the way toward the darkened abbey she had once planned to call home. The heavy door was stuck. Stepping aside, she watched as

Karan put his shoulder against the door and pushed. With a loud creak, it finally budged a little. Combining efforts, they finally forced it open.

Sindara entered first. A strange, unnatural hush hung within the once bustling lobby of the abbey. Having lived there for years, Sindara knew every corner, every door, and every window. With a hint of moonlight filtering through broken glass and tattered draperies, she quietly inspected the deserted ground level. Cautiously climbing a carved stairway to the upper floors, she found only damaged artifacts, scattered personal belongings, and overturned furniture.

Her heart twisted as she thought of the center's teachers and faith leaders she had known and respected. She had heard that some of the talented healers, instructors, and religious servants had escaped westward. They had not dared head north toward Arvacon for fear of running into Breyal forces flooding northern Bramond. She knew several senior faith leaders had fled in different directions, sacrificing their lives to give Master Zoman the chance to escape with the precious book of faith that was now safely hidden.

Going back outside, she removed her knapsack from her horse and pulled a candle and match from a side pouch. The candle's flickering light only served to heighten the sense of tragic solitude now permeating the abbey. With grim resolution, she grasped leather leads and guided the horses through the door. They would all be safer within the abbey's walls.

Karan prayed grace over their food before they ate in silence. Every now and then, a banging door or the scampering feet of woodland animals gave them a start. Later, Sindara scrounged around by the light of extra candles she had salvaged and noticed a pair of heavy draperies that had been dragged down to the floor. She shook them out and then tossed them over the backs of the horses. Then, finding several cushions flung around the office of the abbess, she arranged them for bedding. Using their knapsacks as pillows, Karan and Sindara then huddled together under their blankets for shared warmth and slept, once again trusting their safety to angels and Creator God.

Nagrand's posture was erect and his senses alert as he stood some twelve feet from the tall, elaborately carved chair the demon master claimed as his throne. While minutes ticked slowly by, his mind briefly wandered back in time to when this hall had served as the site of lavish banquets and parties hosted by the late Count Brandere. Meals had been extravagant and the assortment of ales and wines plentiful. Fragrant colognes and aromatic foods had combined delightfully with music and laughter to fill air now permeated by the lingering odor of decay.

A door opened. Breeneth Brandere glided into the room, again wearing a black gown, this one lavishly adorned with gold braid and embroidery. Raven tresses had been plaited and arranged elegantly at the back of her head, their gleaming spirals secured with combs of gold. Holding her chin slightly aloft, her appearance exuded an image of nobility absent from her soul.

"Good afternoon, Nagrand. I do hope you have enjoyed our hospitality." Her voice held a taunting note.

Bowing his head, he quietly answered, "The accommodations have certainly changed since my last visit, but I suppose that should be expected now that your father no longer oversees this grand house."

Her faint smile vanished, and her dark eyes flared with anger. "Do you know what happened to my father?"

Nagrand met her gaze without flinching. "I heard that he died in Bracordia. I was away at the time, so I have no knowledge regarding his premature death."

"I'm sure you don't," she drawled sarcastically. "His fear of death was quite satisfying. I forced him to watch as I killed my mother and my useless sister. He was weak and pathetic...crying, trembling, and begging while I tore their flimsy bodies into pieces. Nothing quite compares to the sounds of screams and breaking bones. Poor Father. He actually spewed vomit all over the floor when I drank their blood."

Nagrand's insides twisted as he resisted gory images rising before his mind's eye. "Your parents always showed me kindness. I consider their deaths a tragedy."

Her upper lip drew into an ugly, sneering curve. "Their demise fed my strength. I can see to it that you avoid such a death. Master and I can use your knowledge of the defenses Ambracor's king uses in his pitiful attempt to forestall our inevitable victory. Quicker victory for us will mean an end to this war and the beginning of a new order."

"And this new order would be what?"

She huffed a frustrated breath that blew stinking air from delicately flaring nostrils. "Power. Power for Master and wealth and comfort for those who willingly serve him. Those who resist will be forced into subservience, toiling to provide the luxuries and ease that Master has been unfairly denied throughout many ages."

Nagrand closed his eyes for a matter of seconds, hoping to calm the acidic rise in his stomach. Meeting her gaze once again, gray eyes studied her features. He remembered her soft, appealing beauty when he first met her years ago. That beauty had lost its glow, replaced now by cold harshness.

"Well?" she demanded, her voice rising sharply.

Nagrand faced her squarely, mentally steeling himself for whatever lay ahead. "You are most generous in your offer, Lady Breeneth, but I must decline. My allegiance is sworn to King Hamund. I am a man of my word."

"Fool!" she screeched. "Do you have any idea of the suffering Master can inflict on you? For that matter, perhaps my own power might give you cause to think!" Throwing up her hand, dark mist jetted from her fingers, lifting Nagrand from the floor and sending him flailing half the length of the room.

Landing hard with the breath knocked out of him, Nagrand lay still. On an intellectual basis, he had known her power. Still, actually experiencing it was shocking. Dragging himself into a sitting position, he realized he wasn't seriously injured...yet. Determined to conquer his own fears, he defiantly refused to look at her and remained silent.

Stalking toward him, she emanated a growing stench that made his eyes water. "You will submit. Sooner or later, you will!"

She reached out and grabbed a handful of his hair to jerk his head upward. Glowering at him as a sharp, stinging sensation shot through her fingers, she released him immediately. Snarling in anger, she again raised her hand and sent him skidding into the wall.

"How dare you resist me? What is this burning that happens when I touch you?" she demanded. When he only shook his head back and forth, too dazed to respond, she shouted shrilly, "Answer me!"

Catching his breath and speaking required considerable effort. "My Lady, I cannot explain that which I do not understand myself."

"Liar!" she shouted again, spitting on the floor in front of him. "Tell me now or prepare to face Master's wrath! He is not as patient as I."

Nagrand watched her spittle disappear in a sizzling burst of steam. He lifted his face and saw her eyes blazing with anger, her skin flushed scarlet. "No matter the consequences, how can I tell you what I do not know?"

A deep, echoing voice filled the room. "You bring pain to my beloved servant. I tolerate no such insolence."

Nagrand's eyes shifted toward the direction of the voice. The image of Breeneth's master exuded a sinister surge that carried with it a foul, reeking odor far worse than the smell around her. Tawny skin and slick black hair only magnified the fiendish smirk and fiery eyes of the demon who now strode forward with a menacing gait.

Nagrand suddenly screamed out from what felt like flames searing his skin. Abruptly raised off the floor, he felt himself twisted and turned in every direction. His own voice, crying out in agony, filled his ears until all he heard was fading laughter as he lapsed into unconsciousness.

Karan's glance shot up as Sindara gasped and dropped the blanket she was bundling. "Sindara! What's wrong? Are you all right?"

Grabbing Karan's arm, she staggered forward. "Help me sit down," she said, her voice weak and trembling.

Karan wrapped an arm around her waist and lowered her slowly to one of the cushions they had slept on. He took her face between his hands and stared into her eyes. Her pupils were dilated and her skin pale. Her breathing was shallow and quick. "Sindara, listen. You must try to breathe more slowly. Take a deep breath. Hold it a second. Let it out. Again. Again."

She strained to follow his instructions. Reaching into her tunic, she pulled out the crystal amulet that glowed brightly inside the shadowed lobby of the abbey. Forcing herself to concentrate, she gazed into the brightly shining light. "Kendra," she murmured.

"Sindara, are you all right?" Kendra's inquiry echoed Karan's words of just moments earlier.

"I will be. I just felt the demon master's power. His dark minions have already begun to rise, but what I felt was more than that."

"Sindara, tell me. What time of day is it there?" Kendra's voice intoned urgency.

"Morning. I'm not sure of the hour. Perhaps six or seven."

"Listen carefully. Are you in a safe place?"

"As safe as any, I think. Why, Kendra? What do you know?"

"Are you alone?"

"No, Karan is with me. Why? Kendra, what's happening? I... felt..." Although Karan only saw light, the crystal allowed Sindara to see Kendra's worried features. "Tell me what's going on."

"The master demon is starting to unleash his powers. I believe he just attacked a prisoner..." She hesitated. "I think it may have been Nagrand."

"Nagrand? Are you sure?" Sindara asked breathlessly, tears brimming in her eyes.

Karan sucked in an abrupt breath. "My brother! What has that vile creature done to him?"

"He's weak and hurt, but he's still alive," Kendra answered, her lower lip quivering. "You must listen to me."

Sindara ignored Karan's anxious grip. "What, Kendra?"

"Sindara, promise you'll do as I say. Swear it, because I'm working on getting critical information to help you."

"I can't just leave Nagrand alone there to face those devils."

"Sindara, do you still trust me?" Kendra asked, desperation saturating her words.

"Of course I trust you," Sindara answered. "Tell me what to do."

"Stay where you are until nightfall."

"Kendra! How…"

Kendra raised her voice. "Stay where you are! Don't risk going out! I promise you'll have help soon. You must listen. If you don't, you'll lose more than just Nagrand. You'll also lose Thehrund."

"Thehrund? What are you saying?" Sindara trembled harder. "Please, Kendra, don't tell me…"

"Yes, he's been taken prisoner. I think he'll be turned over to Breeneth today. That's why it's so important for you to pay attention and wait until tonight. Please, Sindara, I'm begging you. Trust me enough to wait to hear from me later this evening."

Sindara swallowed. Her jaw tensed painfully as tears streamed down her face. "Oh, Kendra, I cannot lose him. I cannot let them take him from me."

"Then do what I say. I swear I'm doing everything in my power to help. Just don't leave until tonight. Promise me, Sindara."

Weeping softly, Sindara nodded. "I shall wait, Kendra. I promise."

Kendra managed what she hoped was a comforting smile. "Keep faith, Sindara, and pray. I'll be praying while I work on getting you more help."

The light faded, leaving the gleaming crystal to appear as no more than a beautifully crafted pendant. Sindara's hands shook so hard she could barely lift the amulet high enough to drop it beneath the neckline of her tunic.

Karan's features were drawn taut with fear and anguish. "My brother...what did she say about my brother?"

"She says he's still alive, but that he's hurt." Sindara pressed her lips together in a vain attempt to avoid crying. "They've also captured Thehrund. He'll be delivered to Iglarm today."

Karan's shoulders drooped. His breath came in painful gulps as he felt like a terrible weight had fallen upon his chest. "I have to go. I have to save my brother," he muttered.

"No, Karan!" Sindara exclaimed, grabbing his arm and holding tightly.

"No! What do you mean? Nagrand needs me!" Tears glazed the priest's eyes.

"Karan, they've got Thehrund, too! Do you think for one second I don't wish to run from this place to save him?" Tears streamed down her face. "Karan, I trust Kendra with my life. Whatever she's doing, she will find a better way to help us. Believe me when I tell you there's no one I trust more to help save Thehrund and Nagrand. If you leave, we will surely lose them both."

Karan stood and paced, angrily kicking debris out of his way. "We'll lose a full day, Sindara!" he exclaimed. "We certainly can't travel in the dark. How can you just sit there and do nothing?"

Her face fell. She dragged in a breath fraught with fear. Closing her eyes, she pictured the Ambracada she had so carefully hidden. She remembered its power penetrating her hands and then flowing throughout her body. Invading calm soothed raw edges of her apprehension. Her breathing slowed to a more natural pace.

"I am doing something," she replied at last, her voice soft and subdued. "I'm placing total faith in Creator God. I shall pray with all my strength. I'll also keep my promise to Kendra. I trust her with more than my own life. I trust her with Thehrund's."

Chapter Twenty-Four

KICCHAK DISMOUNTED JUST OUTSIDE TALL gates of scrolled iron bars. Four of his warriors followed suit and waited by Thehrund's horse as the prince tightly gripped the pommel of his saddle and lowered himself to the ground. Ignoring his guards, he took a couple of steps forward and stroked the stallion's sleek head. Glancing up at Kicchak, his expression was dour. "What will you do with my horse?"

"What would you have me do with him?" Kicchak asked, somewhat puzzled by the prince's concern for the animal.

"He has served me well. I would like to have him set free."

Kicchak grunted. "You are an adversary who merits respect. I will see that the animal is stripped of his saddle and released in the forest nearby. He will be given his freedom and not be taken by my people."

Thehrund dipped his head respectfully. "I thank you for your gesture." He met Kicchak's curious gaze directly. "I sincerely regret that our mutual respect is born of enmity."

Kicchak ordered two warriors to take the horse to the forest and let it go. He then turned to deliver his prisoner to the Brandere mansion. Before they reached the manor's entrance, two Breyal chiefs galloped through the gates, each dismounting and hurriedly approaching the Grand Chieftain. Standing aside, they spoke to their leader in angry voices. Judging by Kicchak's severe expression, Thehrund concluded the news conveyed was bad.

The Breyal chieftain turned a furious expression toward Thehrund. "Go with these men. They will take you to a nearby camp. I will speak with the dark ones before I release you to them."

Thehrund's eyebrows lifted in question. "You will not deliver me now and claim your reward?"

Kicchak's face was flaming red with rage. "For now, you are *my* prisoner. Do not be so anxious to confront Thafalos and his consort. I have had personal experience with their powers."

Curiosity prompted every sort of speculation imaginable as Thehrund was set on a painted Breyal horse for a silent ride to the nearby encampment Kicchak had mentioned. Once there, he unconsciously assumed command mode as he estimated the number of warriors and noted both quality and quantity of their supplies and weaponry.

Within minutes of reaching the camp, he was roughly shoved into a small tent. He glanced around and listened to harsh voices and the clatter he associated with a war-ready bivouac. He crouched down and, unable to support or balance himself with bound hands, clumsily fell into a sitting position. He resigned himself to waiting for Kicchak.

By the position of the sun when he had ridden into the Breyal camp, he reckoned it had been mid-morning. Time alone inside the tent caused every minute to feel interminable. At one point, two Breyals entered. Within his reach, one set a plate in front of him with chunks of roasted meat and round pieces of flat bread crisped over an open flame. The other handed him a crescent-shaped canteen filled with water. The prince gave an elegant tilt of his head as thanks for the food.

Several Breyals later returned to the tent. One removed the plate and canteen while the others escorted Thehrund to a line of canvas-shaded latrines. On the way back to the tent, the prince's brow furrowed. The sun had moved far across the sky. Autumn's early twilight would soon be upon them. Struck by the ironic peculiarity of the thought, he was beginning to worry about why Kicchak had not returned.

"Are you absolutely sure?" Madalyn Amador's brown eyes studied Kendra's expression.

Kendra met the woman's questioning gaze. "I prayed long and hard. My guides and guardians agree."

Madalyn busied herself with packing, being sure to maximize the limited space available. "As connected as I've always felt to the universe's spirits, this goes far beyond any endeavor I ever might have considered."

"You said yourself many times that God gives our souls specific purpose. It is our responsibility to recognize and live the assignments our spirits accept as sacred missions."

"True. I can't argue that point, but this is such a drastic measure."

"No doubt. I just wish it hadn't taken me so long to figure things out."

"You haven't made a mistake in your timing. I'm not sure of the exact situation there, but I must believe this is the right time for a reason."

Kendra gave a slight shake of her head as she finished packing. "Except for an uncle and a few cousins who hardly know I'm alive, I think of Sindara as the only real family I have left. When we met at the Repository of the Guardians, I actually felt what her angel parents meant when they called us sisters-in-spirit. I've also thought repeatedly about what that man on the plane said as we were getting off. While we were chatting, I never mentioned the word *her*, but he knew I was missing a female friend. He also didn't say *if* I saw her again. He explicitly said 'when.' Then, suddenly, poof! He just disappears."

"Makes one really think on the saying that there's no such thing as coincidence," Madalyn remarked as she stuffed a few final items into the small rolling suitcase. Sighing heavily, she set the case on the floor. "Ready?"

"Ready," Kendra answered firmly. "Thanks so much for your help."

"You're welcome. Now, let's get you out into that desert one last time."

Marnee lovingly ran her hand along the dusty rose satin of one of Sindara's formal gowns. The fabric's fine texture was silky smooth beneath the aging servant's fingertips. Smiling to herself, she imagined how beautiful her beloved mistress would look in the gown she'd never had time to wear. The maid sighed, sadly thinking that Sindara had worn very few of the elegant dresses from her bridal trousseau.

Resuming her original task, Marnee selected some blouses and skirts for Irlini. The young woman had moved into a guest suite inside the prince's apartment to maintain the deception of Sindara's return to the palace. With Thehrund away commanding Ambracor's armies and the recent death of Rezda Varacor, palace staff had been informed that the princess desired a period of solitude to pray for her husband and mourn her dead brother.

Suspicious for some time that a few workers in the palace held allegiance to Breeneth Brandere, Marnee had approached Queen Narlina about continuing the masquerade Irlini began in Arvacon. Irlini, whose height and size were similar to Sindara's, could wear some of the princess's clothing and use some of her personal items. Laundry, meals, and discarded waste items would reinforce the impression that Sindara preferred to remain in seclusion. Both the queen and Cleotis Tamazor discussed the matter with Irlini. All agreed that the excuse would easily explain the princess's seclusion in her apartments with her longtime servant as her only constant company.

"I hope you will find these suitable," Marnee said as she carried several garments into the suite where Irlini sat reading a book.

The young woman looked up and smiled. "Thank you, Marnee. I'm certain they will do quite well."

"You were very brave to undertake such a dangerous mission," Marnee remarked as she hung the garments in a large armoire. "What prompted you to suggest impersonating my mistress?"

Irlini set her book aside. Standing, she went to stare through a window overlooking several acres of trees. "After my husband was killed in combat, my outlook on life changed completely. Grief was my constant companion. Part of me wanted to punish those who caused his death. Another part vowed to try to save others from such indescribable sorrow."

When Marnee turned from her task, she noted the young woman's profile and the telltale glistening of tears on her cheek. "I know it isn't the same, but my grief was overwhelming when I received word that my mistress was killed outside Articene. I had cared for her since she was just a baby. She was like my own child."

Irlini cast Marnee a sad smile. "My husband and I married not long before his death. I would give anything to have his child as comfort. Since I have nothing left but memories, I decided the next best thing was to honor his memory.

"I met Sindara years ago at school. Although we weren't close, I knew her reputation. When she arrived in Cahmdurn dressed for combat, I knew immediately that she planned to go to Bramond Province and confront Breeneth Brandere. That's when the idea entered my mind to draw attention away from her and perhaps gain extra time for her to reach Iglarm."

Curious, Marnee watched the play of emotions on Irlini's face. "How did you devise your plan?"

The young woman shook her head as if she could hardly believe the plan had succeeded. "I remembered reading someplace that conjurers and demons gravitate toward blood. I figured the scent of Sindara's blood must have been detected in Articene. Since Erator's wife is my cousin, I visited her and approached Countess Varacor. The countess and I then presented the idea to the princess. She expressed no reservations whatsoever about cutting her hair to reinforce her scent. I admit I still feel somewhat queasy when I remember her drawing a blade across her leg and soaking the blood into a large handkerchief." Irlini pointed at a small pouch lying on the nightstand by the bed. "I keep it with me."

"You think the palace is not safe?"

"Breeneth Brandere is too devious not to have spies among the staff here. As long as she thinks the princess is here, she will concentrate on getting the prince under her control. After that, her evil nature will inevitably bring her here to capture Sindara. She will force Prince Thehrund to witness his wife's murder."

"You sound convinced."

Irlini sat down and closed her eyes. "My husband is dead because of the evil likes of Breeneth. His sister-in-law is a distant relative of the Brandere family. I once thought the stories she told were mere make-believe and born of jealousy. Not anymore. I want that wicked woman stopped. If I thought I could do it myself, I would gladly go to Iglarm. Sindara's return from the dead is proof that she walks in blessed light. If she can't defeat Breeneth, I fear all of Ambracor will be lost. No matter what, I will resist this evil with my last breath."

Marnee gave Irlini a look filled with compassion. "A bit of advice from an old woman, Mistress Irlini. Your anger is justified. I also understand your desire for justice. The one thing you must not do is to allow your anger to build into hatred so great that you lose sight of all but revenge. Your husband died to preserve the peaceful life Ambracorans cherish. Your courage already honors him. You will continue to do him great honor by refusing to let Breeneth's wicked deeds destroy the integrity of the woman he loved."

Leaving Irlini in quiet contemplation, Marnee closed the suite's door and went to her own quarters. Donning a woolen cloak and locking the door to the prince's apartments behind her, the elderly servant walked through palace corridors. Her eyes carefully observed the behavior of everyone she passed. Outside, she breathed in fresh air. She paused to smile at the marble angel so loved by Thehrund and Sindara before going to the chapel to pray. Aware of a shadowy figure following her, she was glad to find others with whom she might share her prayers.

Marnee followed another servant and a soldier from the chapel. She glanced upward to see the moon peeking from behind a cloud. She closed her eyes for a matter of seconds. The night was quiet except for faint rustling from behind some bushes. She dawdled a few moments before continuing back to the palace.

Hearing slow, stealthy footfalls behind her, she maintained her pace before suddenly whirling around to confront whoever dared to follow her. The man behind her stopped short in surprise, but menace clearly marked his expression. She immediately recognized him as a palace groundskeeper.

"Why do you follow me?" she sternly demanded.

The man snorted. "Why do you think, old woman?" He stepped closer, his very posture a threat. "You will take me to the princess."

Marnee laughed. "How amusing. Do you honestly think I would betray my princess to the likes of you?"

The man produced a long, curved dagger and moved closer. "If you value your life, you will. Now, turn around and lead the way."

Marnee stood her ground. "You don't frighten me. Many soldiers patrol these grounds. You dare not attack."

The man's features curved into a snarling expression, and his eyes burned with inhuman ferocity. "I do not jest, old woman. Take me to the princess, and I will see that your death is quick and merciful."

"Perhaps you're the one who needs a quick and merciful demise," Marnee retorted as her arm snaked out with startling speed and snatched the gloved hand holding the dagger. Her grasp tightened with strength that shocked her attacker.

"Drop the knife!" she shouted.

When the assailant would have wrested free and escaped into darkness, Marnee stood firm. Knowing soldiers on guard would appear within seconds, the man struggled harder. Despite his twisting and pulling, the groundskeeper could not avoid the hand that Marnee forcefully shoved forward to place against his forehead. Her touch elicited an agonized howl, and the dagger bounced across the walk and onto the grass.

As soldiers raced toward them, the maid forced her attacker to his knees. When guards reached them and grabbed the assailant by the shoulders, Marnee, scowling angrily, met the questioning faces of the sentries.

"This man threatened to kill me if I didn't take him to Princess Sindara's quarters." She turned her attention to her attacker. Beneath dim moonlight, raw burns on his face were evident. "Your own evil intentions brought this injury upon you. I will never betray my princess. Those like you who desire to harm her will never succeed."

Marnee then spoke commandingly to the guards. "You are both anointed, so you are safe. Take him to a cell and lock him up. First, place a drop of the blessed oil on him and line his cell with sea salt. He will be powerless to escape."

As guards dragged their cursing prisoner away, Marnee closed her eyes for a few seconds and drew in a deep breath. Hurting another being gave her no sense of satisfaction. Resuming her walk to the palace, she paused again to gaze upon the angel sculpted so lovingly from gleaming marble. She murmured almost inaudibly, "Our secret remains safe. Thank you for coming to my aid."

Inside the derelict abbey, Sindara whiled away part of the day by righting furniture and organizing some of the clutter remaining from the hasty evacuation and subsequent ransacking. She even found a broom and swept as occasional bouts of weeping dripped tears onto dirty floors. The activity made little sense, but it occupied her time and shifted her thoughts from constant fear for Thehrund. Being separated from him again had been painful enough. Knowledge that he was being delivered to Breeneth and her demon lover was sheer agony. Tiring of her efforts, she finally rearranged cushions and tried to rest a while.

Karan had barely spoken since morning. Avoiding her, he wandered through buildings where he had also once studied and prepared for his vocation. Like Sindara, idle time wore on his nerves. For distraction, he picked up hundreds of books and piled them in neat stacks away from broken windows and doors where they would not be exposed to the elements. Inspecting damaged interiors, he noted that whoever Breeneth had sent to retrieve the Ambracada had ripped away at furnishings, cabinetry, and anything else they thought might conceal the sacred book. He breathed a grateful prayer that Master Zoman had acted so quickly on his urgent message. Many had died saving the sacred texts, but their spirits would rest peacefully because their sacrifice had not been in vain.

Later, Sindara sat on a step outside. Studying the map in her hand, she prayed for guidance. How hard it was to sit idle as daylight dwindled and twilight approached. She was glad Karan had finally taken the horses off for a chance to feed and drink from a nearby stream. His level of anxiety and impatience had begun to wear on her nerves. She could hardly blame him. Her own anxiety for Thehrund burdened her heart as nothing ever had. Despite swelling fears and apprehension, she trusted her friend. Never had Kendra failed her.

Looking up, she watched Karan slowly reappear from surrounding woods. His posture and his expression conveyed palpable gloom and dejection. He and Nagrand were extremely close. She knew Thehrund considered them both as the brothers he never had. Pausing to give him a wan smile, she returned her attention to the map.

"I'm surprised you haven't memorized that map by now," Karan mumbled crossly. "As hard as you're studying it, perhaps you can just wish us into Iglarm."

Setting the map aside, she gave him a thoughtful look. "Karan, from the very beginning, I planned to make this trip alone. You knew that, but you insisted on coming. If this isn't done correctly, both Nagrand and Thehrund will die. If that happens, I cannot begin to conceive of what will happen to Ambracor. One thing is sure. I'd rather die than lose Thehrund."

After hitching the horses to a nearby post, Karan entered the abbey. When he emerged, he handed Sindara some of their rations and fresh fruit Habron had given them for their trip. Settling himself on the step beside her, he stared at darkening skies. "I apologize. I know you're doing what you think best. I also realize the risks increase with every mile we travel during the day. Traveling by night is a sure way to get lost. It seems we're doomed whichever way we go."

Sindara bit into a tart apple. Chewing the crunchy bite and swallowing, she blinked back tears. "Nagrand once told me how difficult it was to maintain focus as the two of you accompanied Thehrund on the portal journeys. According to him, he had to remind Thehrund on the last trip of something Thehrund himself had said...exactly as you told me. Nagrand said he had urged Thehrund to believe in *when*, not *if*. Not long after, they saved me from that gang of criminals."

Karan released a short, breathy laugh. "I remember."

Sindara leaned sideways against Karan's arm. "We need to live that very same principle here."

Thehrund heard a thundering voice shouting commands outside the tent where he sat in solitude. Within minutes, Kicchak stormed inside to face his prisoner. Even in the tent's shadowy interior, the Breyal's black eyes gleamed with stark fury. "Get up!"

Drawing a deep breath of resignation, Thehrund struggled to stand. He shook his head sharply to flip long strands of hair from in front of his eyes. He met Kicchak's stern gaze without hesitation, but he waited for the other man to speak.

"Come," Kicchak barked as he held the tent's flap open for them to go outside.

Thehrund was surprised when Kicchak raised a sharp knife to cut the ropes binding his hands. Rubbing his wrists, he stared at the Breyal chieftain. Somewhat bewildered, the prince waited apprehensively to learn what was behind the chief's strange behavior and truculent mood. Glancing around, he also noted signs that the camp was breaking up.

"I am taking you to the dark ones, but I will deliver you with the respect due a great warrior. We eat first."

Perplexed, Thehrund sat in front of a large campfire. Kicchak quickly joined him. The two men were handed plates filled with hot food and fresh water in cups of hollowed-out gourds. Saying nothing, Thehrund followed the chieftain's lead and ate in silence, occasionally stopping to drink. There was no way to know how long before his next meal or even if this might be his last.

As he stared at yellow flames dancing above the stack of logs, Kicchak finally spoke. "What does the woman want with you?"

Thehrund glanced around. "You refer to Breeneth, I assume?"

"Yes. I find her determination to have you strange for someone who claims devotion to Thafalos."

"What she wants is marriage that will give her formal right to the crown of Ambracor," Thehrund replied flatly.

"So, she plans to force you to marry her? She wishes to be your queen?"

Thehrund nodded. "That is what she wants, but it is something she will not have."

"Do you not find her beautiful?" Kicchak asked curiously.

"I did once, long ago. I soon realized hers is a character I could never trust. Especially now, knowing things she has done and how she defiles herself with her demon master, I would never marry her. Besides, I have a wife who is beautiful, brave, and strong."

"Ah, yes, the woman who escaped the war party sent to capture her. I understand she now hides away in the king's house in Bracordia."

Thehrund barely restrained a smile. Irlini's idea had apparently succeeded. "I'm certain Sindara does not hide away. My father thinks of her as a daughter. He will keep her under guard for her own safety."

Kicchak emitted a rude grunt. "The dark woman, Breeneth, is hateful and contemptible. She and Thafalos have lied to me again and again. I received word earlier that their promises of help from the underworld proved worthless. Your armies defeated a large number of my warriors as they attempted to cross the twin bridges over the big river five days' ride north of here. Thafalos sent his demon soldiers, but they were few and were quickly destroyed when the heavens awoke with killing winds. I ask you. Why did those winds not destroy our armies?"

Thehrund leaned forward and stared at the ground, grateful that his hair concealed his satisfaction. "My people believe in a Creator God who made all that is in our world and all that we see in the heavens above. In a past too long ago for any of us to remember, some of those he created saw Creator God's power and wanted it for themselves. They rebelled and were cast out of the perfect existence he gave them. They were then forced to reside in dark and distant places.

"Creator God sent his loyal servants...those we call angels...to search for them. They convinced some to return to the light. Many of the rebellious ones were too proud and too hungry for power to listen. The strongest of them are like Thafalos. They seek to take what does not belong to them through violence and torture. They actually feed on fear and death, growing stronger with each life destroyed. As they grow stronger, they free lesser devils to serve them. I can only conclude that Creator God's angels came to banish the weaker demons."

"So, your people believe this war increases power for the dark one?" Kicchak asked.

Thehrund straightened and gave the Breyal a direct, unwavering gaze. "It is so. Even you must have noticed how long it took Thafalos to summon his weaker minions. He needs our animosity...the pain, death, and grief caused by our battles...to feed his power, just as you and I need food and water for our bodies to live each day."

Kicchak thoughtfully considered his prisoner's words. Iglarm's dark ones had already claimed his brother's life. They had then promised him great rewards for fighting their battles and severe punishment for his own wives and children should he fail. He had tasted their power once. He had no wish to do so again.

"It is time to go," he said at length, his expression brooding.

In silence, the two men mounted horses and, accompanied by half a dozen warriors, headed toward the Brandere mansion. Riding through gates opened by armed sentries, the party reached the front of the manor where they were met by two Bramond militiamen and a third wearing a captain's uniform. The Breyals remained on their horses while Thehrund dismounted.

Somber regret showed on Kicchak's face as he cast a final glance at Thehrund. He then turned an intimidating look to the militia officer. "Inform Thafalos and his woman that I have met the terms of our agreement. It is their turn to fulfill their side by releasing my family."

When the chieftain turned his horse to leave, he suddenly stopped. Far in the distance, he and his warriors stared at what appeared to be a spinning cloud emitting sparks of multi-colored lights. The phenomenon lasted only moments and then abruptly vanished. Kicchak sharply twisted his head for a final glance at Thehrund before leaving to rejoin his departing camp. As he galloped away from the mansion, his mind's eye clung to the image of Thehrund's features, especially the mysterious smile that lit the prince's face for scant seconds.

"What's that sound?" Sindara asked urgently as she ran from a lavatory that was miraculously still functional.

Karan cast a worried glance in her direction. "I'm not sure," he muttered in a hushed voice. He hurried to the door and edged it open. Practically paralyzed with amazement, he stared through the narrow opening.

Sindara rushed to him. "Karan! What is it?" she hissed into his ear. When he only shook his head, she shoved him aside and peered out into the night. The sight of a twinkling whirlwind met her astonished stare.

Crackling leaves swirled skyward as a distinct hum filled the air. Following two dull thuds, the hum abruptly ended, and the whirlwind dissipated, leaving in its wake a shower of dry leaves floating downward.

Without thinking, Sindara swung the door wide and ran outside. In the center of the plaza were two large humps and a seated figure swaying drunkenly beneath layers of leaves. Never once considering possible risks, Sindara rushed toward the center of the square and stopped just short of the bizarre image before her.

"D...don't...just...stand there...staring at me..." the familiar voice stammered. "H...help me...up!"

With a wide, disbelieving grin, Sindara hurried forward and steadied Kendra with hands firmly holding her shoulders. "Just breathe. Breathe deeply and slowly. The dizziness passes quickly."

As the dizzy spell gradually faded, Kendra looked at Sindara's features with shock in her eyes. "Remind me of this should I ever again consider this mode of travel."

Unable to restrain laughter or tears, Sindara threw her arms around Kendra and hugged her tightly. "I can hardly believe my eyes! Is it really you? What kind of insanity brought you here?"

With her typical humor quickly returning, Kendra pulled away and gave her friend a wry grin. "I think the insanity is called a portal. I came because you need help. Together, we can set things right again."

Karan lingered a few moments before approaching them. "Kendra, I wish I could welcome you under more pleasant circumstances. You have taken a tremendous risk coming here."

"Hello, Karan," Kendra greeted him with a hug. "Whether or not you believe it, I do know the risks. I also know that Sindara and I together can create a formidable force to stop the evil powers at work. If we don't, the evil here threatens to spill over into other dimensional planes. The demon master in Ambracor is likely the worst of them all."

"Come," Sindara said as she led Kendra by the hand toward the abbey. Karan had already picked up the two bags that had fallen from the portal with their unexpected visitor.

Inside, Kendra cast a wary glance at the two draft horses. "Quite a fancy barn you have here."

Sindara just shook her head, her spirits instantly lifted by her friend's presence. "This was the abbey at our Sacred Halls of Faith Center. Everyone was forced to flee when they came to destroy the Ambracada. We thought it best to keep the horses and ourselves out of sight."

"I hope they didn't destroy the book," Kendra remarked, remembering what Sindara and Thehrund had told her of the ancient texts.

"They did not," Karan replied, "thanks to Sindara's timely warning, a brave courier on a swift horse, and men and women who sacrificed their lives delivering the book to safety."

Regret for lives lost shadowed Kendra's features. "I'm glad the book is safe. My goal now is to help you stop more loss of life. We really should start out now. If we hurry, I think we can reach our destination morning after next."

Sindara's eyebrows lifted. "Kendra, it's dark outside. We'll surely get lost and never arrive in time to save Nagrand and Thehrund."

"Is there a place I can safely stash this?" Kendra asked, ignoring Sindara's comment and pointing to her suitcase before putting her arms through the straps of a nylon backpack.

"You can leave the bag practically any place. The center is deserted, and everyone is afraid to come here. Was I not clear? It's too dark for travel."

Kendra took Sindara's hand and led her back outside. Pointing to clear night skies glittering with innumerable stars, Kendra smiled. "An elderly gentleman asked me to tell you something when I saw you again. I guess it's time for that message. First thing..."

Wrapping her arms around Sindara's shoulders, Kendra squeezed tightly once, then a second time. "He told me to give you two hugs. He then said to remind you to look at the stars and remember that you have a very stubborn guardian angel watching over you."

Golden irises reflected moonlight. With her lips quivering, Sindara whispered, "Grandfather? You actually spoke with my grandfather?"

"So that message really does mean something to you?"

Mystified, Sindara glanced around at Karan. "Grandfather and I always loved stargazing. It makes sense now. We can navigate by the stars without stopping so often during the day to hide from passing enemy patrols. When I was little, Grandfather always promised to ask Creator God to let him be my guardian angel. He also told me what a stubborn guardian angel he'd be."

Kendra smiled curiously. "And the two hugs? He was very specific."

Sindara didn't know whether to laugh or cry. "He always said one hug was never enough. He always wanted two."

Feeling reassurance trickle into his being, Karan breathed out a heavy sigh. "Ladies, it is early. If we really must travel by night, Kendra is right. We should get started."

Sindara paused long enough to squeeze Kendra's hand and kiss her cheek. "A better sister no one could ever have."

Bundling Kendra's backpack with their other travel gear and supplies, Sindara and Kendra mounted one of the horses while Karan rode the other with the travel bags. Grateful for clear skies, Sindara looked up and studied the positions of the stars.

"Thank you, Grandfather," she murmured as they began their trek through the forests of Bramond.

Chapter Twenty-Five

Flanked by two guards and following the militia captain, Thehrund strode through the familiar entrance and corridors of the Brandere mansion. Still clad in leather brigandine over hauberk and gambeson and wearing sturdy bracers on his forearms, he exuded an air of both strength and command despite his prisoner's status. Piercing blue eyes stared straight ahead as his escort led him to the manor's throne room.

Once inside, he quickly scanned the surroundings. Once the site of lavish dinner parties and crowded celebrations, the room's unpleasant odor struck him first. The smell was not one of neglect or lack of cleanliness. It was pervasive and disagreeable. The décor no longer shone with elegant wallpaper, brightly polished chandeliers, or welcoming banquet table and chairs inviting visitors to stay and partake of sumptuous foods and animated conversation. The hall was virtually empty of furniture except for a chaise, a throne, and a small table at the far end. Silver chandeliers and wall sconces now held black tapers topped with yellow flames that cast sinister plays of light and shadow.

Movement at the far end of the room caught his eye. He watched as the fine figure of a man entered and sat upon the throne. Wearing flowing robes of burgundy velvet with extravagant trim, the man projected an arrogant bearing noticeable even from a distance. His right hand raised from the arm of the throne and signaled the prince to approach.

"Welcome to Iglarm, Prince Thehrund. I invite you to approach the throne." The voice was low. Its strange echo reverberated off the walls of the nearly empty chamber.

Cautiously, Thehrund bowed his head and walked forward. Whatever game might be in the offing, he felt his best chance to reach Nagrand would be to play along. "Your welcome is appreciated. You will kindly forgive me if I am uncertain how you wish me to address you."

Thafalos chuckled derisively. "*Your Majesty* will do quite well for the time being."

"Your Majesty," Thehrund repeated smoothly, "I thank you for your unexpected welcome."

The demon thoughtfully studied his prize prisoner. "I imagine you are fatigued after your recent travels. I know you are a well-educated and highly cultured man. I expect your boorish Breyal escort was less than stimulating. I imagine you might appreciate a good meal, a clean bed, and time to rest."

Thehrund could hardly avoid wondering about the intended direction of this audience with the demon. "I do not regret time spent in their company. Observing different peoples can be rather interesting, but continuous travel is tiresome."

Thafalos responded with a smile Thehrund could only describe as cynical. "I suppose you wonder why you are not being greeted by Lady Breeneth."

"Your Majesty," Thehrund began, trying not to choke on the words, "considering you have assumed rule over Bramond, your status makes this initial meeting more appropriate."

The demon again chuckled. "I find you quite curious, Prince Thehrund. You stand as captive before one who holds power to decide whether you live or die, yet you show no sense of fear or indignation. Why is that?"

Thehrund met the black-eyed demon's direct gaze and suppressed a shiver. "I doubt your power for not a single moment, Your Majesty. Any show of fear or indignation would be a meaningless waste of energy. Whatever your intentions, any feelings on my part would have little influence on final results."

Thafalos rose from his throne and approached Thehrund. Assuming an intimidating posture, he slowly circled the much taller prince. "You are an outstanding specimen of the human race. You obviously work hard to build your body into an excellent example of masculine strength. Your bearing is that of one accustomed to privilege and control. Your father, at least what remains of him, must have taught you well in the ways a king should conduct himself."

Thehrund refused to be baited into a display of temper. "My father taught me discipline and wisdom."

Thafalos stopped directly in front of Thehrund, his face only inches from the prince's. "I admire a human with your rare self-control. I better understand why my devoted Breeneth was so insistent that we bring you to our side. The image you project is one that will most certainly expedite Ambracor's acceptance of my reign. You would ease the transition of control over vast resources that will satisfy my desires and give you the life of luxury that is rightfully yours."

Black, sweeping eyebrows rose high. Blue eyes shone with icy coolness. "With all respect due one with your legendary powers, I project nothing for the sake of appearances. This image to which you refer is one developed from a foundation of education and faith. In truth, it is no image; it is substance."

The demon tossed his head backward and laughed heartily. "Such prideful words from a man who stands before one who could crush him within a matter of seconds! I do admire you, Prince Thehrund. Few have ever dared to speak to me as you just did."

The prince's expression remained impassive. He breathed in as deeply as he dared of the reeking air around him. Again, he waited for the demon's next move. With some surprise, he watched the devil step away.

When Thafalos turned back, his expression and his voice transformed from taunting to menacing. "What I expect from you is simple. Your image, however you wish to define it, is required to pacify your people. It is my decision that you will marry Breeneth. Ambracor's crown will then legitimately fall under my scope of control. My beloved servant will be your queen and satisfy desires she dreams to fulfill."

Thehrund stared at a carved figure on the demon's throne. "I will not marry Breeneth. I have a wife already."

The demon's face darkened at the prince's audacity to refuse him. "I will declare your marriage null and void."

Thehrund finally met the demon's gaze with a frigid glare. "You deceive yourself if you think you have such power. My avowal to my wife was made before witnesses and according to the laws of Creator God."

"I do have the power!" Thafalos roared, his pride insulted and his patience evaporating. "Your Creator God possesses no influence here! I will make certain you have no wife to encumber my plans for you to marry Breeneth! Do you understand?"

Thehrund subdued rising rage. He responded in a voice that was both calm and unwavering. "Perhaps you are the one who must learn to understand. My marriage will never be ended by the likes of you or Breeneth Brandere. It bears power you cannot defeat. We call that power love."

The demon cackled with amused sarcasm. "You will learn to obey me," he said disparagingly as he sent Thehrund flying through the air with a mere flick of his wrist. "What you need is time to consider all consequences should you continue your obstinacy."

When Thehrund awoke, he found himself lying upon a scant layer of dirty straw scattered across stone floors. He closed his eyes and mentally assessed his body, which felt like one enormous ache. Slowly moving toes, feet, legs, and then fingers, hands, and arms, he sighed relief that no bones seemed to be broken. Rolling onto his side, he pushed himself up on one elbow before painfully sitting upright.

"Thehrund?"

The prince quickly glanced around at the sound of his name. Sitting with his back against the rock wall, Nagrand's sigh contained both relief and anxiety.

"Nagrand!" Thehrund exclaimed quietly, quickly dragging himself to his friend's side. "Thanks be to Creator God that you're still alive! What have they done to you?"

"Alive only by the grace of Creator God. I've had encounters with both Breeneth and her master. None ended well. I've been thrown into the air, twisted into nearly impossible positions, slammed onto floors, and sent skidding into walls. Their abilities are astonishing. What about you? And why in the name of Creator God did you come after me? That's why you're here, isn't it?"

Thehrund reached out and grasped Nagrand's shoulder. "Had roles been reversed, you would have done exactly the same. You are like my brother. I had to try to save you."

Nagrand shook his head weakly. "I expect the worst now. They will use me as a weapon against you."

Involuntary tears brimmed in Thehrund's eyes. "Nagrand, you mustn't lose faith. You must believe that help will come...that we'll both be saved."

"Faith is all that keeps me alive. That and..." He glanced upward, his eyes signaling Thehrund to be quiet. Footsteps were approaching.

Lying back on the floor, Thehrund feigned continued unconsciousness. Nagrand remained still and quiet. He was surprised when he saw the hurried motions of Berdran, who quickly tossed some bags of food toward Nagrand along with an oilskin filled with water. Furtively glancing around and listening for guards, he gave Nagrand a smile that looked more like a grimace. "I must go before they see me. I will help if I can," he whispered before disappearing around a far corner.

Thehrund sat up again. "That man. Who is he?"

Pity filled Nagrand's eyes. "Breeneth's brother."

"Berdran?" Thehrund asked incredulously. "His face! It's hardly more than scars!"

"He disagreed with his sister."

"Do you trust him?" Thehrund asked, concerned that Berdran might be acting on orders from his sister and delivering food laced with poison or other mind-altering potions.

Nodding, Nagrand opened small portions of food wrapped in leaves that could be eaten, thus leaving no remnants of the life-sustaining contraband. "Here. It isn't much, but it's better than the slop they serve prisoners."

Thehrund willingly drank a little water but declined the food. "I ate quite well not long before they took me to Breeneth's demon. You need it far more than I."

"You're sure?" Nagrand asked, his stomach rumbling with hunger.

"Eat."

Gratefully, Nagrand finished the portions quickly. Drinking from the oilskin and then hiding it under a pile of straw, he wearily leaned back. "Have you seen her yet?"

"Breeneth? No, not yet. Only her master. Which reminds me," Thehrund said in a low voice. "If you haven't heard, his name is Thafalos. Karan said knowing a demon's name gives you more power to resist."

"I wish I had known that days ago. How did you find out?"

"Kicchak told me."

"Kicchak?" Nagrand's dull eyes sparked with surprise. "The Breyal leader?"

"I think the Breyals never would have escalated hostilities had Thafalos not manipulated circumstances. From what I overheard, Thafalos murdered Kicchak's brother and now holds Kicchak's family hostage. He dares not defy the demon."

Nagrand's head drooped. "Never have I felt so weak or so weary in my entire life. Even if it means death, I will be glad when this ends."

Thehrund firmly grasped Nagrand's hand. "You have the strength to resist. You must trust me. I believe with all my heart that we both shall be delivered from this living nightmare."

Prison darkness was alleviated only by light from a single torch stuck in a bracket on a far corridor wall. Nagrand whispered, "The medicine bags...as far as I can tell, they have no effect on the demon. When Breeneth actually touches me, there is a difference. Each time, she jerks away in pain. I rubbed the oily pad on my forehead and over my heart. I'm sure it helps. Remember that."

Clenching his jaw in anger, Thehrund urged Nagrand to rest. Listening to his friend's shallow breathing, the prince retreated to prayer. He begged Creator God to deliver Nagrand safely from the clutches of Thafalos and Breeneth. He pleaded for Sindara's safety and an end to his people's suffering. Tired and hurting, he then escaped into the welcome refuge of exhausted sleep.

Eyes the color of ebony flared with undisguised depravity. Lips of dark red spread into the smile he had once thought excitingly beautiful. Her figure retained all of the voluptuous curves that had so thrilled him when they first met. The form-fitting bodice of her elegant gown accentuated her slender waist. Yards of black satin, embroidered with silver threads, flared from her waist and rustled softly as she glided toward him. Her approach carried an air tainted with a faint, disagreeable odor masked by expensive perfume. When she stopped in front of him, she sighed heavily with satisfaction.

Seeing her attention fixed on him, Thehrund waited for Breeneth to speak while regretting ever becoming involved with her. He could hardly avoid wondering if her relationship with Thafalos had begun before or after his affair with her.

"I have long missed you, Thehrund. Good morning. Welcome back to Iglarm." Her smile softened. "It appears you've had a trying journey."

With a slight nod, Thehrund replied, "I have traveled much of late. Fatigue is natural."

Breeneth laughed quietly. "I know Master has already spoken to you. I will see to it that you are shown to a guest suite where you'll be served breakfast. After that, you can rest while servants launder your clothes and take measurements for new ones. You will need a wardrobe more appropriate for the prince of Ambracor and, of course, new clothing for our wedding."

Thehrund frowned. "Breeneth, I tell you as I told your master. I will not marry you. I have already married Sindara. Nothing you say or do will change that fact."

Invading rage instantly marred Breeneth's features. "Master will declare an end to your marriage, and I will ensure that Sindara Varacor does not live to interfere with my plans."

Thehrund shook his head. "Your master's powers do not supersede those of Creator God. As I already informed him, he has not the power to end my marriage."

"Oh, but he does," Breeneth sneered. "So do I. Sindara will soon die, and Master promises me the pleasure of ending her life. I will not leave the task to an inept band of Breyal warriors this time. I will kill her myself and relish every drop of her blood that I drink."

Sickened by her threat, Thehrund's blue eyes blazed furiously. "I refuse to play your games, Breeneth. Your war is with me, and I swear to you one thing. If ever you hurt Sindara again, you will face my personal retribution."

"Oh!" Breeneth exclaimed in mock fear. She then snarled hatefully, "The prisoner dares threaten the captor who would place him on a throne of man and remind him of the great pleasures to be found in her love."

"You know nothing of love," Thehrund ground out. "You know only that which serves your self-centered, depraved aspirations."

"Ah, my dear Thehrund, how you misunderstand me," she said in a taunting voice as she reached out to caress his cheek. Suddenly jerking her hand away, she stared at him with undisguised bewilderment. "What is this vile thing you do?"

Thehrund stared in surprise. "I have no idea what you mean."

"Your touch! You burned me! I demand to know how!" she screamed.

"May I remind you that you were the one who touched me?"

Every shred of Breeneth's self-control evaporated in fury. Raising her hands, she lifted Thehrund's body into the air and sent him flailing across the room. Storming toward him, she glared at where he lay sprawled on the floor. A flick of her wrist sent him skidding into the wall. "You have until tomorrow to agree to marry me. In the meantime, you can return to your stinking cell with your fellow prisoner. If you continue to defy me, you will watch him die a most unpleasant death."

Nagrand looked up at the sound of boots treading on stone floors. The jailer opened the barred door and waited as two guards shoved a limp Thehrund into the tiny cell and departed. The jailer emitted his shrill, sinister laugh as he turned the iron key in the lock. "Quite a pair, the two of you. A word of advice. It is not wise to make the lady of the house angry. Her master is very possessive and greatly enjoys inflicting agony on mere humans who resist her."

The prince, in pain and severely shaken, glanced upward. "Do you speak from experience?" he inquired hoarsely.

"The human who once lived in this body dared to resist. When Master destroyed him, he saved the body for me." The jailer cackled, his laughter echoing through the corridors long after he disappeared from sight.

Thehrund slowly sat up, rolling his neck and shoulders while trying to restore order to dazed thoughts. He tasted blood in his mouth where his teeth had pierced the sensitive inside of his lip. Nausea assaulted his empty stomach.

Nagrand reached out and placed a hand on his shoulder. "Are you badly hurt?"

"I'm sure I could be much worse."

"Don't blame yourself, Thehrund," Nagrand said in a comforting tone, reading his friend's expression. "No one could have foreseen this."

Thehrund shook his head. "I wish I could believe that. If she carries through on threats she made today, I will never forgive myself."

"What did she threaten this time?" Nagrand hated asking, but he needed to know.

"Thafalos intends to annul my marriage, murder Sindara, and force me to marry Breeneth. He plans to give Breeneth rightful claim to Ambracor's throne." Tears slid from the corners of Thehrund's eyes. He stared at the straw-littered floor. "She said I have until tomorrow to agree. If I refuse, she said they'll make me watch as they kill you."

Nagrand leaned his head back against the wall. "I'm surprised she hasn't killed me already."

"You were right. Your life is her weapon against me." After a prolonged pause, he continued thoughtfully, "You were right about something else. She touched my face and jerked away. She demanded to know how I had burned her. We must think of some way to turn that into an advantage."

Nagrand shook his head. "Even if she allowed either of us close enough to touch her, Thafalos would intervene. No, we must place our lives in Creator God's hands and prepare to face the morrow."

With well-practiced dexterity, Erator Varacor slid his hands into heavy gauntlets and tugged them until they covered the lower edges of bracers studded with sharp metal points. Dressed for battle, he glanced toward his right where King Hamund sat upon a chestnut steed. Both king and horse wore chainmail that gleamed in the light of the fort's torches and lanterns. Erator had strongly opposed the king's decision to join a midnight ride to intercept advancing Breyal tribes. He finally had no choice but to concede to the king's authority and allow him to accompany the battle-hardened regiment preparing to depart Articene.

"I remind you, General Varacor," Hamund called out as the troop rode through the fort's massive gates, "I want no excessive deference shown to me. I will fight as any other mounted officer. If today is my last day to draw breath, then I shall draw that breath defending my people. Is that clear?"

Erator nodded his understanding. "My officers and soldiers are informed, Your Majesty. They know their duty and will offer you no more help than they would any other soldier on the field."

"Command is yours, Erator. May Creator God bless us all."

Although he didn't favor riding at night, an immense war party was traveling so fast Erator was convinced he did not dare delay moving troops into defensive positions. He kept his garrison on rotating shifts just so fresh regiments could be ready at a moment's notice, day or night, to move into combat-ready positions. The day had been dreary with overcast skies as dark clouds moved eastward. Despite their biting chill, he preferred the night's stiff winds over cold rain. Troops and horses' hooves could march without the sucking effect of muddy roads and paths.

Well before dawn, Erator ordered his troops to prepare for combat. Fires from the enemy camp glowed over the horizon. Scouts reported that Breyals had gathered and begun their advance. Brilliant light from a half-moon cast strange shadows across the broad, rolling landscape ahead. Erator glanced up at clearing skies, unsure if the light meant salvation or doom for his soldiers. Holding his right hand high in the air, he watched and waited for the imminent assault. The cries of enemy warriors suddenly filled the night with a great uproar, and the general signaled his regiments to meet the attack.

Archers, lining high points above broad meadows, released waves of arrows at the enemy's front lines. Foot soldiers braced themselves and met the brutal onslaught of ferocious Breyal fighters who escaped the rain of arrows. Horses snorted and stomped as their riders swung swords with lethal power and worked in unison to herd Breyals into open spaces vulnerable to the deadly aim of Ambracor's skilled archers.

Erator shouted a string of commands to his officers as opposing ranks rushed forward to break through the line of defenders. Mounted troops chased down small groups of warriors attempting to circle around and attack the main body of soldiers from behind. The general spared a quick glance and could hardly believe the sight of his maimed king expertly pivoting his horse around and back again as he swung his sword with the ferocity of a man years his junior.

Erator had grown so accustomed to the cries and moans of wounded and dying that he hardly noticed the sound. His mind focused on a single goal...bringing this newest battle to a quick end. In concert with his lead officers, he raced toward enemy warriors in a skilled strategy of preventing them from splintering into separate units that could attack from different directions.

King Hamund drew on strength he never realized was his. He saw every Breyal warrior as a menace to his wife and son, thus taking their attack personally. He charged at many, knocking them over and trampling them beneath the iron-clad hooves of his horse. Swinging his sword with deadly accuracy, he felled warriors unlucky enough to run within the broad sweep of his long arm.

Blood splattered men and horses as the battle raged beneath the golden rays of a rising sun. Breyal leaders roared orders, attempting to regroup their fighters for a renewed push against the soldiers from Articene. Erator shouted fresh commands to his officers and troops, warning them to prepare for yet another thrust.

Suddenly, Breyal soldiers closed ranks and started backing away, their faces raised skyward. Erator raced toward King Hamund and abruptly reined in his horse. The king's eyes had also been drawn to the spectacle taking place in the skies above them. A great hush, broken only by low moans from those felled in battle, descended over bloody chaos strewn yet again across vast grassy fields.

The celestial scene above inspired fear in many, faith and hope in others. Hamund exchanged an astonished glance with his general. Again, he gazed up at the astounding image of two stars beginning to merge as one, their convergence creating brilliant shafts of light shining down from the heavens. Superstitious Breyals huddled together, pointing at the stars and looking to their leaders for direction. Troops from Ambracor mouthed words of praise to Creator God, believing the extraordinary convergence to be a divine sign.

※ ※ ※

Following yet another restless night, Artrian Varacor quietly left bed, donned a warm robe, and slid his feet into fleece-lined slippers. Padding down a back staircase, he walked through his still-sleeping household and went outside through a side door. Strolling along paths he could follow with eyes closed, he hardly noticed chilly breezes blowing through his long hair. His heart ached with unsettled emotions.

He had visited Rezda's grave daily since the somber funeral. At times, he raged at Creator God for taking from him the son whom he loved so much. How unfair it was for Rezda to die when he had such a lovely young wife so close to bearing their first child. As his rages played themselves out, he begged forgiveness. His grief was stronger than his will to bear it.

He pleaded with Creator God to protect Erator, the courageous general leading armies along Ambracor's eastern border with Breyal. Fervent appeals were lifted for divine protection of the daughter who believed her life had been spared so that she might return to protect her home and confront the evil that had nearly killed her. Drained emotionally, he left the cemetery for home each day and locked himself away in his bedchamber. With minimal success, he sought some measure of rest before striving to deal with issues facing the war-torn province continuously turning to him for guidance and wisdom.

Finding himself near the ancient oak tree his father had always loved, Artrian leaned against its sturdy trunk. Wrapping his arms around it and resting his forehead against its rough bark, he let his mind roam into the past. How hard his aging father had pushed him to assume leadership of Arvacon Province. Artrian had argued the point, convinced his father was still entirely capable and the son far too inexperienced to manage the vast responsibilities of Ambracor's busiest, richest province. Those early years had tried his patience and challenged his intellect. He had often resented his father's stubborn insistence on naming Artrian as Arvacon's youngest governor in history.

As of late, Artrian had thought more often of the father who had governed Arvacon when the province had begun to grow and prosper. With a faint smile, Artrian recalled how his father had taken great pains to include him, even as a boy, in meetings covering every aspect of provincial governance. Encouraging his son to ask questions and spending hours explaining fine details, Artrian's father had quickly recognized his son's sharp intelligence, analytical skills, and natural diplomatic finesse. As difficult as it was to admit, the beleaguered count suddenly realized how much he now appreciated that early, rigorous training.

Turning to lean back against the solid support of the nearly naked tree, Artrian closed his eyes and raised his face heavenward. "Father, forgive me for all the times I doubted your judgment," he spoke aloud. "My heart is broken for the son I just buried. I fear for Erator and Sindara. I know now that I'm able to face this because of all you taught me. I want you to know that I always loved and respected you, even when we disagreed."

Swallowing several times, he blinked back unbidden tears. Artrian finally held his eyes open, determined to watch the sunrise create a new day in which he might manage his grief and ease burdens bearing down on citizens of his beloved Arvacon. The sight that filled his vision prompted both shock and awe. Two distinctly different stars were moving toward one another, the sparkling glow of each beginning to touch. Transfixed, he stared as the stars appeared to merge into one great light.

Artrian's lips moved rapidly in silent prayer. The stellar display shone from the direction of Bramond Province. His heart jolted within his chest. A brief memory shafted through his brain. He suddenly recalled his father telling Sindara that one day he would be her guardian angel. Tears rolled down Artrian's face.

"Father, don't let them hurt her. Please...I beg you. Don't let them take my daughter from me again."

Sindara gazed skyward. Twilight receded, and nighttime's velvety hues darkened the heavens. Stars twinkled merrily. Digging deep into memory, she pictured dozens of star charts her grandfather had drawn decades before her birth. Some odd notation teased her thoughts.

"What are you thinking?" Kendra asked as they prepared to mount the horses for their final approach to Iglarm.

"What was it you said my grandfather told you?"

"About what?"

"Something about stars, I think."

"He just said to remember to look toward the stars. Why?"

Before she could reply, a nearby disturbance prompted them to sudden silence. Listening intently, they heard sounds rustling the undergrowth. Both Sindara and Karan quietly slid their swords from scabbards and held them ready. To their dismay, the horse Sindara held tossed his head upward and whickered just as a large, dark form emerged from a moonlit section of forest and snorted back.

Sindara gasped as the stallion trotted toward her. "Kufu!" she exclaimed softly, stroking her fingers through the horse's mane while combing out twigs tangled in the coarse hair.

Karan shook his head as Kendra stared. "I don't believe it."

"Someone has removed his saddle and halter," Sindara remarked as she ran her hands along the horse's back and muscular flanks. He must have escaped a stable or corral. Judging by the dust and brush clinging to him, I'd say he's been loose a few days."

Curiosity prompted Kendra to ask, "Whose horse is it?"

"Thehrund's," Sindara replied worriedly. "It's maybe a blessing in disguise. We now have three horses, which gives us more mobility and possibilities once we reach Iglarm."

Brushing off the horse's back, Sindara beckoned to Karan for help in mounting. "I'll ride him."

"Are you sure you should do that?" Kendra asked, doubtfully eyeing the powerful, spirited steed.

Karan managed a grin. "She was born and bred in Arvacon Province, as was this horse. Without a bridle and reins, she's much more competent at handling a stallion like Kufu than either one of us."

Traveling as quietly as possible, they rode for several hours before Sindara signaled a stop. Gracefully lowering herself from Kufu near the edge of a clearing, she held her hand up, signaling the others to wait. Lifting her eyes again to skies bedecked with jewel-like stars, she heard her grandfather's voice echoing through her mind.

"My sweet Sindara," he had said, "your life holds great purpose. I've always loved watching the stars. They give us many messages. I want you to study my star maps and remember their movements I've charted for you. They'll help you know when the right time has come to fulfill Creator God's call to preserve his light for our world."

Karan finally dismounted and approached her. "What's wrong?" he whispered into her ear.

"Nothing," she whispered back, pointing upward.

Seeing only multitudes of stars and a silver half-moon, Karan shrugged his shoulders. "I don't understand."

"Do you see those two bright stars there?" Receiving his nod, she smiled. "They're moving toward convergence. They will cross just after dawn and still be visible well after sunrise. We must reach Iglarm first."

Karan boosted Sindara back onto Kufu, stopped to tell Kendra what Sindara had said, and remounted his horse. The three riders then picked up their pace. Midnight was hours past when they paused long enough to eat and drink a little. They all watched as the two stars steadily marched across the sky toward one another. Then, hiding all non-essential gear near a road marker, they began the final leg of their journey.

Sunrise lingered just below the horizon when the trio reached the edge of Iglarm. The city slumbered as Sindara confidently guided Kufu toward the Brandere mansion, which seemed to lie directly beneath the two stars whose courses had nearly reached the point of crossing. Sindara finally led them onto a side street still clinging to night's heavy shadows.

"Karan, there's an entrance to the mansion two blocks around this corner. We need to open the gates. That is something Kendra and I can accomplish together. Help me switch one of the bridles to Kufu."

Karan started to question how she was so sure about the location of the entrance and then stopped. A subtle glow shone through the layers of her clothes. Glancing around, he saw the same was true with Kendra. "What do you want me to do?"

Sindara's golden eyes held a determined glimmer as she first turned her attention to Kendra. "Are you sure about going through with this? There is great danger."

Kendra solemnly nodded. "We have a chance to protect both our worlds from the menace here. I'm with you, dear sister."

Sindara quickly embraced Kendra before pulling her amulet out and gazing into its depths. "Nagrand and Thehrund are locked in a cage in the cellar. Karan, you must free them. There's one guard with a jailer. Both are bodies inhabited by the master demon's lesser servants. Take the cloth you have that's soaked with the oil and cedar blend. Wipe it along the blade of your sword and on your hands and face. That will help you against them. Call on the angels to stay with you."

Pulling a similar cloth from a leather bag in her pocket, she did the same with her sword, a dagger she carried, and a knife she handed to Kendra. Swiping the oily mix on Kendra's cheeks and hands and then on her own, she also wiped the cloth over Kufu's face and along his back and sides. She paused for a moment of silent prayer before shoving the material into her pocket, then touched the horse with her crystal amulet.

Sindara glanced up at the sky. Just as her grandfather's astronomical studies had projected and in synchronicity with prophecy from the Ambracada, the two gleaming stars began their convergence. "Kendra, the time is come. Pull out your crystal. We shall hold them together so that they may absorb light from both stars."

Karan watched in fascination as starlight seemed to focus a luminescent beam bearing down on the crystal amulets. Both pendants began to emit glowing, pulsating rays from between two sets of clasped fingers holding them together. Feeling blessed to witness such an event, he lifted his own prayer to Creator God that this day would end the destructive wave flowing over Ambracor.

With Karan's help, Sindara mounted Kufu. He then boosted Kendra up behind her. "Sindara, remember that you, too, should call on Creator God's angels for help."

"I will not forget," she replied. "May Creator God's mighty angels help us all." With that, she nudged her knees into Kufu's sides and ventured onto the street just as dawn's first rays colored the skies in beautiful shades of pastel pink, orange, and gold.

Approaching the back service entry to the Brandere mansion, Kendra grinned. "I only see two guards outside the gate. Shall I see what I can do with them?"

Sindara nodded. "Be my guest. See that block on the side? Open the gate. As I ride past, use it to jump back onto Kufu, then hold on tight."

Kendra slid off the horse and strode nonchalantly toward the guards. The unusually dark color of her skin and her confident pace caused the sentries to bow in respect. Each assumed she must be one of the master's lead servants. Within seconds, she had both guards flat on the ground. Touching each with her amulet, their bodies instantly stilled.

Opening the single gate, Kendra jumped onto the stone block and slid tightly against Sindara's back. Daring a look backward, she saw Karan quickly closing the distance between them.

"That was easy enough," she whispered as Sindara guided Kufu along the grassy perimeter where his horseshoes would not clatter against brick drives surrounding the house.

Sindara finally turned the steed toward a line of closely placed shrubs, positioning him directly in front of the main entrance. "Count your blessings. We're getting ready to make a grand entrance. I doubt the resistance inside will fall so quickly. Hold on."

Kendra looked up at the bright light shining down from the stars that had reached such full convergence that they appeared to be one brilliant body. "Lead on, girlfriend. Let's get this done and over with!"

Freeing her sword and digging her knees into Kufu's sides, Sindara called out, "Angels of Creator God! Help us now in our time of need!"

The stallion's hooves pounded across the brick drive and up granite steps. Sindara could have sworn she heard her grandfather's laughter as ten-foot high doors opened without the aid of human hands. Iron-clad hooves pounded across tiled floors and hand-knotted carpets. Pivoting the horse sharply and bringing him to a halt, she and Kendra leapt from Kufu's back and faced demon-possessed guards who charged at them.

Noiselessly descending stone stairs, Karan reached the cellar and headed toward faint light flickering to his right. With sword at the ready and a call to the angels on his lips, he turned the corner and faced one surprised guard and the jail keeper. Both stood and drew weapons. For the first time ever, Karan fully appreciated the swordsmanship gained through all the practices Thehrund had demanded while they searched for Sindara. Lunging forward, his sword pierced the guard. Falling to the floor, the body quivered within a reeking black mist that dissipated almost immediately.

The jailer sneered at Karan and rushed forward, skillfully brandishing his own sword. Fleet and light on his feet, Karan leapt out of the way and parried the jailer's swinging sword. Karan fought as he never thought possible. He concentrated on his foe and deflected blow after attempted blow. The demon jailer's skills were formidable. Karan, tired after a long night's ride, drew on every ounce of energy left to him. He could not afford to surrender to fatigue.

Suddenly, a rock flew through the air and struck the jailer's head. That second of distraction proved fateful as Karan plunged his sword into his opponent's heart. Just as with the guard, a grisly tremor shook the body as stinking mist escaped the physical form and disappeared.

Looking up, Karan saw a man whose face was scarred from what looked like burns. The stranger's brown eyes looked back with amazement. "Hurry! The keys are there on the wall. The prince's cell is over here."

Not daring to let down his guard, Karan reached out and snatched the iron ring of jangling keys from a metal hook on the wall. He followed the gaunt figure. Within seconds, they stood in front of the cell holding both Thehrund and Nagrand. Keeping a careful eye on the stranger, Karan tossed the keys to Thehrund. "Hurry!"

Thehrund quickly found the right key, pushed it into the keyhole, and shoved the cell door open. "All praises be to Creator God! How in the world did you find us?"

"No time." He nodded. "Who is he? Can he be trusted?"

"I am Berdran, Breeneth's brother," the hooded man answered. "You see what she did to me, and I know what she did to my family. Whatever the cost, she and that demon Thafalos must be stopped."

Nagrand stumbled to his feet. "Karan...without Berdran's help, I would not be alive."

Karan reached out to steady his brother as Berdran stepped forward to help Nagrand. Suppressing anger over his brother's condition, he said, "I'm here. We'll get you to safety." He asked Berdran, "Can you get him out of here? There's a horse just outside the back gate."

"He's weak. I'm not sure we can get that far. I know a safe place here that my sister won't suspect. It's a small storage room behind the kitchen's main pantry. I will not leave him unprotected. I swear it," Berdran offered in an intense whisper.

Karan turned to Thehrund, who had already retrieved swords the guards had dropped. He grabbed a sword from Thehrund and swiped it with an oiled cloth before handing it to Berdran. "Get my brother to safety. We'll find you later. Go!"

Facing Thehrund, Karan handed him the cloth and heaved in a deep breath. "Wipe your sword with this. Sindara has gone to confront Breeneth and her master."

"What?" he exclaimed, a painful expression contorting his face. "How could you let her go alone?"

"Hurry!"

Reaching the stone stairway, Karan leaned back against cold walls and listened. Glancing around, he knew Thehrund was enraged by the idea of Sindara entering the mansion on her own. "Too much to explain, but you know that's what she intended from the start. Thankfully, she's not alone. Kendra is with her."

Feeling urgency surge through his body, Thehrund's eyes widened. "Kendra? How in..."

Karan put his index finger to his lips. Hurried footsteps quickly approached the cellar door and then faded. "Where?"

Thehrund edged around Karan. "The banquet hall. Follow me."

Safely passing through the kitchen and hallways to reach a spacious drawing room, Thehrund peered around the corner of an arched doorway. Chaotic sounds echoed through the corridors. "Karan, stay here. Sindara is my wife. I must go to her. This is my fight."

"This is *our* fight," Karan replied tersely. "We both resist this evil."

Without further hesitation, the two men launched themselves into a dead run through the hallway leading from the drawing room. Sharply rounding a corner at the end of the long corridor, they nearly collided with two sentries also rushing toward the reverberating sounds of fighting. Thehrund swiftly dispatched one and engaged the other who fiercely advanced on Karan. The uniformed guard quickly fell. Thehrund and Karan bolted, neither noticing the stench when pirated bodies expelled demon possessors in puffs of black fog.

Arriving at the embattled foyer, Thehrund and Karan jumped over several motionless bodies on the floor. Sounds of continued fighting echoed from the anteroom outside the mansion's banquet hall. Without hesitation, the two men dashed ahead, dodging a body that flew past them and bounced off a wall. Within moments, they paused scant seconds to assess the astounding scene unfolding outside the dining room's main entrance.

Kendra's exceptional training and agility were astonishing to watch as she whirled in circles, leapt into the air, and aimed precise kicks at soldiers charging toward her. She sent swords and bodies flailing in her wake. Sindara's sword rang out as it slashed against weapons and the mansion's demonic guards. The sight of Kufu rearing and striking others with his hooves added surreal dimension to the vicious battle unfolding before them.

Releasing great cries of fury, the prince and the priest charged into the fray. Swinging their swords with power and efficiency, they quickly thrust at stumbling guards attempting to reclaim weapons and rejoin the fight or those taking flight as the result of Kendra's unique combat techniques. The thought that they had once been citizens of Ambracor was readily dismissed. The powers possessing those bodies needed to be destroyed, and the oil-smeared swords were proving effective at expelling vile spirits into oblivion.

Lunging forward to plunge his sword into one of the last guards, Thehrund dared to look up. The golden eyes of his beloved wife met his gaze for a prolonged moment. Her lips mouthed the words "I love you." He shook his head violently, signaling her not to proceed, but she ignored him and turned to thrust open the polished wood doors of the banquet hall now serving as throne room for Thafalos.

Drawing in several deep breaths, Sindara quickly spotted the strikingly handsome demon who lounged in a relaxed, nonchalant position on his throne. His mouth was drawn wide in a toothy smile. Black eyes glittered with fiery pleasure. His image struck her as that of someone who had just gorged himself with a lavish meal and was settling his substantial repast by enjoying an extravagant show of entertainment.

In front of him stood his consort. Breeneth's renowned beauty was marred by the anger curling one side of her mouth and furrowing her brow. Her breasts heaved with every breath she took, and her hair strayed out in wild disarray. Wearing only a thin camisole over long, ruffled drawers, she had apparently left bed in a rush.

Kendra hurried inside to join Sindara. Thehrund and Karan followed close behind and slammed the doors shut. The odor in the room was decidedly unpleasant, but not one of the new arrivals showed any indication of discomfort as they quieted their breathing in anticipation of the imminent confrontation.

Ignoring Kendra's presence, Breeneth spoke first. "So, the illustrious and miraculous Sindara Varacor has come to brave her rival in her own lair."

"I must correct you," Sindara said, her expression staid and implacable. "I am Sindara Cobrandya now, and I have no rival...especially none here in Iglarm."

Furious disdain further contorted Breeneth's features as she took several steps forward. "You will learn humility today. My master has granted me the privilege of killing you...once and for all. After that, Thehrund will be my husband."

"Think carefully what you do, Breeneth," Sindara warned. "There is still hope for you to reconcile with Creator God, as there is for your master. I have no wish to fight you, but I will do so to defend Thehrund and our people."

"Such brave words," Breeneth scoffed maliciously. "Especially from one who lacked sufficient spirit to do more than hide away in a religious cloister until you connived your way into the affections of the prince who belonged to me. He was mine, you know. He gladly visited my bed for the pleasures he found there."

Sindara refused to respond to taunts that no longer held power to wound her. "I give you a final chance, Breeneth Brandere. Agree to reconcile with the light, or face the inevitable consequences."

Breeneth tossed back her head and laughed, the harsh, cold sound echoing throughout the room. Slowly, teasingly, she began a steady advance.

When Sindara stepped forward, sword still in hand, Thehrund abruptly jerked forward. With lightning speed, Kendra turned and shoved him backward, hissing in a low whisper, "Stay! This is something she must do!"

Karan grabbed Thehrund's arm and hung onto him tightly. In an urgent whisper, Karan told Kendra, "The demon's weakness...his name. It's Thafalos."

Thehrund's fearful blue eyes watched his wife stride confidently toward her wicked adversary. His heart drummed rapidly, even painfully, within his chest. Memory choked him. Breeneth had failed once to end Sindara's life. Sindara had also thwarted her attack on his parents and forced her to flee the palace in Bracordia. Her hatred for Sindara was boundless.

The two women finally faced off with barely eight feet separating them. They walked a circle around one another, warily assessing strengths and weaknesses before hurling themselves into what would surely be mortal combat. Breeneth's entire body shook with unbridled anger and hatred. Sindara's face remained calm, her tall, lithe body emanating readiness to strike at the first sign of attack.

With a flick of her wrist, Breeneth aimed what looked like a black flame at Sindara. Having spotted twitching in her opponent's hand, Sindara swiftly repelled the shaft of energy with the broad side of her sword. Breeneth hastily bent far backward, barely escaping the deflected bolt of her own dark energy.

In an attempt to lure Sindara from her silent state of composure, Breeneth snickered. "You are quick. I grant you that much, but you may as well surrender. You will never defeat me."

Sindara remained mute, her eyes taking in every nuance of Breeneth's expression and movements. With her gaze fixed, she took one step closer to her foe.

Black eyebrows lifted high with surprise. "Aggressive, are we?" Receiving no response to her taunts, Breeneth was quickly losing patience.

"Let me demonstrate real aggression." Both of Breeneth's hands flew up and emanated a concentrated force that caused Sindara to slide backward no more than the length of the sword she held in front of her. A look of absolute astonishment flashed across Breeneth's face. The powerful burst should have sent Sindara flailing into the wall. Instead, barely moving, this woman had again deflected the attack with the broad edge of her sword.

Enraged, Breeneth leapt toward Sindara. The princess quickly sidestepped and simultaneously struck a sharp blow across the other woman's thinly clad hips with the broad side of her forged steel blade. Slamming hard to the floor, Breeneth cried out from the stinging crack against her buttocks. Twisting around, the black-haired witch nimbly leapt to her feet.

Red lips curled with unrestrained fury. "You will pay for that!" she screamed just as she hurled a string of profanities and vile curses at her rival.

Sindara's expression reflected unwavering resistance. Tucked safely inside her tunic, the amulet she wore against her skin had begun emitting powerful pulsations in direct response to the hateful blasphemy and dark spells spewing from her wicked adversary. As the vibrations grew stronger, Sindara felt a surge of righteous anger and slowly advanced toward Breeneth.

Far too arrogant, Breeneth rushed Sindara again. This time, Sindara's hands shot out, grabbing one of Breeneth's arms. Pivoting sharply, she whirled Breeneth around and sent her crashing into the wall near Thehrund and Karan. Thehrund reacted swiftly, bending forward and snatching the fallen woman by the wrist. Breeneth shrieked in agony.

Thehrund shot a look at Karan. "Quick! Her other hand!"

Despite searing pain in her wrist, Breeneth resisted with all her might, twisting and kicking at Karan while trying to free herself from Thehrund's scorching grasp. Kendra turned and leapt, landing a solid kick into Breeneth's stomach. The stunning blow robbed her of breath. Karan fell to his knees and grabbed the free hand Breeneth had tried to protect.

"Enough!" Thafalos roared. His booming voice rattled chandeliers and sent an echoing wave throughout the closed banquet hall. Rising from his throne, the master demon rapidly strode toward those who dared to invade the luxurious lair he claimed as his own. Haughty amusement quickly vanished, and his earlier smirk disappeared. Black eyes glittered with hateful menace, and his features drew into a daunting scowl.

"Release Breeneth immediately!" he commanded.

Glancing downward, Thehrund noted red streaks of scorched flesh on Breeneth's hands and wrists. Quickly meeting Karan's gaze, both men shook their heads as they faced the demon master. Thehrund's voice carried a resounding tone of utter disgust. "Absolutely not!"

Kendra rushed to Sindara's side and firmly grasped her left hand. The two women boldly placed themselves between Thafalos and the men forcibly restraining the fiend's sobbing consort.

The demon's swarthy complexion darkened as his fury swelled. "How dare you defy me? I rule in this place! I demand that you release her! If you do not, you will face punishment more severe and more agonizing than you ever dreamed possible!" By this time, the demon's body had begun to emit intensifying flame-like swirls of inky-black mist.

"Breeneth rejected Creator God. She must now face her time of reckoning for the despicable deeds she has performed," Sindara responded forcefully.

Infuriated by their refusal to submit to his demands, Thafalos flicked his hand toward them, spewing forth a putrid cloud and mighty surge intended to remove the two women blocking the way to his precious servant. Tightening the grasp joining their hands, Kendra and Sindara moved backward only inches.

The demon's forehead drew into deep creases reflecting his bewilderment. Throughout many ages, his maniacal ego and cunning intellect had sustained him through numerous attempts by warrior angels sent to capture and return him to Creator God's presence. He had always resisted and escaped their pursuits. If he had foiled the efforts of superior angelic beings, he would not fail to overpower and destroy these feeble humans who dared to challenge him.

"You!" he shouted as he directed his attention to Kendra. "How is it one with features as dark as yours allies yourself with the likes of the pale woman at your side?"

Kendra offered a daring smile. "The answer lies beyond your comprehension."

The demon snarled and growled like a predatory animal cornered in a trap. "You actually come into my home and dare to insult me?"

"This home is not yours and never was," Sindara countered. "That which is stolen will never truly belong to any thief who possesses it."

Thafalos growled louder, the sound savage and vicious. Ignoring Sindara, he addressed Kendra. "You do not belong with these people. Look at you! You belong on the dark side with my kind. What game do you play?"

Kendra lifted her chin, defiance flashing from her eyes. "I play no games! You exist not in darkness, demon! You dwell in the absolute absence of light! Sindara and I are sisters sharing sacred balance between the light of day and the dark of night. Light shines within our souls at all times. Night gives us rest and day renews our vitality. By shunning the Creator's gifts, you renounced your sacred connection to the universe's great balance. You alone chose your end when you refused to make peace with the Divine One who created you."

Thafalos tilted his head to the side. His eyes narrowed to mere slits. "How utterly presumptuous you are! I am master here! You both will suffer my wrath!"

With an abrupt leap, Thafalos aimed his fingers toward Karan. Thehrund had seen the demon shift his weight and gave a sudden, mighty jerk to the left, dragging Breeneth and Karan toward him to evade the demon's aim. Thafalos bellowed in rapidly burgeoning fury as he watched his shot scorch the wall only inches from where Karan landed.

Black fingers of mist began to billow around the demon as his rage expanded. Uttering blasphemous profanities, he fixed his sights on the two women opposing him. His nose and lips twitched with pure malevolence rising from his evil core. Spiteful wickedness prompted him to charge at them, the black cloud around him crackling with showers of sparks and expanding to conceal his form.

"Archangels of Creator God, we call on you and your light to help us defeat this demon!" Sindara called out loudly.

"Sindara!" Thehrund's resonant voice exploded desperately above the mounting tumult. Tension burned every muscle as he forced himself to maintain control over Breeneth. Releasing her to join her master would prove nothing less than catastrophic.

Feeling Sindara being drawn from her grasp, Kendra clung desperately to her friend. The mighty power dragging her away filled Kendra with unadulterated horror.

"His name! Use it to command him!"

She had nearly forgotten until Karan's familiar voice pierced her terrorized brain. Kendra cried out with complete authority. "Thafalos! I order you in the name of Creator God! Release Sindara! Thafalos! I know your name! You cannot ignore me! Release her immediately! I command you!"

A violent, inhuman roar reverberated throughout the chamber and again rattled chandeliers and shook windows until glass shattered and cracking ceilings rained down choking plaster dust. The demon's throne toppled, crashing onto Breeneth's chaise beside it. Doors at both ends of the banquet hall rattled with such force that locking mechanisms vibrated and failed.

"Sindara! Help me!" Kendra cried out.

Jerking backward with what little strength remained to her, Sindara staggered against Kendra. Both women collapsed to the floor. Facing the demon whose concealing cloud was receding, Sindara issued her own demand in a hoarse voice. "Thafalos! I command an end to your vile existence here! I call on all Creator God's angels to return you to the sacred source of all creation. You must face your judgment!"

The demon's thundering wrath changed in tenor and volume as he offered mighty resistance to commands issued by Kendra and Sindara. Blinding black mist churned around him as his form twisted and contorted into positions impossible for any human to achieve. Pure rage pervaded all that he was as he endeavored to defy their commands.

Slumping weakly against Kendra, Sindara forced a whisper. "The crystals! We must join them!"

Kendra dragged her necklace from beneath her sweater as Sindara reached for hers. Leaning far forward over Sindara's shoulder, Kendra slid her pendant across Sindara's chest until the crystals lay together on Kendra's open palm.

"You are commanded to surrender, Thafalos!" Kendra called out again.

Although weak, Sindara's rasping voice conveyed authority. "Thafalos! Surrender! Creator God's angels come to remove you. Go!"

The banquet room was suddenly saturated with light so brilliant that all were forced to shield their eyes. The joined amulets emitted a concentrated, shimmering beam that held Thafalos motionless as glowing figures surrounded him. With his contorted form firmly in their control, they rose from the floor and gradually vanished.

Breeneth wailed in sorrowing agony for her master. Renewing her struggle against Thehrund and Karan, she started to chant an ancient curse. Before she could finish, a dagger flew through the air and pierced her heart. Horrified as she collapsed, they watched as her body violently shuddered and slowly disintegrated into a pile of smoking ebony dust. Thehrund glanced upward. Just inside the doorway, Berdran stood, his scarred face expressing a heartbreaking combination of sorrow and resolve.

"There was no other choice," he said softly. "Better that it was by my hand than any other. My family does not deserve a legacy devoid of honor. Their memory should not be forever defiled by her shame."

"Thehrund?" Kendra's choked voice interrupted the shocking sight of Breeneth's demise.

Turning, a strangled gasp erupted from Thehrund as he scrambled across the floor toward the spot where Kendra sat with Sindara's head resting on her lap. Rising to his knees, Thehrund pulled his wife's limp form into his arms and cradled her head against his chest. Showering her face with kisses, he repeated her name over and over again. Tears poured from his eyes.

"Sindara," he sobbed brokenly. "Sindara, you cannot leave me now. Oh, dear Creator God, please! Don't take her from me again. Sindara! I love you! I beg you. Please! Don't die! I need you! Sindara!"

Karan swallowed hard as he knelt beside them. Touching his fingers to Sindara's neck, he detected no pulse. Leaning over her, he pressed his ear to her chest. Tears brimmed in his eyes as he looked up. "Thehrund, I... Her heart... I can't hear her heartbeat."

Drawing her lifeless body tightly against his, Thehrund's head fell backward as he cried out in wretched anguish. Burying his face in the silken softness of his wife's hair, he sobbed uncontrollably as his powerful body quaked with grief wrenched from the depths of his soul. "Sindara. My beautiful Sindara."

Karan offered a hand to Kendra and helped her up from the floor. Tears drenched beautiful brown features, and her entire body trembled. He stretched his arms around her and held her tightly. For the first time in his life, he found himself incapable of finding any comforting words born of faith. Instead, he thought only of the terrible loss the whole of Ambracor had just suffered.

Chapter Twenty-Six

RARE AND STAGGERING IN ITS beauty, the convergence of the two stars slowly faded into heavens brightened by morning sun. Mere wisps of clouds remained after night winds blew heavier cloud cover east of Arvacon. Cold air lingered, emerging as frosty mist from the breaths of Ambracor soldiers who secured Breyal prisoners, tended to the wounded from both sides, and arranged bodies for recovery.

Limping around the battlefield, King Hamund paused to grasp soldiers by their shoulders, praising them for their courage and loyalty. Here and there, he took the hands of wounded troops on stretchers to encourage and comfort them. Several times, he stopped before those who had died. Bowing his head, he fervently prayed for their peaceful repose.

The thought continually crossing his mind was that not one had desired to be embroiled in such tragic violence. With their homes and families endangered, they had all delved deep into their hearts and found strength and resolve to defend their homeland. They had yearned to recover the peace that had served as Ambracor's foundation for centuries. So many died. Of those surviving, some would heal from their injuries. Still others would face physical infirmities for the remainder of their lives. Not one would survive unscathed. Their hearts would forever bear scars carved by memories of suffering they had witnessed and deaths they had inflicted.

"Your Majesty," Erator quietly interrupted the king's heavy ponderings, "we're ready to return to the fort."

Hamund nodded before lifting solemn eyes to the general and remounting his horse. For a fleeting second, he remembered Erator as a small boy full of imagination and mischief. "When I saw you as a child,

I never imagined that the fate of our people might someday rest on your shoulders. You have grown into a remarkable man, Erator, and an exceptional leader."

Erator could do little more than nod in gratitude for the king's assessment. Finding his voice with difficulty, he met his king's sincere gaze. "Our people respond to this crisis with uncommon unity, and that unity is inspired from many directions. Leadership from our royal family also stands as inspiration in the face of this crisis."

"I bear profound pride for all Thehrund did to prepare us for this conflict." Hamund's blue eyes reflected sadness as his voice cracked. "How I wish I knew his fate."

"As I wish I knew my sister's," Erator responded. His eyes automatically scanned the horizon for any sign of fresh assault. "The best I can do is to tend matters within the scope of my control and carry in my heart prayers for their safety."

As weary regiments prepared to return to Articene, a lieutenant shouted in warning to Erator. The general turned and stiffened in his saddle. He cast a rapid glance at King Hamund. A long line of Breyal warriors had just come into view. Signaling his troops to stand ready, the general watched a line of seven mounted warriors emerge from the main body of fighters.

Erator's forehead creased in consternation as he watched the Breyal war party approach. The lead rider carried his longbow horizontally on outstretched arms. The six warriors behind him held their sheathed swords in the same fashion. They advanced steadily as the enemy's main line remained stationary. Their intention was clear. They wanted to meet.

Commanding senior officers to remain alert, Erator responded in kind by starting slowly toward the riders with his sword pointed downward. A sideways glance sparked anxiety. Resigned to the fact he was powerless to stop the king, Erator slowed his horse until he rode side by side with Hamund. Tense minutes later, the opposing riders met.

The leader of the Breyals handed off his longbow to one of the riders behind him. He then dismounted and approached Ambracor's king and commanding general. Of average height, the leader's soft leather jacket and ornately trimmed leggings moved with supple grace over his strong, muscular frame. Unkempt hair framed tanned features. His eyes shone with bold intelligence. He waited in silence for his enemy's reaction

Erator dismounted first. Leaving his sword balanced across his saddle, he rounded his horse and offered assistance to Hamund as the king dismounted. Matching his pace to the king's slower gait, the wary general walked with King Hamund to face the dismounted Breyal.

Following several moments of prolonged silence, Hamund tilted his head in an elegant nod. "I am King Hamund. This is General Erator Varacor."

The Breyal leader remained quiet a moment longer, his eyes straying toward the wooden prosthetic upon which the king walked. "I am Kicchak, Grand Chieftain over the tribes of Breyal."

"You wish to speak with us," Hamund stated the obvious.

"On behalf of my people, I do. I have ridden day and night to reach this place of battle. Our mystics inform me that the joining of the celestial orbs and the light they have shone down on us represent a sacred portent requiring change."

"What change do they suggest?" Hamund asked, his eyes fixed on the Breyal chieftain's face.

"They tell me the fighting between our peoples must end."

"My nation never wanted this war, but we were compelled to defend our people and their homes. We are willing to discuss terms for peace."

"Your son told me the same." Kicchak nodded respectfully toward Hamund's missing leg. "I see that his strength and character honor his father."

Hamund's breathing quickened. "You have seen Thehrund?"

Kicchak nodded. "My warriors took him prisoner as he rode toward Iglarm." The chieftain's eyes reflected both respect and regret. "I was forced to deliver him to the dark ones in Iglarm. They had already murdered my brother. They took the rest of my family hostage and forced me to capture your son."

Erator saw the tensing of Hamund's jaw. "The fate of Prince Thehrund. Do you know his fate?"

Kicchak dropped his gaze to the ground and shook his head. "The demon's lover planned to force him into marriage. She wishes to rule your people."

Hamund finally recovered sufficiently to speak. "My son has a wife already. He cannot take another."

Kicchak aimed a puzzled glance at the king. "Among my people, we may have many wives. I had two already, but when my brother was slain, his wife and children also became mine. They were all taken by the dark ones."

Hamund forced himself to remain calm. "That is not the way of my people, but I do hope your family is now safe."

The Breyal chieftain's expression remained impassive. "Your son was a man who commanded my respect. He was brave, strong, and loyal. I sacrificed an honorable man for nothing because the dark ones rewarded me by slaughtering my wives and my children. That is why I come before you. I offer myself as sacrifice in exchange for your son. He told me he would never marry the one called Breeneth. After you kill me, I ask you to consult with my council here to make peace between our peoples."

Erator turned his attention to his king and saw Hamund's face had blanched. His hands clenched into tight fists, but his posture remained erect, his bearing regal. The general imagined his own father had received news of Rezda's death with similar fortitude in the presence of others. He briefly wondered how such grief would manifest itself in private.

"It is not our way to sacrifice one life in exchange for another," Hamund's voice responded quietly. "I do, however, invite you and your council to join us for discussions about how we might put an end to this war and the loss it has brought both our peoples."

"You would discuss such matters with me even knowing that I delivered your son into the hands of the dark ones?"

"I will not lie and extend my hand to you in false friendship. For the sake of my people, however, I will not hesitate to work with you to build a treaty that will benefit both Breyal and Ambracor."

The chieftain quietly assessed the leaders of his enemy. "I must respect the will of a man who rides into battle with but one leg; however, sacrifice in exchange for the life of your son is something my people will expect from me."

Hamund drew in a deep, shuddering breath. His mind raced through possibilities. "Will your people wait for us to impose adequate, acceptable sacrifice after we decide our course to end hostilities between us?"

"If that is your wish as the one to whom my debt of honor is owed."

Both Hamund and Erator released relieved sighs. "General Varacor will discuss with you the details of when and where we can begin our discussions. In the meantime, I will take my leave to return to Articene with our soldiers and your warriors who need treatment for their injuries."

"You will care for our wounded, too?" Kicchak asked incredulously.

With Erator's assistance, Hamund mounted his horse and looked down into the Breyal chief's questioning eyes. "That is our way," the king answered quietly as he quickly turned his horse and rode back to troops anxiously watching the exchange.

Blue eyes lifted, their depths reflecting desolation such as no one in the hall had ever seen. Thehrund's dark hair moved with the shaking of his head. "Karan," he implored, "can you do nothing to save her?"

Karan swallowed and rested a hand on the prince's shoulder. "I am but a priest and a healer. I am not Creator God who can restore life to the dead."

Kendra knelt beside Thehrund. Elegant fingers softly caressed her friend's cheek. Meeting Thehrund's tormented gaze, she remembered her own grief the day she learned her parents had died. That experience taught her that such heartache often evaded any cure. The best one could hope for was fortitude to manage the magnitude of such absolute sorrow.

"She was all I had left, Thehrund...the only person who loved me. Besides her memory, the one thing I will cling to is the love she and I shared. No one, not even Thafalos or Breeneth, can ever take that from me...or from you."

Thehrund choked. His throat tightened, denying him all ability to speak. Kendra stretched an arm around his shoulder and pulled him close. Karan joined them on the floor and also wrapped an arm around his childhood friend. Both suppressed their own grief as Thehrund's body again shook with anguished sobs torn from his battered soul.

Berdran stood silent watch. Many of the household servants had reluctantly yielded to Breeneth's threats and continued their work in the Brandere household. All had secretly hoped for deliverance from her clutches, but none had seen any possibility of escaping alive. One of the grateful approached Berdran and whispered that a room upstairs was being prepared to receive the body of their heroic princess.

The sole survivor of the Brandere family approached Prince Thehrund. "Your Highness," he said kindly, "we have a bedchamber prepared for the princess until you decide on final arrangements."

Although speech still eluded him, Thehrund nodded. Karan stood and extended his hand to Kendra. The grieving prince gathered his wife in his arms. Staggering slightly, he forced himself up off the floor. With Kendra and Karan close behind, he followed Berdran and the servant to a chamber where he gently laid Sindara on a bed covered with freshly laundered sheets of white linen.

Unable to bear letting anyone touch her, Thehrund tenderly settled her head on a pillow. He covered her with the top sheet, neatly folding it and pulling its edge in a straight line across her breasts. Her arms he arranged over her heart so they rested on top of the folded sheet. Bending forward, he kissed her hands. He could not help but notice their coolness now that the warmth of her life's blood no longer circulated in fingers that had once caressed him with feverish delight.

With pale features drawn into anguished lines, Nagrand joined them. Sorrowfully, he observed Sindara's peaceful countenance and Thehrund's kneeling figure at her bedside. Although weakened by his own ordeal, Nagrand was the only one with sufficient voice to offer prayers for her soul and comfort for those left behind who would forever mourn her passing and cherish her memory.

The passageway ahead gleamed brilliantly. Wrapped in a cocoon of light and warmth, Sindara sensed herself being carried along on currents that were velvety soft and saturated with incomprehensible peace. Her soul felt buoyant and weightless. Sorrows and pain were no more than faint memories. Engulfed in a blanket of pure serenity, she allowed her spirit to traverse endless space stretched out before her.

Her journey slowed. Surrounded by a perception of vibrant love, her consciousness rose from its state of flowing freely through all-encompassing light. Her spirit's inner vision perceived familiar figures awaiting her. If such a thing was possible in this place, she felt herself smiling.

"Sindara...my sweet Sindara, how proud you have made me."

"Grandfather, I knew it was you. You kept your promise, didn't you? You watched over me."

"As I always promised."

Another presence caught her attention. "Rezda?"

"Sister, your courage honors our family in Arvacon and all our ancestors who have returned to Creator God's holy light. I watched while you gazed at the body I left behind. You were right when you thought of my spirit finding peace."

"Mother and Father are so sad that you left them. Dalina grieves that you will never know your unborn child."

She felt tenderness in her brother's smile when he responded, "I will always watch over them both, and I will wait. When their lives are fulfilled, I will know them here, within the grace and light gifted to us by the sacred source of all creation."

A rush of questions rose from her soul. "Grandfather, all remains so unsettled in Ambracor. There is no peace. Breeneth and Thafalos left thousands at war and even more to dwell among the ruins. So many need healing and help. Tell me, Grandfather, will their suffering ever end? And what of all the pain Mother and Father will face?" Something lurched within her, its strength pulling at her soul. "What will happen to those whose grief can never be assuaged?"

"Oh, Sindara, questions upon questions. Always you have been a fountain of unending questions."

Uncertain of his meaning, she wanted badly to reach the comfort she had always known in his embrace. Still, that other power tugged at her, drawing her away from him. "Grandfather, will you not help me understand? Will you deny me the consolation of your closeness?"

Her grandfather's voice sounded clear within her mind. "Child, only you can know for sure. Look back from whence you came. Then, you tell me the answer to your questions."

Confused, Sindara shifted her vision. She realized her consciousness was floating, allowing her to observe with curiosity the scene below her. How peculiar she felt as she drifted from one scene to the next, asking herself how and why no one noticed her.

The banquet hall at the Brandere mansion was empty. Pounding outside caught her attention. Boards were being nailed over windows. Shattered glass littered the floors, as did fine, powdery dust from plaster cracks in the ceiling. The throne had fallen on the chaise. A table had also toppled over. Nothing had been righted. Doors at each end of the dining room were nailed shut.

Voices attracted her attention. Drifting toward them, she saw with relief that Nagrand rested on a sofa in a large drawing room. How pale and sad he looked. Karan was urging him to eat something. Another man was with them, someone she didn't recognize. His features were blurred to her vision, but she sensed compassion in his soul.

Another sound caused her awareness to shift from Nagrand and Karan. At the far end of the elegantly appointed room, a tall man stood, his head bent and pressing against a windowpane. His long hair draped forward, concealing his face. Broad shoulders slumped. His muscular frame shook with despair. As she focused her attention on his solitary figure, she felt irresistibly drawn toward him.

"Sindara, I never had time to actually prove how much I love you. How am I to go on without you? I am naught without you."

Thehrund's grief-laden whispers penetrated her soul. Her spirit could not bear the weight of his sorrow. She fled, arriving at a bedchamber in the upstairs of the spacious mansion. Studying the scene below, she saw white sheets neatly tucked over the bed. The body beneath the covers lay motionless. Pale features revealed no sign of pain or worry. In fact, the young woman's countenance showed no emotion whatsoever.

Movement in the room caused her to glance away from the still body she at last recognized as her own. Kendra was approaching the bed. How sad her beloved friend appeared...almost as forlorn as she had looked at the funeral for her parents. Kendra sadly contemplated the face lying on a lace-trimmed pillow. Stretching out long fingers, she smoothed an errant strand of hair. Sindara watched as her friend bent her head and leaned forward.

"Sindara?"

"Yes, Grandfather?" Sindara responded as she continued to observe Kendra.

"There is much left to be done to restore lasting peace in Ambracor. You have felt the light close to Creator God, but you must remember what I told you long ago."

"I remember, Grandfather. I remember everything you told me."

"I love you, my sweet Sindara."

Swiftly returning to the drawing room and glimpsing Karan as he attempted to console Thehrund, Sindara's spirit reveled in her husband's love for her. Drawn back to where her body lay, she watched as Kendra gently grasped the crystal amulet that had fallen onto the pillow and then tucked it beneath the neckline of the torn tunic.

A sudden, forceful vacuum captured Sindara, sucking her into swirling winds with the same swift, spinning velocity she remembered from her journey with Thehrund through the portal. Stopping abruptly, she felt the cold of the gold-framed crystal vibrating against her chest. Gasping for breath, she began to cough.

Kendra jumped away from the bed and stared in startled disbelief. Within seconds, she was back at Sindara's side, dragging her into a sitting position and holding her as violent coughing continued. As Kendra firmly kept her upright, Sindara marveled at the tingling sensation of warmth returning to the fleshly vessel stirring to renewed life. Tears wet Kendra's face as she soothingly cooed encouraging words to the miracle surrounded by her own embrace.

The coughing finally eased, and Sindara stilled, content for the moment to rest her face against Kendra's shoulder. Shivering, she managed a weak, trembling whisper. "I'm so cold."

Kendra's lips quivered and settled into an astounded smile. She eased Sindara back onto the pillow. "I'll get you some blankets. What else do you need?"

"Thehrund," she whispered before she started coughing again.

Kendra ran to the door and flung it open. "Karan!" she shouted. "Thehrund! I need help! Hurry!"

Turning slightly, she noticed a quilted spread had been folded across the bottom of the bed. Rushing to unfold it, she quickly bundled Sindara in the thick coverlet.

"What's wrong?" Karan stumbled to a sharp halt as he stared in utter disbelief at Kendra as she chafed Sindara's icy hands between her own.

Kendra looked up, half-dazed with shock. "She suddenly woke up coughing. She said she's cold and asked for Thehrund."

Karan ran back through the hall. He knew Thehrund had been too engrossed in his own state of desolate shock to respond to Kendra's call for help. "Thehrund! We need you up here! Now!"

Entering and sitting on the side of the bed opposite Kendra, Karan helped support Sindara's shoulders as the body-wracking coughs continued. Glancing up urgently at Kendra, he sent her for towels and a pitcher of fresh water. His calm voice belied his utter astonishment. "It's all right, Sindara. Whatever it is, cough it up. Don't be afraid."

Bolting down the hallway in search of towels, Kendra nearly bowled Thehrund over. Glancing over her shoulder, she shouted at him. "Go! It's Sindara!"

Bewildered, Thehrund's clouded mind could hardly fathom the urgency in Kendra's demand. Still, he quickened his approach to the bed-chamber where he had gently laid the body of his beloved wife more than an hour earlier. Finally reaching the room, he froze at the sight of Karan holding her while the intense bout of coughing shook the entire bed.

"Thehrund, help me hold her upright!" Karan snapped.

Hastening to Sindara's side, Thehrund wrapped one strong arm behind his wife's shoulders and placed the palm of his free hand firmly against the front of her shoulder closest to his body. "Sindara," he gasped breathlessly, "I'm here, my love. You'll be all right. I'm here. I won't leave you."

Kendra reappeared with a stack of towels and passed one to Karan. Kneeling on the floor, she watched intently as Karan held the cloth beneath Sindara's chin. She added her own words of encouragement. "It's okay, girlfriend. Cough it up. Get it out, and you'll feel better. You can do it! Come on!"

As Kendra quickly thrust more towels toward Karan, Sindara coughed up thick, glistening, black masses of mucus. As the coughing subsided, she collapsed weakly into Thehrund's embrace. How soothing she felt the heat of his body. How her soul calmed as the resonance of his rich voice penetrated the depths of her being. "Thehrund," she sobbed softly.

"Shush," he murmured tenderly, planting kiss after kiss against her hair. "You'll be all right now," he whispered, raising his eyes to meet Karan's, hoping and praying this wasn't some cruel hallucination or dream rising from a soul in torment.

Karan gave him an encouraging smile. "She was enveloped in the shroud of mist that surrounded Thafalos. She must have breathed it in. How she revived to expel it..."

Kendra interrupted. "Her amulet had fallen to the side and was on her pillow. I saw it and tucked it underneath the neckline of her top. That's when she started coughing."

Brilliant blue eyes lifted to gaze appreciatively at Kendra's face. "You saved her. Kendra, I owe you a debt I can never repay."

Kendra's full lips spread into a tranquil smile. "The angels gave us those crystals to save your world and to prevent the evil here from spreading to mine. If debt is owed, then I think it is owed to them and to God."

A servant carrying a pitcher of water appeared at the door. Thankfully, she also brought a glass. Refusing to release his wife, Thehrund supported Sindara while Karan held the cup for her to sip water and rinse her mouth clean of the dark residue that she spat into towels. Obediently following Karan's instructions, she repeatedly rinsed her mouth until the liquid in the towels appeared clear.

Smiling with astounded relief, Karan sighed. "I will go prepare an elixir that will help rid you of any remaining traces of that nasty residue.

The coughing won't be pleasant, but you'll regain your strength much faster once it's all out. In the meantime, I want you to rest."

Too weak to argue, Sindara nodded at Karan. She then locked her gaze on her husband's penetrating blue eyes. Those brilliant eyes had haunted her for years. Reflected from those azure mirrors to his soul had been the singular devotion that had inspired her courage and resolve to confront the wicked entities that had threatened their people. "I'm so cold. Will you stay and hold me?"

Tears of joy swam in Thehrund's eyes. "I will hold you as long as you want."

With great tenderness, he lowered her onto the bed. Glancing at Kendra, he grinned sheepishly. "May I ask a favor of you?"

"Of course. Anything," Kendra replied. She stifled laughter when Thehrund, unwilling to loosen his grasp on Sindara's hands, lifted first one leg and then the other. Leaving his boots at the foot of the bed, Kendra followed Karan from the room and closed the door behind her.

Several hours later, the oppressive atmosphere inside the Brandere mansion had brightened considerably as household staff closed windows. Despite chilly air outside, Berdran had earlier helped servants open windows to permit the flow of fresh, clean air throughout his ancestral home. Inside the kitchen, Kendra helped Karan as he simmered various herbs and then blended them into the elixir for Sindara. Cooks quietly worked around the priest and his unusual assistant to prepare decent meals now that the house had been cleared of those who had nearly decimated the Brandere family.

Nagrand sat at a desk in the study that once belonged to Count Brandere. Supporting his head with his left hand, he carefully composed dispatches to Count Varacor in Cahmdurn and to King Hamund in Bracordia. Reports were already flooding in as Bramondan citizens passed along news of demon-possessed guards abruptly collapsing. Weary as he was, Nagrand appreciated the privilege of extending details of the momentous day to those who would be in desperate need to know all that had occurred.

He shook his head sadly as he wrote of the many Bramond militiamen whose bodies lay about the city, their demonic possessors driven into oblivion when the master demon was removed by Creator God's angels. Citizens were celebrating freedom from evil taskmasters. As of yet, there were no reports of any Breyal war parties active in the area. Prince Thehrund was safe. Berdran Brandere bore severe facial scars and other infirmities as punishment for resisting his sister. Still, he had ended his sister's life in defense of those engaged in the courageous confrontation with her and the master demon called Thafalos. Despite victory over the evil ones, the battle's end had left them brokenhearted, mourning over the lifeless body of the princess. Their hearts were later gladdened by yet another miracle when Sindara was once again restored to them.

Nagrand reviewed the two dispatches he had written. After his ordeal, his script lacked the precision of his usual penmanship. He ended with comments that he would send updates as necessary and would look forward to further instructions from Arvacon's leadership. After signing the communiqués, he thoughtfully added a final notation. *All praises to Creator God.*

Rising from the desk, he gave the sealed messages to waiting couriers. Then, returning to the formal drawing room, he held cold hands in front of a large fire blazing in the fireplace. Sighing, his thoughts and feelings were jumbled. The demonic threat was ended. For that, he rejoiced. His brother and their dearest friends had fought and won the most critical battle of their lives. Berdran, who had risked his life during Nagrand's brief captivity, had also survived.

Nagrand's thoughts drifted. Images of battlefields strewn with bodies of Ambracorans and Breyals brought involuntary grimaces to his face. He mouthed a prayer for a prompt end to all hostilities.

Upstairs, Thehrund silently studied his wife's delicate features as she slept peacefully. Long, dark lashes lay sweetly curved just above her cheekbones. With death's gray pallor banished, ivory color had returned. The rosy pink of her lips caused him to long for the taste of her kisses. Golden-brown tresses caressed the cheek not nestled into her pillow. Tears brimmed in his eyes as he surrendered to temptation and placed a lingering kiss against her forehead.

Eyelashes fluttered as softly as delicate butterfly wings. Eyelids slowly opened to reveal amber irises flecked with sparkles of pure gold. Her lips curved into a gentle smile. "Thehrund," she whispered, "you're still here."

"I promised I would stay," he murmured before pressing another kiss against her forehead. "I couldn't leave, not after I believed you were really dead this time."

She closed her eyes. Her memory was suffused with the vibrant feelings she had experienced after the battle with Thafalos. "Thehrund," she said, her voice still hoarse and raspy, "this time, I think perhaps I really did die."

Thehrund's forehead creased. "Karan said..." His voice faltered as he recalled how his own soul had emptied of all but sorrow when he had lifted her lifeless form from the floor and carried her to the bedchamber where they now lay together.

"I know," she whispered, "but I remember." Haltingly, she continued, "Light more beautiful than words can describe. I spoke with my grandfather and Rezda. All the while, I felt your love pulling me back. Grandfather reminded me of something he said long ago." She paused, swallowing with difficulty. "We all have our time to live and our time to die. It was so beautiful in the light...so peaceful...but I realized it really wasn't my time to die. I came back. Your love called me home."

Pressing his lips tightly together, Thehrund blinked. Still, he was unable to halt tears sliding from the corners of his eyes. "I could not conceive of life without you. I lost you once. I could not bear losing you again."

Sindara's eyes glowed. "Someday, death will part us. What I now know is that our love will transcend the death that comes to us here. The time will come when we will reunite in Creator God's presence."

Gathering her closer, Thehrund could not bear to think of such a parting. Not yet. Creator God had returned her so that they might live a full life together. He promised in prayer that he would always cherish her. He also vowed he would never take for granted the love they shared. As her fingers lovingly curled around one of his braids, he closed his eyes and smiled. Never would he fail to give thanks for the gift of his beloved Sindara.

Chapter Twenty-Seven

Count Artrian Varacor thanked the messenger who delivered Nagrand Mezden's communiqué. Dispatching everyone from his office, he sat down and stared at the folded paper in his hand. The courier had mentioned only that he had encountered no Breyal warriors on the roads from Iglarm and that Breeneth and her demon lover had been destroyed.

Swallowing against the knot rising in his throat, Lord Artrian reached for a pearl-handled letter opener and broke the document's wax seal. Slowly, he began to read lines written by a shaky hand. His vision stalled as he reached the part mentioning that Thehrund was safe, but hearts had been broken over the loss of Sindara. Tears scorched the count's eyes as the paper abruptly fell from trembling hands. Heartbreak struck him with staggering force. He could not bear to think how he would face losing his daughter this second time.

A knock sounded just outside his office. The mere attempt to speak choked him. He watched in strangled silence as the door slowly opened. Liana nervously walked inside.

"I heard a courier arrived from Bramond," she said, acutely aware of her husband's apparent distress. Her eyes drifted downward, noting at once the open letter lying on her husband's desk. Her chin quivered. "Sindara?"

Her husband's eyes closed. Unable to answer, he shoved the letter across his desk.

Liana slowly crossed the office. Her hands trembled as she picked up the letter. Her eyes scanned the dispatch. She caught the word brokenhearted associated with the loss of her daughter. Having suffered no sense of dread or premonition, she forced herself to read on. The word *miracle* practically exploded into her consciousness.

"Artrian," she said softly, "you must not have read the message through. Nagrand has written that she lives because of some miracle. Sindara is alive!"

Shocked and confused, Artrian snatched the page from his wife's hand. He read the final lines of the message. Joy instantly replaced the invasion of fresh grief. He had not lost his precious daughter after all! The demon master and his servant had been defeated. Standing, he dragged his wife into a tight embrace. Aloud, he echoed Nagrand's final words. *"All praises to Creator God."*

Following Kicchak's initial contact with King Hamund and General Varacor, longtime enemies observed a wary truce. The Breyal chieftain requested six days to prepare for their first formal meeting. He wanted time to send tribal messengers to distant bands of warriors with orders to end all fighting until results of talks with Ambracoran leadership could be advised. Breyal tribes then settled into a massive camp several miles from Articene while the fort's garrison maintained watchful vigil.

On the day talks were to begin, Kicchak and his tribal council sat uneasily in chairs placed at the large conference table inside Fort Articene's spacious war room. Glancing around, the Breyals observed large maps hung on walls and shelves filled with books and war journals. They possessed written records in the form of rudimentary glyphs but nothing quite so complicated as the printed items inside the neatly organized conference area. They were also surprised by clean cups set at each place around the oaken tabletop and pitchers of fresh water.

When King Hamund finally entered the room, walking with crutches, Kicchak stood first. His council members quickly rose from their seats. After General Varacor and four aides followed the king inside, Hamund smiled tersely while the general invited all to sit.

Although not wishing to prolong the negotiation process with unnecessary social graces, Hamund exercised years of diplomatic practice by treating the Breyals with respect and consideration. He waited for aides to pour water into cups for each participant and then nodded deferentially. "It is our custom to offer prayer to our Creator God before any meeting as critical as this."

Without further comment, the Ambracorans bent their heads and Hamund prayed aloud. "Heavenly Creator God, we come before you today to request your blessings on each of us in this room. Please guide us with wisdom and compassion as we seek lasting peace for both our nations. All praises to you, Creator God."

Erator noted the look of confusion shared among the wordless Breyals as he waited for his king to sit before taking a seat himself. As the day wore on, he began to comprehend fully why his own father held Hamund in such high regard. Although not combative, the Breyals brought a unified, resolute stance to the conference table as they discussed terms acceptable to a people defined by tribal strength, prestige, and pride. Hamund entered discussions fully aware of Breyal tribal mentality. Adroitly using that awareness to ask probing questions, he listened carefully to answers, countered with firm responses, and set a cooperative tone for continued negotiations.

That afternoon, negotiators from both sides welcomed the end of a tense day. Kicchak had described his people's culture with details regarding reasons for their warlike nature. Hamund had outlined a concise list of complaints and demands to end years of violence against peaceful villages. Breyals justified their raids, stressing their people's need to maintain their lives in a country with what they viewed as limited resources. Hamund reiterated his nation's refusal to accept continued surprise attacks. Kicchak listened with interest as Ambracor's king suggested they agree to compile and review a list of specific concerns and difficulties Breyal peoples confronted. They would adjourn the first day's session and reconvene the following morning with a revised agenda.

As the Breyal Council filed out of the room, Kicchak lingered. Although he held his head aloft with ingrained pride, his brown eyes revealed solemnity. Stridency left his voice and was replaced by aloof resolve. He addressed Erator. "I request to speak privately with your king."

Erator turned questioning eyes to Hamund. "Your Majesty?"

Hamund cast his general a slight smile before meeting Kicchak's direct gaze. "You need not ask permission to speak to me. You are free to address me directly."

Erator silently departed and closed the door. With two soldiers at his side, he took the precaution of remaining just outside the conference room.

Kicchak's unsmiling countenance reflected troubling burdens. Steely principles allowed him no slack to avoid what he deemed personal accountability. "I wish to inquire when you will advise me regarding my execution."

"Your execution," Hamund responded quietly.

"Yes," Kicchak said. "My execution is a matter of honor among my people. My deeds sacrificed the life of your son to evil ones to whom I yielded without resistance."

Hamund breathed in deeply and expelled a heavy sigh. He could not bring himself to accept his son's death. Neither could he conceive of punishing a man who had lost his entire family to Breeneth's wicked deeds. How he wished to know current circumstances in Bramond. How he simultaneously feared that same knowledge.

Gathering his thoughts, Hamund nodded. "For the time being, I repeat my earlier assessment. You are needed to help me resolve the enmity between our peoples. It is my decision that any execution should be enacted only after we complete our negotiations. I can make a public declaration if you consider that necessary to satisfy your council."

A single nod conveyed the Breyal's agreement. "That will do. My people must have confidence that I do not avoid your retribution through cowardice."

"Very well," Hamund stated. "I will issue the announcement tomorrow."

Later that evening, Hamund sat on a sofa inside Erator's family quarters and gazed blankly into the roaring fire that warmed the room. A shiver chased along the length of his spine as he contemplated his son's fate. Breeneth's image tormented him. He dared not imagine what punishment she might have inflicted on Thehrund. He harbored no doubt that Thehrund would have elected to die rather than betray Sindara. Recalling the murders of the Branderes and his own confrontation with Breeneth, he shuddered to think how his beloved son might have suffered.

His thoughts turned to the night he had ridden into battle against Breyal forces. He had felt like a madman. His nature was to respect and protect life. That night, he had been overcome by murderous acts that he thoroughly detested. Despite understanding he had killed to defend himself and his nation, he grudgingly acknowledged horrors that would haunt the remainder of his days.

The majesty of converging stars invaded his memory. With battle suspended after the awe-inspiring celestial display, he wondered if he dared to hope that Sindara might achieve victory over Breeneth and her demon master. Unwelcome worry then burgeoned as he feared more grief would besiege Artrian, his highly esteemed friend.

"Your Majesty?" Erator offered his solemn king a glass of brandy.

Nodding his thanks, Hamund accepted the glass and took a fortifying sip of the fiery liquid. Swallowing, he drew in a deep breath. "I have newfound respect for you, Erator." He sighed despondently and added, "You and our armies have willingly faced unspeakable violence, yet you still retain the essence of our desire for peace."

Erator wearily lowered himself into a chair. "We were given no choice but to fight if we wanted to preserve our country's values. Those same values must prove strong enough to carry us into a new state of peace."

"Hmm," Hamund sighed at length. "Kicchak asked how soon I would proceed with his execution as justice for Thehrund's life. I am left with the unenviable challenge of balancing our values, my grief over my son's death, and Breyal's code of honor."

Before Erator could reply, a knock sounded at his door. Rising, he left the king in brooding silence while hoping the late visitor bore no news that might weigh more heavily on him and his royal guest. When he opened the door, he accepted a dispatch from one of his aides. Glancing downward, he immediately recognized the handwriting on the elegant stationery and rejoined King Hamund.

Clenching his jaw, Erator sat and broke the thick wax seal bearing the Varacor family crest and unfolded the paper. His eyes quickly scanned his father's neat, precisely penned words. Shaking his head once, he slowly read the message more carefully. His eyelids closed, and he released a pent-up breath.

Hamund placed his glass on a side table and leaned far forward. His expression was intense as fearful impatience seeped into the depths of his being. "What? Tell me what has happened. Erator!"

Relief revealed itself in the form of a slow smile. Erator met the king's gaze. "Father received word from Iglarm. Breeneth is dead. Her demon master has been destroyed. Thehrund is traveling directly here from Bramond. He brings Sindara with him."

Several moments passed before Hamund could absorb the report's full significance. Tears swam in his eyes as unadulterated joy shafted throughout his entire being. Thehrund was alive! His son and his daughter-in-law had somehow prevailed in their confrontation with the greatest crisis Ambracor had ever faced.

"You're certain?" Hamund choked out.

Erator passed the dispatch to the king. Hamund read Artrian's elegant prose with growing gratitude to Creator God for the answer to fervent prayers lifted by his beleaguered people. The king uttered aloud heartfelt thanks. Fresh confidence swelled that negotiations with Breyals could proceed without fear of demonic interference. Hamund felt suddenly liberated to anticipate healing for his people's suffering and a return to the peaceful prosperity Ambracor prized so highly.

Thehrund slowed his pace and drew his sword, signaling the carriage following him to stop. Riders in the distance were approaching. Sindara, still weak from her near death experience, rode inside with Kendra. The prince cast a glance toward Karan and Nagrand. "Careful. We must be prepared."

As the riders closed the gap, Thehrund recognized Major Lohrdrend in the lead position. Releasing a tense breath and relaxing, he waited. When the soldiers were within earshot, Thehrund's booming voice called out, "Greetings, Major! Such a relief it is to see a friendly face!"

Lohrdrend smiled broadly as he guided his mount closer to his prince. "Your Highness, good morning! Count Varacor sent us to intercept you and escort you to Articene. His Majesty King Hamund is there."

Thehrund shook his head, his long hair swinging from side to side. "My father is in Articene? Why?"

The major's expression beamed with patriotic pride. "He fought in the last major battle before the Breyals surrendered. He now works with their tribal council to negotiate peace."

Thehrund exchanged surprised glances with Karan and Nagrand. "Father rode into combat? The Breyals surrendered?"

"Accounts describe the battle as quite fierce. Breyal warriors had withdrawn to regroup. As I understand, their soothsayers told the tribal leaders that converging stars in the sky were a sign against continued hostilities."

Karan lowered his head for a brief few seconds as he recalled the dazzling spectacle he had been blessed to see. Meeting the officer's smiling countenance, he said, "That was the morning Breeneth and her demon were destroyed."

"You saw the convergence as far away as Bramond?" Lohrdrend inquired curiously.

"The convergent stars were a sacred portent that the time had come to strike against her and her demon master. It is written just so in an obscure passage of the Ambracada," the priest answered.

Lohrdrend's expression turned pensive as he shifted his eyes to Thehrund. "Our people already hail you as a hero. They will undoubtedly proclaim your victory with greater fervor when they learn you defeated the demonic threat with heavenly guidance."

Thehrund gave a mighty shake of his head. "I was naught but a minor player in the drama that freed our nation. Sir Mezden and I were both prisoners in Iglarm when the battle against the demons began. Karan here freed us with help from Berdran Brandere. Our princess and a young woman she calls her sister-in-spirit actually confronted both Breeneth and Thafalos, her demonic master. While we watched angels remove the devil, Berdran bravely killed his sister."

Major Lohrdrend and his troop turned to accompany the prince toward Articene. A quiet reserve descended upon the party. All reluctantly recalled horrific scenes of battle they had witnessed over the past months. Each prayed profound gratitude for the turn of events in Iglarm. More than all the others, Thehrund contemplated the magnitude of a string of miracles that had begun in Articene years earlier when angel voices had echoed inside his mind.

❈ ❈ ❈

Disdaining crutches upon hearing of his son's approach to Fort Articene, King Hamund limped outside and watched as Thehrund led the way through the fort's gates. He proudly noted the prince's regal posture as he urged his horse forward.

"Father!" Thehrund exclaimed, swiftly dismounting and running forward. Strong arms tightly enfolded his father with surging relief. When he finally loosened his hold, he rejoiced to receive his father's affectionate welcome.

"Thehrund, my son! Words will never express my joy that you and Sindara are safe!" Hamund exclaimed with an emotional catch in his voice. Tears freely tracked down his cheeks.

Thehrund turned as Sindara approached. Stretching out his hand to grasp hers, he drew her into the embrace shared with his father. Everyone present beheld the joyful image of Hamund, Thehrund, and Sindara. All heads bowed in unison when the prince's rich voice majestically chanted prayers offering gratitude for the end of the war and seeking guidance to build lasting peace.

Glistening tears filled Kendra's dark eyes as she leaned against Karan's side and watched Sindara in the company of her husband and father-in-law. Intuition, faith, and love for her sister-in-spirit had ignited her courage to venture to Ambracor. With Karan's arm around her waist, she sensed a growing closeness that she never would have found on her own Earth-plane. Her heart swelled with newfound joy as familiar voices spoke inside her mind. Her body had been created in a different dimension of existence, but her heart and spirit belonged in Ambracor.

Epilogue

KING HAMUND SAT UNCEREMONIOUSLY ON the floor of the family drawing room inside the palace. Sandwiched between his grandson and granddaughter, he held a book in his hands and read adventure stories he had told years earlier to his only son. His granddaughter grinned, reminding him that her father had said the king's adventures during Ambracor's time of war had been far more exciting than anything written in the books. His grandson tugged at his grandfather's sleeve and begged him to tell them more about his encounters with the Breyal chieftain named Kicchak.

Thehrund stood just inside the arched doorway, leaning back against the wall with Sindara's body tucked snugly against his. His fingers locked in front of her waist, and her hands covered his. The prince and princess smiled as Hamund described the scene when Kicchak had first approached him and their Uncle Erator to begin a peace process. With the book lying open on Hamund's lap, the king's animated account showed how the great warrior had ridden with his longbow balanced on his arms. He told of the Breyal Council riding behind him with sheathed swords and the many Breyal warriors waiting to see what would happen.

"Grandfather," young Artrian begged, "tell us about when Kicchak wanted you to kill him."

Hamund shook his head. "I could not do such a thing. That is not our way in Ambracor. Just think what a mistake it would have been. Only a few days later, I received news that your father was alive."

"Uncle Erator said you were very brave in the last big battle. He said Breyal warriors were afraid seeing a king with only one leg riding a horse and carrying a sword."

"Good kings and queens must always lead their people, Diana, especially during difficult times."

"Father was brave, too, wasn't he?"

Hamund glanced up at his son and wondered how he had gotten dragged into yet another retelling of the past. "Your father was very brave, Diana. He was the real hero."

"And Mother, too, right?"

Thehrund released his wife and went to crouch down by his son. "Your mother was the bravest of all. Now, it's time for the two of you to let Grandfather rest while you both change for your riding lessons."

As Sindara shooed the children off to where Marnee waited with their riding clothes, Thehrund leaned forward to help his father up from the floor. "I think it may be time for you to write down the entire history from your perspective."

Hamund lifted an age-spotted hand to pat his son's cheek. "The history of those times is already well chronicled in my journals."

Thehrund's blue eyes beheld his father with affection. "Despite all the bad, those tales are worth retelling. I still marvel at all that happened."

"As do I," Hamund remarked as he sat in a comfortable armchair. "Returning home to Bracordia was also a memorable occasion. Besides the rousing welcome from the crowds, I will never forget the shimmering glow of the Ambracada when Sindara and Marnee retrieved it from the chest buried behind the angel sculpture near the palace chapel."

"That was an awe-inspiring moment," Sindara agreed. Placing her hand in the one Thehrund extended to her, she joined her husband on the sofa. "So many lives changed forever."

"No doubt," Thehrund confirmed. "I sometimes think of the suffering Berdran endured, yet still he defied his sister by helping Nagrand and me. How glad I am his fiancée refused when he offered to release her from their engagement. A man so honorable deserves the love and happiness he now enjoys."

Sindara nodded with a thoughtful smile. "She is a woman of exceptional character. His physical scars don't matter. She appreciates what dwells in his heart."

"And then we have Karan and Nagrand. After Nagrand finally married, I never expected him to have four children so close together. I barely manage with two!"

Hamund laughed heartily. "That's because your two are too much like their father."

Sindara giggled and gave her husband a teasing glance. "He is right, you know."

"So your parents and mine continue to remind me." Thehrund grimaced comically. He changed the subject in self-defense. "Is tonight our dinner with Karan and Kendra?"

"Yes, it is. Continuing our earlier discussion, the two of them represent the most impressive change since the war."

Sindara's eyes grew distant. Through the eye of memory, she watched her beloved friend utilize natural empathy and professional training as a counselor to guide many Ambracoran citizens from the precipice of emotional breakdown. Her intervention helped save both individuals and families from the traumatic stress brought on by the ruthless, bloody war. As she plied her professional skills, she also discovered a kindred spirit in Karan.

Smiling to herself, Sindara softly remarked, "I still find Karan and Kendra's decision to marry as one that truly mystifies me. He resigned his role as a priest to teach and practice healing arts, and she left behind a completely different home world."

"I share that feeling," Thehrund said as he gently squeezed his wife's hand. "Their combined vision for helping others is remarkable. No one can deny how happy they are."

Hamund became pensive as he gazed at his son and daughter-in-law. In the years since the war ended, he had watched their love steadily grow.

He would be forever grateful that they had been reunited and then survived the menace that had nearly destroyed the way of life they all now cherished with greater fervor.

Recalling conflicts and joys of the past, he sighed thoughtfully. "Those times changed no lives more than yours. I am convinced Ambracor would have spiraled into total devastation had it not been for your devotion to one another and the courageous deeds you accomplished under the most trying of circumstances." After a prolonged pause, Hamund concluded his thoughts. "With perhaps the exception of Lord Artrian, I can also say with absolute certainty that no father could ever be prouder of his children than I."